THE LONG WEEKEND

Gilly Macmillan

PENGUIN BOOKS

PENGUIN BOOKS

UK | USA | Canada | Ireland | Australia
India | New Zealand | South Africa

Penguin Books is part of the Penguin Random House
group of companies whose addresses can be found at
global.penguinrandomhouse.com

Penguin
Random House
UK

First published by Century in 2022
Published in Penguin Books 2022
001

Copyright © Gilly Macmillan, 2022
The moral right of the author has been asserted

Typeset in 10.37/16.55 pt Palatino LT Std
by Integra Software Services Pvt. Ltd, Pondicherry.

Printed and bound in Great Britain by Clays Ltd, Elcograf S.p.A.

The authorised representative in the EEA is Penguin Random House
Ireland, Morrison Chambers, 32 Nassau Street, Dublin D02 YH68

A CIP catalogue record for this book is available from the British Library

ISBN: 978–1–52915–800–7

www.greenpenguin.co.uk

In memory of Oscar Macmillan
A very good dog

FRIDAY

John shouldn't be driving, they discussed it with the doctor yesterday, but Maggie sees the look in his eyes and puts the key into his outstretched hand. His fingers snap closed around it.

He gets into the Land Rover without loading the bags of clean linen and towels into the back, but Maggie doesn't say anything; she hefts them in herself. The dog jumps in and lies down, bracing her back against the bags, tongue out, gaze taut. Maggie shuts the door.

The wind is cold this morning and cuts right through her. It's only the start of September yet autumn has arrived abruptly. There's the feeling of a storm coming. Clouds race to gather on the horizon, their shadows grazing the solid stone-and-slate farmhouse below where it's nestled in a hollow in the side of the valley.

John starts the Land Rover and, over its growl, Maggie thinks she hears the whine of another engine. She frowns. Their guests aren't due to arrive until later this afternoon. The lane that winds up here doesn't lead anywhere else. If you're on it, you're either on your way to the Elliott farm or you're lost.

Drystone walls divide and organise the land around the farmhouse. Acres of unenclosed rough grazing surround it, steep, harsh terrain, only semi-useful. Beyond lies an unmanageable wilderness of exposed moor concealing boggy wetlands and cleft by isolated valleys and sheer-edged ravines, slippery with scree. Rocky outcrops disrupt the summits of distant peaks.

The boundaries of the farm are ill-defined. Elliott land encompasses some of this wilderness and has done for centuries. John and Maggie shepherd three thousand acres and eight hundred head of sheep. There's good grass and bad; there are good years and bad. The sky is always huge and the stars at night brighter than anywhere else they've ever been. Guests who stay at the barn always remark on this.

Maggie waits for a moment, to see if she hears more, but picks up nothing over the noise of the Land Rover. She doesn't linger. Up here, sound can play tricks on you. And she has work to do.

She fastens her seat belt. 'I thought I heard someone driving up.'

John doesn't react. His foot is down, the Land Rover moving already. She glances at him.

'Are you all right?'

'Why wouldn't I be?' He manoeuvres the car out of the farm gate. It bounces as the wheels hit the potholed surface of the lane.

'Don't be like that.'

'Sorry.'

He stares ahead and she watches his profile. His cheeks and nose are riddled with broken veins, his skin knitted thick on to his bones. He's done a shoddy job shaving today, but his eyes are as full of soul as ever. This is a good man. She knew it the day she met him.

She looks harder at him, searching for outward signs of what's invisible: the areas of his brain riddled with connections as broken as his veins. 'We suspect dementia with Lewy bodies. I'm so sorry,' the consultant said. That appointment lost in a sea of others by now, but she'll always remember hearing the diagnosis and that apology, and John flinching as if he'd been struck.

She's so lost in staring at him that she doesn't see the motorbike round the bend in the lane, tilting, black, and powerful. Coming right at them. Too fast.

John hits the brakes hard, bracing himself at the last instant. Maggie is thrown forward and back, the air punched out of her lungs.

'Sorry,' he says in the shocked silence afterwards. 'Are you OK?'

'I think so. You?' Her heart thumps and she winces at the sudden arrival of pain where the seat belt cut into her chest and her shoulder.

'Hurt?' he asks.

'It's not too bad.'

John nods and looks behind to check on the dog. She shows him the whites of her eyes but seems fine, only a towel fallen on to her from one of the overstuffed bags.

'Good, Birdie,' he tells her.

The bike has skidded to a stop at an angle across the lane, frighteningly close to the front of the Land Rover. The biker's a big man, dressed in plain black leathers and a black helmet. Even with his helmet on, they know he's not one of their local couriers.

He dismounts. The surface of his visor reflects the dark trees gathered on each side of the lane. Maggie is suddenly afraid that he might be angry with them and try to blame them for the close shave. They'd be defenceless against a man like him. She's breathing hard.

John winds down the window. 'You need to watch where you're going,' he shouts. A vein pulses in his temple.

'Don't,' Maggie warns. She used to feel safe from everything except the elements up here. She loved the isolation and the sense of living on the very edge of civilisation. But the change they've been through since John's diagnosis is like today's stiff wind. It has rattled everything, and Maggie is afraid that she and John have reached a stage in life where once something's rattled, it stays loose.

Birdie growls and gets to her feet. Her head pokes between their shoulders. She shows her teeth.

'Birdie!' Maggie puts a hand on the dog's shoulder. The growling stops but Birdie's muscles are tense, her hackles are up, and she doesn't take her eyes off the biker.

He lifts his visor as he moves nearer to the driver's side of the Land Rover. His mouth is obscured by a bandana and his eyes are buried in shadow. 'I'm looking for the Elliotts.' His accent is southern. He's come a long way north to be within a stone's throw of the Scottish border.

'That's us,' John says.

'I've got a package for you.'

'Parcels get left in the box by the farm gate. At the bottom of the hill.'

'I'm supposed to give it to you in person. Special instructions.'

They watch him fetch the package from the back of his bike, his movements unhurried. He hands a cardboard box to John who passes it to Maggie. It's unsealed, unmarked and has some weight to it. Maggie opens the flaps to peer inside and sees another box, this one cuboid and beautifully wrapped in paper and ribbon. An envelope is tucked beside it. Maggie takes it out and retrieves her glasses from her shirt pocket so she can read the small, carefully printed words. 'TO JAYNE, RUTH AND EMILY'.

'This isn't for us,' she says but, as she speaks, she remembers. 'The guest who booked the barn this weekend is called Jayne. It must be for her. For them.'

'There's a note for you, too.' The driver hands over a sheet of paper with typed instructions on it. Maggie reads aloud.

'"Please discard the cardboard box and place the wrapped present prominently on the kitchen table at Dark Fell Barn, facing the door, and lean the letter against it so it'll be the first thing my friends see when they enter the room on arrival. It's a very special surprise so I appreciate your attention to detail. Thank you."'

It's not signed. Maggie flips it but there's nothing on the back.

'Aye, I suppose that's fine,' she says. Her tension ebbs. Sometimes guests do the strangest things. 'We're on our way up to the barn now.' She still feels a little uneasy but also embarrassed for feeling so fearful earlier.

The biker nods. He closes his visor and is away as suddenly as he arrived, the bike spraying mud in its wake, leaving questions on Maggie's lips, such as who and where he picked the box up from, and why all the effort to get it here in this way. Not her business, she supposes, but she's curious about this 'special surprise' and its 'special instructions'.

'That's a first,' she says. 'How far do you think he came from?'

'We could have killed him.'

John speaks through gritted teeth. He's angry because the near miss frightened him, Maggie thinks and she wonders if she should take over the driving, after all, if he's going to get himself in a state. She's about to ask, but the words stick in her mouth. Every offer she makes to help him wounds his dignity and it hurts her to inflict pain on him.

Instead, she lifts the parcel and gives it a tentative shake. 'The lengths people will go to,' she says. 'I hope whatever's in here is worth the bother.'

John glances over, shakes his head and mutters something she can't hear as he fixes his eyes back on the road. She notices him tighten his grip on the wheel, knuckles whitening beneath his thinning skin.

Those hands, she thinks, aware that since his diagnosis she's been prone to moments of reflection and of nostalgia but allowing herself the indulgence. What those hands have built and achieved. She loves the liver spots, the tendons like thick string; sees the happy years of her marriage and the challenges of their farming life in them.

But the tight grip on the wheel, the head shaking and the muttering; it's not him. It's more change that's new and troubling. She's still learning to read his symptoms, and to decipher what they might mean, and she gets a sinking feeling that today might be one of those days where he's lost to a terrible pessimism.

'What are you shaking your head for?'

'It's a bad thing. The parcel is.'

'What gives you that idea? How can you possibly know?'

He inclines his head. He knows, he's saying. She tries to laugh it off, but the sound coming out of her mouth is hollow, and the truth is, she finds herself taking him semi-seriously. John might drown in pessimism or despair; he might exhibit agitation, forgetfulness and sometimes she thinks he even sees things that aren't there, all of which is deeply troubling; but she can't deny that for as long as she's known him, he's been able to sense more than the average person.

She touches the back of her neck, seeking any soreness from whiplash. Her cold fingertips trigger a shudder that runs right through her. She thinks about the parcel, about whether it's a good or a bad thing. After a few silent moments she puts it in the footwell.

The Land Rover lurches and bumps as it climbs the rutted track. Maggie steadies the parcel with her foot when the vehicle's movement threatens to damage it. If whatever is inside it gets broken, her guests may leave a bad review, and that's the last thing she and John can afford.

I wrote the letter and wrapped the package, taking my time over it, to make sure it looked beautiful. I thought carefully about the instructions for the owners of Dark Fell Barn. And I arranged the delivery meticulously so that it couldn't be traced back to me.

And now I've just received confirmation on my burner phone that both letter and package have been handed over, along with my instructions.

Phew.

It really is a great feeling, mostly comprised of relief – but satisfaction too, because I take pleasure in planning. You might, I suppose, call me a control freak.

What happens next is out of my hands, though, and my nerves are jangling at the thought. Directing a piece of theatre long distance isn't easy.

I have to hope the Elliotts do as I've asked, putting the props precisely in place so that the curtain can rise on Act One.

Outside the car, rows of trees crowd the edges of the narrow road, densely packed, trunks straight and foliage overhanging low, absorbing the dying afternoon light. Emily takes out one of her earbuds. 'It looks like a fairy tale,' she says.

She clears the hours of silence from her throat, tugs the sleeves of her sweater over her wrists and wraps her arms tightly around herself. She should ask Jayne or Ruth to turn up the heat, but she's too shy. They intimidate her with their closeness and the decade they have on her. Emily feels like an impostor.

Jayne, in the driving seat, raises her eyebrows. Finally! Emily speaks! she thinks. Emily has been either asleep or plugged in for most of the journey.

'Like a fairy tale in a good way?' Ruth asks, turning round. Emily is a mystery to Ruth and someone Ruth is determined to get to know better over the course of this weekend.

'Not really,' Emily says. The fairy tales that were read to her as a child were terrifying.

Ruth isn't sure how to respond. Emily's relative youth sometimes leaves Ruth at a loss for words. It shouldn't, she knows, but somehow the ten-year age gap is always there between them, making Ruth afraid that whatever she says will sound patronising, even though that's the last thing she means to be. She faces the front again and consults the satnav.

'Not long until we're out of the woods,' she says. 'Literally. And around fifty minutes until we get there, according to this.'

They've been on the road for hours, heading north. Muscles are stiff, minds dull. Ruth insisted on packing lunch for them all, lacklustre sandwiches which she apparently made at the crack of dawn. It adds to the school-trip feel of the journey for Emily.

As the car breaks out of the forest, light floods the windscreen, and the landscape reveals itself. Jayne smiles for the first time since she woke this morning with Mark's hand on her flank. She thought at first that he wanted to make love, but it was a more careful touch, an apology. Phone in his other hand, Mark was waking her with the news that he wouldn't be able to join them on the drive up north today, meaning he would miss the first of their planned three nights away.

Jayne was cross. The news bruised her and so did the row they had over it. They bickered clumsily, both tired and both upset with how the other was taking it, both feeling like the injured party.

But Jayne's sense of wellbeing has grown with every mile they've travelled north, the banality of the motorway soothing her, happy anticipation of the long weekend ahead re-emerging, reframed.

Now the weekend will consist of a girls' night followed by two nights when all six of them will be together. It's not what she expected but it's fine, and she will still be able to surprise Mark, the way she planned to. And as Mark pointed out, perhaps she needs to work on handling change better. And she will. There are always improvements to be made in life and she's not afraid of putting in the graft.

She focuses on the positives. She's been looking forward to this weekend for weeks. She needs a break. And it feels as if she's hardly seen Ruth since Ruth had the baby. It'll be nice to have time to catch up properly. That's sometimes easier when the men aren't with them, dominating the conversation with their in-jokes and reminiscences.

Alone in the back of the car, Emily has fallen quiet again. She blows on the window glass and traces her initials and Paul's there, with a heart around them. Her nails are manicured and painted a pretty pale blue; the back of her hands tanned. A large emerald on her ring finger is a match for her eyes. Paul held it up beside them when he proposed, comparing the green of the jewel to that of her irises. The smile on his face was so broad and unfiltered that it touched her. He looked like the cat who'd got the cream, which is exactly how she felt.

The idea of being a wife is still thrilling to Emily. She never expected to be married at this age, only twenty-three, especially to a much older husband, but she fell in love, tumbled into it, and so far, it's been amazing. She adores Paul and adores their life together. And as a bonus she gets to flash that big rock at the doubters, including her mother, who never managed to get a ring on her own finger. After Emily's dad left them, her mum mostly collected toxic boyfriends, nasty bruises and a deepening alcohol addiction.

Emily's breath evaporates from the window, taking the initials and heart with it and the magical memories. Outside the countryside crawls by. Walls and gates, fields and hills. Many black-headed sheep. A horse, waiting for something. So much emptiness. Dull.

Ruth and Jayne are talking about a play that's on the radio. The play and the conversation sound pretentious and worthy, confirming Emily's impression that the two of them are boring. Though, while she's got no desire to join in their chat, she wishes that she'd accepted Ruth's offer to take the passenger seat for the journey. Sitting in the back makes her feel even more like a kid.

She wants Jayne to put her foot down and get them to the cottage quicker because she's fed up of the drive, but the white lines have disappeared from the centre of the road and it seems to be constantly narrowing and forcing the car to decelerate. It's as if the road is taking control.

She puts her earbuds back in and shuts her eyes, thinking of the holiday in the South of France that she and Paul have just returned from. The business-class flights, the hotel, the spa, the sex. It was lush. Paul is perfect. He was a gentleman. She felt like a princess, even when the air hostess gave her that knowing face, as if to say, 'You're not the only young thing I've seen in this cabin beside an older man, and you won't be the last.' Emily took pleasure in flashing her ring, then.

Marriage isn't all fun, though. She's annoyed with Paul today. She wishes he were here with her. If she's honest it's more than

13

annoyance. She resents him for insisting he had to work today and for making her come on this long weekend ahead of him, with these other women, who she barely knows.

'Come on, Em,' he said. 'It's just one night. Make the effort. It's really important to me that you try to get to know my friends.' Emotional blackmail.

She's been happy to avoid these women until now, shying away from group nights out or Sunday lunches, feeling acutely that she has nothing in common with them. But there it hung, the implication that Paul would be disappointed in her if she didn't do what he wanted. So, she agreed. And now, she wishes she hadn't. Especially since the other husbands aren't here either. Mark and Toby are more fun than their wives, but they couldn't come either, also at the last minute, so now she faces twenty-four hours in the draining company of Jayne and Ruth. Already, Ruth has been fussy and patronising, and Jayne has stared at Emily in that penetrating way that makes her feel vacuous and stupid.

She sighs and once again her breath mists the window. She draws another heart. But this time she's too annoyed with Paul to put their initials inside it.

John's impulse is to take the package back to the farmhouse, to toss it in the dustbin and say good riddance to it. He'd like to toss the guests away with it, if such a thing were possible.

This bloody special delivery is yet another display of ridiculousness and arrogance from the people who come up here to stay in the barn, he thinks. They only want to party and to play.

They're totally disconnected from the land that his family have been custodians of for more than a century.

With every set of guests to arrive at Dark Fell Barn over the past year – since Maggie made a website and began to advertise it – John's unhappiness with the situation has burgeoned along with his sense that something sacred to his family is being invaded. He restored the barn himself, to preserve it for the use of William, his son, and for the generations of Elliotts he hopes will follow.

Hardly a day passes when John doesn't think of the people who walked his land before him, and of how you should learn from the past, how we are all rooted to it.

The past contains warnings, he believes. You must respect it. In this part of the world, deepest Northumbria, the past is bloody and suffused with myth and history. The rugged beauty might photograph well, but it's no playground.

He wants to tell Maggie once again that the barn should not be rented out, to press his case urgently, but she's heard it before, and he can't stand to see any more sympathy in her eyes. She'll understand how he feels but she'll only say, 'We can't vet people before they arrive here,' and 'We need the money,' and she's right so he keeps his mouth shut and concentrates on driving them safely up the track.

The journey up to the barn is difficult. It takes about twenty minutes and the steeper they climb, the more the Land Rover lurches and rolls. Finally, the track curves sharply and they emerge from woodland high in an isolated valley.

You can see for miles, but Dark Fell Barn is the only building in sight. In every direction, below racing clouds, shadow and light play chase across the limitless terrain. Perspective contracts and expands. Layers of detail are shrouded then revealed as conditions change. Colours are fickle, dulling one moment, intensifying the next. Textures look velvety and welcoming, before turning raw and pitiless.

John Elliott has spent his entire life here and loves it with his whole heart. He knows he's losing his memory and knows that reality, for him, is now warped and no longer easily navigable, and that Maggie is his only anchor to it.

But he makes a daily vow to himself that he will never forget his purpose as custodian of this land.

Rain hits the car windscreen like a handful of pebbles. Ruth, in the passenger seat, flinches and looks behind to check on Emily. Maternal habits are hard to break, even if newly acquired. Ruth's baby, Alfie, is only six months old and she feels practically rabid with protective hormones but knows that she mustn't treat Emily as a child substitute just because she's so young.

That would be wrong in so many ways. They are three women of equal status, married to best buddies, and Ruth hopes that by the end of the weekend she'll be able to count Emily as a new friend.

Ruth fires off another text to Toby asking if he's arrived safely at his sister's house. He hasn't replied to any of her recent texts, but he should be there by now, playing the white knight. Like the other two husbands, he found a last-minute reason not to travel up to the barn today and Ruth isn't happy about it. Long weekends away are a ritual for their gang and this year the talk has been that getting away is more important than ever, in the aftermath of Rob's death.

So, what a time for Toby to prioritise a sister who never lifts a finger for him! When does he ever prioritise Ruth, his wife? Or, for that matter, their son?

She knows she probably shouldn't send so many messages – more than ten in the last hour – but it drives her mad how bad Toby is at texting, especially at a time like this when he'll know full well that she'll be wanting reassurance.

It's just not the sort of thing he cares about though. His phone is an old model he refuses to upgrade. His head is always in his research and as a result he's disorganised, overly reliant on Ruth to run their lives. She used to love that about him; it made her feel useful, as if she was an excellent supportive wife, and became another area of life that she could excel in. But since the baby it's become overwhelming.

Alfie should be waking up from his afternoon nap about now. Since she left home this morning, she's felt uneasy, unsure whether her mother will have the patience to look after Alfie the way Ruth would like her to.

Ruth stayed up late last night writing pages of notes on how to care for him, covering every eventuality she could think of, but her mother took them from her almost offhandedly and didn't so much as glance at them. Ruth made her promise she would read them, but who knows if she will. Professor Flora MacNeill always knows best.

Ruth sighs and shifts position. She's uncomfortable in body as well as in mind. The waistband of her jeans is digging into her. There's a coffee stain on her cotton top. A quick check in the vanity mirror confirms that her mascara has migrated to stain her cheeks and it resists a tidy-up with a licked finger. She stops trying when the car jolts over a pothole and she almost stabs herself in the eye. She feels mumsy and frumpy by comparison to the other women. Emily is gorgeous, young and svelte. Jayne is whippet-thin and super-fit, her face bare of cosmetics. She radiates health and certainty.

Jayne turns off the wipers when they start to squeak. The rain has stopped. It was a passing squall, violent but moving swiftly. Nothing to get excited over.

'You OK?' Jayne asks, glancing at Ruth. 'You're frowning.' Jayne is dismayed by how tired and strung-out Ruth seems. Ruth hasn't been as silent as Emily during this journey but has definitely not been her usual chatty self either. There are bags under her eyes and her skin has a pasty, plump look to it, as if Ruth hasn't been taking care of herself in the past weeks since Jayne last saw her.

'I'm fine.' Ruth closes the mirror and tries to stretch, forcing her shoulders back, feeling the muscles resist. Jayne is a good friend. Never effusive or excitable but steady and kind. A safe pair of hands. Worth putting on a brave face for. 'Looking forward to getting there.'

'Are you worried about leaving Alfie?'

Ruth's grateful for the question, for Jayne's thoughtfulness, though it won't do to admit how deeply anxious she feels. It would be embarrassing in front of Emily. 'A bit.'

'He'll be fine.'

Ruth nods, but gratitude has turned to irritation because the comment smarts. People always give bland rejoinders like that when she verbalises her worries about the baby. It's almost a reflex, an automatic response. But what if her worries deserve more serious attention? A follow-up question perhaps? One displaying concern and consideration?

Ruth finds being a new mother the most intimate but also the loneliest of places. She wonders when she last felt connected to her friends. It was before Alfie was born, certainly. A sense of loss comes with the realisation that it's probably almost a year since she hooked up with some of them.

Even being back at work at the surgery hasn't helped her isolation; in fact it's made it worse. Working full-time, which is necessary because she and Toby need the money, means she lost the mum friends she made during maternity leave because she could no longer make it to their coffee mornings or baby groups.

Her days are packed. She's either commuting, dropping Alfie at nursery, or at work racing through her patient list and worrying about what she's missing out on at home. There doesn't ever seem to be time for casual chats with colleagues or after-work drinks with friends. Everything feels hurried. And she feels permanently inadequate, as if she's not doing anything well.

She checks her phone. Her mother hasn't replied to the last text she sent, either, but to be fair phone reception is becoming patchy.

Anxiety feels like pressure that germinates in her chest and radiates into every part of her body.

Before she had Alfie, she was enthusiastic about motherhood. Wanted it, looked forward to it, prepared diligently for it, reading every book on babies that she could get her hands on, consulting recent medical research. No detail was too small for her to take seriously; nothing was going to catch her out.

This was how Ruth had always approached life, how she'd achieved her dream of becoming a doctor and how she'd tried to live up to her family's expectations. Rigour. Attention to detail. Hard work.

She was astounded after Alfie's birth to find out how useless all her planning was. Instead of having a sense of control, she felt feral and instinctual about motherhood the moment they placed her son on her tummy and everything she'd read suddenly became redundant. It was as if she'd undergone a personality change during his birth.

She became obsessed with the vulnerable flop of his damp head, the delicate folds of his skin, every single detail of him. In the last six months she's experienced the most powerful feelings she's ever felt in her life. Sometimes she thinks she could eat Alfie up for dinner and want more of him for dessert. There's nothing she wouldn't do for him.

Toby doesn't feel as strongly about their son. It's obvious and Ruth resents him for it. It's driven a wedge between them.

For weeks, she's been nurturing the hope that this weekend, their first break without the baby, can help them rediscover each other. She's aching for him to touch her again. It's been almost a year since they last made love. Toby stopped touching her a few months into her pregnancy. And she misses the intimacy terribly.

The urge to have a drink arrives abruptly and powerfully. Just a small drink. It would take the edge off her worries and help her to get in the mood to party with Jayne and Emily.

She started drinking surreptitiously after Alfie's birth, during her maternity leave. At first it was a pick-me-up, but soon it was the only thing that held back the feeling that her life was spinning out of her control.

And it didn't stop when she went back to work when Alfie was eight weeks old. Everything got worse. She found she barely had the attention span to listen to her patients properly and resented how much they both expected and took from her.

She knows she's got to stop drinking. It's causing problems. She thinks of the email she received yesterday from the other partners at her surgery and the formal warning it contained about her behaviour. She hasn't told Toby about it yet. Just the thought of it is overwhelming.

And the problem is, she doesn't know how to stop drinking because increasingly, lately, she's felt that it's not just her life that's out of control, but she herself, as if she's slipped loose from the moorings that used to keep her stable.

To distract herself from her rising panic and from the stabbing urge to drink, she looks outside, studying the landscape. The view is startling in its immensity. Moorland. Bleak, even at this time of year. Like something out of a Gothic novel. She worries she's been very quiet on the journey. What must the others think of her? She should contribute something positive.

'I'm actually really looking forward to having a fun girls' night tonight,' she says. 'Just us three. Without the men.'

Ruth looks into the back, to see if Emily heard, but she's plugged in, eyes shut.

Jayne slows the car to take in the view. The countryside resembles nothing they're used to in the south of England. It's wonderful. She feels dwarfed and dazzled by it. The prospect of driving deeper into it thrills her. Mark will love it as well.

Jayne examines how she feels now about him dropping out at the last minute. Not quite as angry as she was this morning, but not happy.

What she can't shake is a nagging suspicion. It's in her nature to question things – in the army she worked in intelligence gathering and lives could be saved or lost depending on the information she acquired, so she was rigorous and second-guessed everything she heard or learned – but the arrangements for this weekend have become such a farce that even the most naive individual would surely smell a rat.

First Paul texted a few days ago to say he couldn't be with them at the barn tonight, but that Emily would come anyway, then Toby messaged with a story about his sister. Mark was the third to drop out. His excuse was that a work thing had come up. But surely, it can't be a coincidence that none of their husbands can be here with them this evening, even though the men are acting as though it is. It's just such an unlikely scenario.

Don't you think it's weird that none of our husbands could come today? she wants to ask, but something stops her. She glances at Ruth then at Emily via the rear-view mirror. They probably don't want to hear it right now. Emily has her earbuds in, anyway. It will only put a dampener on things if Jayne mentions it. She imagines that if they have concerns, they're keeping them to themselves for now, so she should too.

And Ruth is right. The long and short of it is that they can have fun without the men tonight. Jayne knows she and Ruth can, at any rate; it remains to be seen whether Emily will let her guard down.

The upside is that their husbands will join them before lunch tomorrow and whatever those three have been up to, if they have, will come out somehow. None of the men are great at keeping secrets. They're too close to one another.

There is someone else missing from their party, but in contrast to how she feels about their husbands, Jayne is secretly pleased about this additional absence.

Edie declined the invitation to join them for the weekend, saying that it would be too painful to come without Rob. Everyone understood. Rob's death has left a hole in all their lives over the past five months, but especially Edie's. Obviously. Rob and Edie had been a couple since school. Jayne can't help thinking of their daughter, Imogen. The sight of her at Rob's funeral was heartbreaking. She was such a daddy's girl.

Jayne's kept her relief that Edie didn't join the party this weekend from Mark and everyone else, because the men all love Edie so much.

But Jayne can't deny to herself that she'll find the trip easier without Edie. Whether she's in a good mood or a bad one, Edie takes up all the oxygen in a room.

'I'm really looking forward to tonight too,' she says. 'Let's have a blast.'

Here's something that surprises me: you'd think the fact that I can't control what happens up at Dark Fell Barn tonight would drive me crazy after all my painstaking planning, but it's exciting me, making me feel like I'm alive and reassuring me that I can feel something again.

It's how I know I'm doing the right thing.

Rob has been dead for five months and I've been living in a state of numbness. Everyone else has moved on, that's obvious, even though it's felt impossible to me. I've been the straggler, left behind on my own, my only company the ferocious pain of missing him.

And, of course, Imogen. My daughter. My lifeline. I don't know what I would have done without her.

Sometimes I go online and find the description of Rob's death in the *North Devon Gazette*. It's a masochistic habit that I can't seem to kick. I can't seem to stop wanting to read it, yet I always feel upset by the article's cold recounting of the 'facts'.

Friday 17 May 2019

Robert Porter, 37, has drowned in an accident near Hartland Quay on the North Devon coast. Robert was photographing local wildlife along the coastline on Tuesday when he was cut off by the tide and swept out to sea. Friends raised the alert. Swansea coastguards retrieved a body from the rocks at 6 p.m. on Wednesday. Robert is survived by his wife, Edie, and their daughter, Imogen.

Where are the words that mean something? That convey the enormity of our loss?

If I wrote about Rob dying, I would describe how it's broken me as completely as the sea broke his body on the rocks. You would learn that I'm still frequently ambushed by grief. That there are times when I imagine it shutting me down internally: the coagulation of my blood, a thickening of my saliva until my mouth can barely open, the softening of my bones into the consistency of milk-soaked bread.

Honestly, since he died, nothing can be the same.

Which is why I've done what I've done. Imogen and I need a new life.

All being well, the parcel and the letter will soon be in place at the barn, and Jayne, Ruth and Emily won't be far behind.

Dark Fell Barn is compact, built from square blocks of local sandstone. A door punctuates the facade, as do four windows, asymmetrically placed and each one different in size to the others. Each pane of glass reflects the restless cloudscape.

John and Maggie get out of the car and she opens the back. The dogs jumps down.

'Bring the bags in for me?' she asks.

He nods. Why is she asking? She doesn't need to. Of course he'll do it.

She carries the wrapped parcel into the barn. He's distracted by the view. Deep in the valley, a tributary catches the sun fleetingly and glints as if it were forked lightning. It's breathtaking. Is it an omen? As a boy he believed this valley, the most isolated on his family's land, is where the creatures that his father warned him about lived: bogles and brags, shapeshifters who might trick you or lead you astray. Everything up here can change in an instant.

Beyond, far to the north, a veil of rain obscures a rocky outcrop. Heavy anvil-shaped clouds are gathering behind it, dense enough that it looks to John as if the sky might collapse under their weight. The storm is no more than a few hours away and it's heading in this direction. They'll have to get the guests up here before it breaks, or the lane will be impassable.

He follows Maggie into the barn, Birdie at his feet.

'John!' she says. 'The bags!'

'What bags?'

'In the car. Can you please bring them in?'

'You only had to ask.'

'I did.'

She didn't. He's sure of it. But he hates nothing more than to argue with her.

They work through the chores in the barn in silence. Maggie checks everything John does to make sure it's perfect; he says nothing but resents it.

She feels tired and uneasy. Today was supposed to be ordinary but everything that's happened so far seems determined to catch her out. This strange delivery and, even before that, John's behaviour. He's having a bad day.

When everything is dusted, beds made, towels hung, the welcome basket packed with beautifully arranged local produce and placed on the kitchen surface, Maggie takes time to position the letter and the wrapped present on the table, just as instructed. She checks how it looks from the kitchen door, and from the hallway, tweaks the angle slightly and adjusts the envelope so it's propped a little more upright.

John watches with a bad taste in his mouth. One of the things the people who come here don't understand, he thinks, is that this barn, with its three-foot-thick walls, here on the borders of England and Scotland, like all the others in this area, was built to protect people and their livestock from invaders. From outsiders.

'Right!' Maggie says. 'That'll do. Time to go back down.'

He nods. *Goodbye,* he says to the barn, but silently. He always does this when he departs, even though he plans to be back up here in a couple of hours, delivering their guests. He considers it a courtesy.

It was as a child that he first heard the walls whisper back: *We will protect you.* He heard it again, during the long months he spent restoring the place. And he's heard it since.

But for outsiders, those walls have a different message. He senses the restlessness of the walls when he leaves guests here, and he hears them muttering:

We can contain you. We can teach you.

'Why can't we drive up to the barn ourselves?' Emily asks.

She watches the farmer, John Elliott, put their cases into the back of his Land Rover. The farmhouse looks well-kept, but mud slicks the yard and she's afraid it's not just mud, but shit. She hardly dares inhale in case a stink hits the back of her throat.

'You'll see,' he says. Or, at least, that's what she thinks he says. His accent is strangely sing-song to her ears and difficult to understand.

'The track up to the barn isn't passable with a normal car,' Jayne explains, like a know-it-all. 'You need a four-wheel drive. They say it on their website. The link I sent you?'

Emily nods, but the truth is she didn't get past the lack of an en suite bathroom before clicking away from the barn's primitive little website, in despair.

The farmer offers her a hand to help her up.

'I'm fine,' she says. She tries to smile at him, but the effort dies on her lips. She feels intimidated by his gruff demeanour and his swarthiness and is a little repelled by his weathered hand.

The interior of the Land Rover is basic and not all that clean, the bench seat hard. Emily perches on it, wriggling to fit in beside the bags, and straps in. Ruth gets up with a grunt, accepting help from Mr Elliott. He shuts the door.

Ruth makes a freaked-out face at Emily and, in spite of herself, Emily can't help smiling back, grateful that she's not the only one finding everything rough around the edges. Jayne doesn't look bothered – in fact she looks like she's relishing everything as she climbs in the front beside Mr Elliott – but then she and Mark are outdoorsy types. Rain slides down the windscreen.

John Elliott drives aggressively. The pitch and roll of the car makes the journey feel more like sea travel than four-wheel travel. In the front, Jayne's hand is clamped on to an overhead safety bar. Emily feels as if her internal organs are being redistributed.

Ruth tucks her arms beneath her breasts to stop them bouncing painfully and makes another face. Emily giggles – she doesn't mean to, it just bursts out of her – and, bracing her elbows against the back of the seat to stabilise herself, cups each of her own boobs with a palm. Her laughter is infectious, Ruth catches it, and it quickly escalates into hysteria, which both try to manage silently, as if they're naughty schoolkids afraid of being told off by the adults in the front.

They're no longer smiling by the time they arrive at Dark Fell Barn but desperate for the drive to end. The rain has eased but the wind whips at them as they get down from the Land Rover and buffets them as they take in their surroundings.

'Talk about the definition of off-grid.' Ruth raises her voice a little to be heard. She links an arm through Jayne's. 'Well done, Jayney. You've exceeded expectations.' For years, the men have been pushing for these weekends to be spent in more and more remote locations. Jayne has taken them further than they've ever been.

They stare out at the landscape, at the absolute desolation of the place. Jayne's sense of satisfaction burgeons. Ruth can feel panic gnawing at her. She checks her phone. No reception whatsoever. She'd been warned, but it felt easier to cope with in theory. Mr Elliott has carried their bags inside and is about to leave. She has a strong urge to get into the Land Rover with him and tell him to take her back down to the farmhouse. She'll go home, collect Alfie from her mother. It's on the tip of her tongue to call out to Mr Elliott to stop and wait for her but the shame of being a quitter and the feeling of Jayne's arm linked through hers stops her.

As John Elliott drives back down to the farmhouse, he has thoughts about their newest guests. They told him their names

29

and he's already forgotten them, but their faces are clear in his head.

Only one of the women might be worthy of Dark Fell Barn, the one who rode in the front with him. Maggie told him she made the booking. He liked her steady, serious face; plain and pale, open somehow; the flinty grey eyes that narrowed in awe as she took in the sight of the barn and the view. In the car, she had sensible, respectful questions about the history of the area, wondering about the location of the ancient burial chambers that can be found up here, the Neolithic remains. She knew the correct term for them was barrows and he appreciated that. She was dressed appropriately too, unlike the other two who will spend the weekend cold and burn too much wood trying to warm themselves.

The youngest is a slip of a creature, with flaming red hair, the sort who doubtless barely eats. She wore flimsy clothes, full make-up, and dangling earrings and a watch so expensive it should have stayed at home. She's noticeably younger than the others and it makes him wonder for the first time what the absent husbands are like, why they're not here with their wives, who they are. When she took off her dark glasses, he saw that the green of her eyes was watery, and he thought they carried a flinch deep in them the way it lurks in the eyes of wild animals.

The third woman wore tight clothes, though they were not clothes designed to be worn that way. He suspected she had grown too large for them. Her hair curled, dark and unbrushed, as if it belonged to someone wilder, yet everything about her seemed soft and tamed. She looked ready to bolt from the moment they arrived. Preoccupation hovered around her like a cloud of midges. She must have left her mind or her heart behind at home. Her chatter didn't disguise it from John. Amongst the expressions of delight and thanks there were too many questions about what they should do if something went wrong.

'Don't leave the barn in the dark,' he said. It was all they needed to know.

They're on their own now.

Emily watches John Elliott drive away. The clock's ticking, she thinks, until Paul gets here. I just have to endure this. Wind hurtles up the valley and whistles around the barn. It's too much for Emily; it feels as if it's prodding through every seam in her clothing and it pulls her hair out of its topknot, lashing strands of it across her face. She has not dressed or packed for this weather. It feels more like winter than the start of autumn.

She takes shelter in the doorway of Dark Fell Barn. Framed by the thick walls she feels small and intimidated by the building. There's something unyielding about it. Stubborn and cold. She shudders.

Jayne and Ruth stand on the patch of ground in front of the barn, their backs to Emily, looking out over the wide beyond. She notes their linked arms and how they're shoulder-to-shoulder. It's hard not to feel jealous of their friendship.

Emily slips into the barn.

She sees the present immediately. It's at the far end of the hallway, on the kitchen table. With its shiny wrapping it almost seems to wink at her out of the gloom of the barn's interior. It looks like a shiny beacon amidst the muted tones and old surfaces. Emily walks briskly down the hallway towards it and her heart fills up as she does. This is just the sort of gesture that Paul makes: a thoughtful surprise, something to let you know he's thinking of you or that he's sorry.

She touches the present, runs the lovely ribbons through her fingers and picks up the envelope. It's addressed to all three of them.

She's slightly disappointed that it's not addressed to her alone, but Paul's fair as well as generous. He wouldn't want to play favourites. She glances back over her shoulder. The front door's ajar, and the others are still standing where they were before, looking at the view. She doesn't think she needs to wait for them to open this. It can be her treat.

She smiles as she opens the letter.

Hi ladies,
Your weekend starts here! I hope you have a great time!
I didn't come along because I know I'm not welcome.
This is goodbye. I'm going away.
But I wouldn't want you to forget me.
By the time you read this, I'll have killed one of your husbands.
E

It's difficult to concentrate on driving when all I can think about is what might or might not be happening up north. My calm has evaporated and I'm stressing that the owners of the barn didn't

32

put the parcel and letter in the right place, that the drama of the moment I choreographed won't unfold the way I want it to.

I try to quell my nerves by imagining what might happen after the wives have read the letter and opened the gift. It works, a little. I feel a little nub of excitement in the pit of my gut when I think of what their reactions might be.

When my phone rings, the sound slices right through me. It can't be the burner and it shouldn't be my personal phone either. Unless—

My blood runs cold. I've made a rookie error. Stupid, stupid me. I meant to turn off my phone when I made this journey, so I couldn't be traced. I can't pull over here, so with one hand on the wheel, eyes half on the road, I reach across to the passenger seat and scrabble through my bag, finding my phone just as it goes to voicemail.

I see it was Imogen calling and the phone almost slips through my sweaty fingers. She shouldn't be ringing now. I have her schedule memorised and right at this moment she should be rehearsing for the final performance at her music camp, which I'm so looking forward to watching.

What if something's wrong?

I've been thinking so much lately about Imogen. I always longed for a daughter of my own, longed so hard that it hurt.

I pull over into a lay-by created by an entrance to a field. My nerves are skittering all over the place. I must call her back. Ignoring her or returning her call later isn't an option because I promised myself that I would never let her down again.

Plus, I might as well use my phone now that it's pinged every tower between here and the city. That's a problem I'll have to figure out how to deal with later.

Imogen picks up instantly.

'What's wrong?' I ask.

'Can you come and collect me early?' Her words are rushed and tense, simmering with emotion, as if she's on the brink of a meltdown. What the hell has happened? She was fine when I spoke to her yesterday. I pinch the top of my nose, a useless gesture I make when I feel a migraine coming on.

'Why? What happened?'

'I nearly did it again.'

'What do you mean?' I think I know. I feel as if someone has poured icy water over me.

'I wanted to cut myself.'

My gut takes a swan dive. I have longed for her to confide in me more this year. And now she finally does, it's this unbearable thing. 'Oh no,' I breathe.

She talks over me. 'I can't keep up in rehearsal because I'm rubbish and I feel like I'm letting everyone down. Can you come and get me? Now?' She starts to cry and chokes on her sobs.

'Please don't say these things.' It hurts me physically when she talks like this. 'You're brilliant. A star. Everybody says so.'

I mean every word. If your child makes music the way my girl does, it can make your heart bloom, even if you've been through the longest, darkest few months imaginable. I'm not someone who cries much, especially not in public, but the last time I watched Imogen play, I blubbed until my face was red and ugly and didn't care who stared.

Rob felt the same. Her concerts made a mess of him.

'What about your final performance?' I ask. It's tomorrow night. I plan to be there. Front row.

34

Imogen's sobbing escalates, becoming such a broken sound that I feel as if it might shatter me too. But all the closeness we had when she was younger suddenly feels tantalisingly within reach, if I can just support her now, in the right way.

'I can't. Please don't make me stay. Everyone made fun of me at rehearsal today.'

'What? Why?' It's impossible to keep the anger out of my voice, but I could wring the necks of whichever spotty little—

'I kept messing up,' she says. 'I left early. It was then I got the urge to cut.'

'But you didn't?' The thought of her taking a blade to her skin is horrific. I've had nightmares about it since it first happened, soon after Rob died. She told me after the fact, refused to show me the scars on her stomach, she was so ashamed of what she'd done. She was also terrified, she told me, that she wouldn't be able to stop doing it. And here we are.

'No,' she says.

The relief is incredible. I let my forehead rest on the steering wheel, grateful she can't see me. 'That's awesome and it's also awesome that you're sharing this with me and not keeping it to yourself. I'm coming now. Pack up, tell whoever you need to tell, and I'll be there as fast as I can. Five at the latest, I would hope.'

'See you,' she says and the gratitude in her voice is beautiful to hear.

This is unexpected. My plans for today will have to change, but it's also a sign that I've made the right decision to prioritise Imogen.

I reach to turn on the ignition and as I do I get a whiff of something that brings me a feeling of dread. I sniff. *Is that?*

It's a nasty, organic, catch-the-back-of-your-throat stink.

Fuck.

I sniff again and glance in the rear-view mirror. I should check, but I can't bring myself to open the boot until I absolutely must. And what if someone drove past and saw me and thought something was wrong? Pulled over? Offered help?

I try to breathe through my panic and tell myself things are not falling apart. I turn on the engine so I can roll down the window. A deeper sniff triggers a retch reflex because the stink is overwhelming, but I feel like the luckiest person in the world because it's definitely a countryside smell coming from outside my vehicle. Strong, repulsive, but fine by me because, for a moment there, I thought it was something else.

Which would have been horribly problematic, because I don't have time to get rid of the body before I collect Imogen.

Maggie waits anxiously for John to return from dropping the women at the barn. She had planned to drive the guests up there herself, but he'd got ahead of her and had the Land Rover keys in his hand and how could she take them from him in front of their guests?

The three women seemed nice enough. And determined to have a good time in the absence of their husbands. To make the best of it. 'We'll bring the men up to you as soon as they arrive tomorrow morning,' Maggie reassured them.

She chases the chickens back into their coop, enjoying the feathery rush of them around her legs.

Maggie's worries seem insurmountable some days. She often wonders what will happen to the farm when John's health declines further. Maggie can't manage it on her own. She's spoken to their son, William, about it. He's a police constable and loves his job. He has to think about whether he can give up all that he's achieved to come back here and farm. She senses that in his heart he doesn't want to, but he's attached to the land as much as she and John are, so there's hope.

And then there's the not knowing how quickly John's health will decline. Do they need to act soon, or will he maintain a manageable level of function for a year or more?

John is in denial, but his symptoms have gained in frequency and intensity lately, just the way the doctor warned that they might. There are the memory problems, bursts of emotional aggression, moments of confusion, lapses of judgement, repetitive conversations, and the obsessive thinking. He's taken especially against having guests in Dark Fell Barn. It's becoming a real worry.

This morning, something new happened that troubled her. She didn't have a chance to process it in the moment because she was too busy getting everything ready for the barn. But she pauses to think about it now. It occurs to her that perhaps it explains why she felt so uneasy when the biker arrived. Why the day had already gone awry.

John hallucinated. He claimed to see a figure walking away from him, through the morning mist – a tall figure. He described it in detail. 'Shapeshifter,' he said.

'John,' she replied. 'There's nothing there, love.'

He stared into the mist for a long time and had tears in his eyes when he turned back to her. 'But it was so beautiful,' he said. 'I've been wanting to see one of those all my life.'

He talked about it more, conjuring up images from folklore, stories his dad told him, and that he had, in turn, told William, and she humoured him at first as she worked to pack up the bedlinen, thinking that might be the best response, certainly the easiest, until he said, 'Perhaps it's a sign that we shouldn't let the guests stay at the barn tonight. A warning.'

'Don't be so bloody ridiculous,' she snapped.

He fell quiet and didn't mention it again. The incident seemed to have slipped through the holes in his memory after only a few minutes. For once, she felt grateful for his forgetfulness.

What's bothering her is the fact that their previous guests left the barn early, saying they felt freaked out up there, frightened by what they described as terrifying noises in the night.

Maggie couldn't think what they'd heard but refunded them all their money to appease them and prevent bad reviews. The barn is a crucial source of income. They'll need it if they want to be able to stay here when John gets worse. Leaving really would be the death of him. In his right mind, or not, she can't imagine him living out his days in a bungalow on a handkerchief-sized piece of land, or in some kind of nursing home. No, she'll have to do everything she can to keep them both here. She'll look after him.

But she can't deny that since that incident at the barn, she's nursed a worry about the coincidence of the guests leaving in fright and John getting himself worked up about people staying there.

And there's the fact that he's in and out of the farmhouse more than he used to be, especially in the evenings.

She lets herself into the kitchen, and its familiar scents and sights envelop her like a hug, cheering her up. She'll make bread tonight, she decides. That'll be nice. Supper is cold meats and cheese but fresh bread with it will be lovely. There's time. The thought grounds her. She loves this room. So much of their life has played out here. She'll also light a fire this evening. First one of the autumn. It's cold enough. Hopefully her guests will do the same.

As she lays kindling in the old fireplace, her worries fade, and her common sense regroups. Her kind, tender husband cannot be in the business of terrorising guests. That's as much a nonsense as some of the things he says these days. She should know better. She's letting her own anxiety get out of hand and it's not fair on him, or her. One of them needs to keep a level head to cope with what's coming.

She starts to gather what she'll need for breadmaking. It soothes her.

Whatever John's state of mind, she still intends for them to travel further into old age together in the same gentle manner that they've lived their lives so far.

She hears the Land Rover and relief floods her. Birdie stands by the door, tail wagging, waiting to greet John. But he doesn't come in. After a while Maggie goes out into the yard and calls for him, but she gets no reply. He's taken off somewhere on foot, she supposes, and her anxiety bites harder than it did before.

The letter falls from Emily's hand and floats to the floor. Her scream is loud enough to be heard outside. She steps away from the parcel, fearful of what's in it, her eyes locked on to it until the sound of footfall prompts her to turn to the door. Her face is a picture of shock and fear.

'What's wrong?' Jayne is first into the room, first to retrieve the letter. Ruth reads it over her shoulder.

'What is this?' Ruth says. 'This is horrible.' Her voice rises in pitch. 'Is this from Edie?'

They all know that it is.

The edge of the paper crumples beneath Jayne's fingertips. She lays the letter down on the table. Emily hands her the envelope. 'It came in this.'

They look at it, then contemplate the parcel. They can almost imagine it has a pulse, that it might start to throb.

Ruth feels fear gathering in her gut as if something inevitable is coming or has come to a head. Could Toby be in danger? The letter implies murder. There's no doubt about it. She pictures him. He would be so surprised to be killed, she thinks, because he's so affable. He's the good guy, the friendly art-history professor.

She tells herself off for even having this thought. Who thinks such a thing in such a moment? Why has her mind gone so far, so fast? And yet, for some reason, it also feels horribly plausible to her.

And if Toby is in danger, or dead, what about Alfie? She pins her lips together, afraid that she might retch, afraid that she's been right to catastrophise since she had Alfie, even when everyone else minimises her concerns, because now something unthinkable has possibly happened to her family. Is that why her mother didn't answer any texts this afternoon? Ruth's legs threaten to give way.

Emily is sitting at the table. Ruth leans heavily on the back of Emily's chair, puts a hand on her shoulder. Emily dips free of Ruth's touch and leans forward.

This needs to be read carefully, Jayne thinks. Think before you react. Assess. She studies the letter. The words are typewritten and therefore bland and normal in one way, but also undeniably vile. As she rereads them, she experiences the same sort of internal shudder that occurs when she sees nasty online trolling.

Use your training, she tells herself. But it's been years since she and Mark worked together as army intelligence analysts. Both rose to the rank of captain, and worked on identifying counter-terrorism threats, both in the UK and abroad. They monitored enemy communications to inform decisions made at commander level, sometimes providing real-time warnings to troops on the ground. It was intense, high-stakes work; no day was the same. Lives were at stake. Often, they watched the outcome of their intelligence advice play out via live feed. It was always hard, and sometimes they got it wrong.

But Jayne's skills as a soldier and as an analyst are rusty, and this is personal.

She tries to force her mind to clear itself up after the shock, to give logic space to kick in and to ask the right questions.

'Why would Edie write this?' Jayne asks.

Emily's eyes brim with challenge, with a flight response, specifically the desire to separate herself from this place and these two women, as if they're personally responsible for this situation. Her phone is already in her hand. 'I'm going out to find a signal. I need to talk to Paul.'

If she wasn't here trying to force a friendship because Paul put pressure on her, this wouldn't have happened, she thinks. She was right to steer clear of these people.

'Wait,' Jayne says. 'Let's think about this before we panic.'

'No.'

Jayne glances at the kitchen window. It faces the steep hillside behind the barn. Tufts of grass shiver in the wind. The light is a heavy grey.

Emily is halfway down the hall when her confidence ebbs and she stops. She's afraid of setting off outdoors alone and doesn't know which direction she would take. She might get lost, or stuck. Maggie Elliott warned them about bogs and ravines and told them that if they went out, they should be sure to stick to the walking routes recommended in the notes left at the barn. But Emily is hopeless at map reading.

She knows that she can definitely get intermittent phone reception at the farm, so perhaps it's better to go back down there, though she didn't pay attention to the route as they drove up here, didn't note where there were forks in the track, or landmarks, because she was giggling with Ruth.

As she lingers, she hears the others.

'It's a hoax,' Jayne says. 'Why would Edie sign it, otherwise?'

Unseen in the shadowy hall, Emily can observe that Jayne and Ruth are looking at one other, communicating something Emily can't interpret, something from a shared history she has almost no knowledge of.

Ruth's shoulders sag. She rakes her fingers through her springy hair as if she needs to stimulate blood flow to her scalp. 'A hoax,' she repeats. 'Yes.' But she doesn't sound as convinced as Jayne.

Emily steps back into the room. 'How do you know it's a hoax?'

Jayne turns to her and hesitates. This is something she knows better than to say in front of Mark or the other husbands because they've known Edie since they were at school together, when Mark, Rob and Toby were pupils and Paul was their rugby coach. The bond between them all has been intimate and close since then. At times, it has seemed to Jayne to be almost impenetrable.

But why not say what she truly thinks of Edie now?

'There are two sides to Edie. She's fun and lovely a lot of the time – fiercely loyal to her friends, as Paul might have told you – but she also has a mean streak. What I'm trying to say is that this sort of thing is typical of Edie. She's done it before.'

I decelerate as I approach the main entrance where wrought-iron gates hang on pillars that are only a carriage-width apart, a fact that caused me to scrape my car when I dropped Imogen off here almost a week ago. The driveway is long and straight, golden pea gravel bordered by lawn dotted with venerable trees. This is a private school that plays host to camps during August and the first week of September.

Imogen stands on the front steps of the house, waiting for me, holding her cello. There's no one else in sight.

I feel my body relax, but only slightly. I must keep the strength of my feelings packed away, so as not to alarm her. I've been accused before of failing to care about how others feel, but I know enough to understand that, to teenagers, a fulsome display of adult emotion can be like the sound of gunshot to a herd of deer. I don't hug her for the same reason. Public hugs have been taboo since she was ten.

I scan her, looking for signs of harm. I can't help myself. But there's nothing to see. There never is. No doubt intentionally, she's well covered up by her clothing. But she said she resisted the urge and I have to believe her.

Apart from a couple of old scars on her arms, she's never let me see the extent of what she's done to herself, and I'll admit, there's a part of me that feels relieved to be spared the sight of her beautiful young skin scarred in that way. Could any parent stand to see it? I'm not sure.

She's only done it twice before, so far as I know. I bitterly regret that I wasn't able to help her at the time, but I didn't know about it until it was too late.

I can be here for her now, though, which is something I take very seriously. It means so much to me, as we're on the cusp of our new life together. I want her to feel more loved than she ever has done. It will help us both to heal.

'Do I need to speak to anyone before we leave?' I ask.

She shrugs. 'I told them.'

'They were OK with it?'

Another shrug. 'Not really. They were upset. But I went to the nurse and she said I should go home. She emailed.'

Above us, hanging from the columns supporting the building's portico, a canvas banner drifts lethargically in the breeze. 'WELCOME, OUTSTANDING YOUNG MUSICIANS 2019!' it proclaims. From inside I can hear the faint discordant sounds of an orchestra tuning up.

What a shame Imogen won't stay the course, but I must prioritise her health. That's what a good parent does. It's what Rob would have done, and I must play the part of both her parents now.

'Let's go,' I say, with my best smile. I pick up the cello and march ahead to the car because it's important she doesn't open the boot.

I ease the cello into the back seat and take her bag from her, cramming it in beside the instrument.

As we drive away, I hit the gas and, after sitting rigid for a while, she seems to relax and puts her earbuds in and I relax a little too.

So, this was not my plan, and I'm a little shaken up by the change, but that's life as a parent. And that's what it's all about going forward. A simple, loving existence, for me and for her.

Which is how I know I can deal with this.

I can improvise. Why not? And now that I'm thinking about it, it'll be wonderful to spend time with Imogen tonight, just the two of us.

Did I mention that love is a beautiful motive?

I'm standing by that.

'What do you mean?' Emily asks. 'When did Edie do this before?'

It's hard for Emily to believe. Emily has only met Edie a few times, but she is so much more fun than Ruth or Jayne. Edie doesn't take herself seriously. Her sense of humour is wicked, she has fantastic clothes, and there's nothing mumsy about her.

Quite the opposite: she's hot for her age. Emily was surprised when she learned that Edie has a teenage daughter.

In fact, the first of Emily's disappointments regarding this weekend was when Edie announced at the very outset, when they had just begun to plan when and where they would go, that she wouldn't be coming with them.

'Edie pulled a lot of pranks when they were in school,' Jayne says. 'She has a reputation for it.'

'This is really a prank? Are you sure?' Emily very much wants to believe this.

'It makes more sense than the alternative,' Jayne says. 'Seriously, you can't believe she's actually killed one of our husbands.'

She picks up the letter. 'To me, this is a cry for help.' She reads from it. '"I didn't come along because I know I'm not welcome. This is goodbye. I'm going away." Edie wants us to rally around her and beg her to stay. The murder threat is to get our attention.'

'Could the men rally even more than they already are?' Ruth asks and Jayne snorts. Paul, Toby and Mark have rushed to Edie's side at the drop of a hat since Rob died.

Ruth thinks that there's some sense in what Jayne's saying, though. Her eyes fall on the gift, still wrapped and sitting in the centre of the table, shiny and exuberant. 'So, what do we think's in there, then?'

Jayne reaches for it. A confident gesture. 'Let's see.'

She tugs at the ribbons, and they stretch, digging deep into the flesh of her fingers before snapping. Ragged shreds of paper fall on to the table as she rips off the wrapping.

The box that emerges is a bright tangerine orange, the writing on it black and elegantly curlicued. 'Champagne,' Jayne says.

She opens it and pulls out a heavy bottle, with a label in orange to match the box, and places both on the table. They stare at the bottle for a few moments, no one knowing quite what to make of it. Ruth reaches for the empty box and peers into it, as if expecting to find something else, but it's empty.

She looks at the others. 'Is Edie expecting us to drink this to celebrate her going? Or to toast the death of one of our husbands?'

'Do either of you read French?' Jayne asks.

Emily shakes her head.

Ruth reads the label. 'Veuve Clicquot.' Her pronunciation is terrible. 'Oh,' she says.

'Exactly.' Jayne has already translated it.

'What?' Emily can't stand the way these two communicate without her. It's so superior.

'It means "the widow Clicquot",' Ruth explains.

'The widow? As in, that's what one of us is now? Or that's what Edie is?' The urge to speak to Paul tugs hard at Emily again. It feels like a necessity.

'I don't know.' Ruth feels suddenly as if she needs to apologise to Emily for all of this, even though none of it is her fault, because this situation is bad for her and Jayne but must be even worse for Emily, who barely knows them all. She opts for a sort of explanation. 'Edie loves word games. Crosswords, anagrams, that sort of thing. It's just part of the joke. I think.'

When they played games on previous couples' weekends, Edie relished comfortably winning any that were related to words or involved acting out. She could transform herself into other characters with ease, dominate the attention in the room effortlessly. Ruth never wanted the attention Edie sought, but she would have killed for a piece of Edie's confidence.

'It's sickening,' Emily says.

Jayne puts a speculative finger on the foil covering the top of the bottle. She feels angry with Edie and wants to show that this letter is not to be taken seriously under any circumstances. It's not to spoil their weekend.

'What do you think?' she asks. 'Should we open this? Wouldn't it be the best revenge on Edie if we have a great time this weekend in spite of her revolting letter? We could make a toast. How about . . .' She pauses, considering calling Edie a bitch, or much worse, but deciding to keep things civilised, for now, in front of Emily. 'How about: "Here's to not letting Edie spook us"?'

As the car bumps along country lanes, Imogen's phone reception fades in and out. She composes a message and taps her phone repeatedly until it sends.

On my way!

A reply arrives quickly.

Awesome.

What time do you want to meet? Imogen types. A bubble appears, indicating that Jemma is replying, then disappears for what seems like forever. Imogen frowns. When Jemma's reply finally lands, Imogen feels disappointed when she reads the one-word answer.

Later.

When? she asks. 'Later' isn't good enough. She's had to bust a gut to get out of music camp. She might be good at lying to adults, but that doesn't mean she enjoys it. She feels bad about it, actually.

Again, Jemma takes ages to reply. Imogen puts her phone on her lap, face down, and yawns. Camp was tiring. She runs her thumb over the callouses on the tips of her fingers on her left hand. She's had them since she first began playing the cello and has been making this reflexive, self-comforting gesture since then.

She flips her phone over when it buzzes.

I'll message you.

Really? she thinks. That's disappointing. She considers kicking off because it hasn't been easy to get out of music camp and in fact she'd been quite looking forward to the concert.

At heart, Imogen loves to play her cello. It reminds her of her dad. Music is the thread that's kept her connected to him since he died. If she shuts her eyes when she plays, she can imagine him sitting in front of her, listening. He'd been her greatest supporter since she began playing when she was just five years old. Music was a thing they had together. Her mum supports her too, and always has, but not as intensely.

She decides to play it cool. Jemma needs to understand that Imogen is not like some of the desperate girls in her year, who are happy to abase themselves to earn Jemma's friendship and become one of the popular kids. Imogen won't do that. She knows Jemma too well and she's known her for too long.

Her fingertip flies across her phone screen.

If you're not going to the party tonight let me know because there's another one I might go to.

A bluff, but the lie does the job. Jemma's typing bubble appears immediately.

I'm around and party is on.

Imogen smiles and sees Jemma is composing another message.

Message me when you're in Bristol and we'll meet up & make a plan.

Emojis flow at the end of Jemma's message, suggesting how much fun they're going to have. That's better. Now, getting out of camp feels like it might have been worth it.

Imogen feels a little flutter inside her. She can't tell Jemma, but the reason she really wants to go to this particular party is because she's hoping Matt, a friend of Jemma's brother, will be there. Even if she had Matt's number, which she doesn't, she wouldn't dare message him to find out if he's going, because that would be so lame. But every cell in her body is desperate to see him, for him to make eye contact with her across the room and for it to carry the same message it did last time they met: *I want you*.

She shivers almost imperceptibly, from nerves and excitement. Jemma lost her virginity over a year ago, Imogen thinks, and some of the other girls in her year did it when they were way younger than that. If she's going to do it for the first time with anyone, it's Matt. It might not be tonight, and she knows it shouldn't be because she hardly knows him, but this evening could be the start of something.

Cranking up the volume on her music, she stares at the countryside flashing by, enjoying the blur of it, the promise of later. The moment when she walks into that party can't come quickly enough.

Ruth shakes her head. Her urge to drink is strong but, even so, she can't stomach the idea of Edie's champagne.

The thought that Edie has targeted her personally to be the butt of such a malicious joke horrifies her. She doesn't know what she's done to deserve it. Ruth makes a virtue of being the kind of person you don't hate. She's a keen pleaser. This feels like a very personal failure and she has the sense that she's got something fundamental wrong – about Edie, and about herself – and it frightens her.

'I'm not touching it,' Emily says.

'I'll put it in the fridge, then,' Jayne says. 'Maybe later.' She's disappointed in the others.

'Why would Edie do this to us?' Emily asks. She's still finding it hard to understand. Before the others answer, something else occurs to her. 'She must have known the men weren't going to come with us. And known in advance. Or the letter wouldn't have an impact.'

Jayne shuts the fridge. Emily's right. Yet Mark only made the announcement that he wasn't coming first thing this morning. Was it planned in advance? Did he already know he had no intention of coming? Did the other men? For the first time, she feels a little nervous.

'When did you find out that Paul wasn't coming?' she asks Emily.

'A couple of days ago.'

'Toby?' Jayne turns to Ruth.

'Yesterday.'

'Paul's not here because of work, right?' Jayne asks. Emily nods.

'Same for Mark,' Jayne says.

'Toby's gone to help his sister.' But Ruth sounds uncertain.

They exchange glances and nobody's reassured.

'Edie's arranged this,' Jayne says. 'She has to have. She's lured the men off somewhere to mess with us.'

'No way. Paul's definitely working,' Emily says. 'But I want to talk to him.' She feels the urge to lash out. 'How can you lot call each other friends if this is the sort of thing you do to each other?'

'Don't blame this on us,' Jayne says. 'Ruth and I are incomers, just like you. We're not part of the original gang either. Maybe that's why she's targeted us.'

'What gang?' Emily asks. She hasn't heard Paul use this word to describe his friends, before. It seems a bit full on.

'Paul, Mark, Toby, Rob and Edie were all at school together. You know that, right?'

'I know Paul coached rugby at their boarding school.'

'Right. So, you know they all made friends there.'

'Of course.' Emily's aware of this but only the bare details. She's never felt curious enough to ask Paul more. What she knows is that Paul met the others via Mark, a talented player who he mentored, but Paul didn't stay at the school long because he quit to take the plunge and open his first bar. And the rest is history.

'OK,' Jayne says, 'so I have a theory as to why they're all so close. I think it's a boarding-school thing. Kids at boarding school make extremely close friendships and in their case the intensity of that was magnified because their parents were all teachers at the school, so they didn't fit in with the other kids. They weren't posh or rich enough. It made them stick together.'

'But what's that got to do with Paul? He wasn't a pupil there.'

'Because he, like them, lived at the school all year round, on site. Have you ever been there?'

Emily shakes her head.

'It's really isolated. Not quite as remote as here, but not far off. Paul wouldn't have had a chance to meet many other people.'

Ruth says, 'And I think when Edie arrived, she made things even more of an emotional hothouse, because they all fell in love with her. She was the only girl in the whole school. They only let her into the sixth form because they were desperate to hire her mum to teach art.'

It makes sense of Edie's confidence in herself, Emily thinks, if literally hundreds of schoolboys lusted after her when she was still a teenager.

'I bet she relished the attention,' Jayne says.

Ruth thinks about it. 'I don't know. To be fair, she probably didn't enjoy it all the time. It was probably a bit unhealthy for her.'

'Paul never fancied her,' Emily says, because he's assured Emily of that, but Jayne talks over her. 'Oh, Edie was precocious even then, everybody says so. That's why they all assumed she'd end up with Paul. Because he was that much older and more worldly. She bloody loved having them all dote on her; you know she did.'

Emily doesn't bother to repeat herself. She's not sure she even wants to know any of this, let alone get stuck into talking about it now.

'I'm sorry,' she says, 'but I really want to try to call Paul. Will someone come with me? Please?'

'Sure,' Jayne says.

'I'll stay. Somebody needs to unpack the food,' Ruth says.

There are two overstuffed coolbags on the kitchen floor.

'You sure?'

'Absolutely. I'll get everything put away. But if you find a signal, can you call Toby for me? I'm not actually worried, but it would be nice to know . . .' Her words trail off. She will put away the food, but what she's thinking about most of all is the bottle of vodka hidden in her bag.

'That's he's OK. Of course I will.' Emily hands her phone to Ruth and asks her to save Toby's number into it. Ruth has a moment of hesitation, a dropping feeling in her gut. She doesn't want Emily to have Toby's number. She's so young and so pretty.

'Don't you have his number?' Ruth asks Jayne.

'I might do, I'm not sure. My phone's in my coat.'

Ruth looks at Emily's phone. She doesn't know how to refuse to give out Toby's number without it sounding weird, or offensive, so she types the number in.

'Can you call my mother too?' she asks. 'Just to make sure that Alfie's OK?'

She tries to smile, not wanting to reveal how deeply anxious she feels, but it's a watery effort.

'Of course,' Emily says.

As soon as Jayne and Emily have left the barn, Ruth goes to the upstairs landing where John Elliott has left their baggage and kneels beside her bag, delving into it until she finds the bottle that she slipped into an inside pocket.

The warm vodka feels like sedation as it runs down her throat. She breathes slowly, savouring it, takes another long sip. The hardwood floor is uncomfortable on her knees, and she relaxes to sit more comfortably, her back against the landing wall, her toes pressed against the banisters. All the spaces in this house are tight. Above her, the glass in the skylights looks as if it's liquidising in the rain. The others will get very wet. She allows herself one more draught, screws the lid back on the bottle. It dangles from her hand.

I should have gone with them, she tells herself. Because of Alfie. In case Jayne's wrong. She looks at the bottle, suddenly consumed with loathing for it and for herself. What kind of mother prioritises drinking over hearing the voices of her family in an emergency? What was she thinking?

She hurries into a bedroom and peers out of the rain-spattered window to the front of the house, hoping to see Jayne and Emily, but they've disappeared.

Her fear feels visceral. It makes her doubt everything Jayne said earlier, and she feels cross that she was hoodwinked by Jayne's rationality and her reasonableness which suddenly strikes Ruth as pedestrian and a sort of weapon that both Jayne and Mark wield to give themselves the upper hand socially.

But neither Ruth nor Toby buys into it entirely.

Toby's always been quick to point out that Mark used to sound like a West Country lad. It was at their boarding school that Mark got rid of his accent, to assimilate better with the posh boys.

Mark already had good looks, sharp humour and physical prowess of the sort that's lauded at the cruellest institutions, and once he'd learned to speak the right way he yomped across the social divide and was officer class by the time he left university to join the army.

And Ruth can't help thinking of Jayne the same way, sometimes, as someone who might have learned to assume an air of authority but hasn't necessarily earned it.

But then isn't that true of all of us in a way? she asks herself. Toby and Rob pulled themselves up by their bootstraps, just like Mark did. They were at the same school, with similar backgrounds. Likewise, Paul transformed himself from rugby coach to entrepreneur.

And I feel like an impostor in my job, for the same reason, she thinks. Because I've got authority that I don't believe I deserve.

So, what if Jayne's wrong to insist that this is just a hoax? Ruth asks herself.

Edie will know that we'll assume it is. But perhaps that's part of the joke she's playing on us. Perhaps it's a truly sick joke, and Edie has hurt someone.

She unscrews the bottle and takes another long drink.

Her gut instinct tells her that she's right. It convinces her that something very bad has just begun. She drinks again and sinks down, to sit on the floor.

She's so tired. It hits her like a train. Admitting to the fatigue she's been suffering since Alfie's birth hasn't been an option, however debilitating it's become. Not to the brilliant Flora, her own mother, who apparently juggled motherhood and a career effortlessly; not to her friends, who she's barely seen since having Alfie and wouldn't want to admit weakness to, anyhow; and not to Toby, who can't wait to hand the baby over like a baton when Ruth gets home from a late shift, performing that swift, crablike scuttle to his study as if staying in the room with his wife and child would hold him back somehow, tether him somewhere he doesn't want to be.

The light under his study door stays on late, a slim yellow strip symbolising rejection. She knows she should knock on the door, go in, massage his shoulders, talk to him, but something has shifted between them. He hasn't touched her for so long. The physical absence of him is an ache and she doesn't know how to treat it because she no longer feels like his equal, nor does she believe he thinks of her that way. Having Alfie has diminished her in her marriage. Physically, emotionally, mentally. She and Toby don't talk any more about anything of interest. It's all domestic trivia, worries about the baby that preoccupy her. She can see him switching off and she can't understand it.

And there is worse, another layer of fear unpinning these anxieties, but this is all she can face up to just now. She pushes the rest back, things that are too painful to think about, even through the blissful numbness that the vodka is just starting to bring her.

She stands, grateful to ease the pressure her waistband is inflicting on her midriff. And even that reminds her of how much time she spends examining her shortcomings nowadays. How she is reduced to wondering what is wrong with her, to try to figure out the puzzle her marriage has become. How she feels as if she doesn't even recognise or even trust herself any longer.

She returns to look out of the bedroom window and takes in her surroundings a little more than the first time. This is the best bedroom – a glance into the others has told her that. Why shouldn't she and Toby have it, for once? They usually acquiesce to the others, stronger characters all of them, more insistent on what they want. But this weekend is already different. Edie has made sure of that. And the men. By not turning up.

Did Toby lie about needing to see his sister tonight? Is he doing something else? She's not sure and it's hard to think about.

But she is starting to feel calmer and allows herself a scrap of optimism as she looks at the double bed, with its pretty cover, its simple wooden headboard and its endless view down the valley. Perhaps here, away from home and from Alfie, perhaps Toby will want her again.

If he touches her, she'll know that everything will be all right. She'll forgive him the months of sexual drought in a heartbeat, she'll do her best to forget the times when she noticed him look at Alfie as if the baby were a stranger, and at her as if he doesn't recognise her any longer; she'll relegate to history the endless evenings spent in the same house yet apart, and the other troubling things, puzzle parts that she hasn't dared to piece together for fear of what they'll reveal.

She fetches her bag and puts it on the double bed, to claim the room. She scrutinises what she can see out of the window, looking for Jayne and Emily, seeking the bright red of Jayne's coat through the haze of the rain, but they're nowhere to be seen.

The thought dogs her again: If I was a better mother, better wife, I'd be out there with them. Ruth wonders if they've found a phone signal yet. She takes another drink of vodka.

She's going to try to put on a brave face, the way she always does, but it's been harder and harder lately.

The awful truth is that this letter plays into a fear she's been nursing, and trying to forget, but unable to. A fear that Toby is not who she thought he was.

That's why she didn't go out. Because only vodka can treat that fear.

And if she's going to hold it at bay, she desperately needs Jayne and Emily to find a signal and confirm that Toby's alive and well and where he said he was going to be, and that Alfie is still safely in the care of her mother.

'Hey,' I say, softly. We're parked in a small market town, on the high street. Imogen's head lolls against the car window and a slick of drool dampens her chin. I resist the urge to wipe it away with the side of my finger.

'Sleepyhead,' I say. 'Sorry to wake you.'

'Where are we?'

'I have to run an errand and I thought you might want to hang out here while I do. I shouldn't be long.'

'Why can't I come with you?'

Instead of answering, I hand her £100 in cash. 'Something for you to spend. Treat yourself.'

'What? Why?'

'Why not?'

She smiles. 'If you insist,' she says.

'Buy yourself a coffee next door if you get bored of trying things on.'

I watch her go into the boutique. We discovered it by chance on our way home from last summer's music camp. It's stuffed full of the sorts of clothes and jewellery that she loves. I hope it'll cheer her up.

As soon as she's inside, I let the smile fall from my face and put my foot down.

Ten minutes later, I'm driving along a lane at the very edge of town. I pass a couple of bungalows before open fields unfold on either side. At the end of the lane, I enter a small industrial yard containing a couple of rows of single-storey units, each as tumbledown as the next. I pass a row of shipping containers, stacked two high. They block any view of the yard from the lane.

Most of the units here are empty. Only three are occupied. One has a sign advertising lawnmower repair; the other is a garden ornament shop, guarded by a concrete dog with a chipped ear. The third has a forklift truck and stacks of pallets outside it. On the couple of trips that I've made here, I've never seen anyone else visit.

I rented a unit that was out of sight of the others. So far as the owner knows, I'm using it to store furniture and white goods left to me by a deceased relation. To be frank, he didn't seem to be in the slightest bit interested when I explained this to him, and I probably needn't have bothered. He had his eyes on the lump of cash in my hand, which suited me just fine. He runs the mower repair shop. His fingertips were stained green from grass clippings.

When I took possession of the unit, I furnished it with the heaviest padlock I could find. Then I moved an industrial chest freezer in.

I access the unit with some effort and back the car right up to the open entrance. I'm about to get out when I see the forklift truck round a corner and head towards me and my heart almost stops.

I panic and back the car inside, as far as it'll go, thinking that it's best if nobody sees me, but realise immediately that I haven't left myself enough room on either side to open a door, so I drive forward again until the front end of the car is protruding enough to allow me to get out.

The forklift's gone, I can't see where, but I can still hear it.

I almost lost my cool then, and I'm cross with myself. It's this body. It means so much to me. And perhaps having to collect Imogen early has disturbed me more than I thought, putting me off my game, causing my adrenalin levels to spike. I'm all over the place, jittery and exhausted.

But it won't stop me doing what I need to do. I'm so close to being finished and I'll never, ever need to undertake anything like this again.

I tell you, murder is easy in comparison to disposing of the body.

I shimmy past the car sideways to reach the back of the unit. Before opening the boot, I take a deep breath. It swings up abruptly and I'm faced with the corpse.

It's splayed awkwardly, limbs and head at unnatural angles. The sheet I've covered it with is good quality, and drapes softly enough that I can see those familiar facial features and I flinch at the recollection of the wide, staring eyes right after death, the shock that lingered in them even after the body had let go of its last breath.

I couldn't think of it as a person at that point, or at any point since.

But that doesn't stop me gagging now. Fortunately, it's not productive. I haven't eaten for hours.

Once my stomach has stopped heaving, I realise I have a problem. There's too much distance between the freezer and the car.

I'm expecting partial rigor mortis to make shifting the body difficult and I don't want to have to drag it across the floor. There would be no dignity in that, for me or for it. I'm going to have to move the car closer.

The car is a hatchback, which gives me an idea. Leaving the boot open, I get behind the wheel and edge it back to where it was parked originally, right inside the unit, so I can stick to my original plan of pulling the body straight from the car into the freezer. Only this time round, I misjudge and reverse the car into the freezer. Cursing, I inch forward again.

None of the car doors will open wide enough for me to get out now, but I clamber over the seats towards the boot, intending to exit the vehicle that way, though I almost lose my nerve when it comes to climbing over the body. It's not a nice thing to have to do and I don't think I can avoid touching it, but I try, and am partially suspended above it, my back scraping the car roof, when I hear the forklift engine again and it's getting louder.

I scramble out of the car as quickly as I can, yelping as my foot lands on the body. I fall awkwardly on to the floor of the garage in the small gap between the car and freezer. Pain shoots through my knee, forcing me to rest on the floor for a minute.

As I wait for it to ebb, I notice my freezer is sporting a big dent in the front where I backed into it. I run my fingers over the warped metal, hoping I haven't been so stupid as to break something inside it, that the thing isn't going to malfunction as a result. It seems to be intact, but I know it'll be one more thing to worry about.

It's starting to bother me that things have gone awry today. It's hard not to think of it as a bad omen.

The engine noise gets louder. I need to hurry. I pull myself up and open the freezer. Icy air blooms into the space around me. I intend to make use of the body's semi-stiffness to bridge that gap between freezer and car. I start to manoeuvre it but it's not easy.

By the time I close the freezer lid, I'm damp under my armpits. I stand in front of it, panting, and wonder if I should say something to mark the moment, though I'm not sure what, when the engine sound stops abruptly. Someone has killed the engine somewhere very close to my unit. My heart sinks. Perhaps I am cursed today. But I'm not going to get caught. Not now.

Please don't make me have to kill again. Because it will break me.

*

Emily walks a distance behind Jayne, slow and reluctant because her strong instinct is that they should have tried to follow the track back down towards the farmhouse, however long it took, however tough the going was, because there was definitely some phone reception there, but Jayne refused, arguing that it was too far to go, that their best bet was to head uphill where they're bound to find reception more quickly.

Jayne's brisk authority was hard to contradict.

The path is steep, the terrain underfoot uneven, muddy and littered with half-buried stones that bruise Emily's soles if she doesn't tread carefully. Rain spatters her phone screen whenever she checks it, which is often.

She's afraid to step off the path. The turf beside it looks spongy. If she puts a foot wrong, she might get stuck.

I'm doing this for Paul, she repeats in her head as a mantra. Doing it to make sure he's OK. Because I love him. And I hate this place.

A stream rages just below them, swollen with rain. On its far bank a dead animal, rabbit or hare, with limp and sodden tawny fur, looks peaceful, as if it didn't fall there but was laid out. Emily looks away from it.

I'm doing this for Paul, she repeats to herself.

She wore her red dress on the night she met him. She owned one red dress and one green and alternated them for work. Nude heels went well with both. They were in need of resoling, but nobody knew that but Emily. Her hair was teased into a ponytail, her make-up immaculate, as elegant as online tutorials could teach her. She took time shaping her eyebrows.

'Have you made a booking?' she asked him. She loved her station at the entrance to the restaurant, where she greeted guests before showing them to their seats.

'No,' he said. 'But I don't need to.'

He was well dressed, but not ostentatiously so. Handsome too, but there was nothing hasty or showy about him. His energy was confident, low-key and steady. Focused. She liked that. It intrigued her.

But he wasn't going to get away with this.

'I'm sorry, sir, but everybody needs a reservation tonight. We're full.'

'I know,' he said. He looked amused where she was expecting frustration or disappointment. She felt wrong-footed, but she wasn't going to show him that.

'So,' she said and raised her eyebrows before assuming a polite expression of regret. He was nearly old enough to be her father but something inside her curled because he really was very attractive.

'So,' he batted the word back to her.

She broke eye contact first but rallied. 'Can I find you a seat at the bar, sir? We're famous for our cocktails. I can recommend a . . .' Words failed her. She was desperate to suggest a cocktail whose name wasn't loaded with innuendo, but her mind drew a blank.

His polish slipped and he laughed. A loud, cheerful sound. 'Sorry. I should tell you I'm not actually a guest.' He tugged at his collar as if embarrassed to have deceived her, though she suspected he was enjoying it.

'Oh,' she said.

'I'm Paul.'

He didn't need to say more. It was on the top of every menu and above the door: PAUL'S.

She noted that his hand was soft and dry and immediately loved his quiet confidence. He wasn't what she expected.

'Oh,' she said again.

They married six months later, last spring. He changed her life. Saved her. And only he knows how much she needed saving from a life that had fallen apart dramatically because of a single but devastating lie. She would never forgive her father for it.

Maggie Elliott knocks back the bread dough and sinks her knuckles into it as if it were an adversary. A cloud of flour rises when she turns it and slaps it back down. Condensation beads the inside of her kitchen windows, but not so much that she can't see into the yard.

Her mood turned as the dough rose. John should be back by now. He still hasn't come back into the house since taking the women up to the barn.

His dog, Birdie, lies on her bed beside the Aga, but she's not settled either. She glances towards the door as often as Maggie.

'Where is he, Birds?' Maggie asks. 'Where the bloody hell is he?'

She'll leave it a little longer, she thinks, before worrying too much. A year ago, she wouldn't have given the fact of John's going back out in this weather or the length of his absence a second thought. She took for granted how much she could rely on him; she realises that now.

She reshapes the dough, oils the bowl, and looks up when Birdie yips and wags her tail as she crowds the back door.

Maggie doesn't look at John when he comes in. She places the dough in the bowl and holds her tongue while he hangs up his coat and cap, kicks off his boots.

He switches on the kettle.

'Where've you been?' She doesn't mean to snap but she can't hold it in any longer. Why hasn't he greeted her? That's another thing that's slipped. She shuts her mouth and breathes through her nose, but her chest rises and falls with emphasis, as if her feelings are protesting her efforts to contain them.

'Seeing to things.'

'Seeing to what? To what, John?'

'I was seeing to the wall by the paddock.'

'Do I believe you?'

'I don't know, do you?' The look he gives her is sharp. Nothing lacking in it. Disconcerting when she's expecting vacancy. Confusing how there's no predicting when he's all there and when he's gone.

Maggie eyes the bowl of dough. She wants nothing more than to throw it at him, but it won't do any good, so she doesn't. He only responds to a gentle approach these days. Something freezes in him if she gets angry. She'll make him a tea, sit and have a chat with him. While John's upstairs, she places the bowl on the warm end of the dresser, beside the Aga, and gently drapes a linen towel over it.

He clatters back down the stairs and doesn't even look at her on his way outside.

'Where are you going now?' she calls after him as the back door shuts, no longer able to contain her outrage.

He doesn't answer. Birdie whimpers. He's left her behind again. It used to be that he didn't go anywhere without her. He always had a dog at his feet.

Maggie wrenches the door open.

'Don't you mess with those people!' she shouts into the gloom. She can't see him, has no idea if he can hear her, half-hopes that he can't. But perhaps he needs to hear it. He doesn't seem to comprehend that they need the money rental of the barn brings. They can't survive without it.

Him acting on his vendetta against guests is something she suspects, not something she knows. In moments when her confidence in him fails, she feels as if it's something brewing in him. When the previous guests left early it haunted her because John was out that night. She knows he was if she's honest with herself. He got up in the early hours, thinking she didn't notice. There, she's admitted it now.

She didn't confront him about it before because it was only the one set of guests, after all, who weren't pleasant. And things have been fine, since. But maybe she should have.

And perhaps, if she's right about that, it wasn't so bad that she just shouted after him not to mess with these new guests. Perhaps it's time to be firm about these things, even though she doesn't want to face up to it. But there's no point in chasing after him now, to make the point more firmly. She'll never find him.

She leans against the Aga, absorbing its heat. Birdie looks up at her with those crazy mismatched eyes. Maggie slips her a piece of ham.

'I don't understand him either, Birdie,' she says as the dog eats. 'But he still loves us both.'

The dog lays her head down.

I miss the man I married, Maggie thinks.

Jayne scrambles on to a rock to survey the view. The weather conditions were poor when they set out and they're deteriorating. The rain has intensified, and visibility has reduced.

Worse, Emily has lagged further and further behind as they walk, obsessively checking her phone, and they need to press on more quickly if they're going to cover any distance and find a signal before conditions drive them back inside.

Jayne is as committed as Emily to finding reception, even if it's only patchy. If they can get hold of one or all of their husbands, hopefully Ruth and Emily will stop worrying about the letter and they can have the weekend they all wanted.

Jayne also has another reason to be out here.

She's looking for the ancient burial chamber, a Neolithic barrow, that's on the edge of the Elliott land. She read about it after booking this place and couldn't get it out of her head. And then she read something else, something apparently unrelated, but the two things knitted together in her mind with an intensity that surprised her and gave her an idea that she hasn't been able to let go.

It was a partially formed, beautiful idea, which morphed into a plan whose details she has obsessed over. It gives her a more powerful reason to be at the barn than just the desire to spend a few nights away with friends.

The plan involves her and Mark, alone. She'll tell him about it when he arrives. Anticipating it feels intimate to her, and exciting. What she wants to do will lie at the very core of their marriage and, like the intelligence work they did, it'll be their secret.

She waits on the rock, bearing the full force of the elements as Emily catches up. The rain is falling brutally hard, the wind whipping it in all directions. Jayne can't see as far as the burial chamber, but she knows it's close and that's exhilarating.

Emily is bent against the wind as she picks her way along the path. She must be soaking, Jayne thinks. That's not a waterproof coat.

She feels a little guilty about how irritated she felt with Emily earlier because Emily's having a miserable time, which is only made worse if you hardly know the people you're with. Jayne resents Edie powerfully for the letter. It isn't just a horrible thing to have done, it's verging on endangering them. Emily probably shouldn't be out here, in these conditions, without proper kit.

Resenting Edie isn't new, for Jayne. There have been times before now when Edie has felt like the third person in her marriage.

Jayne wasn't prepared for this when she and Mark first left the army and moved back to Bristol, his hometown. She hadn't reckoned with the dominance of Mark's friends in their life, with how Mark would welcome it and how she would struggle with it.

It might have been OK if Mark's friends were all men, or if Edie were a different kind of woman, but there was something about the way Edie interacted with them all, something possessive, that rankled with Jayne. That Edie was undeniably attractive, that even the most loyal men tracked her with their eyes, didn't help.

But she didn't complain, even when Edie began to grate on her, even when things Mark said made her suspect that he might have fallen in love with Edie while they were at school together, because she believes that the past is the past, and she also believes in loyalty. You do what you have to for the people you love.

Jayne clambers off the top of the rock and extends a hand to Emily to help her up the last, steep bit of the path. Emily grips tightly, her hand wet and slippery, her wedding ring digging into Jayne's fingers. Once she's up, she clings to Jayne's arm. The wind blows Emily's hood off her face, and within seconds rain has painted strands of hair down her forehead.

With her free hand, Emily holds up her phone and moves it from side to side, searching for reception. This is almost the highest point around, and Jayne feels hopeful, but they get nothing.

'I haven't even got one bar,' Emily says. 'The whole way up here. We should have gone down.'

Her forehead is creased in a frown beneath her wet locks. Jayne thinks Emily might be right, but she wants to keep going, just a little. She thinks Emily can cope with a few more minutes out here. Jayne feels inexorably drawn onwards by the possibility that she might be able to glimpse the site of the burial chamber.

It feels urgent that she sees it if she can. She points to higher ground.

'Come on,' she says. 'Just a little further. It's worth a try now that we're here.'

She keeps close to Emily, this time, encouraging her. The hiking is difficult, the ground more unstable by the minute, and Emily's drag on her arm weightier with every step until Jayne starts to regret her decision to push on, but then they come up on the brow abruptly and Jayne pulls Emily back, away from the edge.

Below them is a void. The land beneath their feet, which moments ago felt so solid, collapses into scree. There is nowhere else to go. Jayne kicks a stone as they move back. They hear it tumbling down for what seems like forever.

Emily checks her phone once more.

Over her shoulder, Jayne sees it. To the west. Not too far from here. The hillock where the chamber lies.

'Still nothing,' Emily says, and Jayne feels guilty.

'I'm sorry,' Jayne says. 'We should have gone downhill in the first place. Let's go.'

'We can still go down.' Emily looks as if she might cry, and Jayne realises how desperate she is to speak to Paul and suddenly understands how much more frightening this must be to someone who doesn't know them all.

'We can't,' Jayne says. 'It's too bad out here. You're freezing.'

Emily shakes her head. Her lips are tinged with blue.

'Let's go back to the barn and decide there,' Jayne says but she already knows that Emily needs to warm up, that it would be an unnecessary risk to go down to the farmhouse.

When they turn the wind strikes their backs. Emily slips on the path going down, rights herself, wipes her muddy hand on her jacket, leaving it a little bloody. In places, it's hard to see where the path lies, as if nature shifted things behind their backs, while they teetered on the edge of the brow.

The rain solidifies as they make lower ground, sheets of it pulleyed across the sky.

At the barn, Jayne heads for the door. Emily stops on the path.

'I want to keep going down.' Her skin is alabaster polished with rain. There is determination in her expression, but Jayne also sees indecision, and that Emily has begun to shake.

'Come inside for a little while, please. To dry off and warm up so you don't get sick. We can go out again later when the rain's eased up. There are a few hours before it gets dark. I promise I'll go with you.'

Emily looks uncertain, still. She must really love Paul, Jayne thinks. Or there's something I don't know that's giving her a real reason to worry. She feels another little sliver of doubt about her insistence that this is just a prank but knows she mustn't let it show.

'The letter's a hoax, I promise,' she says. 'Please, come inside.'

Emily looks at Jayne, at her outstretched hand and the pleading expression on her face. She thinks of Edie, writing the letter just to spoil their weekend. And she thinks of Paul, sitting dry as a bone in his office, working hard so he can join her tomorrow.

She steps into the barn.

*

It's not a bad mirror – could be more flattering, could be less. Reflected, the changing room behind Imogen looks lush: a deep red curtain, funky string lights, retro chair, heaped with the garments she pulled from the racks, most of which she can't be bothered to try on. The stuff in here isn't really her style any more. A year ago, maybe, but she's changed.

She takes off her sweater and slips into a blouse made from a slippery turquoise fabric. She buttons the cuffs and creates a perfect French tuck. Skipping breakfast was a good choice. Her midriff lies perfectly flat beneath her waistband. There's a zipper at the neckline and she plays with it until it reveals the perfect amount of cleavage.

Next, she applies lip gloss until her lips are glistening and she pouts into the camera, kinks her hips to the side, takes a dozen photographs from different angles. Her fingertips rake the back of her scalp as she lifts her hair. They hover on her waist as she alters her pose.

'How are you getting on?'

'Fine,' she tells the shop assistant while her fingers are busy cropping and filtering.

She wants to post the photo in case Matt looks at her feed because she thinks she looks good in it. But she can't bring herself to do it. It's the sort of selfie that all her friends post and that Imogen used to, but not since her dad died. He hated social media, hated how the girls in her year put up pictures showing their bodies off. 'Never feel you have to give in to peer pressure to do this kind of thing,' he told Imogen. And while she didn't think much of disobeying him when he was alive, now it feels like a betrayal of him, especially on a day when she's already told one big lie that he wouldn't have approved of.

She wipes off her lip gloss and stares at herself. She wishes she could see more of her dad in her own face, but it's not there. All she sees is her mum.

'Just so you know, we close at five.' Imogen jumps at the sound of the assistant's voice coming from right behind the curtain and checks her phone. It's 5:03. She takes off the shirt, slips her sweater back on, sorts out her hair, sweeps the curtain back.

'How were the clothes? Did you see anything you like?' The assistant is trying to look interested, bless her, but you can tell she wants to lock up and go home. It's Friday night.

'No, thanks,' Imogen says. 'But lush things.'

It's chilly outside. Next door, she takes a table by the window and orders a tea. She checks her phone, but Jemma hasn't been in touch. A man in the corner is eating sausages and egg. He stares at her until she flips him the finger.

Imogen never used to feel lonely. But now it's as if all the things she used to enjoy are being swallowed up by a big hole inside her. She thinks of her mum. Edie's trying to be a good mother, Imogen knows that. But she's been so distracted lately, as if something else is gnawing at her, something more than the grief that they've both been crushed by. She really hasn't been herself. And it's scaring Imogen. More than a little.

Emily's in the shower, her eyes shut, and her head tipped back beneath the paltry jets of water. She's trying to warm up.

Downstairs, Ruth peels potatoes. The beef stew she made and froze before travelling here is defrosting in its Tupperware on the side. She made enough for six, so there'll be leftovers.

She curses when the knife slips. It almost cuts her and would have if it wasn't so blunt. Tears spring to her eyes. The vodka settled her at first, but now she feels agitated, and upset, the way she always does before her emotions well up and she feels as if she might drown in them.

The news that Jayne and Emily were unable to get a phone signal when they went out has rattled her, more than she'd like to admit.

Jayne watches from the other side of the kitchen. She notes Ruth's exaggerated wince when the knife slips, how hard and for how long she grips her finger, even though there's clearly no cut. She's not herself.

'Do you want me to take over?' Jayne asks.

'I'm fine!' Ruth says. If she keeps busy, she won't be able to think bad thoughts. It's one of her coping mechanisms. 'You know I enjoy it,' she adds so as not to sound snappish.

Jayne thinks that might have been true on previous weekends away but that on this occasion Ruth is a bad liar. She doesn't challenge Ruth, though, because she wants to ask her something she's never broached with her before.

'I was thinking,' Jayne says, 'about how when I first got introduced to you all, I found it very strange, how close you were. You lived in each other's pockets.'

'I liked it. For me it was like being handed an instant social life on a plate. It was a novelty because I was that girl at school and at uni who didn't really hang out in groups.'

Ruth trots her answer out before she properly considers Jayne's question.

Had it felt strange? She can't really remember. At the time she was dizzy with her achievement of having found a boyfriend who she had real feelings for and who her mother accepted. It had felt like finding the holy grail. Flora had welcomed Toby with open arms. Adored him. Ruth had revelled in her mother's approval and Toby's attention. It had felt too good to be true. Was it?

She shakes her head to bring herself back. She mustn't let her thoughts spiral. 'I remember the night Mark introduced us to you,' she says. 'We were so surprised! Everyone thought he and Paul were settling into happy bachelorhood.'

Jayne smiles. Tactful Ruth is omitting to say that they were also surprised that handsome Mark Pavey had chosen such a plain woman to marry, but Jayne knows what everyone thought and she's at peace with it. Mark wants someone strong by his side, not a trophy wife.

There have only been a few moments in their marriage when she's wondered if he regretted his choice, when she's taken a long look at herself in the mirror and felt doubt.

Once, Mark suggested that Jayne dress more like Edie and that cut to the core of her confidence. It took days for her sense of inadequacy to disappear even though he apologised profusely, saying that he didn't know what he was thinking, that it had been careless talk.

Jayne tries another angle. 'But it did feel strange to you when you first met Toby, how close their gang were? Because it's unusual how much Edie has this sort of hold on the men, don't you think? I mean, not always, but since Rob died it's been very intense in that respect. Don't you think?'

Ruth feels tears prickle. The last few months have been a nightmare. The room suddenly feels too dark to her. It's hard to see what she's doing, and everything looks a little fuzzy, and ill-defined. I need more light, she thinks.

She snaps on the overhead. It illuminates the room harshly, taking away some of the cosy, showing up the worn edges of the cabinets, a dark stain on the scrubbed pine table. The letter, no longer dissolving gradually into shadow, looks a bright, clinical white. Ruth stares at it.

'Ruth, are you OK?' Jayne asks. Did her question touch a nerve? And when was it that Ruth last appeared to be herself? Jayne can hardly remember. All eyes have been on the baby since he was born and Ruth wanted him so badly that Jayne assumed she was ecstatic after having him, snug in a fluffy cloud of maternal bliss.

But perhaps not.

Ruth feels blindsided. No one ever asks if she's OK, not like this, with *feeling*, as if they truly want to know the answer.

It's hard to know what to say. Growing up she learned that you report success, not weakness. With her childhood vitamin supplements she absorbed the idea that love, and friendship, are conditional, that you can be disliked if you don't present your best self, that no bond is so close as to be unbreakable.

The thought of sharing even a little bit of her true self is alarming, let alone her darkest worries, the ones that are laced with shame.

She puts on a smile before turning to face Jayne. 'I'm fine, really,' she says. 'I'm tired and working too many hours and Toby is hopeless with the baby but it's my new happy place.'

'I thought Toby would be great with Alfie. He's so . . .' Jayne searches for a word. 'Immature' presents itself, but she's not sure she knows Ruth well enough to say it. Their friendship is still more careful than that.

'Such a child himself?' Ruth cuts in.

'Well, I wasn't going to say that exactly,' Jayne says. But, yes, Professor Toby Land has never grown out of his boyish looks (not handsome, but almost), his clowning around, his open-hearted affability. He wears his hair long enough to show off a charming cowlick, his eyes are rarely without a soft twinkle.

The gang love to tease him about the tweed suits and bow ties he sometimes wears. These are playful affectations and eccentricities he delights in. But he's also, apparently, brilliant in his field and much loved by his students. It's not difficult for Jayne to imagine. Toby is far from her type as a partner, but she's always felt herself slightly softened and quietly charmed by him.

'I thought he'd be good with Alfie too. I never considered that he might not be, but he struggles.' Ruth feels safe sharing this much, a fraction of her burden. 'I don't think they've bonded very well, but that's probably my fault because I don't trust him to do a lot of stuff with Alfie. But I think it's not uncommon for men not to bond with small babies. I've read quite a lot about it. When Alfie's big enough for Toby to do stuff with him I'm sure it'll be different.'

She stops abruptly, afraid that she's talking too much and too fast. She does that sometimes. She turns back to her peeling, hoping she's shared enough to prevent Jayne from prying further, afraid that if Jayne pushes her, she'll spill everything.

From upstairs, the sound of the shower ceases. Emily will be down soon, Jayne thinks. She lowers her voice.

'Emily's so freaked out about the letter that she was trying to head down to the farmhouse even though she was freezing out there, actually shaking from cold. Can you help me reassure her?'

'I don't know how.' The words are out of Ruth's mouth before she can stop them, and she regrets them instantly. She doesn't want Jayne to know how scared she feels. 'Will you find a pan and fill it with water for me?' she asks. 'A big one.' She halves a peeled potato. The knife thumps on to the board and the pieces scatter, one falling on to the floor.

'Fuck!' Ruth says. She seals her lips and shuts her eyes. That was an overreaction. When she opens her eyes again Jayne is looking at her with concern.

'Ruth—' Jayne says.

'No! Look! I'm fine. I just want to get this done.'

'We can do it later.'

'I want to get it done now. I'll reheat it later.'

And it'll go to mush, Jayne thinks, but says nothing. She's never seen Ruth as agitated as this.

She touches Ruth's arm gently and Ruth drops the knife as if burned. It clatters on the kitchen surface. Her self-control fishtails. She's strongly tempted to share everything she fears with Jayne, and there is so much more that frightens her than the letter.

But she can't. Why is she even considering it? Is she unravelling because she's so far away from home? Or because the letter, hoax or not, feels as if it's bringing everything to a head?

The truth is that Ruth has been feeling crazy lately, and she can't admit it. It's mortifying. And it's a secret she's been keeping for long enough that it feels impossible to share. She's afraid that if she does, she might find her life is too shattered to put back together.

She has a powerful urge to get out of here, to return to her normal life, where she feels less exposed, where it's easier to distract herself from what she's afraid of.

'I wish you'd got a signal,' she says to Jayne. 'You know, maybe I'll wander down the track to the farm myself. It would be nice to be reassured, don't you think? I'd like to hear Toby's voice and to check in with my mum.'

This seems like a terrific idea to Ruth, suddenly. She'll be the one to brave the weather and put all their fears to rest. The thought of being a sort of saviour for their little group appeals to the dormant teacher's pet in her.

But her thoughts immediately turn negative. What if she manages to call Toby but he doesn't answer his phone and the other men do? Or what if her mother doesn't pick up? It would be unbearable.

'The letter's a hoax!' Jayne says.

'But what if it isn't? Why does she say in the letter that she's leaving? And make a point of saying that we didn't want her here? Does she think we've done something to her? Is she blaming us for something, and this is her revenge?'

'What? No. Don't believe a word of the letter. Not one word.'

Ruth glances at the window. Rain is still lashing down, the slope at the back of the barn is saturated. Jayne looks too.

'Listen, if you want to walk down at least wait a bit to see if the rain eases up. You saw the state of Emily and me when we got in. I'll go back out with you later if you like. I said the same to Emily. But please know that whatever your mind is telling you right now, this letter absolutely isn't a real threat. I promise you. And you know it. Remember the stories about the hoaxes that Edie did when the gang were at school? The ones they always tell when they're drunk? And don't forget that she's grieving hard. She's not in her right mind.'

Jayne is shocked. She never expected Ruth to react like this. Jayne feels like she's playing catch-up; that her friend's mental state is far more fragile than she ever imagined.

Ruth catches the depth of concern in Jayne's words and her expression and is horrified to be the object of them.

'You're right,' she says. 'I'm sorry. I know it's a hoax, of course I do. It's just that since Alfie, I've been a little anxious. You know? Hormones maybe?' She sounds unconvincing to herself. She's fudging the facts, understating what it's been like. She notices that her hands are clenched into white-knuckled fists and unclenches them.

'Don't let Edie get into your head.'

'I won't. I'm not.' Yet Ruth knows why she feels that her family is the intended target. The reasoning has fully assembled itself in her head and sits there now, a small, hunched figure in silhouette, waiting.

But it feels impossible to articulate this to Jayne because if she does, she'll have to admit that it might be true.

In the silence after the engine dies my breathing sounds unbearably loud.

I crouch down behind the car reflexively, and my knee hurts like hell. I hear footsteps approaching.

'Hello?' A male voice. I don't think I have any choice but to stand up.

'Hi,' I say.

The sun is behind my visitor so it's hard to see his face, but I think it's the man who rents this place to me, which is good news. He wasn't a man of many words or much curiosity when I met him the first time.

'How are you?' I add. I raise my voice a little because I'm behind the car. It's a vulnerable feeling.

'Have you got yourself stuck in there?' he asks. It's definitely my landlord. He has a gravelly West Country accent with a flat undertone of world-weariness.

'No, no! Everything's fine. I'm just loading the freezer.' I wish I hadn't said that, but it's too late. And don't they say that the best kind of lie is one that's close to the truth?

I'm glad he can't get near enough to observe the sweat patches forming under my arms, or to hear me swallow as I speak. I wish I was in the car. I imagine driving into him, solving the problem of him with a little tap on the accelerator.

He squints and peers, trying to see me better. It unnerves me. I must distract him.

'Moving some stuff around?' I ask, nodding at the parked forklift.

'I'm emptying another unit for a mate,' he says.

I nod. When will he go?

We hear an indistinct shout from the other end of the yard. My landlord raises a hand in its direction.

'That's him, then. Sure you're not stuck?' he says to me.

'No. Nope. All good here. Very good.' I force a smile. 'Nice to see you.'

'Right,' he says.

I watch him leave and sag with relief once the forklift is out of sight. I'm a little wobbly as I climb back through the car and drive forward far enough that I can get out, shut the hatchback and lock the unit. I wonder why the landlord came up here at all. Perhaps he's nosier than I thought. I tell myself not to get paranoid. Not now.

Once I've made the unit secure, and you can believe I triple-checked the lock, I get back into the car. Every nerve in my body is jangling. It's hard to stay upbeat. I can feel my ability to focus starting to wane, weakness creeping in. But I give myself a pep talk and tell myself that the worst is over.

People have got exactly what was coming to them and I'll finally be able to have what I deserve.

I'm just not sure why I'm crying.

The pile of peeled, bone-pale potatoes sits on the counter in front of Ruth. 'We'd better get these in water,' she says, 'or they'll go brown.'

'Sure.' Jayne locates a pan, fills it, the water out of the tap surprisingly cold. She puts it on the hob and turns on the heat.

They've fallen into an awkward silence, broken only by the sound of the rain and the clatter of the pan lid as the water comes to the boil.

Everything feels messy to Jayne, suddenly. She's seen more complicated emotion in Ruth these past few minutes than she has in months. Years, maybe. Ever? Is it something that's happening in her life? The letter's undeniably a stressor for all of them, but surely it shouldn't have knocked Ruth for six like this.

Ruth is struggling to know what to do with a strong impulse to share her feelings. It feels wrong, terrifying, and possibly humiliating, but necessary, as if she can't help it. If anyone will try to understand, Jayne will. She might be straight-laced, she might even be boring (an accusation Toby has made in private), but Ruth knows Jayne to be level-headed and kind.

Ruth looks at her friend and Jayne breaks the silence.

'I'm sorry,' she says. 'If things have been difficult since Alfie was born.'

And Ruth knows she's going to share. 'Jayne,' she begins, 'I—'

'Hi,' Emily says from the doorway. Her eyes flick from Jayne to Ruth and back again. 'Am I interrupting something?' Her hair's wet. She scrunches the ends of it with a towel.

'No,' Jayne says.

'No!' Ruth speaks over her; she sounds a little manic, her voice too loud. 'Of course not. How are you feeling? Have you warmed up? Would you like a cup of tea?'

'I was wondering if either of you have a hairdryer?'

'Isn't there one upstairs?' Ruth asks.

'No,' Emily says.

'Because you wouldn't be asking if there was. Sorry. I've brought one.'

'Can I grab it from your bag?'

'No! I'll get it for you.'

'Sure,' Emily says. 'Thanks.' Ruth, she thinks, is exhausting. And why doesn't she want me to go in her bag? Does she think I'm going to steal something?

As they head upstairs, Jayne notes how swiftly Ruth morphed into mother-hen mode. It was as if a switch had flicked in Ruth's mind, reverting her to what Jayne thinks of as normal Ruth. But perhaps it's not normal at all. Perhaps 'normal' Ruth is a coping strategy. Jayne feels guilty that she might not have noticed fault lines when she should have.

The pan is billowing steam now, its lid rattling urgently, catching her attention. Jayne adds the potatoes and turns down the heat a touch. There's no extractor fan in this little kitchen. She supposes it would be impossible to install one beneath or between the heavy beams. The windows are misting up quickly. She cracks one open, and the wind immediately bullies its way through the small gap. She shuts it, makes a cup of tea, and sits amidst the thickening fug.

Should I be as worried as Ruth and Emily are? she wonders. Be rational. Think it through. What would Mark say? She imagines him raising his eyebrows, asking what all the fuss is about. 'Don't get sucked into their paranoia, Jayney,' he would say. 'You know better than that.' She agrees.

The answer is that she should keep her cool and the reason for it is that Edie isn't capable of killing another person. The idea's ridiculous. Edie's been at the heart of the gang for two decades. She's the glue that holds them together, the sun they orbit.

And it's not just about Edie. Toby, Mark and Paul have been like uncles to Edie's daughter Imogen all her life, even before Rob died.

Why would Edie hurt any one of them?

Jayne has always kept her distance from Edie as much as possible. They're such different people. It's as if I've studied her, she thinks. Like a specimen of the sort of woman I'll never be. What have I learned? That Edie is funny, and charismatic. That she's beautiful and sexy, but also sharp and intelligent. She takes offence.

Jayne thinks of the letter. 'I didn't come along because I know I'm not welcome,' Edie wrote. A typical dig at them. I'm missing out and it's your fault. It's chagrin and exactly the sort of thing Edie might say to manipulate the men.

So, *should* they be worried about the letter?

No, Jayne thinks, the intention of this letter is to hurt me, Ruth and Emily. Maybe because our husbands are not dead, because we get to go on couples' weekends as couples, not as a widow. Edie's hurting and she wants us to know what it might feel like.

She reaches for the letter and rereads it. It's mean. Edie has gone too far. And it wouldn't be the first time.

It's definitely a hoax.

With brisk movements she refolds the letter, stuffs it back into its envelope and puts it aside. Out of sight, out of mind.

She takes a tour of the downstairs of the barn, though there's not much to see.

The front room is as compact and claustrophobic as the kitchen, with the same heavy beams overhead. One small window is sunk into the deep wall and faces the front. A wood burner sits within the exposed stone fireplace. Two sofas gather around it, and a bookcase holds a smattering of holiday novels, a pack of cards and some board games. Nothing special. Comfortable enough.

She's drawn to the window, the pale grey light filtering through it a lure. She feels as if she herself is little more than a shadow as she passes through the dark room.

Lost in what she can see – the volatile storm, the land cowed yet proud beneath it – her mind wanders as wide as the horizon stretches and finishes where it always does: with Mark.

She never thought he would look at her when they met. Her conversation with Ruth has reminded her of this. Memories of her early days with Mark are a mix of elation and surprise because the attention he paid her was so unexpected. She'd never thought of herself as the type of girl to find 'the one' because she's never been conventionally pretty or girly, never really known or wanted to know how to flirt. She was a tomboy.

It seems a miracle to her, still, that he wanted her and that their lives knitted together so perfectly. It's amazing how life can surprise you, she thinks, with a smile. How her idea of her future changed in a heartbeat, marriage to Mark becoming her life's work.

And it is work, but Jayne accepts the imperfect, relishes the challenge. She's up to it. When she's set her mind on something, she doesn't give up and she gives it her all.

She turns back to the room and pauses for a moment to examine a framed black-and-white photograph hanging over the fireplace. She leans in to read the inked inscription on the mount identifying it. It's hard to decipher as it's written in spidery brown ink, but she knows what the image is of. She knew it immediately because she's studied every picture she could find online. It's the Neolithic burial chamber, taken from an angle that emphasises its menacing solidity and its ancient significance.

In this image the stone-lined entrance is still partially intact, which makes Jayne think that it must have been taken decades ago because she knows the chamber is in more disrepair now. It sends a shiver up her spine.

From upstairs, she can hear the whir of the hairdryer. How long does it take Emily to do her hair? Ruth hasn't come down yet either.

She tears herself away from the photograph and decides to light a fire. As she lays firelighters and kindling in the wood burner, her thoughts circle back to the letter and to its sender, and they darken.

If she's brutally honest with herself, she has to question whether it's right to assume that Edie isn't capable of murder. How can we really know who has the potential to use violence? She and Mark move amongst the general population freely and they both have blood on their hands.

Granted, it got there in service of their country, and it got there indirectly, because neither of them wielded a weapon outside of training. But it's there, nevertheless. An invisible stain.

How many others are like them? Others whose motives are not as acceptable?

Is Edie?

'I found my hairdryer for her,' Ruth says. Jayne startles. She didn't hear Ruth coming. The narrow stairs are thickly carpeted.

'I hear it,' Jayne says and smiles. Ruth isn't the only one who can put a game face on.

'Do you think the rain's easing?' Ruth asks.

It's not. And whatever her personal doubts are, Jayne is clear in her mind that it's not a good idea to leave this house while the weather's like this. It's a safety issue. It can't be argued with. And in her view, if the weather stays bad until it gets dark, they're going to have to wait out the night here until, hopefully, the men arrive in the mid- or late morning tomorrow.

So, for now, she won't share her own fears about Edie. It will only escalate Ruth and Emily's anxiety. And that's bad situation management.

'Not yet,' she says. Ruth goes to the window to look out, blocking the light.

Jayne strikes a match and a firelighter catches. She shuts the stove door and sits back on her heels, staring at the flames.

She has to admit that there's a small, selfish part of her that's desperate for this weekend to go ahead as she planned it, no matter what else is going on.

She looks up at the photograph of the burial chamber. It's almost as if I'm a supplicant, kneeling here before it, she thinks. But that's letting her imagination run too far.

She glances at Ruth and notes the defeated slope of her shoulders, the way her arms hang limply by her sides. Jayne suspects that Ruth's in no state to make sensible decisions.

And whatever her own intentions, objectively, the best way forward is to stay here, stay safe and ignore the letter as best they can.

'What do you think?' she asks, looking at her watch. 'It's almost six o'clock. Time for a proper drink?'

I close the front door behind me.

The car's in the garage and Imogen and I are safely home. I lean my back against the door, shut my eyes and feel sweet relief.

All I need to do now is to keep Imogen with me. She's ruined the alibi I set up for this afternoon and tonight, so she has to become my alibi. It's not strictly necessary that my time is accounted for, a nice-to-have rather than a need-to-have, but I would like to have her with me. Now that she is, it feels essential somehow. I can't tell you how important to me it is that this night be a good one because it's the first night of our new life together. Not that she knows any of this yet.

'I'm going out later,' she says. Her cello is leaning against the wall, her hand lingering on the scroll end of the case. She, and it, look timeless. I'm so lucky to have her.

'Out? Where?' I ask, keeping my tone light, feeling a little bud of panic unfurl in my chest.

'With friends.'

'Which friends?'

'Jemma.'

'Jemma and who?'

'What?'

'You said friends. Plural.'

'I meant just Jemma.'

'Do you think she'd like to come here? She can join us for takeaway and a movie?' I can tell from the mildly disgusted expression on Imogen's face that I might be sounding a little desperate.

'You don't like Jemma.'

She's right. She must remember when I lost my temper with Jemma all those years ago, when I thought Jemma was being unfair to Imogen. But I'm not going to admit it. 'I do like Jemma. She's a nice girl.'

'You could say it like you mean it.'

Deep breath. Most convincing expression. 'I mean it. She's most welcome to hang out with us tonight.'

'I don't think she's going to want to come here. We were thinking of going out.'

'Going out where?'

She shrugs, but I'm not buying it. Of course she knows what they're planning to do tonight and, whatever it is, it's not going to happen. Rob used to say that it's best to back down when you're dealing with Imogen, give her space and she'll come around. I didn't always agree, but I try it now. My shrug is as nonchalant as I can make it and I turn away to pick up the post on the mat.

'Well, she's welcome. And don't you think you should take it easy tonight and stay in? You weren't in a good place when we spoke this morning.'

She hesitates. I can sense her mental cogs turning. She knows I've got a point. Though I suspect I haven't won this yet. 'I guess I am tired.'

'Why don't you relax, take a bath or something?'

When she's upstairs, I rummage through my bag and locate the burner phone. I don't need it any longer.

Removing the SIM card only takes a moment. I pocket it and carry the body of the phone into the garden. Before Imogen mucked up my plans, I had a different idea for the destruction of this phone, but it's no longer viable. This is Plan B. It will have to do.

I kneel at the edge of the pond and sprinkle its surface with flakes of foul-smelling fish food. The fish rise, eyes bulging, gobbling, always so greedy, and I let the phone slip from my hand into the water where it sinks soundlessly with barely a ripple between the churning bodies. Imogen won't be able to see me here. Neither her room nor the bathroom have a window overlooking the pond.

The phone settles invisibly into the depths. I'll retrieve it later and dispose of it properly.

The SIM card goes into the kitchen waste disposal unit joining saturated Cheerios and the wilted remains of some salad leaves. I switch it on, and it grinds noisily. When the sound changes, I stop and flush with water. I can just get my fingers in to feel that the card is still intact, but badly damaged. I retrieve it carefully. I'm pretty sure I've destroyed it but, to be sure, I take it into the sitting room and put it in the grate. I arrange a pyramid of kindling over it, making sure it's perfect. Lastly, I tuck a firelighter in and light it.

The flames are so pretty. You could lose yourself in them and I do for a while. I watch until the card curls and melts and a sense of satisfaction settles inside me.

That's another job ticked off, another obstacle removed, bringing Imogen and me that bit closer to starting our future.

Emily is drying her hair. It's not easy because Ruth's dryer is primitive and blows too hot. No wonder Ruth always looks dishevelled.

Emily peers into the small mirror on the chest of drawers in her room. Her hair looks shit from every angle. She'll have to tie it up and if Paul tries to take it down tomorrow, the way he sometimes does, tugging at her hair clip and saying that he prefers her to wear it loose – if he tries that, there'll be hell to pay, and it'll serve him right.

Emily's not afraid of a row. Nor is Paul. They can fight like cat and dog, but it doesn't mean they love each other any less. He says she's fiery, like her hair, that he likes a woman who'll stand up to him.

She turns off the dryer and her bravado disappears with the sound, as if it were wired to the same switch.

They can only fight *if* Paul comes tomorrow.

She wishes she could have reached him on the phone. She's determined to get down the hill and back to the farmhouse as soon as the rain has eased. Jayne said she would go with her.

In the meantime, she'll make an effort. No point in making enemies, especially if she wants Jayne's help.

Plus, she'll ask more about Edie. What kind of hoaxes she's pulled in the past. Perhaps she can be convinced that Edie's just messing with them. Perhaps then her heart will stop beating so fast and the twist in her gut that's making her nauseous will loosen.

She scrapes her hair back into a ponytail. She looks younger with her hair back and she might have cared about that this morning, but not now. Her face in the mirror reminds her of her mother at the end of her life. She seemed to grow younger as the illness stripped her of anything that was left after the years of addiction.

It's a painful memory. Emily turns away from her reflection.

Outside, the clouds have dipped so low it's as if Dark Fell Barn is being squeezed between land and sky. The valley is veiled with rain. The place still feels like a fairy tale and definitely not one with a happy ending.

She's angry with herself for not recognising Edie for who she is. A hoaxer at best. At worst . . . it's unthinkable.

You should know better, she tells herself. In the world you came from you had to be on your guard 24/7. First, from her mother's boyfriends, then from the cancer and what it would do next to Mum. Perhaps she's lost her edge since living with Paul, got too comfortable, bought into a happy-ending fantasy. She should have known better.

She thinks about the times she's spent with Edie. There haven't been many occasions. A few nights out, the gang gathered in a pub, loud and happy. Edie was compelling. People gravitated to her naturally. She was beautiful, elegant and witty but didn't act like she was above you. She complimented Emily on her own looks and her clothes and Emily was flattered and seduced.

Was I being played? she wonders. And if so, why? Jealousy, maybe? Has Edie found it impossible to relinquish a claim to these men, even after all these years? Did she resent Emily and

Paul being together? Was all that niceness on display just to ensure that nobody was ready when she decided to unsheathe her claws?

It hits her then, the stuck-in-your-throat feeling of a difficult memory. Rob's wake. Emily travelled there separately from Paul. The men had orbited Edie that day, acting as pall-bearers, gathered around her and Imogen like a security detail before and after the service. Edie's grief was towering, desperate, amplified by her elegance and her beauty.

The wake was crowded when Emily arrived at Edie and Rob's house. She couldn't find Paul anywhere downstairs or in the garden. She went upstairs.

'I don't think so.' She heard Paul's voice, slightly muffled, but couldn't see him.

'But you promised.' Edie. Upset. Where were they? Should Emily interrupt? Probably not, but she couldn't resist listening. She crept up to the landing.

'I didn't promise,' Paul said.

They were in a room at the top of the stairs. Bathroom? The door was shut.

'Please,' Edie said. She was begging. Emily was shocked.

Then, silence. Perhaps the sound of fabric against fabric. Had Paul gone to Edie? Was he embracing her? Kissing? No. Surely not. Emily couldn't help herself. She turned the door handle and pushed. The door was locked. 'Hello?' she called. 'Paul?'

She rattled the handle again, imagining them in there hiding from her, and rested her forehead on the door. When it opened suddenly, she stumbled into the room. Paul caught her by the arm.

Edie was sitting on the edge of the bath, still wearing her coat and hat with its scrap of black veil at a coquettish slant. Her face was blotched and the tip of her nose red from crying.

'I'm sorry to hijack Paul,' Edie said. 'I couldn't face downstairs. This is hard.' Her smile seemed somehow cracked.

Paul didn't meet Emily's eye. He looked tense.

'Mum?' It was Imogen, coming upstairs. Emily stepped aside to let her into the room. Edie snapped to attention. She checked her face in the mirror before turning to her daughter.

'Sweetie,' she said.

'Why are you up here? People won't leave me alone downstairs.'

'Aren't Mark and Toby looking after you?'

'They're talking.'

'I'm so sorry,' Edie said. 'I had a funny moment. I'm fine now, I'm coming.'

Paul stuck to his story on the way home. That Edie had needed his moral support to get through the wake. It was plausible, though it didn't feel right to Emily. But she couldn't put her finger on why. Something in the atmosphere between them?

Or was she paranoid that Paul would turn out to be as big a liar as her own father?

Paul knows he must never lie to her because Emily's father told a lie so bad that it ruined her family, and her life. He told Emily and her mother that they were the only ones, his darlings. But one day he made a mistake and they discovered that he had another family. With two little boys and a wife who he chose over Emily and her mother after the truth came out. It broke Emily's mum. She never recovered. It turned their lives, their convictions, their identities, to dust.

Paul promised that he would not lie to Emily when they married. They are one hundred per cent honest with each other. It's the deal they made, because she insisted on it, the thing that separates them from other couples. Not their age gap, like everyone thinks, but this: honesty.

Paul also told Emily never to fall down that rabbit hole of comparing him to her dad. But perhaps, she thinks now, she should have. Is he really working today?

Emily stares out of the window. Is the rain easing a little? It looks like it. Maybe she can go back out again soon and try to reach the farmhouse.

Because what if Paul was lying about what passed between him and Edie in the bathroom that day? What if there's some business between them that Emily isn't aware of? What if Edie has a reason to hate Paul?

But there can't be, because that would mean Paul's kept things from Emily. Or can there?

There's only one circumstance she can think of in which Paul might lie, and that would be to protect her. But she can't imagine what he might need to protect her from.

Jayne is calling upstairs, offering a drink. Emily takes some deep breaths, summoning strength.

She'll go down and find out what she needs to know. Her questions feel urgent.

The last few weeks have been some of the most challenging of my life. Reinvention is very hard work.

It's nice, this house, but I won't miss it. We need to move on.

From overhead, I can hear the bath taps roaring and Imogen's footsteps as she pads between her room and the bathroom. It occurs to me that the towels haven't been washed in a while, that she might like a clean one and she might think it thoughtful of me to bring it to her. I'll earn Brownie points wherever I can.

On the half-landing I delve into the airing cupboard, emerging with the best towel I can find. 'Imogen,' I call but she doesn't answer.

I'm careful not to invade her privacy and I put the towel, nicely folded, on the landing floor, right in front of the bathroom door, which is ajar. But as I turn to go down, I glimpse her in her room across the hall.

She's wearing just pale pink knickers and a vest top. Her body is utterly transformed from the child I used to help build sandcastles on the beach and tickle on the grass. Of course this should be no surprise, because I've watched her grow up, but somehow it always is.

She has earbuds in and she's dancing, her back to me, her slight hips swaying. I see the front of her reflected in a full-length mirror. Her eyes are shut, and she's so absorbed in the music she almost seems to be in a trance, and I can't tear my eyes away. Her skin is perfection, as smooth as silk. Her body is so young and pert. I envy that youth, I'll admit it. I miss the days when everything felt possible, but it also makes me feel more determined than ever to protect her. She has everything to live for. She slowly raises her arms as she sways, lost in the music, and her top rises over her tummy.

I step away quietly, smiling. I'll take this glimpse of her sweetness and store it in the mental space where I put the things that help me get up in the morning.

But when I'm halfway downstairs, something stops me.

Imogen has lied to me.

Because on the midriff of that glorious, young dancing body, there wasn't a single sign of self-harm.

Which is good, of course it's good. A relief so massive that I can hardly process it. But it also means, and this is hard to get my head around, that she's lied about self-harming, that she's been deceiving me for months, deceiving all of us.

It's so bold.

And why would she lie about it? Did she want attention? Is the threat of self-harm a way to manipulate people?

I'm confused. And I can't help thinking how lonely she must be to have done this and how it's up to me to make her feel wanted and heard and understood. I'm tempted to confront her about it right now, but I think twice. It's not the right time. She doesn't need to know that I know yet. I'll talk to her about it when the time is right.

And when that time comes, I'll make it clear that it's not acceptable to deceive me. There will be consequences.

The cork pops, flies, hits a beam, skitters across the sitting-room floor, coming to rest in front of the window. Champagne drools from the rim of the bottle.

Jayne thought about asking again if the others wanted to drink the champagne and decided against giving them the choice. She opened it anyway, hoping to provoke Emily and Ruth into being more defiant in the face of Edie's attempt to sabotage their weekend.

It's not too long until dark now, and Jayne's hopeful that if she can distract them by encouraging them to enjoy themselves, they'll give up on wanting to go out.

She pours.

Ruth glances at Emily. With her make-up off and hair tied back Emily looks like a teenager. It's disconcerting.

Perhaps, she thinks, it's the very existence of Emily, her young body, the beautiful blank slate of her, ready for a man to draw on, that has piqued Edie beyond reason. Edie can offer a man a lot, but not that. Has her grief provoked jealousy in her?

Though that only makes sense if Edie wanted Paul for herself, after Rob died. And then found she couldn't have him. Ruth wouldn't have thought of this if Toby hadn't made a recent comment about it, suggesting that it was well known that Paul had always been Edie's second favourite in their gang, the one they all thought she'd pair off with before she chose Rob.

It does seem far-fetched. But it would be a better explanation than the possibilities that have been tormenting her. She glances at Emily again. It's quite unnerving how young and innocent she looks. And her skin is perfect. Flawless. How, Ruth wonders, have I been so comfortable with Toby being around Emily?

'What about a toast?' Jayne says. She nods at Emily, encouraging her to pick up the glass.

'Oh, sorry!' Ruth has taken a drink already. The bright sparkle of the liquid on her tongue thrills her, builds on the warm glow of the vodka she's just helped herself to more of upstairs, holds the promise of obliterating some of her anxiety.

Jayne raises her glass. Ruth mirrors her. Emily picks hers up reluctantly, as if it might bite. Jayne is pleased with how cosy the room feels now the fire is lit. It took well. The swarming flames are reflected in their champagne glasses.

'Here's to us, to our tradition of weekends away, to friendship and to having a great time in spite of everything,' Jayne says.

'Cheers!' Ruth lifts her glass and drinks. The champagne is tartly delicious. Almost a punishment. A little bit like spending time with Edie herself. The compliments, followed swiftly by the sarcasm, or the gentle put-down. Toby tells her she imagines those, that she's too sensitive to Edie, but she thinks he's wrong. The back of her nose prickles. She can't remember when she last drank champagne. It feels like such a treat.

Ruth has always admired the way that Edie can make you feel special when she wants to. She wouldn't even need champagne to make you feel good. She could do it with a look, a smile, a thoughtful gift.

But why is she thinking like this? This champagne isn't a special gift from Edie, or not in the right way anyway, because it came with that horrible letter. It's bittersweet. Backhanded.

But she can't help taking another sip.

She decides it's special *in spite of* Edie.

Emily raises her glass but sets it back down without drinking. 'I can't,' she says. 'I'm sorry. It doesn't feel right. I need to know more about Edie's hoaxes.'

'Oh!' Ruth says. 'I could tell you a story or two about that!' Suddenly she feels on a high, awash with optimism that's verging on mania. The vodka has hit her system with a bang and she happily anticipates the champagne kicking in too. 'Edie played lots of hoaxes at school. All the usual stuff,' she says. 'Hiding nasty things in people's bags. Gluing the pages of books together.'

She laughs, the way she always does when Edie and the men reminisce about this stuff, because the gang loves solidarity, even though behaviour like that would have humiliated Ruth if she'd been its victim and, behind her laugh, she's always painfully aware of that. She drains her glass.

Jane snorts. 'Edie did far worse than that. Paul didn't tell you about the "love letter"?'

'No,' Emily says.

'When they were in school, in the sixth form, Edie faked a love letter from one of the teachers, a man she hated, to a pupil. She claimed she found it somewhere in school and handed it in. She copied his handwriting well enough that it convinced the head.'

'What happened?'

'The teacher denied writing it and the pupil denied receiving it. There was a moment when Edie might have come forward to admit that she'd written the letter, but she didn't.'

'Were Mark and Toby aware of this?'

Jayne nods. 'Paul was, too.'

'And none of them told the truth?'

'They didn't want Edie to get into trouble. Her mum could have lost her job and they would both have had to leave the school.'

'Wow. What happened to the teacher?'

'He fought it. They suspended him while they were looking into it. I believe there was some explicit stuff in the letter, so it was thought necessary. Basically, it spiralled. And then, a little bit later, the pupil, who had denied knowing anything about it at first, came forward to say that he'd had a previous letter from that same teacher but had thrown it away. That was enough. The teacher lost his job.'

'What happened to him?'

'I don't know,' Jayne says.

'Why did the pupil come forward?'

Jayne shrugs. 'Your guess is as good as mine.'

'Did Edie ask them to?'

'Maybe.'

'Or one of the others?'

'You'd have to ask Paul.'

'Paul can't have known. He was a member of staff.'

Before she can think better of it, Jayne laughs at Emily's naivety. 'He knew. He was just as protective of Edie as the others were. I believe the staff member Edie targeted was unpopular with their group, Paul included.'

Her words sink through Emily.

'But Paul doesn't lie,' she says.

'Everybody lies.'

Jayne's right, Ruth thinks. Everybody. No matter how vociferously they claim that they don't. She refills her glass and tops up Jayne's. Emily still hasn't touched hers.

'No. They don't.' Emily needs to believe this. That there are people in the world who are strong enough to do the right thing for the person they love. 'When Paul asked me to marry him, I said, "I'll marry you if you agree to one thing: never lie."'

Jayne thinks of Paul's lifestyle now, of his success in business. Who gets that far by playing one hundred per cent by the book? Does Emily really believe this? 'And what did Paul say?' she asks.

'He agreed.'

'Uh huh.'

'What? You don't believe me?'

'I believe he said it, I don't believe he's never lied to you.'

Jayne sees a hard, bright challenge in Emily's eyes. It's new to her.

Emily leans towards Jayne. 'Are you saying this because you don't approve of our marriage? You think I'm a gold-digger and he's a cradle-snatcher? It's not like that. I'm not after his money. Do you know why I told him he has to be honest with me? It's because I love him. Because we're meant to be together. He is my forever guy, believe it or not. And I know that here.' Emily presses a palm to her heart, covers it with her other hand. A grand, ancient gesture, it seems to Ruth. Something like the marble statues she and Toby have seen on holiday in Italy. She's impressed by it.

'Of course we don't think that!' she interjects but the other women don't pay attention to her. She knows she shouldn't be oversensitive, but she feels chastised and withdraws into herself a little and realises that she's already more drunk than she probably should be.

She can't deny that her jealousy of Emily is growing, because she and Toby are not close like Emily is describing her relationship with Paul. There has never been a grand passion between Ruth and Toby. Friendship, yes. A passable sex life, yes; nothing too exciting but quite nice in its way. Intellectual compatibility, sure. They admire each other's achievements, or they used to. Ruth is convinced that this, too, has been a casualty of Alfie, as if she was relegated in status to just a body, a vessel, as soon as the baby began to grow in her, and that didn't change after the birth. If anything, it became worse.

Unexpectedly, Jayne also finds herself moved by Emily's speech because she shares Emily's belief in the possibility of finding the exact right partner. In Mark, Jayne is convinced she's found the one man she's supposed to be with.

But Jayne's also irritated by Emily's naivety and the urge to correct her is strong. This is what bonding means to Jayne: protection. Hard truths. Better to know everything than to be surprised.

'Everybody lies,' she repeats.

Maggie Elliott folds sheets. She enjoys the feel of the clean fabric, the smell of washing detergent as it wafts into the room. John isn't home yet. Her anxiety is peaking.

She pulls the edges of the sheets together precisely and smooths the cotton out with her palm, flattening it now so it'll be easier to iron tomorrow. The investment in good-quality bedlinen felt extravagant but has been worth it. Guests have mentioned it positively in their reviews.

Usually, she takes pleasure from this job, from the feeling that she is building a successful rental business, that it'll help to keep them afloat as John's health declines.

Though whether it will or not remains to be seen.

It feels impossible to remove him from this land, so she can't bear to think of the alternatives.

She places the folded sheets in the laundry basket, ready for ironing in the morning, and returns to the kitchen. Birdie follows her, as does her own dog, a soft little terrier called Annie. She checks her dough. It's ready to bake. She puts it into the Aga and sets a timer.

It is unspoken that John will need to live out his days here, whatever they are like. He can't move to a home. It would kill him and would be a miserable end to a dignified, quiet, loving life. He's never done any harm to anyone.

Or so she wants to believe.

But what if the changes in his brain are more sinister? What if they've unlocked something else in him? Her fear that he has begun a pattern of intimidating guests won't leave her. She's going to have to confront him about it.

The worst thing, she thinks, is that there's no one she would rather talk about this with than John.

But that already feels impossible now. He's so often beyond reason, lately, as if he's regressing from man to child, robbing her of a partner and casting her, instead, in the role of his caretaker.

It makes her feel desperately alone and she doesn't want to be, doesn't know how to be.

William might come up here and take over the farm, she supposes, but he might not. She won't put pressure on him to live a life he doesn't want.

At least, she thinks, as she puts the kettle on and sits down to wait for it to boil, at least John and I have loved each other unstintingly all these years.

It has been so good, their modest, beautiful life together here. A sort of miracle.

Ruth's head is spinning. She can't tolerate listening to Jayne and Emily any longer. Her mood has flipped.

Talk of the hoax Edie pulled at school has seeded an idea. Is this where it all started, where Toby got the idea to have a relationship with a student? With someone who's barely an adult? Did it start there? Or perhaps it didn't need a catalyst because an attraction to younger women is just in him.

She stands up, mortified to feel herself swaying a little. 'I should check the potatoes,' she says. Jayne frowns. Did I slur my words? Ruth wonders. Perhaps I need to slow down on the drink. The elation she felt earlier has drained away. Desperate to hang on to it she pours more champagne into her glass before taking it with her into the kitchen.

She finds that Jayne has put the stew in a casserole pot, the potatoes are neatly mashed and in a baking dish. Ruth has a sense that time has slipped.

Of course the potatoes can't still be boiling. They'd be mush by now. She forgot about them when she went upstairs but is irrationally and powerfully annoyed by Jayne's competent rescuing of the situation. She feels it's made a fool of her.

She pulls out the cutlery drawer and lays the table. Two lumpy pottery candlesticks go in the centre. She punctures a packet of paper napkins and extracts three. She suspects the other two look down on her domestic efforts and feels a wave of self-hatred. She's convinced they think she's pathetic, but has no idea how else to prove herself except by pleasing others.

Alfie. She can please him. That's easy. No. Don't think of him or you'll cry. What happened to all the optimism she felt a few moments ago?

Everything she's placed on the table seems to shimmer, to replicate itself. She blinks.

Ruth finishes her glass of champagne. The beautiful constancy of alcohol. It's poetry to her. A meditative song, smoothing out her highs and lows, her louds and quiets. It numbs.

Everything on the table swims and doubles again and won't stay still. It's unbearable to look at. Her body is uncomfortable. Underwear pinching and crawling. Clothes too tight. Her internal organs seem to be jostling and chafing against one another, unhappy sharing space. No wonder Toby doesn't want this. It's only a collection of flesh and bone.

The truth is that time sags, drags, wears out and she used to think she'd married a man who would find beauty in that.

The sound of the rain seems infernal. It falls unapologetically, bowing the grass on the slope behind the kitchen, spreading shadows. Drops tremble on the glazing bars.

But it's better than staring at those flames licking in the room next door as her anxiety builds again, zero to sixty in no time at all; better than Jayne's implacable rationality and the seduction of Emily's beauty.

Her feelings towards Emily harden. Women like her are predatory. They tempt men.

No. That's not right. Emily is blessed, Ruth tells herself. She can't help that she's beautiful. It's older men who shouldn't be tempted by young flesh.

But Toby certainly finds beauty in the images of women he studies. He's published books about it. Degas's bathers and ballerinas, in their tutus and nakedness. He has intimately described their bodies, their poses, the sensuality of paintwork and form. The bathers and ballerinas are younger women, some of them girls.

Is he attracted to younger females?

There. She's asked the question. A muscle in her cheek judders.

Images she doesn't want to see come to mind, invading it, upsetting the prudish part of her, but she can't keep them away. Of Toby making love to a younger woman. She is faceless; a perfect sum of tits, ass; smooth, gentle, soft, curves, taut, lips. A banquet of perfect flesh. She is young, too young. It is disgusting. Criminal. Ruth is appalled by how graphic her imagination is.

She raises her glass and tries to drink. It's empty. She craves more and opens a bottle of red wine. Drink is where she is seeking answers. How pathetic. She almost laughs at herself. Perhaps she's no better than Toby. No. If she's right about him, she is better than him.

Her mind runs in frantic loops. She doesn't have enough evidence to support her suspicions. She's imagining it all.

Except that she isn't. Because her suspicions began months ago when another letter arrived at their home.

It was posted through their door, by hand, one evening, when Toby was out at a departmental function. Ruth had stayed at home, heavily pregnant with Alfie.

The envelope was unmarked, and Ruth opened it.

This letter was long, rambling, and handwritten on cheap lined paper, the kind a student buys in the supermarket, holes pre-punched in it.

'Dear Mr Land,' the letter began. It was for Toby. She scanned the first few lines, wondering if it was from a neighbour, but stopped when she saw a mention of Degas. She glanced at the end of the letter. It was signed 'Lexi MacKay'.

She must be one of Toby's students.

Ruth sat down and began to read in earnest. Lexi MacKay had a point to make, that Degas was a paedophile. 'Wow,' Ruth said out loud. This accusation was old news to academics, but the letter had no time for Toby's view that Degas's work still deserved serious study. It was furious and violent in its condemnation of the artist. Another paragraph began:

Mr Lane, do you think of Degas when you see young women in intimate settings? Did you think of him and his artist's gaze when you were watching me in the library? Did that make it OK to you? Did it turn you on?

Ruth covered her mouth with her hand. Now she wanted to look away but couldn't. She felt very cold, and very still. Her flesh crawled.

Degas had his favourite models. Am I yours? Degas brought girls to his studio to pose, hunched naked over bathtubs. Or to stand for hours in the painful postures of ballerinas. You told us that with a laugh but I didn't find it funny. I imagine he walked around and around them, staring, until he had drunk in every detail. I imagine him correcting their poses, touching them, letting his hands linger on them.

I don't spend time in your spaces, but I think you follow me into mine, to gaze at me. Study me. Am I right? Will the touching come next?

On and on it went, until the devastating final line.

Do you want to fuck me? If so, you need to be a man and say so. Or I'll call the police.

And then, that name, at the end.
Lexi MacKay.
Not the name of any old student. The name of an accuser.

Toby denied it, of course, when he got home. Lexi MacKay was troubled, he said. She could be hysterical. Everyone in the department made sure to keep their office doors open if she came for a one-on-one meeting. The letter disappeared into his pocket and Ruth never saw it again. But she remembered the name on it. And Lexi MacKay wasn't difficult to find on social media. Ruth learned everything about her she could. Learned her face. Her friends. What she did and where she went.

But she gave birth two days later and, while she hasn't forgotten the letter, she hasn't looked up Lexi MacKay since then. But she will now, as soon as she gets phone reception.

And she's had another very worrying thought.

Imogen. Edie's daughter. Toby has been tutoring her.

Is that all he's been doing?

Because that would give Edie a motive to kill him.

I can't stop thinking about Imogen lying about self-harming.

The first time she admitted to doing it, she showed me that horrible scar on her arm, which was so shocking that it gave her subsequent admissions that she'd hurt herself, or thought about it, the urgent weight of fact.

Everyone was hurting so much after Rob's death. Did she need the humiliation of raising her shirt to prove that she had ugly scars criss-crossing and defiling her belly? She was capable of tending to those cuts herself – she had made assurances that they weren't deep – and I assumed she had.

I was preoccupied with attributing blame at the time. Whose fault was this? The question tormented me. Was it Rob's fault, for dying? It made me think of him as a bad father. Troubled, I weighed up my own role in Imogen's life and took the resulting guilt like punishment.

I vowed to make things up to her, to make her life better.

Not once did it occur to me that she might be lying and casting herself as a victim in order to manipulate me. And not just me.

But I can't focus on this too much now. It's too destabilising. I'm afraid it'll nudge me off the path I need to be on. Too much is going wrong as it is. For now, I need to process the fact that I have her with me when I didn't expect to.

Tonight was supposed to be about making final preparations for tomorrow. And for recovering. The work of murder is many things, endlessly discussed in literature and philosophy, involving ethical and moral concerns, affairs of the heart, revenge. But the prosaic is rarely delved into. Murder, the disposal of bodies, is also exhausting. I need to batten down the hatches tonight, and rest.

But there's no reason I can't do that with Imogen here.

Before she went for a bath, she was obsessively checking her phone, hunched over it as if it was the answer to everything. In fact, she's been like that since I collected her. More than usual, I'd say.

Now that I understand that she lied to me to get broken out of camp, I also have a hunch that she might have plans for tonight that don't involve me. And she still has the cash I gave her.

The smell of bath oil trails Imogen into the room. She looks nice. Her face is flushed. Without a word she settles on to the sofa opposite me and lays her phone, a nail file and polish out on the coffee table. She gets to work.

Upstairs, she's left the bathmat crumpled on the floor, a Rorschach blot of damp in the middle of it, a partial wet footprint severed by its edge. I piss. Savour the relief. Wash my hands.

The steamed-up bathroom mirror paralyses me momentarily, the opaque white sheen on it reminding me of a frosty coating, and I think of the flesh in the freezer, and of ice crystals forming within it. I scrub at the condensation with my hand and a bout of violent retching brings me to my knees over the toilet bowl. It's painful and unproductive. My stomach is empty. Just some bile emerges, sticky swags of it.

I clean myself up and take a moment to lie on the floor. The tiles are cool. I bury my face in the bathmat, in the damp traces of Imogen, the one I'm doing all this for.

The doorbell rings. Shrill. One blast, two. An insolent third.

I get up, panic driving hasty movements, and watch from the top of the stairs as Imogen darts across the hall and opens the door.

To Jemma. Her friend. I guess Imogen invited her here after all. I wish she'd told me. They greet each other with the enthusiasm of puppies. When Jemma sees me, she composes herself and smiles sweetly. She and I both know that no one considers her a good friend for Imogen. Jemma is too wayward. Perhaps the self-harm deception was her idea.

I paste myself against the landing wall as they dash upstairs together and the door to Imogen's room slams shut like an insult. I hear giggling.

Jemma is a problem I have to solve. I cannot have her here tonight. I thought I could cope with it but I can't. It's one thing too many. She hypes Imogen up, brings out the selfish in her. I'm craving peace. And now I have another thing to raise with Imogen: don't invite friends round without double-checking that it's OK. Parenting is hard.

I should be relaxing, and I try, while they're upstairs, because I need a clear mind to think what to do about Jemma, but I'm so fired up now that I google Dark Fell Barn on my laptop, combing through the website like I haven't done that a thousand times before, trying to imagine Jayne, Ruth and Emily within it, players on my stage.

Which room are they in? How are they feeling? Are they driving each other crazy yet, trying to figure out if the letter's a real threat or not?

Thinking about their men? Wondering who the victim is?

All our lives are going to be so different from now on. They have no idea.

I shut my laptop and notice that Imogen has left her phone on the table. What a bonus. Something going right at last. I pick it up, make sure it's on silent and slip it into my pocket. If I separate her from it for a while, at least she won't be able to do anything else behind my back. I find a home for it deep in a kitchen cupboard.

'Hey,' Imogen says. I snatch my arm out of the cupboard. Imogen and Jemma are standing together in the kitchen doorway like a pair of twins.

'We're going out,' Imogen states. Jemma gives me that smile again.

If Imogen goes out, I'll have to be anxious about what she's doing and who she's with. I'll have to wait up for her to get home. I won't be able to rest.

'I'm sorry, but absolutely not. I collected you from camp because you were distressed, Imogen. What is this you're going out to? A party?'

Jemma puts on her poker face, but a twitch of her lips gives her away and tells me I'm right. Imogen looks embarrassed for a moment before gathering some outrage. The bravado of the young exhausts me sometimes. What they don't know is a lot.

'You've got no right to stop me,' Imogen states, defiance in her stance and her expression.

'I have every right.'

'You're not my mother!'

'But I'm in charge until your mother gets home.'

Which, of course, she won't.

Jayne and Emily stare at the fire in a silence that's not quite companionable.

'Is Ruth OK?' Emily asks, eventually. 'Should we check on her?'

Jayne considers how much to say. It feels horribly exposing to have this relative stranger come into their group, uncomfortable to watch her learn things about them that show them far from their best. She'll spare Ruth. 'She's fine. I think working full-time with a six-month-old baby at home is tiring. She needs this break.'

'She drinks a lot.'

'She's unwinding.'

Their eyes meet. Jayne looks away first.

'Does she have a problem?' Emily asks.

It irritates Jayne that Emily would ask so boldly. And perhaps it's the alcohol, this lovely champagne, but she's also aware of the weariness creeping into her bones and her mind. She's tired of firefighting, of protecting Ruth and Emily from their fears about the letter, and now of protecting Ruth from Emily. Her patience with the others is running out. She bites the inside of her cheek, half-enjoying the heavy pinch of her molars on the fragile membrane.

Emily persists, 'I smelled alcohol on Ruth's breath earlier, when we were upstairs. And it was worse after she shut herself in her room for a while.'

It was a faint ethanol fug that Emily smelled, unmistakable and not to be ignored, in spite of Ruth presenting as both Mother and Homemaker of the Year and brilliant doctor. You don't work in the hospitality industry for as long as Emily did without meeting some very high-functioning alcoholics. Emily knows one when she smells one.

'Ruth's fine,' Jayne says.

They're startled by the sound of glass splintering, of Ruth crying out.

A glass of wine has smashed to shards on the kitchen floor. Ruth is on her hands and knees, trying to pick up the pieces, apologising too much. Spatters of wine drip down a cabinet door.

'Here, let me help.' Emily kneels beside Ruth, afraid that Ruth will cut herself.

Jayne steps away. This job doesn't need three of them. She finds she feels a little disgusted with Ruth, for having this accident just as Jayne was defending her.

Upstairs, her bag is the only one left on the landing. The others have claimed bedrooms and left her and Mark the smallest one to the side. It's narrow and dark but will do fine. They don't need luxuries.

She opens her bag. Most of the clothes it contains are practical items, her only concession to prettiness a rumpled blouse that she thought she might put on for dinner; otherwise, there are technical fabrics, non-iron, thermal layers, in blues, greys, black.

The blouse is a pretty aqua. Mark says it makes her eyes look more blue than grey.

She lays it over the edge of the bed and tries to smooth out the creases with her palms. She'll wear it tonight. It's important to make an effort even under the circumstances. To keep the others calm.

I envy Emily, she thinks, the same way I envy Edie. They are both beautiful and I am not. It's not that she wants to admire herself in the mirror every day. Jayne's aesthetic sense is not developed enough for that. She wants the power that beauty brings. The way it seems to make a woman sufficient, even without other attributes.

Mark has never admitted that he was in love with Edie at school, but Jayne knows he probably was because of what he omits to say. He talks a lot about how both Toby and Paul fell hard for Edie, even though it would have been a taboo relationship for Paul, as a teacher. He describes how upset both of them were when Rob won Edie, but never mentions his own feelings and shuts down the conversation if Jayne asks about it, with a derisive laugh or a swift change of subject, which doesn't fool her even a little.

In fact, it makes her wonder if Mark has ever slept with Edie. Though she doesn't dwell on it. It would have been before they met, after all.

A fierce longing to see him wells up in Jayne. She's proud that she sees beyond his public persona, to the man beneath, the man she believes needs her as much as she needs him.

She unpacks more clothes, doing it hastily, messily, letting her emotions show because there's no one to witness them, throwing each item across the bed as if it were garbage, and exhales sharply with relief when her hand reaches the bowels of the bag.

A hard, cold item. A pistol. The feel of it sickens and reassures her. It makes her feel strong, sure of herself. Powerful. She doesn't pull it out because she doesn't need to, doesn't want to. It must stay here until the right time. A smatter of hail strikes the window, and she shivers. It's draughty up here.

She checks her watch. It's six forty-five. Dusk isn't supposed to be for another hour but the sky's so dark, you'd think it had already arrived.

The truth is that if Ruth or Emily get down to the farmhouse tonight, and try to phone their husbands, the whole shape of the weekend will be changed because Paul's booked a town car to bring all three of the men up here tomorrow morning. They plan to leave early and to arrive before midday. But if Ruth or Emily gets through to them, and if they're hysterical enough, the men could decide not to bother making the trip and encourage them all to come home instead. Which would tear Jayne apart. She can't let it happen. She's too close now to executing her plan at the burial chamber and the thought of giving it up is painfully disappointing.

She turns on the bedroom light and changes, adding a vest top beneath her blouse because she's chilly. Her reflection in the window stares back at her. Resolute.

A version of herself that seems more real than herself. More honest.

Since they left the army, Mark and Jayne have both struggled to settle into civvy life. Like her reflection in the glass, Jayne imagines them trapped on a different plane from everyone else, somewhere between now and their past.

For her part, on one side, she enjoys her time amongst the novelties that are the small indignities and beautiful surprises of married life and the pleasures of her training as a physiotherapist.

On the other, the backward pull of the past is strong. She can't erase the death she witnessed that happened as a result of intelligence she had gathered. Death filmed by drones or body cameras and seen by Jayne on multiple screens. Pixelated death, but as powerful to her as any other kind.

They witnessed it all.

The destruction of intended targets, saving lives.

But also the collateral damage, the mistakes made. Women, children, families killed. Innocents. She could vomit when she thinks of it. Sometimes, when she remembers, her skin runs cold and she believes it will never warm up.

She slaps her own cheek, hard. A short, sharp shock. It's enough. Her thousand-yard stare breaks. Her reflection stares back at her, chastised. Then resolute. That's better, she thinks.

Remorse has a vicelike grip on her, driving her to put things right the only way she can think to. She needs to. And she will. With Mark. Tomorrow.

Until then, she has to keep control, to ensure things go her way. The risk that Edie's letter carries a real threat is infinitesimal, negligible. The risk that Jayne might fail to do what she intends to do if the other women break camp is higher. It cannot happen.

This is a calculation she made earlier, but one that is worth revisiting. The fluidity of risk has always fascinated her. It was a particular skill of hers when she was serving, this ability to react swiftly and effectively to rapidly evolving situations.

It's clear to her now: she must double down on doing everything she can to keep Emily and Ruth here until the men turn up as planned.

She and her reflection exchange curt nods. In agreement. Yes, she thinks, I am resolute and I look calm and friendly.

Ready.

She turns out the light and makes her way downstairs towards the voices in the kitchen. In the hallway, she adds a smile to her expression.

John Elliott crouches in the shadows outside Dark Fell Barn, staring at the kitchen window.

Rain and hail pelt him, and particles of early-evening light settle on his shoulders to dissolve in the damp patches there. He has no idea what time it is, but tonight daylight is surely dying earlier than it should and he can feel the valley gathering itself, braced for an onslaught. The storm isn't done with them yet.

Condensation on the windows smears the scene inside the kitchen. John sees smudged silhouettes: two women around the table, the wine bottle between them, gestures of intensity.

He senses their building excitement, predicts the incipient drunkenness.

Excess upsets him.

People being here upsets him.

This, he knows.

Upstairs, in the bedroom above the kitchen, the third woman appears, clear to see because there's no condensation. She pulls off her top. Beneath, she wears a plain black bra. He assesses her as he might one of his sheep, as a physical specimen. Her breasts are small and her bare shoulders bony, the muscles on her arms gently sculpted. There's little to no meat on her, but plenty of strength.

He has the idea in his head that this woman is different from her friends. He can't quite think of the reason why, but he's sure this is the case. It's something he can feel in his chest. He can't rely on his brain. He thinks of it as Swiss cheese with gaping holes in it, blanks he must bypass before he can understand things. It can take time. Sometimes he gets lost on the way. The disorientation and confusion that result are horribly draining.

'We can't go on like this,' Maggie said. He hears her voice clear as day. But she's not here, it's something she said earlier. Not now. But when? He has no sense of that. He looks around him. She's not here. Why not?

The woman in the top window moves, recapturing his attention. He watches her pull on a vest top, then a blouse and fasten a necklace. She stares out of the window towards him, at him, and terror leaps unexpectedly in his throat. He swallows it down laboriously. She can't see me. I'm well hidden in the shadows. I know where I can be seen and where I can't. Though the woman stands there for so long, her face turned in his direction, that after a while he wonders if he's wrong. But he holds his nerve and stays frozen in place, until she turns away and the light goes out.

His gaze reconnects with the two downstairs. At the table, leaning towards one another. Still with intensity. Are they arguing? Plotting? Who are they, even?

Strangers in Dark Fell Barn are a bad thing. He feels that as an incontrovertible truth. As inarguable as the commandments he learned at Sunday school.

He realises suddenly that he doesn't know why he's here, but he feels compelled to stay even as the rain drives harder, as hail stings his cheeks, wondering what the skinny woman was thinking about as she stared at him. Did he and she connect? Was she warning him? He can't remember what he thought about this earlier, what conclusion he came to.

Frustration at his brain's inability to put the pieces together drives him back, away from the barn. He takes the sense of a threat with him as he heads home the steep and secret way, on foot, cutting down through the valley and through fields and woodland, circumventing bogs and crevasses. A route you could never recommend to guests. You have to feel it as much as know it.

He can't go down the way he came up because the lane leading to the farmhouse is flooded now, just as he knew it would be.

Maggie knows it too. Knew it when they drove up to the barn this afternoon and saw the clouds massing in the distance. Knew it as well as he did.

In another time she might have cancelled guests in this weather or offered them a night in the farmhouse for free, for safety, but they need the money. She speaks to him again. 'We need the money, John.'

Is that what she says? He thinks so, but why they need the money is beyond him. The farm is doing well. They've spoken about expanding their flock. Maggie would like to take on some more specialist breeds.

He walks on. Stops. Things around him feel familiar. The trees, bent with the wind; the contours of the valleys; the texture of the stone, the grass, the earth, the sky. Even the feel of the rain slicking down his face is a link to something.

But to what?

Fear curls and grows inside him. He needs to decipher why he's here. It's getting late and his mother wants him home for dinner. That's it. He calls for his dog, Meg. His father has given him a pup of his own to look after. She's almost a year old. The first sheepdog of his own. It's a big responsibility. He's running her himself.

She doesn't come. He looks around. He's on a route he recognises but he's not sure where it leads.

But he needs to get home. To the farmhouse.

A tear slips down his cheek.

John looks at his hand resting on the handle of his stick, feels the carved thistle beneath his fingers. His father's stick before his. John notes how cold his fingers look as an observer might, how raised the veins are, how calloused the skin beneath the slick of rain.

He turns, looking to each side of him, behind; feels as if he's been swallowed up by a landscape that he is almost familiar with, but not entirely.

He wants to get home.

But he has no idea how.

*

The girls are holed up upstairs. Imogen stomped off in a huff, eyes gleaming with tears, and Jemma trailed after her, throwing me an apologetic smile over her shoulder that I didn't buy. It suggested that she and I were in cahoots. We're most definitely not. I've had the measure of her since I caught her trying to persuade Imogen to steal glittery hairbands when I was supervising them on a playdate.

And somewhere, behind that smile, I'm pretty sure I caught a measure of scorn.

That playdate was a low point. Not fun to supervise. I had words with Jemma's parents when they collected her. But it was only one bad fruit in a basket of wonderful experiences.

You see, Edie and Rob liked to have time together, without Imogen. They had her when they were so young, barely out of university. And all of us in the gang were happy to oblige by babysitting her when we were able to. We felt like uncles to her. She so resembled her mother it was like having a mini-Edie to play with and I know I'm not just speaking for myself when I say that. She was such a novelty. Such a miracle. So much fun! Between us, we would look after her for evenings, sometimes for weekends. It was normal for us to be *in loco parentis* whenever needed.

And it wasn't just a 'needs must' arrangement. We'd take her out because we enjoyed spending time with her. It wasn't like we needed asking. She had a huge extended family in us. She kept toothbrushes in our homes the way girlfriends do. Each of us had a little box or drawer of toys for her. And Imogen wasn't any bother. No tantrums, no side to her, just daisy chains and big, wide smiles.

It makes me happy to remember those days. Such a perfect little girl deserved all that love.

And isn't it wonderful that I felt that way about her even before I understood that she was mine?

I drum my fingers on the kitchen surface, feel its hardness punishing my nail beds. Jemma has disrupted things, cranking my anxiety up a notch too far. She will not be a part of our future, that's for sure.

I follow the girls upstairs. I feel self-conscious, overly aware of the sound of my footsteps on the treads as if I have elephant feet. I clod across the landing, feeling daunted by the prospect of knocking on Imogen's door. Girls her age have so much power. Some don't even know they have it, and only a few, like Edie, retain it as they age, but we men feel it as viscerally as the thump of our own hearts.

The only thing I can think of comparing it to is the contemplation of unwrapping something you've always wanted for the very first time.

Jemma understands her power. Imogen doesn't. Not yet. But whatever their state of self-awareness, they need protecting from themselves, these girls.

I raise my hand to knock on the door and hear my name, followed by a burst of laughter.

My fingers unclench in stiff slow motion. I lower my arm. Clearly, they didn't hear me come up; I must have imagined the terrible noise I was making.

I grab a small pile of laundry from my own bed and return to stand outside Imogen's door. Carefully, silently, I press my ear to it.

*

Emily wipes condensation from the kitchen window. The sound of the hail pulled her here and now it's passed. She peers out.

'The rain's easing.'

Ruth nods, concentrating on moderating the speed of her gesture, to stave off any nausea or spinning it might bring on. She must be careful. She's let herself get drunk, which wasn't her intention.

She's been trying to imagine how Emily will look in ten years' time. Will she keep her looks? She'll get work done, of course. Not that it's helped Paul much. He's looked strained and tired lately, apparently, in spite of the cosmetic enhancements. Toby remarked on it. Ruth remembers because she thought it would be nice if he noticed how tired she was.

She suspects Emily and Paul have embarked on a course of aesthetic treatments together. Emily's teeth are not the imperfect, stained set she had when Paul first met her. Money has been spent.

And why not, if you've got it, Ruth supposes, with bitterness. She's jealous of Paul and Emily's money. She and Toby never have enough. They borrowed too heavily to buy their home and it's always been a struggle to keep up repayments. Especially now, with childcare costs.

She tries not to think of the fact that she might lose her job. The email she got from the partners mentioned that colleagues and surgery staff had noticed worrying things about her behaviour, and practice. They worried about the impact on patients and wanted to meet her, to discuss any difficulties she might be experiencing, whether she considers herself fit to work.

Maybe it wouldn't be a bad thing if she quit, she thinks. Maybe they sell the house, move somewhere cheaper and she looks after Alfie full-time. Maybe she and Alfie leave Toby behind. But then she'd need to work. There's no easy answer.

She tries to remember if Toby ever talked realistically about having a child before Alfie came along. She doesn't think he did. In her mania to consult written material about babies, to prepare herself to be the best mother she could be, she never thought to ask what he was expecting, or experiencing.

'He's jealous,' she says.

'What?'

Ruth didn't realise she'd spoken aloud. How long has Jayne been standing in the doorway? She looks nice.

'He's jealous of what?' Jayne asks. 'And who is he?'

Ruth sighs. She's going to say it. 'Toby is jealous of the baby.' Her eyelids feel heavy when she blinks. Jayne looks nice because she's changed her outfit. It must be dinnertime, nearly. Time they ate something. She should do the same. Change. She picks at the hem of her cardigan. It's the one she travelled in. There's a little baby sick on the shoulder that she noticed when they were in the car. Where was she?

'I fell in love with Alfie right after he was born, it was ferocious, did I ever tell you how ferocious that feeling is, and Toby didn't fall in love. I kept waiting for it to happen, but it never did. He had a big emotion, he felt something huge, but it wasn't the one he was supposed to have. It was the green-eyed monster.' She draws the words out, mimes the horror with wide eyes and clawed fingers. 'He hates his son,' she says. A conclusion that sounds true now that she's said it. She drinks to moisten her mouth which feels dry, replaces her glass on the table with too much force.

'No. Surely he doesn't. Don't talk like this. You don't mean it.' Jayne sits beside her friend. Ruth pours wine into another glass and pushes it towards Jayne in a wobbly operation.

'I really mean it. And do you know how hard it is to admit it?' Is Jayne really going to minimise this too? Ruth's mouth settles into an expression of obstinacy.

Jayne is alarmed by Ruth's words because in no way does this resemble the Ruth she knows, but also irritated because this looks and sounds like drunken self-pity. Ruth's escalation into inebriation has been rapid. She's slurring her words.

It's almost as if Emily was plying her with wine while Jayne was upstairs. Would she do that? But perhaps Ruth doesn't need anybody else to ply her with drink. She can do it well enough herself. Emily is still at the window, her back to the others.

'The rain really is easing,' she says. 'Finally.'

'Can we talk about that?' Jayne says. 'I think even if the rain eases it's too dangerous to go down. Really, it's getting too dark already and everything must be flooded.'

Ruth gets up and fumbles with the oven knobs. 'I need to eat,' she says. 'Is this on?'

Jayne nods and Ruth puts the tray of mashed potato into the oven, slamming the door shut. She fumbles to open a large packet of crisps and pours them into a bowl, capturing and eating the escapees that tumble across the surface as if she's starving.

'You said you'd come with me if the rain stopped,' Emily says.

'I did, but I meant when there's plenty of light left.'

Emily glances at the time on the oven display. 'It's nearly seven. It won't get dark for, what, another hour or so?'

Dusk starts at seven forty-five, Jayne knows because she looked it up before they travelled here, but she bluffs a little. 'Dusk is in half an hour. But I mean, look out there; it might as well be dusk already.'

Emily can barely contain her upset. She's been waiting, and checking the weather, and waiting some more, while Ruth gets drunker and Jayne pretends it's not happening, and now her chance to go is surely almost here and Jayne is refusing?

'You promised,' she says.

'I never promised.'

Ruth looks from Jayne to Emily and back again, as it dawns on her that their voices are raised.

'Crisp?' she asks, holding up the bowl.

Emily glances at her. Ruth's a mess. She's been guzzling the booze. And what has she got to be so sorry for herself over? Nothing, so far as Emily can see. Absolutely nothing. Paul always says that Ruth and Toby have had a charmed life. That they've been shuffling around in slippers like an old married couple since they first met, finding easy friendships with their peers, Toby taking shelter in institutional life, Ruth glowing with the prestige of being a doctor, of having it all.

'They don't know what it's like to live,' he says. 'You've lived so much harder than they have.' Paul's pride in what Emily has overcome is intense. Her mother's drinking is not a source of shame to him; the role of her mother's boyfriends in facilitating her alcoholism is not something Emily should ever castigate

131

herself for being unable to prevent. 'You were a child, babe,' he insists. 'A teenager. What could you have done? It's a fucking marvel you kept her alive that long.'

The pride Paul feels in my resilience sometimes feels so hot it could burn, Emily thinks. 'I *wish* I'd been there to protect you,' he repeats. 'I *wish* you'd never had to see any of it.'

He talks about the violence he would have done to her mum's boyfriends, holding back words sometimes as if he's afraid of going too far; he talks about how he would have got them out of Emily and her mother's life. He speaks as if he's convinced that he's a hero and the look in his eyes when he says those things is the look of an animal. A wolf. It almost scares her, how much he wants to shield her from the world. Sometimes, she half-expects him to say he would have cured her mother's cancer too.

If he has a fault, it's this. A saviour delusion. She loves him for it, acknowledges that he rescued her from a dark place, but she pushes back, always, on this kind of talk when it goes too far. Interrupting him, if necessary, and raising her voice. She loves him but she's not his possession. If they fight, it's over this. He was her saviour, yes, but she had begun to save herself when they met. She is not to be underestimated.

Her eyes pass over Ruth dismissively. Emily feels betrayed by Jayne's refusal to walk to the farmhouse and she has an urge to cut back.

'Let's say', she says, 'that the letter isn't a hoax, and Edie has harmed one of our husbands. Who do you think it would be?'

Ruth feels cold to the core.

'I'm not going to speculate about that,' Jayne says. 'It's horrible.'

'Really? You haven't given it any thought at all?' The disbelief in Emily's voice holds the satisfaction of information withheld until the right moment, the scorch of imminent triumph.

'Because I think it's obvious it would be Mark.'

'When's your mum coming back?' Jemma asks. She sounds bored. She's lying on her stomach on the bed, scrolling her phone. Bursts of sound fill the room.

Jemma looks amazing, Imogen thinks. Her clothes. Hair. Jealousy tears a little rip inside her. No wonder Jemma's become such a popular girl in sixth form. She's transformed herself and Imogen feels as if she's been left behind. What if Matt's there tonight but he fancies Jemma more than Imogen? It's happened before with boys and is why Imogen isn't going to tell Jemma that she likes him. She doesn't trust Jemma not to try to get him for herself.

'Tomorrow.' Imogen has an impulse to copy Jemma, to lie on the bed just the same way as her friend. She looks around for her own phone, pats her pockets. She must have left it somewhere. The bathroom, maybe.

She sighs. The thought of going to look for the phone, even across the landing, is off-putting because he might be hovering anywhere in the house, overattentive, asking questions. It's not that she doesn't love him in a way. She's fond of him because he's always been like an uncle to her, and she's grateful to him for springing her from camp, or, rather, for falling for her story about the self-harm.

She wasn't going to pull the self-harm cry-for-help thing again. She really did cut herself once. She didn't know how else to let out the pain of missing her dad, but Edie was so devastated when Imogen told her that she felt horribly guilty afterwards. The next time, Imogen didn't actually do it, but she told her mum she had because she didn't know how else to get Edie's attention. Imogen felt awful about it, but it worked. Edie snapped out of a terrible, dark funk and began to talk to Imogen again, to care for her.

Imogen really shouldn't have done it to get herself out of camp. The problem was, she couldn't think of a better excuse for leaving. She knew he was one of her emergency contacts and that he would fall for it like a charm. And he did. She was just lucky he hadn't already gone away for the weekend.

I am fond of him, she thinks, though the thought doesn't make her smile because she kind of feels like she's having to persuade herself that she likes him. It's an effort.

It's because she finds him hard work. She's noticed it so much more since her dad died, how people who don't really know her think it's OK to act like they do. Sometimes she feels like she might scream or start to shudder from loneliness when they try to talk to her familiarly.

No one can replace her dad. All she wants is to be left alone to hold on to her memories of Dad and keep them safe for herself and her mum to share. Her grief is intense and private.

'Where is your mum, anyway?' Jemma is typing on her phone.

'At a spa retreat in the middle of Wales. The kind where they make you hand your phone in. She's having some "me time".'

Imogen makes air quotes around 'me time' to make a joke of it, even though it hurts. She would have loved to go to the mountains with Edie, to curl up in a room with a view, to breathe, to be near her mum. But she couldn't admit it to Edie. It would have felt babyish. Imogen felt obliged to pretend that she was happy to be at camp when she knew it would be a horrible reminder of her dad. And it was.

'Sounds selfish.' Jemma puts her phone down and rolls over to prop herself up facing Imogen. Her nose is scrunched in disapproval. Piggy face, Imogen thinks, and looks away, revelling in how ugly the expression makes Jemma look, even if only temporarily, then regretting the thought. Imogen doesn't like that she might have inherited her mum's bitchy streak.

'Super selfish.' Jemma doubles down, wanting a reaction from Imogen.

'Yep,' Imogen agrees softly because Jemma's right in a way, and it hurts, but Imogen won't slag her mum off to Jemma. Life's difficult for Edie right now. She's gone somewhere in her head where Imogen can't reach her again, and Imogen is so sick with worry she thinks it might choke her sometimes.

'Everything hurts so much since your dad died, I know,' Edie said to her a few days ago, right before she left. 'But he'd want us to be strong. Can you do that for me?'

Imogen nodded, though she didn't know how to be strong. And she had the idea that something else was bothering Edie, something big. It was like Edie's grief had been put on hold because of a larger preoccupation, but Imogen struggled to put her finger on what it was, and it felt impossible to ask. She wasn't sure she wanted to hear the answer. She's too desperate to be

135

mothered right now and ashamed of it because she's nearly an adult.

Everybody tells her over and over that time will heal, and she hopes they're right, though it's hard to imagine. Imogen has developed a hatred of time. For its refusal to move any faster, or slower, than it wants to. For its inability to be rewound so her dad never went swimming that day.

'We should get out of here,' Jemma says. 'The party starts at eight.'

'I don't know how to leave without a row.' This is a problem she wasn't anticipating. He's normally much more chilled out than this. She's not sure what's got into him. Imogen has never done anything to upset her parents' friends.

Though she remembers that Edie also said before she left that they need to wean themselves off the help that the gang has given them since Rob died, but without upsetting anyone. That was important, she said. To do it discreetly.

Jemma sits up suddenly, a naughty gleam in her eye. The mattress bounces. Imogen leans on a hand to steady herself. She's finding Jemma's energy a lot to deal with today. Her friend seems shallow, her view of everything selfish and too simplistic, when Imogen's life consists of complicated, painful layers.

'Why's he looking after you, anyway?' Jemma says.

'I called him from camp. He was the only one I could get hold of from my emergency contact list. You know what my mum's friends are like. It's like they compete against each other to be the most helpful.'

Jemma picks up the note of resentment in Imogen's voice. 'It sucks that you got him.'

Imogen considers that. Does it? She likes them all equally, probably. They all have their pros and cons. She shrugs.

'We could just leave,' Jemma says. 'Sneak out without telling him and get the bus to my house. My parents can drop us at the party. Once we're out of here we send him a message to say you're totally fine and you're staying the night with me. It's not up to him whether you go out or not.'

Imogen is seduced by the idea. While Jemma is a lot, Imogen will feel more suffocated if she stays here, the subject of too much intense attention. And Jemma is right, he's not her dad. It's not up to him if Imogen goes out. Edie would encourage her to. And Imogen is desperate to lose herself in other people's chat tonight, other people's noise. To dance and forget about everything for a while. To look for Matt. Her stomach flips at the thought of him.

If her mum is going to go off and hide in a spa, surely Imogen can do something for herself too.

'Sure,' she says. 'But I need to find my phone.' She checks her face in the mirror, runs a brush through her hair until it hangs like a silky sheet.

Jemma shrugs her bomber jacket back on and reapplies lipstick. Something makes her glance suddenly at the door. She puts her finger to her lips.

'What?' Imogen mouths.

Jemma points to the door and mouths: 'It's him.'

Imogen's eyebrows raise. Has he been listening? For how long? Before Imogen can stop her, Jemma flings open the door.

'Hello!' she says brightly.

He's standing right on the other side of it, a pile of laundry in his arms. He looks artificially surprised.

'Hi!' he says. 'You caught me putting away my clean smalls.'

Eww, Imogen thinks. She's used to him talking like this, old-fashioned and kind of unfiltered, he's never been any different, but it's embarrassing if he grosses out Jemma.

'Actually, Jemma, now that you're here, could I borrow you for a minute?' he asks.

'Just me?' Jemma points at her chest. Eyes wide. Don't, Imogen thinks. Don't encourage him. It looks like flirtation. This is a new side of Jemma that's emerging. Flirting with any man, of any age.

'If you don't mind.'

Why is he smiling like that? Imogen thinks. 'Why just Jemma?' she says.

'I want Jemma's advice on something.'

Jemma follows him downstairs and Imogen flops back on to the bed feeling weird, like everything is extra annoying and tiring today. She remembers again that her phone is gone.

The bathroom is as she left it. Her phone isn't there. She picks up the damp bathmat and drops it over the side of the tub. From downstairs, she can hear muffled voices, but not what is being said.

The sound of the front door slamming startles her.

From the top of the stairs, she can see him in the hallway, but not Jemma. The door is shut. He turns to look up at her.

'Jemma had to go,' he says.

'She had to go?'

'She got a call from her mum.'

'Why? What happened?'

'She didn't say, and I didn't want to ask. It felt like prying.'

She starts down the stairs. This feels strange and the thought of being here with him is the thought of an empty evening, of depression creeping in.

'I should say goodbye,' she says. She wants to beg Jemma to stay, or to ask Jemma's mum if she can go with them.

He moves between her and the door – not completely, not so he's blocking it, but a little, so that she would have to go around him to reach it. There's plenty of room, but she'd still have to make that extra effort. She frowns.

'Her mum was waiting for her in the car outside. They've already gone.'

'I didn't hear a car.'

'Perhaps it's one of those electric ones. They're practically silent, you know.'

Perhaps, Imogen thinks. But they're not really that sort of family.

'That happened quickly,' she says. It feels strange, almost unbelievable that everything she was looking forward to tonight has gone up in a puff of smoke. The disappointment is severe and the possibility that Jemma might go to the party without her hurts. Especially if Matt's there. And there's no way Imogen can go alone because it's being held by another friend of Jemma's brother and Imogen doesn't even know where it is. This feels like one more thing in a long line of things that have happened this year and are crushing her.

He shrugs and smiles, and she hates it because it's like he thinks this is nothing. 'So,' he says. 'Just you and me again.'

'Sure,' she says.

They stand in silence. She wants to go back upstairs and disappear into her room, but she needs to find her phone first. Perhaps she can call Jemma to see what happened and try to work out a way they can go out tonight anyway. And she's thinking of calling the place where her mum is staying to see if they can bring Edie to the phone. Because she wants, all of a sudden, to hear her mum's voice.

'I lost my phone,' she says.

'Oh! Can I help you find it? Where did you last see it?'

'In the bathroom, I think, but I already looked there.'

'Perhaps you brought it down? Let's have a look, shall we?'

In the sitting room he pulls every cushion off the sofa and armchairs, slips his fingers into the crevices where the covers are tucked and runs them around. He does it twice.

Watching his eager efforts, she feels queasy, as if he's choreographing a performance, just for her. Her thoughts cycle. It's unlike Jemma not to say goodbye. I need my phone. Panic rises at the thought they might not find it.

She wonders now if it was worth getting out of music camp. She was playing really well. She even had a solo in the concert. I've let them down, she thinks. But she also knows it would have been impossible to play, without crying for her dad, and that would have been humiliating.

'Imogen?' He's staring at her so hard she finds herself blinking.

'What?' Her voice is whisper quiet.

'Are you feeling upset about the phone?'

Wariness of him has crept up on her out of nowhere. She's not sure why. It's in her gut, and it stops her from fully sharing her feelings. 'A bit,' she says, hedging.

'Maybe it fell underneath the sofa.' He drops to his knees, his backside in the air, buttocks straining against the seat of his trousers, and uses his own phone to illuminate the dark gap.

'It's OK,' she says. She wants him to stop searching because this feels weird.

'What?' He turns back to her, his voice too loud, his face too red.

'It's OK. I think I left it upstairs. I'll go look.'

'I can help.'

'No! It's fine. I'll do it myself.' He looks rumpled when he stands up. The redness leaches from his face.

'OK,' he says. 'Well. Give me a shout if you need help.'

She runs upstairs. Her feet pitter-patter on the treads, like when she was a little girl.

She searches for her phone in the bedroom, starting with the obvious places and, when it doesn't turn up, pulling at the bedcovers, opening drawers, delving into spaces she knows it can't be, frantic with urgency and increasingly upset but keeping her sobs muted, so that he can't hear.

She's confused about why she's so upset. But this happens sometimes.

And now she doesn't even know why she was so bothered about the stupid party but what she does know is that she wants her phone and she wants her mum even more.

Emily spits out Mark's name. Jayne stares at her, searching her expression for clues as to where this is coming from.

'That's ridiculous,' she says, eventually. 'It's nasty speculation.' But Emily has touched a nerve.

'Is it? How much money did Rob and Edie invest in Mark's Dovecote "opportunity"?' Emily hangs the word out there in quotation marks that she shapes in mid-air with her fingers, making it an object of mockery. 'Or, perhaps I should ask, how much did they lose?' The bland veneer of prettiness has fallen from Emily's face, Jayne thinks, replaced by an energy that looks more like aggression. It's as if she's snapped into life, into three-dimensionality, the way a pop-up illustration does.

Dovecote. Jayne wishes she'd never heard the word, never encouraged Mark's enthusiasm for the scheme. It was a planned upscale housing development, the conversion of an old mansion and its grounds, including stable buildings and barns, a historic dovecote lending it its name.

Mark was utterly persuaded that it was a winning opportunity by the men who hired him to find investors. But still, he did his due diligence.

Jayne watched him pore over spreadsheets. She witnessed his excitement building. The numbers made sense, every way he worked them, and he stayed up late, bathed in the light of his laptop. Once he was convinced by what he saw, he threw heart and soul into recruiting people, friends, fellow veterans, serving officers who had held him in high regard; he had a hunger to make life on civvy street a visible success to all. His authoritative bonhomie became his greatest asset, and he successfully persuaded many people they knew to invest.

Jayne understood that what drove him was his fear of failure. It stalked him like a soft-pawed fox. Leaving the army wasn't easy. His friends filled a gap, but Mark wanted to show he could make it professionally on the outside too.

When Dovecote failed . . . when Mark understood that he'd been conned . . . that he had effectively conned others . . . Jayne can hardly think of how hollow it left him. He was broken. And she so desperately wanted to help him get over it. She's been struggling to figure out how best to do so ever since. Her plan for this weekend is one of the solutions she's throwing at the problem in the hope something will stick.

'Dovecote was a very long time ago,' Jayne says. 'Long before your time.' Emily's slow blink acknowledges Jayne's intention to insult by drawing attention to her immature status in the group, but her gaze remains stubborn and focused, demanding an answer.

'Mark made his peace with Edie and Rob after Dovecote,' Jayne says. That's all she's willing to share with Emily.

Ruth watches. She's not getting involved. She and Jayne discussed the whole affair in depth when it happened. Thank goodness Ruth and Toby hadn't had enough money to invest at the time, because they'd just bought their house. Their lack of cash felt like a failure to Ruth at first, especially because Paul gave generously, and Rob and Edie gave what they could. Ruth felt as if she and Toby were lesser adults. Until it became clear that they'd dodged a bullet.

It made Ruth a safe haven for Jayne at the time, breaking the ice between them. Jayne and Mark could talk to Toby and Ruth about Dovecote without fearing recriminations.

Ruth is stuck on Emily's question: if Edie has harmed one of our husbands, who do you think it would be?

Of course it's Toby, she thinks, and feels a knot in her stomach tighten. Even if she didn't harbour a suspicion with outlines strong enough to support her conviction that Toby could be in danger, she can easily imagine it. Toby is not as big a man as the others, he's slender and bookish, he likes to chat, to open himself out to other people, he's a pleaser.

With the right words, the right look, it would have been so easy for Edie to persuade him to drop out of this weekend, to come up with that excuse that he had to see his sister.

She suspects that Toby might have slept with Edie, or, if he hasn't, to have fantasised about it so comprehensively that the act itself might even be redundant, or disappointing. She's seen him sneaking looks at Edie, over the years. Edie in a bikini, in a pretty dress. Toby has drunk her in. But then he's not the only one. Mark and Paul are no better.

She hardly dares think about how much Imogen resembles her mother. She puts it right out of her mind.

Out of the three men, without question it would be the most straightforward to physically overpower Toby, even if you are a woman. If that's what you wanted. Needed. In order to do what you wanted to do. Had to do. There's barely a muscle on him. His limbs are slender, downy rather than hairy, and when they used to make love, his arms would sometimes shudder with effort as he held himself above her.

'What makes you so certain that people have forgiven Mark?' Emily asks.

Ruth looks at Emily, finding her barely recognisable from earlier, and is unable to think why. It's because she looks mean now. Aggressive. As Ruth stares, Emily doubles. Jayne too.

144

Ruth is drunk enough to wonder if she herself has doubled. The idea makes her laugh. Now there are six for dinner, she thinks.

'What's so funny?'

Yes, Emily definitely looks different because she's angry. She's not soft any longer. Her red hair seems to blaze. The green in her eyes is envy. She's jealous of all the girlfriends Paul had before he met her. All the girls just like Emily. Except that none of them got a ring on her finger.

She looks at the ring on her own hand, her budget engagement ring, a tiny, simple diamond, blink and you'd miss it, beside a slim, plain wedding band. Her flesh bulges around them.

'What's so funny, Ruth?' Emily repeats the question and sounds meaner this time.

Ruth looks up. Two Emilys, still. Which one to focus on? She has no idea. The note of aggression in Emily's voice takes its time to reach her and, when it does, a feeling of shattering splinters inside her. Confidence in herself as mother, wife, doctor, friend – all of it becomes rubble, worthless.

'I don't know,' she says. 'I really don't know what was funny.' She's telling the truth. She's forgotten. Her mouth is turned down now.

She feels ugly. Self-pity isn't attractive, Flora once said to her. Ruth ceased calling Flora 'Mum' when she was a teenager. It seemed wrong by then. There was so little that was maternal about Flora.

'Really?' Emily asks. It seems to Ruth that she's sneering.

'Leave her alone,' Jayne says. 'She's drunk.'

'No shit.' Emily hates drunks. Women who drink should not be allowed to have kids. It ruined her mother. She didn't deserve to be called a mother after she started drinking.

Ruth grabs her phone and opens the photos. She needs to see Alfie. Nothing else matters. She scrolls through her images of him, relishing each one. The sight of his face is as powerful as ever.

She'll sort herself out and she'll do it for Alfie. The disgust on Emily's face is fair. It's what Ruth deserves. But she wants to do something to avert it; she wants to convey how much she loves her son.

She finds a favourite photograph of Alfie and turns the phone, shows it to Jayne first.

'Lovely,' Jayne says, but her tone is flat, the word doesn't ring true. She's mocking me, Ruth thinks.

'Don't humour me!' she snaps.

'Hey!' Jayne says; then, more softly, 'Ruth, I'm not mocking you.'

Ruth's hand trembles as she offers her phone to Emily. 'Here,' she says. 'Please. Look at him. I'm going to get sober for Alfie. Even if Toby is dead.'

'Toby is not dead!' Jayne snaps this time, exposing her frustration. She doesn't mean to. Emily has got to her.

A feeling of looseness takes over all of Ruth's body, like a melting. She begins to tremble. Her phone tips from her fingers. Emily catches it before it falls, and feels bad. Ruth's decline is alarming.

Emily studies the phone screen. 'I see Alfie,' she says. 'He's really cute, Ruth.' She swipes, looking for another picture, something else to admire. 'He's grown so much since I last saw him.' Her words sound hollow to her, but she means them. Alfie is a beautiful baby. He has his mother's gentle eyes.

Ruth stands. Her chair almost falls backwards. She wobbles too, clamps a hand on Jayne's shoulder to steady herself, her fingers digging in painfully.

'I feel sick,' she says.

She covers her mouth with her hand. She can't vomit into the kitchen sink. It would be too humiliating. She makes it down the hallway, steadying herself against the wall. Jayne helps her upstairs. Ruth is almost bent double by the time they reach the bathroom.

'Do you want me to come in?' Jayne asks.

'No.'

The door shuts in Jayne's face. She flinches.

Emily keeps scrolling on Ruth's phone. Back, back, back. Alfie gets younger and younger. His face loses definition. His eyes expand in proportion to his head. His hair disappears into wisps. It fascinates Emily, the rolling back of time, the undoing of what is done.

Her thumb freezes over the next image. She stares at it. It's an anomaly amongst the baby photographs.

It shows the gang. Minus Rob. She checks. It was taken earlier in the summer a few weeks after his funeral.

In the picture she sees Edie and Imogen, Toby, Mark, Paul. They seem to be at Glastonbury Festival. Emily sees the Pyramid Stage behind them. Jayne isn't in the picture and nor is Ruth. But the men are clustered around Edie and Imogen.

She feels tension spread along her jaw. Paul lied about this. He is a lying bastard. Filthy words, curses and insults she learned from her mum's boyfriends, and heard spew from her mother's mouth when her mother was drunk – Emily applies them all to Paul.

She knows exactly when this weekend was, and Paul lied about where he was going. He told her with shameless, barefaced dishonesty that he was going on a weekend away with the guys from the gang. Canoeing, he said. He came back suntanned.

He never mentioned Edie, nor Imogen. And Emily has begged Paul to take her to a festival. But he refused. He felt too old, he said. He'd been to enough festivals. She should go with her friends. It would be more fun.

And here he is, in T-shirt and shorts, looking as if he's having the best time. Everyone's smiling at the camera, except Imogen.

If Paul lied about this, then what else is untrue? Emily feels a shattering sense of betrayal and, with it, shame, that she fell for Paul's promise that he would always be completely honest with her.

It was all she ever asked of him. People assume it was his money that she married Paul for, but what she really wanted was all of him, nothing hidden.

Jayne appears in the doorway. 'Ruth's being sick,' she says.

'Have you seen this?' Emily shows her the photograph.

Jayne glances at it. 'Sure. Why?'

Emily covers her face with her hands.

'Emily?' Jayne asks. 'What's wrong?'

In the darkness behind her fingers, Emily breathes in, then out, deeply. Liar, she thinks, but it's impossible to accept. Perhaps there is more to this. Perhaps he lied for a good reason. But maybe not. There's only one way to find out. She has to phone Paul. She needs to hear his voice and his explanation. Staying here a moment longer is not an option. It's a torment.

She gets up. 'I'm going down to the farmhouse,' she says.

Jayne shakes her head. 'No. You can't. It's too late. It's about to be properly dark.'

She gestures to the oven clock which displays the time: 19:35.

But Emily doesn't care. She pushes past Jayne and, as she does, she senses that Jayne is holding herself strangely tightly as if she has an urge to grab Emily, to keep her here in the barn, and she thinks, Just you try. She feels ready to fight, tooth and nail. To claw and to run.

In the hall, as she pulls on her jacket and boots, Jayne tells her all the reasons she shouldn't do this and each one sinks in and frightens her, increasing the rate of her already rapid heartbeat, but she's resolved. She didn't get where she is today by being a coward.

If Jayne gets any closer, Emily thinks, I might slap her.

She opens the door and the wind buffets her, causing her to stumble, but she feels as if the weather is challenging her to meet it and she steps out, hauling the door shut behind her, drowning out the sound of Jayne calling her name.

Emily runs.

Imogen watches as I spoon two teaspoons of hot chocolate powder into a mug and add an extra teaspoon of cocoa powder, the finest on offer in my local supermarket. I bought it just for her. A can of whipped cream and a bag of mini marshmallows also stand at the ready. Since she was little, my tried and tested way of cheering her up is to make her my very special deluxe hot chocolate. It never fails.

She's hardly spoken for the past half-hour, just sat at the kitchen island and stared listlessly out of the window.

'The cocoa . . . ' I say, and I leave the words out there, waiting for her to finish my sentence, the way she used to.

But she doesn't. She just looks at me with dull eyes, her elbow propped on the kitchen surface, her head resting heavy on it. I've helped her look everywhere for her phone – well, almost everywhere – and she's depressed that we can't find it. It's understandable. I'd be lost without mine.

'The cocoa stops it being too sweet,' I say, completing the sentence myself because I know I shouldn't expect too much. Especially as she doesn't yet know who I am to her. But she's going to cheer up when she tastes this, she always does.

'Remember I used to settle for microwaving the milk?' I say. 'Well, I don't do that any more, because I have a new gadget! Ta-da!'

I hold up my milk-frothing tool.

'That's cool,' she says but her voice sounds flat.

I pour milk into a pan and watch it closely for bubbles. It's easy to get distracted and let it boil over.

'This is an all-new technique,' I say. 'Please admire how I've refined it and reinvented the perfect hot chocolate for you. When the milk is hot enough you pour a little on the chocolate powder and mix them together like so, do you see?'

I whisk the mixture vigorously and keep doing it for what feels like an inordinately long time until she drags her eyes back to look.

'You want to do this until all the powder has dissolved and there are no lumps.'

She's staring out of the window again. Obviously, it's disappointing that she's not more engaged but this is the perfect moment to take two little green tablets from my pocket, drop them into the chocolate mixture and give it a final stir.

'Here comes the magic,' I say. I froth the remaining milk in a metal jug I purchased just for the purpose. It's a lovely thing to do, to make something for someone and to take care over it. The milk foams and balloons to perfection. I've been dreaming of this scenario for such a long time. Imogen and I. Together.

'Cream?' I ask, the can in the air, ready to squirt. I'm thinking, lots of marshmallows, an obscene number, piled on top of a tower of cream. Decadent. Fun. To show her how I feel about her. That I'll look after her. That I know what she likes.

'No, thanks,' she says.

I feel hurt. I know it might be childish of me, but I can't help it. I try to ignore the feeling, but the hurt evolves into paranoia. What if Imogen's lying about not wanting cream, to undermine me on purpose? If she lied about self-harming, what else could be untrue?

'You sure?' I ask. My voice is a little high-pitched. I'm still holding up the cream, my finger poised to squirt it.

She nods and reaches for the mug of plain hot chocolate, pulling it towards her, the mug scraping painfully on the kitchen-island surface. I open the packet of marshmallows, and tip some into my mouth as she takes her first sip.

I watch her out of the corner of my eye and, though she says nothing, I'm very satisfied because she finishes the whole thing, and when she's done, she has the cutest speck of froth on her upper lip, and it reminds me so much of when she was younger, which makes me feel better.

How much of a special affinity did I feel for her, I wonder, before I knew she was mine, when I still believed she was Rob's? If I noticed a detail like that, then I guess I must have.

To trace a line from here to our past is thrilling. I must find photographs where Imogen and I are both in the picture. New frames will have to be bought for our new home together. With a little Photoshopping, I might be able to create a picture of just the two of us. The idea of recording and making our new history together cheers me up immensely.

I look at her fondly and she returns my gaze with what looks like wariness, or, at least, boredom. But I'm used to unrequited feelings and I'm nothing if not an optimist. I know she will learn to love me.

'Shall we move into the sitting room?' I ask her.

She'll be feeling sleepy very soon and the last thing I want is for her to fall off the stool she's perched on.

'Sure,' she says. 'Why not?'

'We could put the TV on?'

'Fine.'

I watch her settle herself down on the sofa and I hand her a blanket. She snuggles under it like a baby. I take the chair beside her from where I can see her out of the corner of my eye, but she can't see me looking.

When she starts to look sleepy, I relax a little and I'm seized by a sort of euphoria because I believe that what I've done has been incredibly daring, thrillingly so. It's a vast step away from what everyone expected of me, a rejection of the tedium of those well-worn paths you're supposed to travel in life.

I've ripped myself away from cliché and embraced originality, casting aside the staggering tedium of marriage in search of a true, blood connection. As I cross my legs quietly, careful not to disturb Imogen as she slips into semi-consciousness, I feel almost drunk on the power of being the architect, the creator of something so bold, and within that hurtling, tumbling slipstream of a feeling, I dare to wonder, when *will* Imogen show me that she loves me? How will it happen? Just imagining it is electrifying.

I want to get up and shout to the heavens. I want to release the tension I've been feeling and start a celebration. But I mustn't. Not yet. So I sit and watch her and, though I remain as still as a statue on the outside, I relish the feel of my love for her burning hot inside me and I wait that way until she shuts her eyes.

When I'm certain that she's properly out of it, I fetch my bag and ready the kit. I've read the instructions many times and done this on myself, so I know what to do.

I ease her mouth open gently, marvelling at the pink inside. 'Sorry,' I say, because this is an intimate thing to be doing. I swab carefully. She stirs a little and I stop, but she relaxes again, and I get the job done.

I put her swab in the sterile tube and seal it. I package it up alongside my own swab and message the service.

The courier arrives an hour later. I'm impressed. You get what you pay for, I guess, and I paid a lot for an express service. The result of the DNA paternity test will be sent to me within twenty-four hours, and I intend to present it to Imogen when I let her know that I'm her biological father.

Perhaps, one day, we'll even get it framed and hang it alongside our new family portraits.

Jayne pulls her boots on. She doesn't believe Emily will try to get down to the farmhouse on her own. She'd put money on finding her somewhere close, near the entrance to the lane, having second thoughts.

She hesitates before leaving the barn, remembering Ruth, and calls upstairs but Ruth doesn't answer. Jayne's boots are covered in mud. She runs upstairs anyway, leaving damp prints on the treads.

Ruth sits on the bathroom floor, her head resting against the wall. Her mind is on a rough drunken journey, one minute trying to fathom her surroundings – it's a compact bathroom, she's aware of that because she hit her head on the underside of the basin the first time she tried to get up – another minute thinking of Toby and his student, Lexi MacKay – did Lexi think she was special? How many other special young women have there been? – and then her doctor brain kicking in – you vomited because you drank too much, you need to rehydrate, see if you can keep some food down. But cutting through it all, like a note so high and so strung out that it's painful, a longing for Alfie and each thought of him makes her limbs feel heavier, the air she's breathing thicker. All of it compounds a crushing sense of uselessness. Of abject failure.

A pounding jolts her into a more functional consciousness. Jayne is on the other side of the door, calling her.

'I'm fine,' Ruth says. 'Just a minute. I'll be down in a minute.' She feels as if words are sliding from her mouth, over numb lips.

'I'm going after Emily. She's trying to walk down to the farmhouse.'

I would like to go too, Ruth thinks. She doesn't register the danger it might put her in, and she tries to get up, but can't.

'Ruth?' Jayne calls. 'Did you hear me? Are you OK?'

'I'm fine,' she repeats. Am I upset with Jayne? she wonders, but can't remember why she might be. Perhaps it's Emily she's cross with.

She feels animosity but isn't sure where it should be directed. It must have come from somewhere. She listens for Jayne's reply, but hears nothing. Maybe Jayne said something, maybe she didn't. Ruth's head settles back to rest against the bathroom wall.

It comes to her. It's Toby. He is the cause of her hostility. It's always him.

The Lexi MacKay letter was horrifying. But there have been other, smaller incidents she let slip but can't ignore any longer.

Ruth thinks of a wedding she and Toby went to. They brought Alfie. He was tiny. When he soiled his nappy and Ruth went in search of somewhere to change him she saw Toby chatting to one of the young waitresses outside the marquee. They were standing very close to one another. When she called him, Toby leapt away from the girl and rushed to help with Alfie. He wasn't usually so concerned with Alfie's needs. It made him seem guilty.

She winces at the memory. Her problem is that she never knows if what she saw was *something*, or nothing. Is she piecing together innocent actions and catastrophising, or is Toby fatally attracted to younger women? She doesn't trust herself to know.

But she does know that he wouldn't be the first professor to take advantage of his position. Are there other students, apart from Lexi MacKay, that he's bothered?

Is Imogen one of them?

She knows what her gut is telling her and shuts her eyes, taking a bitter, defeated sort of consolation from the warmth of the tears slipping down her cheeks.

She needs to stop fighting the truth and accept it. This is what giving up feels like, she thinks. My marriage is over.

And the thought that perhaps Edie knows this about Toby, too, and has taken revenge on him doesn't feel all that strange at all.

She doesn't move, just sits where she is and drunkenly tries to imagine a new future, not even reacting when lightning illuminates the bathroom window and a clap of thunder rips across the valley.

*

John walks beside the river. In the darkness the rushing water has a solid quality; it looks like molten lava. He imagines it coming up from the earth. The noise of it fills his ears.

He's walking his land; he knows that much. Maggie would tell him to come in, stay safe from the rain and the lightning that's crackling and approaching from the west, but he feels exhilarated.

A dead hare lies on the riverbank. He stops to look at it and finds it beautiful and sad. The darkness makes it look as if the ground is absorbing it.

Clouds race above him so fast that he feels breathless just to turn his head up and gaze at them. He senses how vast they are, rather than sees, until the lightning reveals their immense, agitated architecture. He feels as if the rain is cleansing him.

He has no idea how long he's been out here. But he knows where he's going.

He wants to pay his respects at the burial chamber. To the people of this valley. His people. They roam this place still, just as he does.

He walks doggedly uphill. Lightning electrifies the horizon when he reaches the edge of the bogland that put fear in him as a child and, in the brightness, he sees a figure rise ahead of him, towering above the saturated ground, dripping, and beckoning to him, but he's not afraid. Rather, he salutes it with one hand, and after a moment he believes he can see through the darkness that it salutes him back, and then it's gone, and as thunder rolls in waves across the valley he feels as if he was understood.

He wonders what he's carrying in his other hand, this fleshy and limp thing, and why it's dead. He recognises that it's an animal and it has a name, but he can't think of it.

'I know,' he says, after a while. He knows what the figure in the bog was telling him.

He turns back towards the barn.

Jayne opens the front door of the barn, hoping to see Emily outside, but it's almost pitch-dark. The storm has accelerated dusk.

Light spills from behind Jayne, from the hallway, but doesn't travel far. It creates falling shards from the raindrops and pools on to the slick paving stones just outside the entrance. She steps out and pulls the door shut behind her, fighting the wind.

Upstairs, Ruth startles at the slam, before blacking out again.

Jayne is enveloped in a cloak of darkness. Only the dimmest of outlines are visible beyond the barn, not a single star and no sign of Emily. Lightning flashes. Thunder follows, only a few seconds behind, menacingly loud.

Jayne turns on the torch provided by the owners of the barn. It penetrates the darkness disappointingly; its beam is dimmer than she would like, long but narrow, not much better than a laser pointer.

But she has no better option. She scans the area outside the front door with the torch. There's a mess of footprints in the mud where the path ends, each indent filled with water, but it's impossible to know if any of them are Emily's or were made earlier.

'Emily!' she shouts, but the wind snatches her words and swallows them before they can be carried any distance. The temperature has plummeted. Lightning ripples across the horizon behind her but is gone too quickly for her to see much.

Beyond the yard her torchlight picks out a small lawn of rough grass, barely tamed, a wooden fence beyond it and a pergola-type structure, partially walled, built into the fence's corner, like a lookout post. Perhaps Emily is there, praying to the gods of phone reception. Jayne's feet sink into the grass and, below it, into watery, uneven ground.

There's nobody in the shelter, just a barbecue cowering beneath its flapping cover and some sturdy wooden furniture. 'Emily!' Jayne bellows but the wind ensures that the word only churns in the air around her, travelling nowhere, before it's obliterated by another clap of thunder.

Jayne knows she should find lower, open ground, or get inside. The storm will be over them soon. But suspicion that Emily might really have tried to return to the farmhouse is reluctantly growing in her mind. She's afraid for Emily and upset with her. People think they're bomb-proof, fire-proof, getting-lost-proof. Death-proof. Until it happens. And it can happen in an instant. She has watched it happen, multiple times.

If Emily's on the lane now, she's surely very afraid. Jayne makes her way to the front of the barn and approaches the thicket that marks the start of the lane.

'Emily!' she calls again.

Across the valley, the gibbous moon, a pocked yellow stone, emerges briefly, beautifully, between storm clouds that roil its edges. Seconds later, they close around it and it's gone. The end of a brief act. As if in answer, lightning ripples again.

She pauses at the top of the lane. It's darker than its surroundings, a black tunnel. Even she feels nervous.

Emily must be very scared for Paul if she's run off down here. It's extreme. It makes Jayne wonder whether Emily's right to be worried about him.

What she does know is that Paul's not the straight arrow Emily seems to think he is. Not by a long stretch. He wears the uniform of success: expensive shirts, collars stiff and proud, striped cotton straining over his belly and parting sharply at the neck releasing an unruly triangle of chest hair. A pair of black jeans. Brogues. The latest phone. A fat watch and wedding band. Cufflinks. His laugh is loud enough to turn heads. The same when he barks an order. The impression is of a man blandly enjoying success, and life, whose arms and wallet are open to those he loves.

But if a bead of sweat springs out on his brow, he doesn't leave it there; a new shirt is pulled from his office drawer if so much as a hint of perspiration darkens his armpits.

Jayne suspects that the grip Paul has on his business affairs is made of steel. When the Dovecote investment failed it was the thought of telling Paul that frightened Mark the most. He came home shaken afterwards. And yet when they next saw Paul, he was open arms and the waft of aftershave, bonhomie and tales and promises of the best this and the best that and taking a call, just a min, I'll be right back. His company is a train you ride on. You don't remember boarding, but you feel it when you're standing alone again.

And what about Toby? The image that springs to mind for him is a shaft of dusty light, illuminating a bookshelf, dust motes turning in it. Mr Professor. He's earnest. A talker. Too many words tumble from him at once. You can struggle to follow them. His mind is a Catherine wheel, the sparks it throws out ideas; some so serious you want to take them away and consider them, you feel as if they might pierce your own confusion about life; others so frivolous, so downright silly and self-effacing, it takes you a moment to process them and, in the meantime, you've already laughed with him.

Lightning flares again and, in the flash of light, Jayne sees that the lane is barely passable.

Emily is just foolish, she thinks. Anyone going down here tonight needs their head screwing on and I mustn't get sucked into her paranoia, or Ruth's. Edie hasn't killed anyone.

Jayne walks a little way down the lane, torch beam aimed at the ground, so she doesn't slip. It's dangerously slick underfoot.

'Emily!' she shouts.

She turns back to face the barn. It looks so simple in outline, like something a child would draw, an uneven little cube punctuated by glowing windows, a rim of light around the door.

Lightning strikes again, closer now. Powerful. Briefly, it makes lacework of the foliage above her. Jayne's chest tightens.

'Emily!' she calls again, at the top of her voice.

Her answer is a roll of thunder.

Emily runs down the lane. Her phone torch guides her, its beam shrouding the space in front of her in a mist of light, bouncing off what's close and pulling it into focus. Her pink rubber boots, the boisterous green of the crowding foliage, occasional flashes of colour in the monochrome. The rest is darkness. Shadows on shadows.

Except for when there's lightning, which feels as if it's above her. The thunder scares her just as much, so loud that Emily imagines it's shaking the valley, rearranging the landscape around her to cut off all routes down to safety.

Even so, there's no way she's going back up now. She needs to find open ground. She needs to keep going.

Between bursts of thunder and lightning she can hear the wind, rustling, pulling, pushing. The wet slap of her boots. Her breathing is rasping, staccato.

She swerves to avoid a low-hanging branch, and a foot lands too heavily in a deep rut, jarring her knee. She has to contort herself awkwardly to regain her balance.

She stops once, to check her phone for a signal. Because if she can talk to Paul while she's going down, this will be easier. She's almost forgotten the letter and her anger at him over his lie. She just wants to hear his voice, wants him to talk her back to safety.

But there's no signal.

She carries on, slower now. The path is degrading. Her heart is thumping. Another round of thunder and lightning stops her in her tracks.

When it's over she starts to move once again, but even more cautiously. Trees close in tighter. The ruts beneath her feet become deeper and flow with rainwater. She recalls the precarious tilting of the Land Rover as they drove up here, the engine alternately gunning and groaning.

She takes to the edge of the lane and must walk now, her balance precarious, but she keeps herself going by imagining emerging from the trees to see the farmhouse lit up and welcoming. Her determination swells, driving her faster, and, as if in punishment, her foot slips into a rut, submerging her boot in muddy water.

Emily tries to pull it out, too late feeling the suction grip of mud hanging on to the sole, and her foot pops out of the boot, sock dangling. She wobbles. There's nothing to grab on to.

Lightning crackles again, but the trees are so dense here it doesn't give her much to see by. Thunder comes quicker this time. It's almost deafening.

One hand goes down on to the verge, on to a pile of nettles and its little darts spitefully puncture her palm and the soft undersides of her fingers. She has to lean into the pain harder before she can regain enough balance to snatch her hand away and try to right herself. When she does, her knees buckle as she loses her balance again, and her socked foot is submersed in slick, cold mud. She cries out with frustration but gets up again, inserts her foot back into the boot and carries on, though more slowly and carefully.

Her hand throbs. Cold is creeping into her bones. She walks on, feeling helpless and possessed suddenly by the fear that Paul might not answer even if she calls him. What will she do then? Does it mean that Edie has harmed him? Right now, anything seems possible.

The rain worsens as the trees become sparser around her and the canopy above splits. She doesn't know if she's safer with more tree cover, or less.

She stops. Questioning herself. Should she turn back? She has no idea how far she's come or how far she has to go.

She points the torch back in the direction she's come from, to assess her options, and sees at once that it will be harder to go back than to keep moving forward. The slope behind her looks steeper than it felt when she was coming down, and slicker, as if everything solid has melted and is descending with her. As if the only momentum is down, towards the farmhouse. She carries on down, slipping and sliding. Yelping.

A feral shriek cuts through the dark. She stops and points her torch into the forest, first in one direction, then another, standing as still as possible, breathing tightly through her nose, as if this could make her invisible. Her hand shakes.

She doesn't see the movement but hears it. Behind her, something approaches, not quickly, but deliberately. She swings the torch wildly in its direction but sees only foliage, teased by the wind. A shudder ripples through her. Lightning strikes, but it only confuses her, white light glancing off every tree trunk, picking out every leaf and thorn and bramble.

She feels spotlit by it, intensely vulnerable, and takes off down the hill, running as quickly as she can, not caring what she steps on, or whether she risks falling. She feels possessed by fear, driven by it. The torch beam bounces, illuminating things at random. A tree, the ground, a face.

Emily doesn't see the log across the lane. Her toes hit it, hard, and she falls heavily. Her phone flies from her hand. For a moment, the large puddle it lands in glows, lit from within, before reverting to oily black.

Emily lies still, wet, shocked, cold to her bones, and in the deepest darkness she's ever been alone in. She begins to push herself up and her whole body starts to shake.

A few feet from her, a hand reaches towards the puddle where her phone has sunk, dips into the water, and removes it.

Jayne walks through the darkness and calls for Emily. The rainfall is more intense than ever. She should go back inside because the storm is almost overhead, but she feels obliged to check around the barn thoroughly, at least. If she doesn't, she won't have done her job properly.

The incline behind the barn is steep and the passageway cut out of the hillside between the two is narrow. She'll be amazed if Emily is hiding back here but you never know.

As she steps into the passageway a blur of sharp teeth and black and white fur bolts past, almost knocking her legs out from under her. Too close, too big, too strong, too quick. A badger. She yelps and swings around, trying to track the animal with the torch beam but failing. She doesn't know where it's gone, and she can only hope it's not coming back.

She inches along. The kitchen light glows through the small back window. It's fogged with condensation, but the room looks empty. Ruth must still be upstairs.

It feels surreal, looking in, as if she's an outsider at her own weekend, and that change of perspective gives her pause and makes her question everything she's felt certain about, and persuaded the others of.

She feels a surge of fear. From out here, looking into the barn, as if it was a doll's house, or an alternative reality, the thought that Mark might be in danger doesn't feel as far-fetched as it did earlier.

And she regrets making Emily walk uphill towards the burial chamber earlier, when they were looking for a phone signal. If she'd agreed to go back to the farmhouse, they might have made it down easily and they wouldn't be in this situation now. If Emily is hurt, will Paul ever forgive them?

Breathe, she tells herself. As she takes her next step something crunches beneath her foot and simultaneously from behind her an animal shriek of pain cuts through the night. The badger again? Has it caught prey? Got itself hurt somehow? Or did the noise come from further away? It's hard to tell. The wind is whistling.

She hurries back out of the passageway and aims the torch in the direction of the sound, then in wider and wider arcs, but it's futile. She sees nothing apart from shivering foliage and branches bent taut, but can't help feeling that things are happening around her, larger movements, laced with menace, that her regular senses can't detect.

She concentrates hard, willing herself to remain calm and not to give in to fear, but she fails. Her chest is rising and falling rapidly. The muscles in her neck and shoulders are knotted.

And now she'll have to punish herself because she equates feeling fear with cowardice. It's what she did when she was serving. If something made her feel weak, or vulnerable, she pushed herself harder and faster, doubled down, volunteered over and over for things that made her blood run cold until she'd taught herself a lesson.

It made her feel better about the death she witnessed and felt responsible for.

She moves forward, consciously putting one foot in front of the other, but not too quickly. Part of the challenge is that she must do this slowly enough to feel her fear as it knits itself into every bone, muscle and tendon in her body and walk with it, uncowed by it.

She emerges around the front of the house and thinks she'll make herself check the lane one more time. As she approaches the thicket of hedgerow at its entrance, she senses movement again, even though she doesn't see or hear it clearly. The hair on the back of her neck prickles.

'Emily?' she calls, hopeful. Perhaps Emily is hiding, ashamed that she didn't have the courage to go down the hill on her own in the end. It would be a relief, but there's no reply.

Lightning rips through the sky, thunder on its tail, and Jayne sees something in front of the hedge. She shrieks involuntarily and tries to direct her torch towards it with an unsteady hand. The bulb flickers and fails. She shakes the torch, but it won't come back to life.

She forces herself to approach the hedge, praying for her eyes to get used to the dark but feeling as if the darkness is fear itself, pressing in around her, claiming her.

When she's close, she can make out an outline that looks anomalous. A person?

'Edie?' she whispers. The idea that Edie might be out here comes to her unexpectedly, but it's convincing. Why not? Has

Edie come to witness the meltdown she triggered with the letter? Or to do worse?

'Edie?' she repeats, louder. Her hair blows across her face and she pushes it away. The outline is motionless. Jayne forces herself to step through the darkness towards it in spite of her building fright. From prey to huntress. This is what she trained to do. The torch hangs in her hand as she approaches, heavy enough to be an effective weapon.

A sheet of lightning bleaches the valley, followed by two more, strobing everything around her.

The face is suspended on a stick and is moon-round, made from sacking stuffed crudely with straw, a cruel mouth painted on with one slash of a brushstroke. Where the paint has dripped, Jayne sees drool. Slavering. The nose is a large safety pin, attached at an angle. Hair is draped over the top of the head and looks fat-white and bloody. She realises with a spasm in her own gut that it's fashioned out of entrails.

'Jesus!' she says. Somebody must have put this here in the last few hours. Or minutes. Was it here earlier? She can't remember how carefully she looked. Who did this? Emily? Edie? Someone else?

She backs away. The blood isn't good. Her heart rate increases. This mustn't start. Not here, not now.

She kicks at the scarecrow, hard, and it topples. A fucking broom. She keeps kicking until all its component parts are scattered and robbed of their power to frighten and half-hidden beneath the hedge where neither Ruth nor Emily should be able to see them tonight. The badger will have the entrails quick enough, or any other hungry creature around here lucky enough to come across them.

She kicks at everything some more and, when she's finished, she stops, panting, and knows that things have got way out of hand, beyond her ability to rationalise what's happening. She's very afraid and she needs to shelter. The storm is almost on her.

And she and Ruth need to make a plan, but Jayne won't mention the scarecrow. Whoever put it there wants to terrify them and she's not going to let that happen to Ruth.

She thinks of her gun. She brought it here for one reason, but might she need to use it for another?

But she knows she can't go back inside just yet. She needs a few minutes to calm down first because Ruth shouldn't see her like this.

Nobody should.

She strikes out into the darkness once more, to circuit the barn, however many times it takes, until she regains control and proves to herself that she's brave.

John thinks he wanted something like this to happen, that it's right, somehow, this sense of fear emanating from the young woman he's found on the lane. But he's also horrified.

Accustomed to the dark, his eyes can make out the whites of hers, the outline of her body, her arms outstretched as if she fears a gust of wind could tip her over.

She hasn't taken a step since he touched her fingers. She is immobilised. Effectively blind until the lightning strikes. Her eyes dart from side to side, her body sways as she tries to stay upright. Her breathing is no more than fast, shallow panting. He can't smell her fear, but Birdie would be able to, and every living creature out here must be paying attention, sniffing, listening, pupils dilated.

I'll help you, I'm here to help you. The words are stuck in his throat.

He's standing very close to her, but she's so seized by panic that she can't see him.

He's seen terror in the eyes of animals but never in a human before. It wasn't meant to go this far, he thinks. Whatever I did.

He feels guilt, terrible guilt, and fear, for this, for whatever else he's done, though it could have been his brother Danny getting up to mischief, he supposes, and feels briefly reassured until, in the next moment, he remembers that Danny died years ago.

'It's OK,' he tells her.

'Who's there?'

'John Elliott. From the farm. Do you need some help?'

She turns towards his voice. 'Did you touch my hand?'

'Don't cry now,' he says. 'I'll see you're safe. Are you hurt?'

'My ankle is.'

'Take my arm here. It's OK. I'll get you down the hill to the farm, rather than back up, if you're injured. Maggie will take care of you.'

She sees him now, in another flash of lightning. He offers her his arm, grazing her elbow with his to coax her to take it, and at first her touch is feather-light but then she slips her arm through his and grips his forearm hard.

'Yes, yes, please,' she says. She's tiny, but John's not young any longer and he wonders how easy it'll be to get her down safely.

She shudders against him. He feels as if she's got heavier.

'Here,' he says. 'Don't cry. There's no need to cry now. John's got you. I'll see you safe, I promise.'

As Jayne walks through the storm, she asks it to purge her of her fear.

She faces up to the lightning, doesn't let herself recoil from the thunder and vows that she'll stay out here until she's hollow inside, reduced to a shell of herself, every cell in her body dedicated just to staying upright in the middle of this onslaught of weather, and she prays that the effort will obliterate the terror she felt.

If she doesn't succeed, she may dissociate. For years she didn't know what dissociation was, didn't understand what was happening to her when she spontaneously clocked out of a situation emotionally. She had no answers to questions about why she lost periods of time and memories, why she entered a kind of fugue state sometimes.

The therapist she saw after leaving the army put a name to it, which was a relief in a way, but also alarming. Now, Jayne is desperate to avoid it happening. A few things can trigger it for her, and the sight of blood is one of them. Fear and potential loss of control of a situation are others.

Gradually, as she walks, battling the elements, the image of the scarecrow and the bloody entrails fades, and she feels as if she might be able to stay present, to go back inside and be helpful to Ruth, but the effort exhausts her.

She slows until she's trudging rather than pacing. She feels utterly depleted, physically and emotionally, frightened for Emily and afraid of the state she might find Ruth in, but she's also scared for herself and of herself. Of her own mind.

And just to be sure, even though she's desperate to be inside, to confess to her friend that she too is frightened, she walks on until she doesn't think she can keep going any longer.

John guides the young woman down to the farmhouse. It's not easy. She has collapsed on to him, and she moans if her bad ankle has to take any weight. John feels a stab of remorse every time it happens. A strong sense is building in him that he's done a bad thing and that this young woman is hurt as a result and could have been hurt worse.

How will Maggie react if it's true?

The guilt he feels is tremendous though its exact source still remains vague.

What has he done?

'Can you tell me your name?' he asks.

'Emily.'

'Come on, flower. Come on, Emily. We're getting there. Maggie'll see you right.'

When they come to the flooded area of the lane, he climbs the wall first and helps her over. She falls into his arms on the other side. Sheep loom out of the darkness and surround them. She flinches when he shouts them away and trembles in his arms.

He is wholly focused on keeping her close, on picking a safe route. The darkness doesn't bother him. The rain rolls off him. She has no choice but to trust him, he knows that, but he likes that she doesn't question him, or panic, that she'll let her weight fall heavy on him when she needs to. She is totally helpless.

But he feels the same way he does when one of his ewes is injured or struggling to lamb. He knows what he has to do. His mind doesn't wander.

As they descend into the valley, he pieces together that she's not properly dressed for outside. Her wellington boots are flat-soled and pink. The jacket she's wearing might hold off a shower in the city, but in this rain it's soaked through. No wonder she's quivering, and her hands are white with cold. Where he's touching her skin, he feels as if it might dissolve.

Ahead is an oak tree, very old, its trunk split. He is pleased to see it. It means something, but he doesn't know what. He stops. Another flash of lightning illuminates the tree's silhouette, and it appears animated for a moment.

She looks up at him, sensing his hesitation. 'What is it?'

He doesn't reply. How can he tell her that he recognises this tree because it's been there all his life, was already hundreds of years old when he was born, and he recognises the fork in the path beside it as well as he knows the path of veins on the back of his hands, but he can't remember how either of them relate to the route back to the farmhouse.

Emily's grip tightens on his arm as he prays silently, to the land, to all it is home to, real and unreal, solid and magical, to help him get her home safely. He has never prayed so hard.

*

Ruth wakes. She has no idea how much time has passed. Her head is a ball of pressure, her limbs stiff. She stands, awkwardly. The room spins. Her bladder is urgently full. She pees, gratefully, and fights off a surge of nausea and dizziness before she can stand up again.

The small bathroom window is a blank square of darkness. She stares at it and has the impression that what's beyond it is hostile. Lightning flashes, making her jump, and as she braces herself for thunder the memory of the letter crashes into her consciousness and, with it, the rest of the evening.

I lost it, she thinks. I drank too much. What did I say? She's acutely embarrassed that she got so drunk in front of Jayne and Emily. She has been slipping more and more like this lately. The drinking is no longer a matter of having one too many glasses of wine in the evening. Her colleagues made that clear to her. Toby did. Flora, her mother. She didn't listen to them, in fact she resented them for it, and now this.

She feels a heavy, maudlin sense of shame. A drunken shame. I'm still pissed, she thinks. She unbolts the bathroom door with difficulty. 'Jayne,' she calls from the landing. No reply. 'Emily?'

Her headache is bad. A vice. She locates her bedroom and empties her bag, in search of pain relief. That would be a start. She can't find any. Back in the bathroom she uses the tooth mug to drink water and opens the cabinet over the basin. Empty.

The headache feels like the thing that's stopping her from functioning, from regaining sobriety so that she can grovel, apologise, make amends. Depending what time it is, she thinks, with a flash of hope, and if I can get the pain under control, I can maybe go down and serve dinner. It's hard to remember whether they had reached that stage of the evening or not yet.

It occurs to her that it's ironic that she hasn't brought with her this most basic first-aid supply. She, who doesn't leave the house with Alfie without packing everything he might need, hasn't attended to her own needs. She resists the urge to sink into self-pity. The inside of her mouth tastes metallic, her saliva is tacky. She spits, washes her mouth out, brushes her teeth. Leans her head against the mirror for a while to try to absorb the cool temperature of the glass and realises she can't hear any noise from inside the house.

Where are the others?

She pauses at the top of the stairs, gripped by the fear that something terrible has happened downstairs, that she will go down and find blood, bodies, a massacre, Jayne and Emily brutally murdered. Her head pounds. She sits on the top step. 'Jayne?' she calls. She feels frightened in a way she hasn't done since she was a child. The raw terror of being afraid of an intruder in the dark.

She stands up, takes a few steps, peers down. The movement makes her headache worse. But she sees Emily's shoes in the hall and remembers. Emily went to the farmhouse and Jayne – well, Ruth can't remember, but perhaps Jayne went after Emily, or with her.

The images of their corpses don't recede completely, but she feels a little reassured. She's pretty sure it's a reliable memory. It makes sense.

And if Jayne is out searching, Ruth ought to make herself useful. She should go out and search too, though perhaps that's not a good idea. She has a child to get home to and the storm is the biggest she thinks she's ever experienced. If they're out there, she dreads to think what state they're in. At the very least she should make sure that she seems sober when they get back. Her head is troubling her most. Surely, Jayne won't mind if she looks for painkillers in her stuff. They know each other well enough.

She checks Jayne's washbag, and finds just a toothpaste and toothbrush, damp from having been used earlier. Jayne's deodorant, an unfussy brand, is out on the side. No medication. There must be some somewhere, Ruth thinks. Jayne always has a first-aid kit. They've had to use it before on weekends away. For cuts, scrapes and hangovers. She turns to Jayne's bag. The side pocket is empty. She unzips the main compartment.

Ruth's head snaps up at the sound of something screaming outside, a swift, shrill sound that dies into a moan. It chills her. She strains to hear more, but only registers the low whistle of the wind wrapping itself around the barn. The windows rattle and judder in Jayne's room, as it seeks a way in. The scream came from a something, not a someone, Ruth tells herself. It was definitely animal. Her head and heart pound in unison, crescendoing.

Jayne's bag is sparsely packed, everything folded and tucked into place with military precision. No excess included, Ruth notes, and feels as if Jayne's neatness is rebuking her for her own haphazard packing.

She grabs the metal object and yanks it out of the bag before she feels its weight, interprets its shape or understands its power. When she sees what she has in her hand, she screams and drops it.

Her chest heaves as she stares at it. That, she realises, was a very dangerous thing to do.

Jayne's gun lies on the bedroom rug, pointing towards the door. It's small, what Ruth would think of as pistol-sized, though she knows nothing about guns and has no idea how to check if it's loaded or safe. She's never handled one. They've always struck her as malevolent objects, even their appearance loaded with menace.

Why has Jayne brought a gun here? Why does she even have a gun? Ruth's mind races, trying to find answers. It sobers her up, but not completely. Nothing makes sense.

Except.

What if Jayne has been playing the puppeteer this weekend? What if she wrote the letter? Could she have wanted to scare them? What if she has some other terrible act in mind, some final act to which the letter is just a prelude?

But why? Jayne's rock-steady, a port in a storm. She and Mark are so well suited, so stable. What possible reason could Jayne have to do something like this?

An answer settles in Ruth's mind and as soon as it does it feels inevitable, obvious, the same way her suspicions about Toby aren't new, but have been shoved under the carpet for too long as suspicion built.

Ruth has always wondered how Jayne worked for so long for military intelligence and emerged with no signs of trauma. It's obvious from what they don't say about their time in the military that Jayne and Mark were involved in some difficult and secretive operations. She knows they did tours in Libya and Afghanistan.

But what if, Ruth wonders, I haven't been looking closely enough at my friend? Is Jayne's measured demeanour, her calm, the way she wields rationality almost like a weapon – is it all hiding some serious mental instability?

The world snaps back into place. John doesn't just recognise what he can see, but the tree and the fork in the path relate to one another once again and relate to the rest of his land, to his destination. He knows where he is and where he needs to go. The farmhouse. Home. Maggie.

'Come on,' he says to the girl. He's forgotten her name, but he's certain that she needs him, that he's helping her.

Her shaking has worsened. It's more of a tremor, coming from deep within her. Whether the cause is pain or cold, it doesn't much matter. It's dangerous. Shock can take you as quick as anything else. He's lost livestock that way.

His relief when the farmhouse comes into view is as strong as he's ever felt, yellow light from the kitchen window as close to a guiding star as he's ever seen up on the moors.

'Oh, dear God, you poor thing,' Maggie says, her arms outstretched to take the young woman from him. Birdie sniffs and backs away, tail low, submissive. Concerned. No barking. She senses, as well as he does, when something is wrong and he's afraid that wrong thing is him.

'She'll be all right,' he says, not because he knows but because it's what he's hoping.

He shuts the door behind them. It's a relief to be out of the storm. He takes off his coat and boots and by the time he joins them in the kitchen, he's not exactly sure who the young woman is and why she's here in his home. He wonders what her name is. But she looks as if she needs help, and Maggie is providing it. That part of it makes perfect sense to him.

But he can't shake a sense of dread and a crawling feeling of guilt. But for what, he's not sure. Perhaps it's to do with the girl?

'Why's she here?' he asks Maggie.

'Not now, John,' she says. The look on her face breaks something in him.

Responding to the warning in Maggie's voice, he leaves the room quietly to let her tend to the young woman. She'll know what's right. Maggie is the kindest person he's ever known.

In the boot room, he stands, head hanging. He hardly has the energy to take off his boots. When he sits heavily on the bench something in his pocket clunks against it.

He reaches in to see what it is and finds a phone. It's wet and clearly broken and it's not his. He has no idea why he has it or who it belongs to.

Worse, he notices that his hands are bloody. He puts the phone on his lap and turns up his palms. Smears of blood cover both. Watery, somewhat washed away by the rain, but clearly blood. It's beneath his fingernails, between his fingers, it's in the cracks on his knuckles.

He doesn't know why it's there, or what he's done. Queasiness rises in him and he drops the phone into the crack between the bench and the wall, to hide it. He's afraid for Maggie to see it and suspect him of something, the way he suspects himself.

There, in the room where he has sat chatting with his father after a day's work, where he has kneeled to tie the laces on his son's shoes, where he has held Maggie's coat for her as she puts it on, where he has fed generations of beloved dogs, he's terrified of what's become of him. After a life of responsibility, he feels nothing but a dread, horror and hopelessness that he's no longer in control of his actions. And, most terribly, that he might be dangerous to those around him.

His hands clench, one locked into the other, until his fingers turn white. He's trying to hide the sight of the blood. The effort and horror of it all makes him cry. Silently.

Ruth tries to pull her thoughts together, to keep panic at bay and think rationally about Jayne.

Jayne's never spoken directly about her time in the army to Ruth, but Mark has shared some of his experiences with Toby who related them to Ruth, in awe. They were difficult, troubling things. Horrific, even.

It intrigued Ruth. For a while, when they first met, she watched both of them but especially Jayne for signs of her past. She wasn't rewarded. Jayne seemed happy. She wasn't plagued by ambition or tormented by comparing herself to others. She spoke in cheerful, no-nonsense terms about the challenges of her work as a physiotherapist. She referred to the armed forces in clipped, jolly tones. While she never confided in Ruth in any depth, she was a good listener. She demonstrated her devotion to Mark and drank in the attention he lavished on her.

But there were maybe little signs of trauma. Times when Jayne seemed distant, or jumpy. When she spoke of nightmares but never shared their horrors.

And there was that time on the beach.

The gang was on a weekend away, in Cornwall, shortly after Jayne and Mark married. Ruth and Jayne were lying together on the sand, towels side by side, chatting amiably. The men and Edie were surfing. Mark came out first. They watched him walk up the beach, his thickset, hairy torso shining. It took a moment to register that blood was running thick down his shin. Ruth stood. Jayne froze. She slipped into a cover-up as if she was ready to help, to take action, but she couldn't look at the wound or at Mark, didn't even approach him. She was useless. Checked out.

It was Ruth who drove Mark to A & E and stayed there with him while they put stitches in. And that seemed to be no surprise to Mark. 'Jayne hates blood,' he said, as if it was no big deal. But it was odd. In every other circumstance Jayne was so attentive to him.

Ruth is no psychologist, but she wonders if Jayne has suffered greater psychological trauma than anyone imagined.

If Jayne's dangerous.

I should have worked harder to get beneath her surface, Ruth thinks, if I was really her friend. Why was the time we spent together so shallow? So focused on drinking and acting as honorary members of the gang. Did we ever have real conversations or was it bluff and bluster from the men and Edie, with Jayne and I playing along?

We were, she thinks, a very privileged group until Rob died.

And at what price? How much was hidden?

Self-pity wells up in her. She feels confused, fuddled, overwhelmed, too drunk to know anything. Are her instincts about Jayne fantastical or possible? She picks up the gun, marvelling at its cold, smooth surfaces. It's surprisingly heavy.

Why bring a gun unless you plan to do harm, or you believe harm will come to you?

She feels her own terror creep up on her again. It's the fear of the unknown. Of what's here, in the house, of what's outside, of Edie, and now, of Jayne. Her muddled brain doesn't know which to tackle first or even if she can.

She looks at the gun in her hand. She's uncomfortable holding it, doesn't really know how to. But if Jayne believed there was a threat, then Ruth must defend herself in Jayne's absence. From the threat. Or from Jayne.

It feels like good logic. It's the best she can do. Alarmingly, her hands start to shake and her resolve wobbles. I'm still drunk and this is too much for me to handle, she thinks. I can't do it. Even for Alfie. A sob escapes her. The urge for another drink arrives suddenly and powerfully. It'll help.

She tries to deny it. She must check the house. For Jayne, Emily. For threat.

Fear makes her jumpy as she goes downstairs.

The kitchen's deserted. Table laid, food out on the side, cooked but not served and cold to her touch. The utility area seems to reproach her with its ordinariness: white cabinets too bright, overhead lights glaring. The sitting room is empty, the fire died down to embers. A trace of woodsmoke still scents the air.

Satisfied she's alone, an idea strikes her. Jayne is not here, and neither is Emily. They have gone. Left her. So, Ruth must lock the door to protect herself. This is what she will do for Alfie. She will protect herself because he needs his mother. He's all that matters, really. She runs the bolt across and leans on the back of the door. It's solid. The bolt is a good one. She feels safer.

Tomorrow, as soon as it's light, she'll leave here and get down to the farmhouse, she tells herself. She'll go home to Alfie and never leave him and never drink again. She'll confront Toby.

She thinks that Jayne and Emily are probably both down at the farmhouse by now, safe and warm. On the phone to their husbands. She feels jealous. And unable to fight the urge to drink any longer.

The gun comes upstairs with her, to her bedroom. In the bottom of her bag, where she left it, is the vodka bottle. She sits on the side of the bed and drinks deeply from it. The gun lies on the duvet beside her. She drinks again, hating herself for it, wiping her face between sessions of guzzling the vodka. But after a while letting it drip down her chin. When the bottle is empty, she drops it.

She touches the handle of the gun. Picks it up. Considers that this is how some people end their lives.

She puts it on the bedside table. No, she thinks, that's stupid. If someone breaks in, they'll snatch it. But it needs to be where she can reach it.

She gets on to her knees and tries to push up the mattress so she can hide the gun underneath it, but the design of the bed means that the frame has tall sides. It's impossible to get the gun beneath it. She wouldn't be able to extract it quickly, or at all.

I need it, she thinks. But it's important to be safe with it. And it's important that I'm safe.

The room spins around her. She thinks again of the possibility that Jayne is dangerous and her face crumples. She squeezes her eyes shut. A tremor runs through her and she feels it in every limb and every organ. Even in her lips. It's as if she's falling apart.

She's terrified of what will happen next. She knows she's drunk, knows she's confused, knows she could be wrong, so wrong, but she's very afraid of Jayne.

It's the worst terror she's ever felt.

Curled up around the gun, all she can think is that she must protect herself at all costs, for Alfie's sake.

She blacks out.

Maggie has bundled Emily into a rocking chair in a snug just off the kitchen, where a fire burns bright and hopeful. A dusty swag of dried hops is draped over the mantel. Dull brass ornaments, horse-themed, are fixed to the low-hanging beams.

Emily is wearing Maggie's clothes: strange elasticated trousers, worn and stretched in places that don't relate to Emily's body; a fleece top that smells alien and scratchy woollen socks.

Her own clothing has been taken from her, to be laundered, or dried off – she wasn't really listening when she first got here. She just knows that it's gone and that she feels as if she's in another woman's skin and finds it uncomfortably intimate.

She's ashamed of how John found her. It's horrible to think how quickly she came undone and helpless out there.

John disappeared as soon as they arrived here. She doesn't know where he's gone and doesn't ask. It's easier without him. He witnessed her humiliation.

His dog has stayed to lie at Emily's feet with mournful eyes, her head resting on her paws, watching as Maggie fusses around Emily, her nose twitching at the plate of biscuits Maggie delivers with a hot tea, loaded with sugar Emily hasn't asked for. Emily drinks every drop of it and gobbles down the biscuits.

Her injured leg rests on the seat of a chair Maggie pulled up for her. The sock is rolled down to expose the ankle, which is swollen, an angry pomegranate red that the firelight intensifies. Emily leans forward and adjusts the bag of frozen peas Maggie gave her to take down the swelling. The peas are almost at room temperature, the bag soggy and soft.

'A phone,' Emily says. 'I need to borrow your phone.' She remembers her manners: 'Please.'

Maggie gives her a handset. 'Best if you use the landline. The mobile signal isn't reliable.'

'Thank you,' Emily says. 'I'm so sorry to keep you up this late.'

'It's no bother. I'll leave you to make your call.'

Emily presses a button on the phone and the dial tone is one of the most delicious sounds she's ever heard. She wonders if Paul will pick up this late.

But as she makes to dial his number, her thumb hovers over the keypad. She's dyscalculic, can hardly remember her PIN number, let alone phone numbers. Sometimes it's possible if she drills them, repeats them like a mantra, but even then, they slip away from her. Paul told her to make sure she learned his mobile number by heart, but she's never been able to.

Some of the digits from his number suggest themselves to her but not enough of them, and not in the right order.

She puts the phone in her lap, feeling utterly impotent. It seems cruel that she managed to reach the farmhouse yet lost her phone on the way.

'Are you all right?' Maggie is watching from the kitchen.

'I can't remember my husband's mobile number,' she says and is ashamed to feel tears pricking.

'Is he home?'

A twinge of terror means she doesn't know how to answer that at first. Edie's letter has polluted all rational thought, upended all reasonable assumptions. Of course he should be home. But is he?

Pull yourself together, she thinks. Of course he's home.

'Yes,' she says. 'He might be asleep.'

'Do you know your landline number?'

Emily shuts her eyes. She does. She thinks she does. That one she practised more than the mobile.

'Yes,' she says, not wanting to admit to her uncertainty. 'Sorry. I can't think straight.'

'It's understandable, pet.'

She taps in what she thinks are the right numbers and stares at the dog as she waits for the call to connect. Hundreds of miles away the landline sings its electronic tune. It's a comforting sound to her as she imagines Paul stirring in bed, reaching for it. After the sixth ring, it's answered, and she catches her breath with anticipation.

'Hello?' A woman's voice, croaky with sleep.

'Paul?' Emily asks, even though it's obvious it's not him.

'Who?'

'Paul?'

The woman clears her voice. 'There's no Paul here.'

'Edie?'

'Who?'

It doesn't sound much like Edie. But. 'Is that you, Edie?'

'I think you've got the wrong number.'

'Sorry.'

She hangs up, embarrassed but also afraid. Was it a wrong number? Or is there another woman in her home? She's never considered the possibility of Paul's infidelity before. Not once. Until now.

She tries again, and though she does her best to redial accurately, she really has no idea whether she's dialling the same number as before.

This time, there's no answer and she doesn't know what to do. How to put this right. She moves her leg and pain lances her ankle. She winces.

It's moments like this that she wishes her mum was still alive. The home phone she had as a child is the only one Emily has ever been able to remember reliably. But it's useless to her now.

If she keeps her leg very, very still, the pain ebbs. She shuts her eyes. When she next opens them, the fire is little more than embers, and somebody has dimmed the kitchen lights. She blinks. It all starts to come back to her.

'You're awake.' Maggie is standing very close. Emily feels as if she is looming, blocking the light.

She props herself up. Her ankle pain reintroduces itself, crawling within the joint, shooting up her leg. Things around her swim before falling into focus. Her brow is sweaty. The dog has gone.

'What time is it?' she asks.

'Nearly midnight. You've been asleep for a while. I think we should move you to a proper bed so you can get some decent rest.'

At least it's almost Saturday now. How long until Paul gets here? Ten hours? Eleven? She imagines his arrival. His face when he sees her. Her relief.

She scrabbles in her lap for the phone handset, remembering the calls she tried to make earlier, casting off a blanket that's been placed over her. She can't locate the handset but she has to know if Paul is OK and she has to know now.

'Please,' she catches Maggie's sleeve. 'I need to call the police.'

The barn door won't open. Jayne tugs on it, rattles it, kicks it, curses herself for not bringing a key, but it doesn't budge. She raps on the windows of the downstairs rooms. No response. All the motion is out here, in the storm.

The barn is stubbornly impenetrable. There's no sign of life from inside. She throws a pebble at the upstairs windows and waits for the curtains to part in Ruth's room, but nothing happens.

She needs to get inside. Every part of her feels wet and cold in a way that she knows is dangerous. It's hard to know how long she's been outside, but it's too long. She's pushed herself too far.

She chooses the kitchen window because it's at the back of the house, as sheltered from the weather as possible. She takes her coat off, bracing herself for the rain to assault her even harder, and wraps it carefully around her hand and forearm. She picks up a stone and is shivering even before she's managed to break the glass and carefully bash away the shards remaining around the edges of the windowpane. It's a noisy operation. If Ruth is inside, it should bring her to the kitchen.

Jayne slithers in through the gap. It's not easy. She falls on to the kitchen counter and the soft edge of her hand misses a sharp piece of glass by fractions of an inch. She carefully twists her body to avoid cutting herself, to avoid the blood, and in the process falls awkwardly off the counter and on to the floor, landing hard on the kitchen tiles.

It's a shock. She feels winded and lies still before moving different parts of her body cautiously, testing them to see what's hurt.

She knows she'll be bruised tomorrow, but otherwise everything seems to be OK apart from her knee. She winces when she examines it. It's cut. Her breathing quickens. She can't just bandage it up and hide the blood because there's a shard of glass stuck in the wound. She won't be able to walk if she leaves it there; it has to be extracted.

She grasps the edge of the glass and turns her head away before giving it a decisive tug. She gasps as it comes out and throws the shard towards the corner of the room, out of sight. Beads of blood cluster along the incision and she pulls her torn trouser leg down over it and presses as hard as she can.

Out of the corner of her eye, the oven clock turns to midnight.

Why hasn't Ruth appeared? The noise should have woken her. Jayne calls for her, hears nothing in reply. The house feels empty, too empty.

She relieves the pressure on her wound and glances at it. More blood wells up, bright and persistent. She applies pressure again, but the blood has soaked into her trousers and she can't look away from it. It horrifies her. She feels faint. All her senses start to tingle. It's happening. She knows it, even before she blinks once, twice, then rapidly. This is the start of full-on dissociation.

As if through a muffle, she hears something. A scraping noise. From upstairs? Or from the front of the house? She's not sure. She pulls off a boot and sock and ties the sock around her knee as tightly as possible, then makes her way, hobbling, into the hall. There's no sound. Perhaps the noise was from outside.

She checks the door. It's locked, as she expected, but the bolt has been drawn, too. Somebody's in the house with her.

As silently as possible, she slides the bolt open. Better to be able to make a quick exit, if needed. She leaves the lock engaged. Opening it from this side of the door doesn't require a key.

'Ruth?' she calls again. She hears another creak, and stops still. After a few moments she tells herself it's just something in the barn responding to the draught whistling through from the broken window.

'Emily?'

Was the door bolted because Emily returned to the barn unnoticed by Jayne, and wanted to lock her out, even if Jayne had a key? As punishment for Jayne not going with her as promised? Or is that paranoid? It's hard to know.

Her thoughts bundle and swirl. Her heart races. Her ears buzz.

Could young, pretty Emily be behind the letter? she wonders. Is Emily the 'E' on the signature? Is there threat here? From within this building and their little group? Has she badly misread the situation?

Or is Emily still outside, at risk of harm, because she and Ruth let her go?

She tries to fight the dissociation, to stay in touch with what's happening, but that never works. She feels as if she's stepped into an alternative version of her life, as if she has only the slightest of connections with reality. Reason deserts her. A sense of danger pulses.

Emily. Ruth. Who are they, really? Anyone can be a danger to others. Who left the remains outside? Who fashioned the hideous scarecrow? It was designed to frighten.

She needs to check this whole place. She needs her gun.

Her brain short-circuits. Blanks. It restarts. Her thoughts are in shreds.

She finds herself standing in the doorway of the sitting room. It's empty. She's unsure if this is good or bad. No threat is good, she has to remind herself. It's as if her logical brain has been wiped.

She moves to look into the other downstairs rooms – a small loo, a cramped utility area – with robotic slowness as her thoughts swirl faster and her heart continues to thump, thump, thump. The buzzing is ceaseless and increasing in volume.

She doesn't know how long it takes her to check downstairs. The air in the barn feels as thick as treacle. So do her thoughts. The rooms, though small, and the way they interconnect, which she knows rationally to be simple, feel somehow confusing. At one point she sits and only snaps to when the throbbing in her knee becomes insistent. She's back in the sitting room but has no idea how long she's been there. Her wet coat is on the sofa beside her. Sometime later she finds herself staring out of the kitchen window and can't remember how she got from one place to the other. It's all a blank.

The oven clock tells her it's 1:30 a.m. But wasn't it just midnight? Time has become a trickster.

She has to concentrate on climbing the stairs. She daren't look at her knee. She should call for the others again but can't make herself open her mouth. It feels sealed shut.

She first dissociated while she was in the army. You can have a fight, flight or freeze response, the therapist said, when you experience trauma in the moment, or when you are triggered afterwards.

You learned to freeze, because in the moment you couldn't fight. You weren't in a trench with a gun in your hand, and you couldn't flee because you were working. Doing your job. You were in a room, at a desk, or watching a monitor. You had no choice but to freeze. It happened because your brain couldn't cope with what was happening. You contributed intelligence that led to air strikes where there was collateral damage. Murder of innocents. You watched it happen and it was too much for you. Which is why it crept into your dreams and has stayed with you.

As Jayne climbs, she's aware of a stickiness between her injured knee and her trouser leg. The back of her neck prickles, as if there's a target on it. The buzzing gets louder. Her clothes are damp. She peels off her blouse and lets it fall.

The light on the landing is on. The bathroom light too. Rain batters the skylights. It's relentless. Jayne looks up at the glass. She has a sense of clear and present danger.

192

It feels as if she's gone too far to be able to bring herself back to reality. She's been taught techniques, but right now can't remember, let alone enact them.

Someone has ransacked her bedroom. Her clothes are everywhere, her bag empty.

The gun.

She searches, frantic, picking up every item, throwing it behind her. Pulling the bedding up. She looks beneath furniture and opens and slams drawers.

She finds herself sitting in the middle of her room, surrounded by her things. She must search the other rooms. If Mark were here, he'd take her in his arms, comfort her. He'd make her feel safe. Her knee hurts.

She marshals her courage as best she can, though she feels her grip on any helpful emotions is loosening. Search for other people, she tells herself. Do it carefully. A weapon is missing.

She steps carefully and quietly on to the landing. The first room she comes to is Ruth's. The door is part open, the room dark inside. She peers in. A sound from behind freezes her. Another creak.

Her rational brain tries to tell her that it is the house, the weather, but the animal response in her is so strong that she feels she can hardly breathe. Her spine stiffens, as if ice water were dripping down it. 'Mark,' she whispers. A sob half-breaks from her.

Pull yourself together, she castigates herself, but the words sound like a joke.

She reaches for the light switch, flips it on, but the bulb is broken. She waits for her eyes to adjust to the dark in the room.

Helped by a shaft of light from the landing she can make out a shape in the bed and she draws breath sharply.

Her fear level skyrockets as she makes a careful approach. Ambush, she thinks. It could be.

But it's Ruth. Asleep.

Jayne sits on the bed, calls her friend's name, shakes her vigorously, but Ruth won't wake up. She's as heavy and limp as a sack of grain. Breathing, though. The smell on her breath is pure alcohol. Jayne reaches for the bedside lamp, turns it on and sees an empty vodka bottle on the floor. Ruth is sleeping fully dressed, beneath a mess of bedcovers.

Jayne feels her strength ebb away swiftly and completely. Dissociation is exhausting. It drains her, robbing her of every impulse – even, now, the instinct to stay safe.

Her gun is gone. Somebody else has it. And Jayne is too afraid to search for it any longer.

All she wants is safety.

She turns out the bedside light and makes her way around to the other side of Ruth's bed. She climbs on to it and lies down beside Ruth. Her eyes fall shut. Pixelated death dances on the back of her eyelids. The flashbacks will ebb. They will.

The buzzing settles to a manageable hum. The sense of danger doesn't abate, but she can only wait now. Sleep will turn this off. It will slow the pounding of her heart. She will come back to life later. She will be herself again.

She moves closer to her friend, until she can feel the warmth of Ruth's body through the duvet. She curls up, like a baby, her back to Ruth, in contact with Ruth's arm.

Her brain starts to shut down. Another safety mechanism.

All she wants is to burrow here until morning, when Mark will come, but still she tries to justify her actions. I'm keeping Ruth safe, she tells herself, in case she vomits in her sleep.

It helps to tell herself that, even as she's succoured by the heat radiating from Ruth's arm. She turns and curls up facing Ruth, her forehead touching Ruth's shoulder. Jayne's hands are clasped, gently, in front of her. Her breath warms them. Her clothes are wet but she can't move to take them off. She is in the foetal position.

This feels like safety for now. It's all she wants.

Her brain demands rest, and she can't fight herself any longer. She sleeps.

Imogen has been asleep for hours and I haven't been able to move from my spot on the chair beside her, have only angled it so as to see her better.

These are the most peaceful few hours I've spent for a long time. I can feel the tension in my shoulders easing and a small sense of satisfaction creeping over me.

It's nice to get a chance to study her. I'm searching for signs of myself in her and I think that maybe there's something of me in the shape of her chin. Truly, she's a beautiful young woman. The image of her mother.

I take out my phone and crouch on the floor beside her, my back against the sofa, my face as close to hers as I can get it. I try to take a selfie, including both of us.

I know, she's asleep, so it won't be perfect, but you don't want to let the perfect be the enemy of the good and I want a memento of this, our first night together as father and daughter. It won't be one for framing, I agree, but I'll keep it to myself and enjoy it.

But it's very difficult to find an angle that's flattering to us both. I put the phone down and rearrange her, pulling her body a little way across the sofa so her head tilts at a better angle. I tuck the blanket over her more neatly, and all the time I'm doing it I hold my breath in case she wakes, but really, there's no need to worry. She's as floppy as a rag doll.

I kneel down again and try taking another picture. This time, it's as close to perfect as it'll ever be and I know I'll treasure it.

Now, all I've got to do is figure out how best to move her from here.

SATURDAY

William Elliott drives up the valley, towards the farmhouse where he grew up. He wears his police uniform; his cap sits on the passenger seat beside him.

It's been a terrible night up here.

The storm only passed an hour ago, just before dawn. Still air has congregated in its wake, inspecting the damage that was wrought overnight, respectful of it, careful not to press too hard where things might hurt: on the tree trunks bearing fresh wounds where branches have been ripped from them, on unearthed roots which are glimpsing daylight for the first time.

William drives through bands of fog and thinks of them as a cool salve on the landscape, treating it gently while it decides how best to recover.

Ahead of him, a barn owl takes flight from the edge of the woodland, wings beating powerfully. It gathers its shoulders, its wings taking on the shape of an embrace, white plumage on their underside reflecting the milky yellow sunlight disrupting an ashen horizon. The owl is completely still for a perfect moment before it plummets, talons spread, to take a mouse from the field and carry it away.

The sight is ethereal. His dad would be transfixed by it.

Maggie Elliott hears William's car as it approaches the farmhouse. She steps outside, thankful to get some respite from being in the same space as the young woman, Emily, who's been so distraught.

They made an official call to the police, but it was impossible to get anyone to come up to the farmhouse and speak to Emily last night. The letter wasn't considered enough of a threat while there was no proof that Emily's husband was harmed or missing. The storm was too violent to allow a courtesy call. It could wait until morning, was the official advice. Then it would be followed up if necessary. It seemed sensible to Maggie, but not to Emily.

Afraid that Emily would become more hysterical, Maggie called in a rare favour from her son, William. He promised to come as soon as he could.

She opens the gate. His car headlamps push through the fog and into the yard. Visibility is very poor.

She and William embrace when he gets out of the car and she feels her heart grow and the relief of having another adult with her, to bear some of the responsibility for all of this. John bathed and went to bed while she was tending to Emily.

'Bacon sandwich?' she asks William.

'I wouldn't say no.'

She already has bacon out, beside the hob. Four rashers. Her skillet is ready.

'Egg?'

'No, thank you.'

He kneels down to fuss the dogs, lets them lick his face.

'You'll have hair all over you.'

'It doesn't matter.'

'But your uniform.'

'Mother,' he warns and scoops Annie's hind legs up, lifting her so she's sitting on his lap. Birdie lies down and rests her head on his lap. He pets them both.

Maggie watches. 'You look handsome.'

'Mother. Stop.'

She smiles. 'Thanks for coming, love. The young lass, Emily, is asleep upstairs. You should have seen the state of her last night.'

William eases the dogs off him, stands and brushes at his trousers though Maggie's face says it won't do any good if what he's after is getting rid of their hair.

He takes his usual place at the table. She puts a cup of tea down for him.

'Tell me again what happened now that I'm awake enough to take it in properly,' he says.

'She's one of the guests at the barn and your dad found her on the lane last night, in the middle of the storm. Just her, she'd gone out on her own. She turned her ankle on the way down so she was stuck there when he found her, absolutely freezing, soaked through. I don't know what would have happened if he hadn't been out there.'

William notices the unfamiliar clothing draped over a clothes horse in front of the Aga. Nothing suitable for last night's conditions.

'What was she thinking? Didn't you warn her about going out at night?'

'Of course we did! But she was determined to phone her husband.'

'Because of this letter they got?' He feels as if he doesn't have a complete understanding yet of what's happened. It sounded like such a tall story when his mother recounted it on the phone in the middle of the night. He could barely keep up with it.

'The letter arrived here by a motorcycle courier along with a present and your dad and I took it up to the barn and left it out for them. There were special instructions telling us what to do. I thought the letter was something nice, but apparently it wasn't at all. It contained a threat against their husbands. She was terrified. Your dad knew, you know, that it wasn't anything good. I wish we'd never left it there now.'

'Did she bring the letter down with her?'

'No.'

'It's still up at the barn?'

'I suppose so.'

'I'll have to take a look at it.'

The bacon spits in the pan and the smell of it fills the room. Maggie puts a bottle of ketchup on the table in front of William. As she slices bread and butters it thickly, she describes in detail how the letter was delivered and what the instructions meant for her and John said.

As he watches and listens, he pays close attention but he's also aware that this is how he thinks of his mother when he's not here, working in the kitchen with fluent movements. Her strength, her big heart and her sharp mind have been the glue that holds their family together.

'Right,' he says. 'And she dialled 999 with this, did she?'

She nods. 'Asking them to get a car out to her home, to see if her husband was alive. I think she believed the threat in that letter with her whole heart.'

She puts the sandwich down in front of him and sits opposite him. He eats it in a few bites. It tastes sweet and smoky. Bacon fat and melted butter oil his lips.

Maggie says, 'She got very upset when they said the letter wasn't enough of a reason to get a car out.'

'It wouldn't be. Not in the middle of the night.'

'So, I called you.'

'And I take it the letter wasn't signed?''

'Only with an initial. An "E". That's how they know who sent it.'

He raises his eyebrows. 'Not even a name? That's a bit cryptic, isn't it? How can they be so certain about who this "E" is? I think if I was them, I'd be asking myself questions about that because it sounds as if someone's playing games with them. What a strange affair.' He finishes his tea in two big gulps. 'I'd better have a chat with her, then.'

'She's sleeping like the dead.'

'Can you wake her?'

As she leaves the kitchen, he asks, 'What was Dad doing out there in the middle of the night anyway?'

Her shoulder blades twitch and freeze. This micro-movement is another memory he holds. How you can wound her, but only in the seconds before she gets her guard up.

'He wanted to check on the sheep in the top field.'

If she turns round, she's telling the truth, he thinks. And if not . . .

She continues into the darkness of the hallway, the patterns on her housecoat claimed by shadows.

'Where's Dad now?' he shouts.

'Out again.'

'Without the dog?'

She doesn't reply.

William removes a notebook from his pocket and lays it on the table, placing his pen parallel to it. The sound of his throat clearing makes Birdie open an eye.

He gazes out into the yard. After a few moments, his dad emerges from the barn and walks round the back of it, glancing at William's car as he does. It's unlike him not to come in and say hello.

John looks unkempt, William thinks, definitely more so than when he was last up here, which was only a few weeks ago. He feels his stomach knot. You might not notice the change that's happened to John over the past year if you didn't know him, because you wouldn't know how dapper he was. How he took pride in his own appearance as much as his farm's.

And now, neither the farm nor his father is what they used to be, no matter how hard Mum tries to paper over the cracks. Something will have to be done, and quickly, there's no avoiding it, though none of them want to face up to it. He wishes his parents had talked to him and sought medical help sooner. They've let things go too far. Maggie has taken too much weight on to her shoulders.

'Hello.' Her voice is small, and she is slight, drowned in what he recognises as his mother's clothes. Most of her face is obscured by her hair but what he can see of it is puffy and pale. Her eyes are red-rimmed. She's favouring her ankle.

'Hi,' he says. He stands, reaches to shake her hand. Her grasp is weak. 'I'm Police Constable William Elliott. My parents own this place and the barn. Mum called me and told me about your . . .' He doesn't want to say 'fears' in case it sounds patronising, so he opts for 'situation'.

'I need to talk to my husband,' she says. No introduction, nothing.

He encourages her to sit. She takes the chair at the end of the table, beside his, and reaches out a slender hand as if to grip his arm but thinks better of the impulse and retracts it, her fingers curling into a fragile fist as she does.

'Help me?' she asks.

'Imogen!'

She dreams her dad is calling her, at first. She knows he's dead in the dream, but even so she floats towards the sound of his voice on a gentle wave of hope until her brain registers that the voice is wrong, the tone is wrong, that the man calling her name is not Dad.

It's him.

She stirs, waking in a confused state, heartbreak from the dream wreaking havoc on her mood even before she opens her eyes and an unsettling feeling that she is being watched making her skin crawl.

She blinks, her eyelids feeling sticky and heavy, and lifts herself on to her elbows to peer at her surroundings, which emerge slowly out of the dark morning.

She's in his spare room. The one he says is really her room. But she can't remember anything about yesterday evening or going to bed. She feels terrible. Groggy and exhausted. Confused.

The door is cracked open. Perhaps that's why she felt watched. A hand appears suddenly in the gap between door and frame. She pulls the duvet over her mouth to mute a scream but the hand only reaches for the switch and the overhead light snaps on, its brightness disorientating her more, and the door swings open all in the same moment.

'Morning, sleepyhead!' he says.

He places a mug on the bedside table. 'Tea for you!' He's smiling like a goon.

'What time is it?'

'It's just after nine.'

'Thank you. What time did I go to bed?' Why doesn't she remember?

'About twelve hours ago. You said you wanted an early night.'

She lifts the covers up a little and sees that she's fully dressed.

'I slept in my clothes?'

He shrugs. 'I guess you really were tired!'

'I've never done that before.'

'How would pancakes for breakfast suit you?'

'No, thank you.'

'Eggs?'

'I'm not that hungry.'

Actually, she's starving, but he's too much for her this morning. She can't make herself smile back at him.

It doesn't make sense that she's lying here in all her clothes and she's unused to things not making sense, but her brain is running at quarter speed so she's struggling to find an explanation. And didn't she have plans last night? To go to a party with Jemma? To see Matt if he was there?

And why does she feel so incredibly tired, as if she has a terrible hangover? Or as if she's been drugged?

That thought gives her pause.

She can't have been drugged, can she? Because she's been with him since last night. So how could it have happened?

Unless he did it? Her blood runs cold. But there would only be one reason to drug her that she can think of, and surely that can't be what happened. Horrified, she tries to take stock of her body. I feel normal, she thinks. I'm in my clothes. I'd be sore if he'd done anything to me. I'd know if he had, wouldn't I?

Slowly, her breathing settles down. Of course she'd know. She's fine.

'Are you sure you don't want food?' he says. 'You look a bit pale.'

She shakes her head. His face falls and she can't help thinking that it's a babyish reaction, and sort of gross. Although she's as certain as she can be that he hasn't touched her, the thought lingers like a foul taste.

'Maybe I'll feel like it in a bit,' she says, throwing him a bone, and he brightens, which seems weird. What's wrong with him? Why is he so needy right now?

She glances at the bedside table, sits up and pats the bedcovers. 'Did we find my phone?'

At least she remembers something from last night, even if it's bad. The lost phone.

'I looked again,' he says. 'But I couldn't see it anywhere. I'm sorry, Imbo.'

Why is he calling her by that name? It's what her dad called her.

She slumps back against the pillows and looks at the ceiling. This is an extreme level of tiredness. She should be bouncing after twelve hours' sleep. He should just leave. She glances at him. Why is he still staring at her?

'OK then,' he says when the silence gets uncomfortable. 'Enjoy your tea.'

'Can you turn out the light?' she asks, moving to face the wall. 'Please?' she adds after a moment. There's a click and the room falls dark. She hears the door close softly but not completely.

Above her, there's a window. Around the edge of the curtains, she can see the sort of depressing grey light that makes her want to curl up and stay in bed all day.

She tries to piece together the night before but nothing comes back to her. A headache ripples across her temples and settles into her forehead. She feels as if something is pinching her all over her body. Depression. It likes to get its hooks into her and tether her to dark places, away from light and from people, places where blankness is a virtue, where you forget how to smile.

Her tea cools, untouched. He's whistling, somewhere close.

The longer she listens the more the sound cuts through her and the more convinced she is that something isn't right at all, though she doesn't know what.

What was it that Mum said about him a few weeks ago?

'I swear, I think he's lost his mind.' Edie had just put the phone down and her eyes were tightly shut as if she was trying to unsee something. The memory induces a cramp of fear. She'd been arguing with him, pleading, repeating his name in a tone that bled. Though Imogen hadn't heard enough to know what the argument was about.

She hated the way that fatigue was etched into Edie's face. It had been since Dad died. Imogen wanted her mum to be able to smile sometimes.

'What do you mean he's lost his mind?' she asked.

'Oh, I didn't see you there! You should knock, you know.'

'What did you mean?'

'Nothing, darling. It was a joke. We had a little argument, that's all.'

But it hadn't sounded little.

'Were you listening to all our conversation?' Edie was lying on her bed. There were clothes everywhere, bags on the floor where she'd dropped them, teetering piles of magazines, even a plate with food crusted on it on the dressing table. It wasn't right. Edie was a neat freak, usually.

'No,' she said, because she was afraid of the distress in her mum's eyes, afraid that it would worsen if Imogen admitted the truth, or that Edie would get angry with her.

Lately, Edie's heavy grief has been punctuated with scarier moments when she seems frightened and lashes out, though she tries to cover it up afterwards, to pretend everything's fine.

Imogen felt as if this was what was happening. She didn't want a row over eavesdropping. Anyone could have heard what Edie was saying. Her side of the conversation wasn't quiet.

Now she wishes she hadn't lied that morning, that she'd questioned her mum about what was going on, because there's definitely something off about him and off about how Imogen's feeling and the fact that she can't remember last night at all and it's totally freaking her out.

The Land Rover rumbles uphill again, slower than yesterday, because the condition of the lane has deteriorated so much overnight. It's like being on a slow-motion roller coaster, powered in fits and starts. William drives. John sits beside him.

In places, the fog is so dense that branches and twigs look like arms and hands reaching towards them with bent fingers. Emily flinches when they scratch the windows.

Emily sits in the back, beside Maggie and the dog, and her ankle protests every bump and turn and lurch. The pain is hot and white.

All Emily can think about is whether Paul is on his way up here. Is he halfway yet? Did he leave extra early, as he promised? She expects him to arrive mid- to late morning at the latest and it's already nine o'clock.

Changing out of Maggie's clothes and back into her own this morning was a relief. She let Maggie's strange, frumpy garments fall to the bedroom floor with relish. They lay in a heap like a discarded skin, and not a skin Emily ever wants to wear again.

When Emily said she was going back up to the barn with the men, Maggie argued that she should do no such thing, that they should take her to the hospital to have her ankle looked at, but Emily's priority is to borrow a phone from Jayne or Ruth, who will have Paul's number, or be able to get it.

She's going to collect her stuff while she's there and get back down to the farmhouse and call Paul, who, hopefully, will be on his way here and the bad dream that was last night will evaporate.

She's trying to be strong but it's a fragile act, the brave face she's putting on in front of the Elliotts. She feels as if her lip might wobble at any moment. Humiliation at what happened to her last night and terror that Paul has come to harm lurk just beneath the surface.

Every so often, William stops the car and John gets out to pull debris from the track in front of them. They barely speak. The family are strangely muted, Emily thinks, but she's grateful for the silence.

When the vehicle emerges from the forest track, high up, she glimpses the sun rising through the mist. It's hardly spectacular, more of a pale yolk uncertain on the horizon. She can't feel any warmth on her face when she turns towards it but something about the spreading light encourages her to be strong.

She exhales and shuts her eyes.

It will be OK, she thinks, I'll see him soon. If he's alive.

Her fingernails dig painfully into her palms.

Eggs. She said she wasn't hungry but sometimes a parent has to take the initiative.

I'm doing them over easy. They look messier that way, I know, but who has the patience for the perfect sunny side up? Life's too short.

I open the bread bin to find we haven't got any fresh bread. I check the freezer. It isn't large, just one of those small spaces beneath our fridge. It doesn't resemble the chest freezer in my lock-up at all, but the combination of the sound of the plastic suction breaking as I open it and the shock of the cold does something to me.

Proust's madeleines, if you like.

How to describe the effect on me? Stone-cold horror would cover it.

I grab two slices of bread and slam the freezer shut, but the bread transfixes me. I see ice crystals embedded in it and I imagine Edie's face, frozen the same way, skin glimmering, shimmering with cold beauty, eyelash tips laden with snow-flakes, eyes so clear you could float in them, set sail across them. I wish I could have.

Why did she have to listen to other people? Why did she have to believe them? I would have made life good for her, loved her, looked after her, completed her family, made us whole.

But someone got between us, whispering into her ear, telling tales, poisoning her against me until I had no choice but to say goodbye to her.

The eggs burn. I bin them. The bread goes into the toaster.

I feel deeply sorry that Edie has to be cold in death. She hated the cold. Is Imogen the same? That's something I need to find out about her.

Before cracking more eggs into the pan, I turn up the thermostat just in case.

To Emily, the barn looks even smaller and grimmer than yesterday. It has an obstinate hush about it, like the satisfied smirk of a bully.

William helps Emily down from the car and Maggie offers her an arm to lean on. They make slow progress up the path. John hangs back. The dog sniffs the air, turns, and makes a beeline for the hedge, disappearing beneath it, only her back end visible. Her underbelly contracts rhythmically as if she's gulping something down.

John watches her.

Emily tries opening the door. It's locked.

'Hey!' she calls and knocks. When nobody answers she hobbles a few steps around to the side of the house and shouts again, aiming her voice up at the bedroom windows. The curtains are shut.

She gets nothing in response. The windows reflect the sky, and the glass looks as solid as the stone walls.

Emily feels a surge of anger. What if she'd made it back here last night, to find the place locked up? Did Jayne and Ruth not think of that? She could have died out here. Of shock. Of exposure. It was one thing for them not to come after her, quite another to ensure that if she did get back, she was locked out.

William raps on the front door louder and for longer than Emily did.

'What's Birdie into?' Maggie says.

'She's fine,' John says.

'Birdie!'

'Leave her!'

Maggie looks at him, wondering why he snapped.

'Hello!' William knocks again. 'Anybody up?'

'Do you have spare keys?' Emily asks. Maggie hands her a set.

Emily unlocks and limps into the barn. It's cold inside, as if the storm seeped through the walls last night and chilled everything within.

'Hi,' she calls, though without confidence. She peers into the sitting room. The emptiness feels hostile. Down the end of the hallway, the kitchen is gloomy, shrouded in shadows that the tentative dawn hasn't lifted.

It feels as if there's no life here at all. Her heart starts to thump.

She makes her way towards the kitchen and stops in the doorway, taking in the broken window, the food, the shards of glass on the floor, the small patch of blood.

William is just behind her. He sees what she sees and starts towards her when she seems to buckle but she's only reaching for the letter. A ragged blot of wine has dampened it but it's legible.

She hands it to him and walks back past him, as if in a daze.

A phone, she thinks. I need a phone.

William reads the letter as Emily makes slow progress up the stairs, dragging her ankle.

Every bedroom door is shut.

'Hey!' she calls. Her voice sounds weak. 'It's me.' She clears her throat, tries again. 'Hello! It's Emily. I'm back.'

She knocks on Jayne's bedroom door. Nothing. Knocks again, harder and with more urgency. Calls for both Jayne and Ruth. No answer.

Perhaps Ruth got so drunk that she passed out. But Jayne should be OK. The feeling that something is wrong is growing.

Footsteps behind her alert her to William, following her upstairs. His face is scrubbed out and grey in the uncertain light falling through the water-pocked glass of the skylights. He hovers at the end of the landing, watching Emily, afraid of barging up there himself in case the other women aren't dressed.

The sheer nastiness of the letter shocked him on one level, but on another it seemed petty and trivial, playground nonsense for the over-twenties and -thirties, for people who should know better. It makes him wonder, who exactly are these people?

Emily opens Jayne's door. She's not there, though her stuff is. Her bag is wide open on the floor and her stuff has been tossed around everywhere. It looks as if the room has been ransacked, and the bed hasn't been slept in.

Emily moves to Ruth's door and, affecting more bravery than she feels, goes to knock on it, though her fingers retract from it the first time she tries. But she gathers her courage, closes her fist, raps sharply and opens the door without waiting for a reply.

'Breakfast's ready!' I call. Imogen hasn't emerged from her bedroom yet.

I assume she's keen to come and see what I've made for her but is still suffering the after-effects of the drug. I believe it can leave you feeling fatigued and strange for some hours after you come round. But I'm here to help her. If she'll eat something, that'll be a start.

I shouldn't have slipped her anything, I know. But I was exhausted. And if you discover someone has lied to you, when you've been doing everything possible in your power to support them, when you've bust a gut, and then you overhear that they're going to try to deceive you again – to sneak out of my house for the night without telling me! – then I don't think anyone would blame you for a little loss of patience.

So, I drugged her after I got rid of Jemma. Jemma wasn't happy when I asked her politely to leave, but I slipped her some cash and told her to humour me, just this once. I only gave Imogen a couple of roofies. I hope she doesn't suspect it. She is, after all, a very intelligent young woman and I'm proud of that.

After waiting for a while, watching the eggs go cold on the plate, where I've arranged them so nicely, I decide to take them to her. Knocking softly at her door again excites me, just as I felt like a real parent when I put her to bed last night and tucked her up. Providing food for someone is similarly intimate. It's how you show people you love them.

Edie said that to me once, when we were watching Ruth cook. I've never forgotten it.

Imogen croaks a 'Come in' as I'm opening the door. She doesn't look much more awake than earlier. Her tea is untouched, which annoys me, but I don't say anything.

I move the mug aside and put the plate beside it on the bedside table, but she doesn't look at it right away because she's curled up facing the wall, and the back of her neck looks so delicate.

'Eggs,' I say. 'For you.'

When she turns towards me her face is her mother's. Her eyes shards that flash as they catch a shaft of sunlight penetrating a gap in the curtains.

'I hate eggs,' she says. 'Sorry.'

The stab of irritation I feel is surprisingly strong. Why, at every turn, is she so determined to prevent me from caring for her the way I want to? It makes me feel a little shaky because I've longed all my life for a daughter.

Everyone says it: the daddy–daughter bond is special. I never wanted a son because I watched my own father dote on my sister and felt the back of his hand across my cheek when I pissed him off. I'm afraid of repeating the cycle. My very own daughter is what I yearn for. I want her to look at me the same way my sister gazed at my dad. Adoringly.

I listened to Rob show off about his relationship with Imogen for years. 'My girl,' he would say fondly, not understanding that every time he said it in the last year, since I've known that she couldn't be his, the heinous part of me found it harder to stay hidden. God, the jealousy I felt.

I discovered that Rob wasn't Imogen's father by accident. He was messaging Edie and I oversaw it. I'm only a little bit sorry that we couldn't have a child together because I love Imogen just as much as if she was mine. And the upside is that at least I'll never need a vasectomy, he wrote. Laughing emoji attached. She sent one back, along with an emoji blowing a kiss and a heart emoji. They got under my skin.

I couldn't question him about it because their messages were private, and I felt it wouldn't be appropriate anyway if they'd kept it a secret this long.

But my mind began to race, wondering who Imogen's father was.

I made calculations, put two and two together.

The answer was obvious and startling. It's me.

And to think, Rob never even knew it. Not even at the end. I was tempted to tell him, but I never got the chance. The ocean will have to whisper it into his barnacled ears on my behalf.

But I think the dead stay with us somehow, don't you? So, he knows now.

This is partly why I plan to be the perfect parent to Imogen. Not in memory of Rob, who doesn't deserve it because he had Imogen to himself for too long, but for Edie. It's what she would want. And it's what I want too.

'Don't you even feel like trying the eggs?' I ask. My words don't come out quite as casually as I'd have liked them to. I might have sounded a little testy but it's only because I care so much.

It gets her attention. She rolls on to her back and stares at me.

'OK,' she says, her voice small. She arranges pillows to prop herself up. I perch on the end of her bed.

I know it'll be a tremendous shock for her to learn that I'm her real father. I anticipate denial, anger, grief and eventually, hopefully, joy.

As I sit, she draws her feet up, away from me, even though there's no need to. She won't do that when she knows who we really are to one another.

'I was thinking we could do something nice today,' I say. 'How about a walk?'

She doesn't answer. A small shred of egg dangles from her fork and she brings it to her mouth tentatively.

I can't keep my eyes off it. I want to see her eat it. I'm possessed, suddenly, by the belief that if she'll just eat the egg, it'll be a sign that we're going to be OK together, the two of us.

In it goes, her lips close around it. I smile. Relief and satisfaction flood through me.

But are her eyes watering?

She semi-smiles back at me and gags. The egg lands, with a gobbet of saliva, in the palm of her hand.

What an insult.

I don't think any of us ever really means to get angry. I mean, who *wants* to be that person?

But sometimes it happens.

Sometimes, we might not have even seen our limit coming when we smack hard into it.

Emily peers into Ruth's bedroom. The curtains are shut. She squints and can make out a lump in the bed. She flicks the light switch, because Ruth deserves to be woken abruptly, but it doesn't work.

She hobbles across the room and snatches the curtains open, rattling them to exaggerate the sharp metallic jangle of their rings on the pole. She's angry. Mostly because she felt so scared. She turns, expecting to see Ruth covering her eyes, nursing a tremendous hangover and what Emily hopes is a punishing headache.

But it's Jayne in the bed. Jayne, who is scrabbling to sit up, her hands on her neck, her mouth open, letting out a rasping gasp, as if waking from a dream of being suffocated. Emily, not expecting it, screams.

Jayne's chest heaves. She swallows laboriously as if she has something stuck in her throat. There's panic in her eyes. 'What happened?' she asks.

'Fuck!' Emily says. 'Don't do that! You scared me.'

Jayne blinks, confused. Her hands fall from her neck. She feels out of sorts, a form of hangover but knows that it's not from drinking. Her heartrate is elevated. With rising dread, she recognises these as symptoms of a bad night, of a possible episode of dissociation. Fragments of the night before swim in her head and she tries to piece them together.

'Isn't this Ruth's room?' Emily asks.

She's right, Jayne thinks. This is Ruth's room. Why is she in Ruth's bed? And, clearly, she hasn't slept there alone. The covers have been ripped back on the other side of the bed and the sheet is rumpled.

She explores the source of pain in her knee. A cut. Her trousers are ripped. There's a small patch of dried blood on the bedcover. She avoids looking at it, and remembers the entrails, the storm, the broken window as she tried to get back into the barn and her fall to the kitchen floor. But what happened afterwards?

'Where's Ruth?' she says. 'What time is it?'

'It's nearly a quarter to ten and I don't know where she is,' Emily says and finds she cares that Ruth is missing, but not as much as she cares about reaching Paul. 'Can I borrow your phone?'

Jayne is still trying to make sense of the earlier part of the evening. Why is she wearing just a bra and skimpy top but also her walking trousers? 'Did you get down to the farmhouse?' she asks.

'Yes.' Emily isn't going to go into detail. She'll only share what Jayne needs to know. 'I dropped my phone in a pool of water on the lane, it's lost, and I can't remember Paul's number so I couldn't call him. I need to borrow your phone. Can I?'

Jayne nods. 'I'll get it.'

Emily watches her get up. She seems sore. And there's something Emily wants to know. 'Why are you in Ruth's bed?'

Jayne thinks and finds an answer she believes is right, but she's not sure. 'Because she was really drunk. I was afraid she might vomit in her sleep.'

There is more, she knows. It will come to her, she hopes, but she also has a feeling that she might not want it to.

'Perhaps she slept in my bed,' Emily says. She lowers her voice. She has to warn Jayne. 'A policeman is here. He's the farmer's son. He's come to see the letter.'

'Why?'

'They need to see what Edie's done.'

Jayne's brain is running slow. On the landing she nods at William. 'I'll come down,' she says.

Emily opens her own bedroom door. 'Ruth's not here,' she says. She checks the bathroom. It's empty too.

Jayne is frozen in the doorway of her bedroom, transfixed by the sight of her belongings strewn everywhere.

She remembers: the gun. It disappeared. The police cannot know.

And where is Ruth?

Emily is behind her. 'Is your phone there?'

'I'll look,' Jayne says. 'Give me a minute.'

She grabs a top from the floor to cover herself up and shuts her bedroom door because she instinctually feels that she should hide the mess, and whatever it might be evidence of, from Emily.

A little more trickles back to her: the feeling of Ruth's warmth in the bed, the comfort Jayne was seeking. She fights the urge to dissociate again. Her brain wants her to.

The truth is, her gun is gone and she doesn't know what she might have done and she's not sure what Ruth, dead drunk last night and surely still drunk this morning, might have done either.

'I'm sorry!' Imogen shouts. 'Please, stop. I'll eat, I'll eat.'

The egg she puked up has fallen from her hand on to the bedcovers. She picks it up, retches again but puts it in her mouth anyway and chews. Tears spill from her eyes.

He looks grotesque. A vile smile spreads beneath a sticky layer of egg. He smeared it all over his mouth and his chin in circular motions; bits have gone up his nose. The yolk is bright yellow. It glues the rubbery globs of white to his skin.

She chews and chews the piece of egg and knows she can't swallow it. It seems to have expanded in her mouth. The consistency is disgusting. Rubber. She reaches for her tea and takes a gulp. The egg won't go down. She retches again. It feels as if every muscle between her tongue and her tummy wants to expel the egg. She takes another gulp of tea, praying this time it'll help. It's lukewarm, over-sugared and over-milked, almost as disgusting as the egg. But she forces herself to swallow and, thankfully, the egg goes down with it.

She pants in the aftermath. She wants to puke it back up.

'There,' he says. 'That wasn't too bad, was it?' There's even a bit of egg stuck on his eyebrow.

Imogen shakes her head. She's never felt so afraid. 'No,' she says. 'Thank you.'

*

Imogen's words are polite, and she worked valiantly, if a little melodramatically, to swallow the egg I made her, but her eyes, bright with unshed tears, betray her true feelings, as does a muscle that's twitching in her jaw.

She's appalled by what I've done, and quite rightly.

I've smashed the egg on my own face, pasted it messily across my mouth like whore's lipstick. Just the way my father used to if I didn't eat everything up.

I'm very embarrassed. It's a terrible lapse. I don't know what came over me. I'm better than this.

'I'm so sorry,' I say. She's pushed herself right back into the pillows behind her, putting as much distance as possible between us. 'What must you think of me?'

She only stares at me in response. Why won't she relax? I'm apologising!

'I'm sorry,' I repeat. 'I really am. It was just a joke, but a really bad one. I haven't had much practice at being a parent.'

'You're not my parent.'

And it's not time to tell her yet because I want the results of that test first. 'What I mean is, being *in loco parentis.*'

She frowns.

'Translation: standing in for a parent.'

'I want to go home.'

She looks desolate. She doesn't want to be with me. This is the last thing I wanted.

'But your mum's not back until tonight.' Or ever.

'Please.'

I consider it for a moment. I don't suppose it can hurt. It might even make things better between us. And anyway, we'll have to go back there sometime so she can pick up her stuff, because even if she and I choose to live there together eventually, it can't happen now.

She points at her mouth with an unsteady finger.

'What?' I say before realising. 'Oh, yes! This mess on my mouth.' It's hardening and starting to feel unpleasant. 'I'd better wash that off before you think I'm completely mad.'

I laugh. She doesn't.

I pause in the doorway before I leave her.

'It means a lot to me, to be able to spend this time with you,' I say.

But perhaps I didn't pick the right moment to say it, because it looks as if those tears might fall.

Emily lies on the sofa in the barn, her foot up. She wanted to be long gone from here by now, but Ruth has disappeared, so the others are searching for her and nobody will drive down until she's found or considered so lost that reinforcements need to be called in.

How they hope to find Ruth in this fog, Emily can't imagine. She can hear them calling for Ruth and their cries, stretched and desperate, shatter the still air of the valley.

Jayne swears that Ruth was beside her when she went to sleep. 'She was blotto,' Jayne told William. 'I couldn't rouse her, and I was worried about her. I thought she might vomit so I fell asleep with her beside me, and I wasn't aware of anything else until Emily woke me. I didn't hear Ruth get up.'

Emily watched Jayne as she spoke. There was an undertone, barely detectable, but definitely present, of strain in her voice, as if Jayne was holding something back, something she was afraid of.

It frightened Emily, tightened her sense of claustrophobia, her desperation to be away from here.

She watched on as they decided to search for Ruth themselves, before calling for help. They reasoned that Ruth could have gone out for an early walk, to clear her head after last night. It didn't seem likely to Emily. Not considering how drunk Ruth was.

Emily shuts her eyes. She is useless, lying here. Last night felt like a fever dream and this morning is no different. She can see out of the window from where she lies. Swifts are carving dizzying ellipses through the fog, as if distressed.

She hears voices and they sound urgent. She sits up, trying to figure out where they're coming from, and who is talking. It sounds like the farmer and his wife but it's impossible to hear what they're saying because their voices have the hushed quality of people trying not to be overheard.

Emily limps into the hall. She wants to hear more. The voices aren't coming from behind the front door but via the broken window in the kitchen. She sidles closer, down the hallway, until she's standing as near to the kitchen as she dares but can't be seen. She has to strain to hear.

'I've done something,' John Elliott says. 'I tried to scare them away.'

'Dear God, what did you do?' Maggie's voice is tense with desperation. 'What is it, John? Tell me!'

'It's my fault that she's gone missing.'

'What did you do?'

'I scared them.' He murmurs the rest of his answer. Emily struggles to hear. Something about a dead animal, a scarecrow, the intent to terrorise them so they left the barn. She feels as if someone is dragging an ice cube up her back.

But she also hears his remorse, and how Maggie's muted anger turns to reassurance.

'We'll find her, it's fine. It'll be OK, you'll see.'

Neither of them speaks for a while after that, or not that Emily can hear, but then she hears a breath sharply drawn in, a half-swallowed sob, muted grunts.

'John, no,' Maggie says.

It sounds like a physical struggle. She doesn't know if harm is being done or if someone is being restrained, but it's unbearable to listen to. After her dad left, when her mum got lost in drink, Emily learned how to hide while conflict erupted around her: punching, kicking, the rhythmic sound of a head being pounded against a door creating a low beat beneath the turned-up sound of rock music on the stereo.

She was too afraid to intervene then, but she's not now.

The kitchen seems miles wide. She makes it to the table, leans on it heavily, and says, 'Who's there?'

From experience it's best to sound as if you're stumbling on conflict innocently, not to give away the fact that you've been listening.

She hears nothing in return at first, only silence, eventually followed by a muted scuffling. The sound of people putting themselves back together. More silence, then she hears Maggie

Elliott calling Ruth's name; John Elliott too. They've put distance between themselves and the barn.

Emily digests what she heard, and it occurs to her for the first time that perhaps some real harm might have come to Ruth and it might have come from John Elliott. She remembers how he loomed out of the darkness last night. She never asked what he was doing there. The thought that he could be violent horrifies her. To think that she let him lead her down the hill like a lamb to the slaughter.

The barn no longer feels like a safe place to wait on her own.

Imogen wants to pee, urgently, but she's afraid to leave the bedroom.

A joke? Is that what he thought it was? It looked crazy, proper crazy. A sob convulses her. She cries as silently as she can and feels as if her tears will never stop falling but when they do, eventually, she finds that she's angry with him. He didn't even answer her question about whether she could go home, but she's old enough to just do it. She doesn't need his permission.

She gets dressed, gathers her stuff, and goes downstairs and fetches her cello.

'Hello, you!' He's cleaned himself up, thank goodness. He clocks that she's holding her bag and cello and gives her a smile that stretches his lips taut and shows a lot of teeth, the way adults do when they're trying too hard. The television is on, a chat show. The set is garish, the presenters look old.

'Hi,' she says.

'Feeling better?' What a question to ask, as if she was the one who disgraced herself earlier.

'Yep,' she says. 'Can you drive me home now? I can wait for Mum at home on my own.'

He objects, saying he can't possibly leave her alone, blustering away about his responsibility and promises made to her mother to care for her.

'But I'm seventeen,' she says. 'You don't need to stay with me. Why are you acting like this?'

He starts up again, sounding more manic this time, reeling out even stupider reasons for having to stay with her, and her sense of claustrophobia escalates, as does her anxiety.

Trying to be rational with him isn't going to work, she realises, but she has an idea. She'll have to lie to him again, to stop him going on and on and to make him do what she wants. She figures that if she can get him to take her home then once she's there she can tell him to go.

As he continues to try to justify his position in more ridiculous ways, she stands with her back to him, staring out of the window, and opens her eyes as wide as she can until they're awash with tears. The way she's feeling, it's not difficult to summon them back.

When he's finished gabbing, finally, she turns to face him and blinks. One hot tear runs down her cheek. Others follow.

She says, 'I've got the feeling again and I think it's because I'm homesick. I *need* to go home.'

His face has gone very still. 'And what feeling would that be?'

'That I want to cut myself.'

There's an odd moment before he answers, as if he's deciding what tone to take, and the expression on his face is strangely composed and there's hardness in his eyes. It scares her. If she was faking before, she isn't now. She blinks rapidly. Real tears roll down her cheeks and she feels desperate.

He continues to stare at her and it feels almost like he's toying with her. Fear curls inside her. She wipes her eyes and feels acutely vulnerable.

'Actually, it's OK, you don't need to drive me, you've done enough. I can get the bus.'

'Sit down.' She hesitates and he repeats the instruction, harshly. She sits. 'Now listen,' he says. 'Your mum won't be home for hours, not until this evening, and I can't leave you at the house on your own, especially if you're having thoughts of self-harming.'

The way he says it is strangely clinical, as if the words are sticky in his mouth. She's never heard him sound like this before.

'Unless . . .' he says.

'Unless what?'

'Unless you've been lying to me about that.'

'About what?' she asks, but she knows what he means.

'About self-harming.'

'I haven't,' she says, but she swallows reflexively, guiltily, and her voice sounds small and unconvincing. How has he guessed?

On the television, the audience applauds wildly as a new guest takes their seat on the couch. Somebody wolf-whistles. He clears his throat sharply. She flinches as if he's made a sudden movement towards her.

'Imogen are you absolutely sure about that?'

Her answer catches in the back of her throat, where it changes from 'yes' to 'no' and back again. She's not sure which he wants to hear but she senses, in precisely the same way a young animal in danger might understand it's cornered, that all hope is lost, that she needs to say the right thing.

Or else.

William Elliott peers beneath the hedge, looking for the remains of the scarecrow that Jayne described to him.

Her recounting of what happened has set off alarm bells. He worked hard to keep his expression impassive as he recognised elements of what she described from tales his dad had told him growing up.

The scarecrow figure. The entrails. Both are familiar.

When William was a child, John Elliott worked hard on the farm all day and then worked hard in the evening to pass down the local folklore to his son. Bedtime stories were terrifying and fascinating, his father's gentle voice bringing alive fabulous creatures that could weave spells around you, save you or doom you. The power they wielded was horrifying and reassuring.

You're a part of this, his dad would insist. It's in your blood. It's in your DNA. So don't be afraid. You should never fight what's out there, because if you respect it, it'll look after you.

He would kiss William on the forehead and pull the curtains tight. A fine man – William knew it even back then, in his heart. Everybody said it too. He's always tried to live up to his dad.

But has John become a version of himself now, a man who would make a grotesque scarecrow to frighten guests away from the barn?

It's possible. And would he do worse?

Jayne told the story about finding the scarecrow strangely without emotion, but she must have been scared.

Beneath the hedge he finds an old broom handle, which fits with her story, but there's nothing else. No face made from sacking, no raw entrails. He's relieved. But also aware that the offal wouldn't have lasted the night up here.

And if it had, he saw Birdie beneath the hedge earlier. She was eating something.

Evidence?

He rubs his face with his hands. He believes Jayne saw a scarecrow out here. He thinks his dad made it.

What a mess.

He's thought more about the letter too. The way it was delivered here and the threat it contains is a cruel joke at best and at worst an extraordinary act of malice, or a set-up of some sort. He's curious about the situation. Who wouldn't be?

He thinks about how Jayne and Emily interacted with one another at the barn. There wasn't much love between them as far as he could tell. 'Careful' is how he would describe their manner towards each other. He's also aware of Jayne's background because she described it to him, and he knows that a certain kind of military training can provide you with the means to tell a good cover story. He wonders if there might be more to Ruth's disappearance than meets the eye.

It feels very odd to him that the women have described themselves as friends. It's as if he's stumbled across a group too dysfunctional to know the meaning of friendship. After all, the alleged letter writer is supposed to be a 'friend' of their husbands.

And there's the matter of Emily having fled the barn alone last night, and risked her life doing so. It takes a strong measure of fear to make someone do that and a notable lack of trust in the people you're with.

He can't help thinking that if the threat in the letter is real, and one of their husbands is dead, or if Ruth has come to harm, this will make a very juicy case.

He doesn't spend long checking out the hedgerow. They need to find Ruth.

He's tasked with searching for her in the close vicinity of the barn. His mother has struck out into the high terrain at the back of the barn; she will search the edges of the moorland, where the worry is that Ruth might have strayed into boggy ground.

Jayne is retracing the walk she and Emily took yesterday, keeping to the path. His father went with his mother but will diverge from her, towards the ancient burial mound that lies high and exposed near the edge of their property.

William doesn't think Ruth will have struggled up there because it's a difficult route, but it's worth a try because John will get a useful bird's-eye view of much of their land from its vantage point and might be able to spot her. If he can remember what he's there for.

William takes the opposite direction from his parents, cutting directly downhill, which might be where you'd go if you were drunk and letting gravity guide you. It's steep. Easy to trip and fall even in daylight.

If they don't find Ruth soon, he'll call for backup. If she's unconscious they could easily miss her in these conditions. He wishes they had some idea of what time she left the barn.

William's progress is slow and careful. When he reaches the bottom of the slope, he notices a stone dislodged on top of the drystone wall, moss freshly disturbed. Could be a sign she was here, could be anything. An animal. Storm damage.

He feels the sound of the shot as much as he hears it. The crack explodes across the valley, and his whole body stiffens. Crows rise from the trees below. The echo of the shot ricochets, confusing him momentarily but his senses settle, and he knows where the sound came from. It is not a direction from which he would expect to hear shots fired.

He runs uphill as fast as he can, fighting the sheer slope with all he's got.

Imogen sits in the car beside me, her face turned away from mine.

Her apology was remarkable. It moved our relationship to another level.

'I'm sorry,' she said. 'I should never have lied about harming myself. I was desperate to get out of camp and I didn't know how else to do it.'

I had intended to be firm with her, to deliver a lecture on the inadvisability of lying, the necessity for honesty between us, but I cracked. I looked into her eyes and saw within them a vulnerability that moved me, and also courage. It takes guts to apologise, and I admire her for it. I told her so. I think I handled it very well.

It moves me to think that she got some of her strength from me, but also from her mother who fought me tooth and nail in the moments before she died, even as I made heartfelt vows to her that I would take the best care of Imogen because I knew that she was mine.

It was different when Rob died. As he slipped beneath the water, I stood at the edge of the shore, knowing I'd tricked him into swimming then and there, when it was almost certainly a risk to his life, and I felt preternaturally calm as I watched the moon brighten the dull swell into which he disappeared. Beneath my feet the rock was slippery, but solid. He resurfaced just once.

You'd have thought he might have fought harder if he was a better man.

I didn't run or shout for help, I didn't stride into the water to try to pull him out. I knew about the dangers of swimming that night, about the rip tide and the merciless currents.

I knew when he went into that water that he was unlikely to survive, and I was happy when he sank beneath the surface for the final time.

I could have saved him, and I didn't.

I remember well carrying his coffin, the brutal heft of it, how I worried my knees would buckle. All of us in the gang were pall-bearers that day, apart from Edie. I wonder, were we paying our respects to Rob as we walked past her with that coffin on our shoulders, teeth clenched and sweating? Or taking part in a beauty parade?

Edie looked so grateful. She didn't yet know that one of us was responsible for Rob's death.

But she was soon to discover that another one of us had suspicions about that.

Which was a surprise to me when I found out.

And a problem.

I turn on the radio. I'm realising that, unfortunately, the silence between Imogen and me isn't comfortable. Some silences you can breathe deeper in, stretch out wider in, but others constrict you, making every gesture horribly self-conscious. She flinches when the sound comes on. It's a play. We let the overwrought dialogue wash over us as I drive her home.

Edie's home is a two-storey stable conversion on the edge of a village just outside the city. It's situated at the end of a lane and completely isolated from its neighbours.

Rob and Edie didn't bother with security. They weren't that sort of couple. Too golden. It was as if they thought nothing bad would ever happen to them.

When I killed her yesterday morning, nobody heard Edie scream.

Imogen tries to open the passenger door before the car has stopped dead but I've got the central locking set up so she can't. 'Hey,' I say. 'What's the hurry?'

Her fingers stay on the handle until I've turned the ignition off and released the locks, then she shoots out like a cat with its tail on fire.

I follow. By the time I reach her, she's at the front door of the house and has let herself in.

'Thanks so much,' she says and extends a hand to take her cello, which I'm holding.

I put my foot against the door. 'Hey,' I say. 'There's no way I can leave you here alone.'

Emily hears a gunshot.

She straightens and strains to hear more but all she picks up are the raspy *kraa*s of startled crows. She shudders and tells herself that it can't be unusual to hear shooting out here. Can it? Don't people shoot all the time in the country?

As the crows settle into silence a bird of prey screams and every muscle in Emily's body tightens again. Her sense of claustrophobia is mounting, her flight instinct intensifying. But she can't go anywhere without help.

She isn't certain what she's hearing at first or whether she's imagining it because she's so desperate. She listens hard. It's a low drone, a car engine, she's increasingly sure, faint but unmistakable. It's not close, but it's in the vicinity.

She doesn't know what time it is, but she guesses it's something like eleven o'clock. Could it be that this is Paul arriving? She thinks it could, and a sob breaks from her chest as she hobbles to the front door.

She opens it, knowing Paul's car won't be able to reach her up here at the barn, knowing she can't see back into the valley where the farmhouse lies, but feeling the urge to step outside, to wait here for someone to drive her down.

She sinks to the ground to sit in the doorway. The dense stone walls gather around and above her like an apse. She lifts her injured leg and balances her heel on a boot scraper, to elevate it. The metal digs into the back of her foot, but she doesn't care.

It will be Paul in that car. It will be him. It will.

She tunes out the shouts that are coming from around the house, from up the hill. Tunes out the rising urgency in them, the note of panic.

She stares down the hill, willing it to be Paul, willing him to be on his way to her.

'You can leave me,' Imogen says. 'It's fine. Like I said. I'm home on my own all the time. Thanks so much. For everything.'

I'm fed up. I've made it clear to her that I wish to stay with her and she needs to respect me. 'I don't think so, sweetheart.'

I put my hand on the door and push it firmly, so that there's room both for me and her cello to enter the house. It's not difficult to overpower her.

She steps backwards and doesn't take her eyes off me.

'You don't need to stay here!' she says. 'I'm seventeen!'

'Enough!' I say. 'End of discussion. I'm staying and that's that.'

She flinches and I realise that I raised my voice but needs must. I'm her father and she's going to have to learn to listen to me.

I step inside and close the door. She walks towards the open-plan space at the back of the house where she drops her bag on the floor and I follow, making sure to step around the area where Edie fell after I struck the side of her head with my fist. I prop Imogen's cello against the wall in its usual spot in the living room. 'Shall I make us a cup of tea?' I ask.

'Sure,' she says in a small voice.

The living room connects to the kitchen and dining area, which have a view of the garden out back. Imogen and I could live here, I suppose; it's pretty nice but I think I prefer we have a clean start.

I make tea. Tucked beside the tea caddy I spot a brochure for the meditation centre where Edie is supposed to have gone this weekend. Yesterday morning, I made sure to send them a message from her phone, cancelling her booking. Acting as her, I explained that something had come up, said I wouldn't be seeking a refund.

I glance at Imogen. She's distracted and I fold the brochure in half and slip it into my pocket. I don't want her to think of calling them. It would complicate things needlessly.

Imogen sits on Edie's favourite chair, upholstered in yellow velvet. Sunny, like Edie was. She holds a cushion on her lap.

'I really can stay here alone. I do it all the time. Mum and Dad let me stay on my own since I was, like, thirteen. And it won't even be dark by the time Mum gets home,' Imogen says and, while it annoys me beyond measure that she's still going on about this when I've made my position clear, I can't help admiring her tenacity.

Before I can reply, something catches her eye. She frowns and gets up, unfolding those colt legs slowly, the way you might if you had been feeling unwell, or if something unaccountably strange was happening, and she sinks on to her knees to peer beneath the sofa.

'What is it?' I ask. My heart skips a beat. Just inches from where Imogen is kneeling, I laid her mother's head down after I'd choked the life out of her.

It wasn't as bad as it sounds. I didn't leave her lying unsupported on the hard stone floor but took a cushion from the sofa and put it beneath her head. There was no blood. Once I'd adjusted her scarf to cover the red marks on her neck, she looked really quite peaceful.

I can visualise her there now.

Imogen reaches beneath the sofa.

I can't see what she's trying to get but I'm very afraid that I might have slipped up. Did I clear up properly? What did I forget?

It was hard, after she died, because I was sobbing. I cradled Edie on that floor for a long time, pressed my skin against hers until the warmth left her, ran my fingers across the contours of her body the way I always longed to. I didn't think it was possible to feel so sad.

Imogen is staring into her hand.

'What's that?' I ask.

She unfurls her fingers and stretches out her hand to show me.

There, in the middle of her palm, is Edie's engagement ring, the one Rob gave her. There's total incomprehension on Imogen's face.

I can't tell her I eased the ring from her mother's finger after she was dead, and I thought I'd placed it safely in my pocket. I can't mention how afraid I am that she'll see something else: a strand of her mother's hair, a blood spot, even though there should be none. But the mind plays tricks on you when matters of life and death are concerned.

My heart thumps.

'Mum'll be thrilled that you've found that,' I force myself to say. 'You can give it to her tonight. I know it means the world to her.'

Jayne freezes when she hears the gunshot. The sound is muffled by the river, which is swollen, the water rushing noisily beneath her. But it's unmistakable.

She knows that gunshot is not uncommon in the countryside, but the fact that her weapon is missing is enough to fill her with fear. It was loaded.

Has Ruth brought the gun out here? Is she still drunk? Has there been an accident?

Oh, dear God, no.

Has her friend unravelled that far?

It's hard to know where the shot came from. It could be almost any direction. Jayne pivots and starts back towards the barn.

What will Mark say if this gunshot comes from her weapon and if someone is hurt? How will she live down how stupid she's been? How irresponsible? How will anyone explain this to Toby? And what about baby Alfie?

The questions arrive so fast and so insistently that she feels as if she might scream. She clamps a hand over her mouth. And runs.

And yells for Ruth, desperate to hear a reply.

Her voice carries up and around the valley, penetrating the mist further than before, until it reaches the place where Ruth is.

*

Imogen stares at the ring, turning it around, looking at it from every angle, as if it's a treasure she just dug up. I sincerely hope this isn't going to be a problem.

'Mum doesn't go anywhere without this. She never takes it off, even to wash her hands.'

'I know.'

'What does it mean that it's here then?'

'Just that she lost it. It happens. Rings can loosen.' I have no idea if this is true, but I say it as authoritatively as possible. 'Like I said, she'll be chuffed to bits that you've found it. You'd better put it somewhere safe.'

Imogen balances the ring on her knee while she unclips her gold necklace. She loops it through the ring but struggles to do the clasp back up.

When frustration gets the better of her, she says, 'Can you help me?' and I can tell it pains her to ask.

I put on my reading glasses, take the necklace from her shaking hands and ease the tiny hoop into the clasp, let the chain fall back against her lovely skin and step away.

'Thank you,' she murmurs, putting distance between us.

'I'll fix us something to eat,' I say. 'For lunch.'

'I'm not hungry. I'm probably going to go up to my room.'

'Well, I'll fix something anyway and you might feel hungry by the time I've made it.'

'No.'

'What?'

'I'm not hungry. Please go away. Go home. I don't need you to stay with me.'

Her voice is raised and she's shaking with bravery.

I'm transfixed by the way her fingertip is touching her mother's ring where it rests in the delicate hollow at the base of her neck, as if she's drawing strength from it. I'm transfixed by it and Edie's death plays out in front of my eyes: every moment, every sound she made, the scent of her, the warmth of the struggle. Murder is not how you think it will be. It's intensely intimate. Time stops.

Afterwards I found I was sweating.

And I realise that I'm sweating now, which isn't a good sign.

I mustn't lose control.

William scrambles up the lower slopes of the barrow, towards the burial chamber, feeling the mist's dampness on his face. The sun is struggling to break through, and for every few yards he covers the mist seems less dense and more crystalline, as if it plans to reveal something to him.

His legs ache but he pushes himself onward. His hands are filthy where he's clawed his way up. His knees are damp and matted with grass.

He emerges from the claustrophobic whiteness into watery sunshine. The air seems liquid, the sky huge and the brightness startling.

As his eyes adjust, everything seems to shift around him, settling into place. The vast long-distance fades away and the foreground comes slowly into sharp focus, every tussock gleaming damply, every stone patterned with vivid shades of lichen.

The body is face down, lying in front of the crumbled entrance to the ancient burial chamber.

He walks towards it as steadily as he can, trying to exhale fear and inhale courage.

'Just let me make you some food,' I tell Imogen. 'And I promise I'll go after that.' I don't mean to sound as if I'm pleading, or being overly insistent, but I'm afraid that I do. My self-control is slipping. It might be best if I take some time out. She's not going anywhere, after all, and I could use a moment to compose myself. It's all a bit much and I'll be able to look after her better when I've rested.

'I'm not hungry. But a cup of tea will be fine.'

I suspect she's humouring me, and I want her to want me to look after her. 'Wouldn't you like another special hot chocolate?' I ask. I hear a sob and I'm afraid it's me.

Tears spring to her eyes. Reciprocal tears? Are we connecting? Or is she still frightened?

She's shaking her head, but says, 'OK,' in a voice that breaks like a fine crack running through a piece of porcelain.

'OK? Are you sure?' I feel a rush of pleasure even though she's nodding as if she can't stop, like one of those dogs on the dashboard, and you wouldn't think so many tears could fit in someone's eyes without spilling.

'Well, then,' I say. 'I'm on the case. One more super-luxurious hot chocolate coming up, or as luxurious as I can make it without the trimmings. We should have brought the cream and marshmallows from my house, but never mind.'

Luckily there's enough milk in the fridge and I whistle as I work, totally focused, and it steadies me, cheers me up. I can do this. This is going to be all right. I can leave her safely for a little while. We're both under pressure. I acknowledge that.

But after some minutes, I hear a door shut. Slowly, carefully. Too slowly, too carefully. Not how Imogen usually enters or leaves a room.

I look up from the pan of milk and hear the sort of weighty silence in which you know you're alone.

Imogen has escaped.

I don't know how long I stand there in shock. The idea that she would do this to me while I was trying so hard to do something nice for her crashes around my head, destructive and enraging.

The milk boils over and burns black on the ceramic hob. It brings me back. I turn off the heat beneath the pan. Still no sound.

'Imogen?' I call but I already know that she's gone. That she's deceived me again.

As if I was someone else entirely, I see myself from above, and note how violent my movements look as I bolt after her.

It's an ugly sight.

Ruth is nestled as if hibernating in the right angle where two drystone walls meet.

Stones dig into her back, her head has slumped forward, the long stretch of her neck looks unnatural, and the vertebrae at its base protrude, damp skin stretched taut and white across them. Her hair is clumped and wet, a few strands twined through the lily-white fingers of a hand that's curled against her face. Her eyes are part open, the whites showing.

She's completely still. Not a breath seems to enter or leave her body.

But the gunshot rouses her. She wakes suddenly and her heart kicks in her chest. She sucks in air, forcing her ribcage and her locked-up shoulders to move. She aches all over, inside and out. She's soaked through and cold has numbed every part of her. Her head is pounding, and her mouth is sticky dry. She has no idea where she is.

Someone calls her name and she shouts a reply but her voice only croaks. Pathetic. She's pathetic. She's lost. Out here. She knows she was drunk. Very drunk. She thinks she might have blacked out.

Standing up feels like a feat almost too challenging to achieve but she needs perspective on where she is. It doesn't help. Fog blankets the area she's in, thick and impenetrable. All she knows is that she's in a field, but she can't see further than a few feet.

She hears her name again and replies again, but her voice still sounds weak, and she knows it hasn't travelled. Breathe, she thinks, gather some strength from somewhere.

And then she thinks, How stupid I am. She's drunk, lost, her clothes are so wet she's not even sure if she's soiled herself or not, though she fears she might have, and what she's been most afraid of in the months since Alfie was born has come to pass: her loss of control is so complete that all the threads connecting her to her sanity have been severed.

She tries to reason, though she's trembling so much it's hard to do anything.

Gunshot. It must be from somewhere on the farm. They're hunting. But that's so dangerous, in the fog. Is she safe here from stray bullets?

She remembers something. Jayne's weapon. Is that what she just heard?

In a rush she recalls how she found Jayne's gun, but not what happened after that, only the feeling of being terribly frightened by Jayne.

What the hell has happened?

She leans against the wall, desperate to be somewhere safe. She's afraid of seeing Jayne, or anyone else, coming out of the mist towards her but also afraid to leave this corner, remembering the warnings from the Elliotts about the treacherous landscape.

Why is she out here? There must be a good reason. She would never have endangered her own life, surely, for nothing, even if she did drink too much. Because what kind of mother does that?

Her clothes give her few clues as to what her intentions were, other than to suggest that she left the barn in a hurry. She is wearing a coat, which has probably saved her from exposure, but it's not done up. Her shoes are inappropriate, her trousers the ones she left the city in yesterday. The hems are clammy with wet mud.

She has never felt so cold, so unwell, so hollow, so scared, so alone. She shifts position and steps on something solid and very hard.

A gun.

It triggers a muddled, partial memory. She reaches down to pick it up, cautiously. It feels familiar. She's held it before, thinks it was in her hand last night. It must be Jayne's gun.

She wonders, as she stares at it dangling from her fingertips, as the fog around her seems to lighten a touch, threatening to expose her, as her heartrate ticks up: Who am I hiding from?

William approaches his father's body. Birdie lies against John. She whimpers. William rests a hand on the dog's flank and tries to find his father's pulse but can't.

The bullet hole in John's forehead is neat. Blood and brain matter cover the side of one of the small standing stones that mark the entrance to the chamber. His father must have sat here, against the stone, and fallen on to his side after shooting himself. His handgun lies beside him. It's not a weapon John uses much. He occasionally has to dispatch livestock with it. William can't imagine why he brought it up here with him. Some misguided notion of protection? Or did he know he was going to take his own life?

It's impossible to be sure, and he acknowledges that there's no point in trying to find sense in anything his father has done lately.

This hiatus of calm, where William's training tells him to try to assess the scene objectively, only lasts a moment before he feels the full force of his emotional loss, the first hefty blow that grief will land on him, and he drops to his knees beside his father and presses his own cheek against John's. His dad's skin is warm and damp. You could, if the evidence wasn't so brutally clear, almost imagine he was still alive.

But William knows he's not.

Up here, above the fog, is the highest point of the Elliott land. The view stretches to the horizon in every direction and William is happy to know that this is the last thing John saw before he died. He understands why John chose this site for this act. His father revered this place.

He looks down the hill, into the whiteness.

'Mum!' he shouts.

It doesn't occur to him to spare her this. She would never forgive him if he moved his father's body without her.

Things have gone wrong. John's mind betrayed him, and he knew it had and knew it wasn't going to get better. William wonders if he could have helped them more, could have avoided this. But he also knows the alternative was never going to be pretty.

Questions will have to be asked, but in this moment John's suicide both profoundly shocks William and doesn't surprise him at all.

What he hopes, sincerely, desperately, is that his father has not done something in the past twelve hours that will taint the legacy of a beautiful man.

He calls for his mother again, hoping his voice will reach her, or that she will have followed the sound of the gunshot, as he did.

Maggie will want to hold John one last time, in this place that meant so much to his father, to both of them. She'll want to end her marriage how it started. Just them, together, in love.

Imogen bolts across the back garden, ducks beneath the hedge and scrambles up an embankment. The old railway line behind the house has been abandoned for decades, but the tracks and sleepers remain, framing weeds and rubble.

She doesn't linger on the top of the embankment but scuttles down the other side where shrubs and bushes grow densely, tethered together by rangy, savage brambles. What Imogen knows, because she used to play here as a child with her neighbours, is that if you burrow to the back of the shrubs there's a swampy area abutting a brick wall.

Underfoot, it's thick with the blackest mud, but the roots of the shrubs and brambles don't stray there, so a sort of tunnel has formed over the years, shielded by the foliage around it. At this time of year, she knows it will keep her hidden.

She fights through the rampant brambles. Fat blackberries streak her purple, and thorns rip at her, yanking her hair and opening slender cuts on her exposed skin, one running from the side of her nose to her earlobe, the other across her midriff where her top has ridden up. Blood beads along them.

She's terrified of him. He's turned into a horrible, frightening version of the man she's known all her life.

When she reaches the wall, she has to crouch. She doesn't fit as well as she used to in the small space. A fleeting memory of childhood play comes back to her, her smiling dad waiting on the track for her to appear with a bucketful of mud and helping her make pies with it. Her feet in yellow wellington boots to match her rain jacket, a plastic shovel in her hand.

She waits, unsure whether she's doing the right thing staying here or if she should have run further. She waits for a while and it feels like forever. Eventually, the jagged rise and fall of her chest settles into a calmer rhythm and she starts to doubt herself.

What will her mum say when she learns that Imogen ran away from him because of a bad feeling? Because he smashed an egg on his face? Because Imogen found the ring on the floor?

Will Edie say that Imogen is being hysterical? Silly? Oversensitive? Insulting to a close family friend? Or that she did the right thing, to follow her gut and protect herself?

Imogen's not sure and it's agony because her mum's advice and approval mean everything to her. Edie's not perfect, Imogen knows that, and they've had a very difficult year, but Imogen also knows how ferociously and unconditionally loved she is by her mother.

She pushes Edie's engagement ring hard against her lips, feeling the smooth facets of the diamond, the fussy detail of the platinum it sits within. The metal feels as if it might rip the skin on her lips if she's not careful.

She shuts her eyes and speaks a wish into it, for her mum to arrive home now, hours early. To make all of this go away. It feels as if she's living a nightmare.

Jayne keeps calling for Ruth and she thought she heard a reply at first, faint but close, but now Ruth has gone quiet. Jayne tries to hold in her head where the sound of Ruth's voice was coming from.

Her sense of urgency intensifies. She's afraid Ruth is hurt; wonders guiltily how many hours Ruth has been out here for. If Jayne hadn't dissociated, she might have stopped this from happening.

A drystone wall runs alongside the path then deviates from it and disappears into the fog ahead of her. Jayne follows it. This is what I might have done if I was Ruth, out here last night, she thinks. If it was hard to see the path in the dark, I would have stuck by a wall.

It might as well be dark now, she thinks, visibility is so poor. It's disorientating. As her ears strain for clues as to where Ruth is, she notices minute detail. Moss and lichen on the stone.

She comes upon Ruth suddenly where the wall turns ninety degrees at the edge of the field. Ruth is crouching, wedged into the corner.

'Stop!' Ruth says.

'It's me. Ruth, it's Jayne.'

'I said stop!'

Ruth is holding Jayne's gun with both hands, pointing it at her. The barrel shakes as Ruth trembles.

'Ruth,' she says. Her military training takes over. Handle the situation. Keep it calm. Assess whether Ruth is still inebriated. 'I'm not a threat to you. Can you please put the gun down beside you?'

Ruth shakes her head. Her finger is on the trigger. She clearly has intent. She looks terrified. The distance between them is about fifteen yards.

'I don't know what happened to you last night,' Jayne says. 'But I'm here to help you. I promise. And I'm not the only one looking for you. The police are here. John and Maggie Elliott are up here too.'

Jayne takes a cautious step closer. Then another. She sees that Ruth is freezing and wet through, but also that she's looking at Jayne as if Jayne is her worst nightmare come true.

I'm the threat, Jayne understands. It's me. What did I do?

It's a shock, but she has to control the situation.

'Can you put the gun down for me? Then we can get you to safety.'

Ruth lowers the gun a fraction and Jayne feels a prickle of hope. She steps closer and slowly, carefully lowers herself down to sit a short distance from Ruth, her back against the wall, just the way Ruth's is. She keeps her body as relaxed as possible.

'Are you cold?' she asks.

The gun tips a little in Ruth's hands.

'Should we call for the others?' Jayne asks. 'They're not far.' She doesn't know this but hopes it's true.

Ruth wipes her eyes with the back of her sleeve. Jayne flinches as the barrel of the gun swings past her.

'Why did you bring this?' Ruth asks. She waves the gun dangerously. 'What for?'

Be honest, Jayne thinks. However drunk Ruth may still be this morning, however untethered she's become, she's an intelligent woman. She'll smell a lie. It's time to be wholly honest. 'Because I had an idea for something that Mark and I need to do when he arrives this morning. You know, the men are probably nearly here.'

'What do you need to do?' Ruth asks.

Even now, it's painful for Jayne to share this. She hesitates, but feels she has no choice. 'We both struggle with what we did when we were in the military. The deaths we played our parts in. The innocent deaths. I wanted us to dispose of the gun up here at the Neolithic burial chamber. It was an idea I had, for a sort of ritual. It seems very, very stupid now, but it was supposed to be cathartic. I thought it would help both of us to start fresh and put violence behind us.'

Jayne sees that Ruth is trying to decide whether to believe this or not.

'I promise you, it's true,' Jayne says. If not now, when? 'I know you haven't heard this before from me; it's not something I've ever been comfortable talking about. I have a whole host of feelings about it that, frankly, scare me.'

A tear slips down Ruth's cheek. Something is getting through to her.

'And I never imagined,' Jayne continues, 'that you and I would end up out here with my gun in your hands. It's loaded, Ruth. Did you know that? You could do some damage with it – to me, to yourself or someone else. Is that what you want? Really?'

Ruth looks at the weapon, as if she hadn't truly considered its potential before. She's drunk still, Jayne thinks. Which makes her even more dangerous.

'If I thought bringing the gun up here would lead to you or anyone else being endangered, I would never have done it,' Jayne says. 'You have to believe me.'

'I'm scared,' Ruth says. Her face crumples.

'You don't need to be scared of me. I promise. I'm your friend, remember?'

Ruth stares at Jayne through her tears. The fog is still dense around them, as if only the two of them exist in the here and now, cocooned from the rest of the world.

'Let's go back to the barn, shall we?' Jayne says. 'And collect our stuff and go home. And after that, let's talk, Ruth. Properly talk. I think we need to. I'm here for you. But right now, we need to get you out of here. You don't look well. Let me help you. Please.'

The barrel of the gun is pointing at the ground between Ruth's knees. Slowly, Jayne makes to stand up.

Ruth watches her, still wary, before a look of defeat settles over her, a moment of laxness, of sheer physical and emotional exhaustion. Her guard is down, and Jayne makes her move. She seizes the weapon.

Within seconds she has emptied the barrel. The bullets go in one coat pocket, the gun in the other. She is very angry. She has an impulse to strike Ruth across the face, to shout, 'Do you know what could have just happened? Do you have any fucking idea how dangerous that was?'

As if reading her mind, Ruth cowers.

But Jayne controls herself and extends a hand to her friend.

'Come on,' she says. 'Let's get you somewhere warm and dry.'

Ruth looks at Jayne's hand and hesitates at first but takes it. She lets Jayne help her up and support her as they make their way back to the barn and, in the foggy distance, they tune into the echoey shouts of the others and, whatever's happening, it doesn't sound good.

In the dark, intimate moments while she's crouching amongst the brambles and wishing with all her heart for her mum to come home, Imogen hears, floating down from the embankment, from not too far away, a jaunty whistle and her blood runs cold. It's him. She's certain because of the tune: 'Fly Me to the Moon'.

He loves Frank Sinatra. He can whistle it very fast and used to if he wanted to make her laugh.

Now, the tune is slow, mournful, deliberate. It drags. Taunts. He wants Imogen to know that he knows she's there and listening to him.

How he's found her, she's unsure. But he has.

She shrinks down and breathes as quietly as possible. There's nowhere else she can run to. She'd have to go either left, or right, alongside the wall. It would be noisy. She'd give herself away.

The whistling gets nearer and louder. The sound cuts right through her, pinning her in place, before stopping abruptly. He's close, but how close? She holds her breath for as long as she can, until she feels as if her eyes might pop out of their sockets, as if she might burst.

The whistling starts up again. *Fly. Me. To. The. Moon.* She exhales. It gets quieter. Is he moving on?

Shot through with pale veins, the whites of her eyes show as she tries to see through the tangle of bushes. She tracks the fading sound of the whistling until she can't hear it any longer.

In the silence all her senses strain to detect him. They strain so hard she feels sick. After a while, she's semi-confident. Stiffly, she half-stands, it's all the space allows her to do, and begins, slowly, to work her way back through the foliage.

She doesn't see him coming.

He grabs her upper arm and shakes her so hard she cuts her lip on her incisors and, when he stops, she leans forward and a drop of blood falls from her mouth on to his shoe and she starts to scream but the sound is deadened when he covers her mouth with his other hand as if he's going to suffocate her.

'Sweetheart,' he whispers in her ear. 'Stop it. Stop now. You're OK. Daddy's here.'

William drives the women from the barn back down to the farmhouse. Maggie and the dog have stayed with the body. 'Your dad shouldn't be on his own,' she said, and William agreed. He wonders if he'll ever experience a love story as powerful as his parents'.

He wants these women to go, to leave his family to themselves. He no longer cares about them or their letter. It's hard not to think of their presence here, and their behaviour, as a catalyst for what his father has done. Whether that's fair or not, he doesn't care right now.

Emily sits in the passenger seat.

She watched Jayne and Ruth emerge from the fog as they walked back to the barn, Jayne holding Ruth up, and she couldn't help hating them. If they'd just all gone back down to the farmhouse the moment they'd read the letter, the way Emily suggested, none of this would have happened.

Ruth isn't well. She slumps on the back seat of the car, leaning against Jayne. They've made sure she's hydrated and warmed her up. She has no other injuries.

Jayne is awash with relief that there was no accident with the gun. It's safely back in her bag. But the 'what if's' are tormenting her.

Emily's nerves build, the closer to the farmhouse they get. She can't stop thinking about the car she heard earlier, coming up the valley, although she hasn't mentioned it, not after hearing what happened.

As William drives, it feels as if they must hang on for dear life. He blinks back tears and has his foot too hard on the gas.

Jayne thinks about the scarecrow and whether John Elliott put it there, or whether someone else did. She feels as if she has no idea about anything any more. Her lapse of judgement with the gun was so profound, it's knocked her sense of herself. Nobody apart from Ruth must ever know that Jayne brought a gun up here.

What was she thinking? Her plan seems ridiculous to her now. She'd read about a Viking burial ritual, where weapons, which were considered to have great power, were maimed and left in the ground alongside the bodies of their owners after death, and she got the idea that she and Mark could do this to his pistol. That it would be symbolic. Healing.

She'd intended that they would hike together to the burial chamber. Obviously, the chamber on the Elliott land was Neolithic, not Viking, but for Jayne it was loaded with just as much symbolism. Once there, they would permanently disable the gun, dig a deep hole and bury it with its ammunition. They would walk away from it together and not look back and would never return. It would be their last link to violence, an ending of sorts. They left the military six years ago after Mark had been passed over for promotion. Jayne might have had a future, a chance to progress beyond captain, but they decided on a clean break for both of them. They just didn't count on trauma tracking them across the years. But this could have marked an end to it.

If they did it right, she was convinced that the difficult elements of their past could be left respectfully behind.

Now, she wonders, what kind of disordered mind comes up with such a plan and puts so much store in it? Would Mark really have bought into it?

And did she plan it more for her, or for him? After all, she's the one who dissociates, not him. If she's honest, it's she who's struggling to cope with the trauma. Mark's done much better than her.

A plan that felt perfect and pure, healing and hopeful to her a few hours ago now feels foolish, selfish and incredibly reckless. She's ashamed.

As the Land Rover descends it's clear the fog hasn't lifted in the lower reaches of the valley. And as it rolls into the farmyard, Emily feels crushed by disappointment when she sees that the only vehicles in the yard are their rental and cars belonging to William and Maggie.

But a few seconds later, Jayne and Ruth's phones both start to ping.

'I'm sorry,' Imogen says and can't stop repeating it, as if she's unable to form any other words. His grip on her arm is a vice. She stumbles and bumps against him as she tries to keep up with him. Attempts to meet his eye and connect with him don't work. He stares firmly ahead, won't even glance at her.

She thinks she might throw up. Her brain can't keep up, can't process this. It feels like violence. But this, she knows, is hardly violence at all.

They pass nobody. Imogen sucks in air as if she's been starved of it. When she tries to shake her arm out of his grip, he tightens it in response. It hurts. She feels as helpless as a toddler.

He takes her the longer route back to the house because there's no way they'll both get through the hole in the hedge. She prays they'll see someone – a dog walker, maybe, anyone – but they don't. She considers shouting for help but it's a risk. Who would hear? Will it make him angry?

What would she say anyway? He's a family friend.

And what might he do? She's never seen him behave like this before. Would he hurt her properly? Or hurt whoever she pleaded with for help?

The ease with which he's holding her is terrifying. He has a strength she wasn't aware he possessed. She knows, of course she does, that men are stronger than women, but she's never personally experienced how effortlessly a man can physically overpower a woman, how it seems built into them naturally, packed into their muscles, written into their brain's pathways.

His strength isn't the worst thing, though, or the fact that he's ignoring her pleas. The worst thing is what he said: 'Daddy's here.'

She doesn't know what he means.

As the Land Rover pulls to a stop, Emily leans over the back of her seat. 'Your phone,' she says to Jayne. 'Please? Can I?'

Jayne looks at her and feels contempt. Emily is so selfish, she thinks. If she hadn't run away from the barn last night, none of this would have happened.

'In a minute,' she says. 'I need to help Ruth out.'

'What's wrong with you? Don't you want to find out if Mark is OK?'

'Mark's fine. All the men are fine.'

'I need to make some calls,' William Elliott says. 'Come into the farmhouse if you need to before you go.'

It sounds as if he's emphasising the word 'go'. Jayne gets the message.

'Of course,' she says. 'Thank you.'

They watch him walk away across the yard. Emily wants to ask him to use his phone, but she'll have the same problem she had last night: she won't be able to recall Paul's number.

Emily opens the car door and squints down the lane, into the fog, willing a vehicle to come into view. She manoeuvres her legs to the side so that she can get out and pauses. It will hurt her ankle, but she's going to lower herself down and drag herself around to the back of the car so she can wrestle a phone from Jayne or Ruth if they won't give her one.

She takes a deep breath in. As she starts to move, the fog in the lane brightens and headlamps emerge slowly, belonging to a black car. It crawls towards them. 'Oh my God,' Emily says. She drops too hard down from the Land Rover and her ankle screams in protest.

She hobbles towards the car in the lane. It looks large, and sleek. A town car. The type Paul likes to use.

'Paul!' she cries out. The fog dampens her shout.

Jayne, watching, helps Ruth out of the back of the Land Rover. Ruth collapses against the side of the vehicle, doubles over and retches.

'Paul!' Emily calls again. She can only inch down the lane. It feels as if it's taking forever. The car is parked about a hundred yards away. The headlamps extinguish.

Emily's heart lifts as two men get out of the car. It's Paul. She knows it because he's wearing his overcoat, the cashmere one they bought together, and beside him, it's hard to say who it is.

Emily accelerates her pace, pushing through the stabbing pain, and wonders why Paul isn't throwing his arms wide open, the way he usually does, why he isn't jogging to greet her.

She hears footsteps behind her. Jayne catches up with her, passes her and stops dead a few feet ahead.

Ruth shivers as she leans against the Land Rover. She can't move but is transfixed, though it's hard to see what's happening through the fog. She thinks there are two men approaching Jayne and Emily. She doesn't know if she wants one of them to be Toby or not, but she's desperate to know if Alfie is OK. She reaches into her pocket for her phone.

Maggie Elliott's little terrier scampers past Ruth and appears on the path beside Jayne. She yaps at the men before sidling up to greet them.

The thicker-set man in the big coat leans down to pet her. He makes a fuss of her.

'Paul?' Emily says. Paul never pets dogs. He doesn't like them. She feels as if her heart might stop.

'No, it's me,' the other man calls.

'Toby?' Jayne says.

'Hello.' Toby emerges from the fog. He's dressed for the weekend, in jeans and walking boots, an old waxed jacket, a messenger bag slung across his torso. 'This is quite the welcome party. What's happening?'

The first man stops petting the dog and steps forward too.

'Who are you?' Jayne asks.

'I'm the driver. You all right if I head off now, mate?' He looks at Toby.

'Absolutely. Of course. Thanks a lot. Drive safe on the way home. And good luck to your nephew!'

The driver salutes him with two fingers and turns away.

Emily has caught up.

Toby kisses Jayne on each cheek and leans towards Emily to do the same. 'You're both freezing,' he says. 'And what happened to you?' He looks Emily up and down. 'Hey, it's OK, oh dear, what's wrong?'

'Where's Paul?' Emily grabs Toby by the lapels. 'Where is he?'

'And where's Mark?' Jayne asks.

'Well, here's the thing. I have no idea,' Toby says. 'When the driver picked me up, he said Paul had contacted him to say that he should bring me up here on my own. No further explanation than that. Obviously, I tried calling them both but neither of them's answering or responding to messages. I thought you might know something.'

'Give me your phone,' Emily says. 'Give it to me!'

He pats his pockets, looking for it, and when he can't find it, he delves into his bag. Emily's distracted by the car, which is starting to back down the lane.

'Wait!' she shouts. Perhaps the driver has more information about Paul. Maybe they spoke this morning. 'Stop the car! Toby! Stop him going. I want to talk to him.'

Toby runs, slaps the car bonnet, and it stops. He has a word with the driver. The car crawls back towards Emily and stops. She leans in to talk.

'What's going on?' Toby asks Jayne as they watch. It's starting to sink in, that he's walked into a situation, that something is very wrong.

'It's a long story,' she says. She feels sick with fear. Where's Mark?

'OK,' he says. 'Where's Ruthie?'

Jayne points towards the farmhouse and Toby looks past her to where he can just see Ruth, who's still leaning against the Land Rover. He raises an arm and walks towards her.

Jayne pulls out her phone. She has one missed call from a colleague and a couple of texts regarding appointments next week.

Nothing from Mark.

She tries calling him. His phone rings and rings but he doesn't answer.

Emily is still talking to the driver. Her voice is raised. Jayne turns to watch Toby approach Ruth and feels jealous.

She tries to call Paul. He doesn't answer either.

Ruth ignores the notifications on her phone and dials her mother's home number.

'Flora? Oh, thank God. It's me. How's Alfie?'

Her knees almost buckle as her mum says, 'He's absolutely fine. Why aren't you off enjoying yourself? You sound hysterical.'

She barely hears Flora's words. My boy is safe, she thinks. He's fine.

From the corner of her eye, she sees Toby. Her stomach flips.

'I'm OK,' she says. 'I'll call you later.'

She's unexpectedly grateful to see Toby. Alfie has not lost his dad. Her suspicions about Toby seem less credible in the light of day, faced with the fact of his presence and the way he's smiling sweetly at her.

'Hello,' he says. 'What the hell's been going on? Are you all right? You look terrible.'

He kisses her cheek.

'Something happened,' she says. She doesn't know where to start or how to explain everything. 'I want to go home.' She begins to cry.

'OK. Don't cry, Ruthie. That's fine. We can go home. What happened?'

She loves him for understanding, for not questioning her but agreeing to take her away from here, but when he tries to hug her, she finds herself going rigid.

Emily and Jayne confer with the driver of the town car.

'I got a message from Paul,' he says. His expression is defensive. 'I didn't speak to him. It was yesterday.'

'Yesterday? At what time?'

'I'll find it for you if you like,' he says. He checks his phone. 'Here it is. He sent it at 11:03 yesterday. Friday morning. Telling me just to bring this chap Toby up here.'

'He sent it when we were in the car on our way,' Jayne says.

Why didn't Mark or Paul try to call us if they already knew by then that they weren't coming today? she wonders. Both would have known that we'd still be on the road and easily contactable. She checks her own phone again, wondering if she missed a call or message from Mark, but she didn't. Not on any of the platforms.

The driver reads out Paul's message.

"'Hi Tony. It's Paul. About the car tomorrow. There's been a small change to arrangements. Same time, same route, but it's going to be one passenger instead of three. Just the pick-up for Toby Land. Thanks, mate.'"

He looks at Jayne and Emily. 'And there was a last-minute address change. Mr Land texted to ask me to collect him from Addison Court this morning.'

Jayne frowns. Addison Court is a familiar address, but it's not Ruth's home address. She's sure it's in Bristol but can't place it precisely at this moment. She can't imagine it's Toby's sister's address either, because she lives on a houseboat in the Wiltshire countryside.

Emily makes him show it to her. 'I don't understand,' she says. 'Was that it? No more messages?'

'That's it.'

He looks upset. 'There's not a problem, is there? I did what I was asked to do. Paul's always been happy with my work.'

'No,' Emily says. 'You're fine. Are you going back to Bristol now? Can you take me? Please? I'll make sure you get paid extra.'

"'Course I can,' he says. 'But I'd like to get going asap if you don't mind.'

Emily doesn't hesitate. She climbs into his car. Before shutting the door, she looks at Jayne. 'My bag,' she says. 'Please?' And Jayne understands that she's not invited to share this ride.

She fetches the bag and watches as the car backs down the lane and its headlamps disappear into the fog.

Imogen's crying. She's been crying for a while, almost silently apart from the odd small hiccup.

It makes me feel awkward. I sit opposite her, and I repeat, 'I am your father. Your daddy.'

It's as if she doesn't hear me, though I know she can. She keeps looking between me and the digital clock on the oven, obsessively checking the time. I suppose she wants to know if Edie will be back soon.

I hoped very much that this moment, when I revealed our true relationship, would be different. I had intended to wait until I had the results of the DNA test so that I could present them to her as a way of delivering the momentous news, so that it was proven.

I've fantasised so often about watching her read the results in front of me and finding out that way that I can hardly believe I've just denied myself that pleasure. And now I know I should have stuck to my plan because she's distracted and the moment isn't going how I want it to, and how stupid and impulsive am I when the results are due later today?

I'm angry with myself but I try to focus on her, on how she's feeling. I desperately want to be a good parent in this moment.

Her growing concern about Edie is exquisitely moving, in its way. It makes me hope she'll be as eager for me to return to her one day.

But it's a distraction.

I need her to grasp the facts of our new situation and the shocked expression on her face tells me that's not happening. She hasn't absorbed the news.

I understand that it might be because I frightened her earlier, and I blame myself for that. I hate it when that happens. It's always a cause of bitter regret.

If I can say one thing for my wife, it's that she's never shown any fear of me. Rather, and I'm not sure where she gets this from – possibly because of what she's been through personally – she brings a loving approach to our union where others in the past have sometimes run scared.

There's very little else to recommend my wife, though. Her self-delusion about the state of our marriage is remarkably immature. She believes we're happy together; she plans for our future. It's an extraordinary misapprehension. Though it has suited me because it makes her very tolerable as a partner. But what kind of ambitious man settles for tolerable?

The forced march back from the railway track was a terrible idea in retrospect, an unforgivable loss of control on my part. But my anger has ebbed now, and I will apologise for what happened.

I move slowly and cautiously to sit beside her, so as not to provoke alarm. 'Hey,' I say, once I'm in place. Her face is crumpled and sad. She makes to get up. 'Stay,' I say. She draws her legs away from me, hugging them. 'I'm sorry for dragging you back home earlier, but I was worried! You have to admit your behaviour was concerning. Why'd you run off and hide like that, sweetheart?'

She won't look at me. She's sniffing as she cries now, which isn't as enchanting as the hiccups. Her sniffs are so loud and replete with what I take to be self-pity that they almost sound like snorts. It's unattractive and it annoys me because she's not the only one suffering here. But I make another effort.

'It's a good thing I remember all your old hiding places,' I say. 'Or I wouldn't have found you on the railway line. What would Mum say if she got home and I'd lost you?'

'I'm seventeen,' she says, her voice almost as steely as her mother's can be, though I detect a little shake in it. 'I don't get lost. Why are you being like this?'

'I'm only looking out for you and I've said I'm sorry.'

'You can go now,' she says.

'It's polite to acknowledge an apology.'

She says nothing.

'I was going to leave you earlier, but I certainly don't feel comfortable doing it now. What if you run off again? No, I shouldn't go until your mum gets here.' And when Edie doesn't arrive, Imogen will beg me to stay.

'Go away!'

My focus loosens at the periphery of my vision in my left eye and my hands feel twitchy, loaded with violence. If I'd spoken to my dad like that, I would have got a slap, at the very least. But I won't be like him. I take deep breaths.

Looking at my daughter, I understand that I need to back off for now and leave her alone for a while. If I don't, she'll become too afraid of me. She's bright and vulnerable and today hasn't gone how I wanted it to, but it is salvageable if I can appear to give her what she wants. But I need her to let me do one thing for her before I go. We can't leave each other with bad feelings unresolved.

'I tell you what,' I say. 'I still really want to make you that hot chocolate – you know, the one I was making when you ran away – and if you'll let me this time, I'll leave you alone for a while when it's done, because I need to pop home. But I'll come back later to cook supper for you and Mum. Does that sound good?'

I see a wary flicker of hope in her eye. I'm encouraged.

'OK,' she says. 'But I don't need a hot chocolate. A glass of water's fine.'

'I'll make it.'

'I—'

I cut her off. 'I'd like to.' My voice, unfortunately, comes out a little too loud and perhaps too harshly. But this is important.

She nods. 'OK,' she says.

'It'll be nice.'

'Great!' she says, though the word sounds hollowed out. But her cheeks twitch, eking her mouth up into an echo of a smile. That's better! She's trying now. If we both try, everything will be fine.

I make the drink. There's just enough milk left after the disaster with my earlier attempt. I'll have to go shopping and bring some more back with me later.

I watch her have her first sip. The drug will take effect soon. It's a slightly smaller dose than before. I just want her too dozy to leave the house, not necessarily unconscious for hours, because when the DNA results arrive, I'm going to present them to her just the way I planned originally, and we'll have a version of that beautiful moment together after all.

She takes another small sip.

'I'll see you later then,' I say. 'I'll lock the door on my way out.'

I have keys to Edie's house. We all do.

Ruth sits in the farmhouse front room. It's simply furnished. A cat naps on a sofa upholstered in red. She and Jayne and Toby are going to leave as soon as she feels ready.

She has sobered up and her hangover is crushing. Trying to process everything that's happened is beyond her just now. She feels numb.

Toby looks at the letter.

'I don't know what to say,' he says. 'I'm speechless. I can't believe Edie would do a thing like this. It really is a bit much.'

'A bit much?' The phrase infuriates Jayne. 'Don't make excuses for her. It's unforgivable. Emily is injured and Ruth . . . ' Her voice tails off. She's not sure how much of last night Ruth will want Toby to know about. They haven't given him all the details yet.

'Where are Mark and Paul?' Ruth spits. 'Did you ask yourself that since you read this?'

Jayne has been trying and trying to phone Mark, but still he isn't picking up.

'Of course I have! But I'm sure there's a reasonable explanation.' He looks at them. 'What? I'm sorry. I'm trying to catch up with what's happened, but for what it's worth, I'm sure Edie is not a murderer. Come on. She's a prankster, we all know that. You girls have got yourselves in a terrible state about it and I'm sorry for that but—'

'How dare you,' Ruth says. Her voice is quiet, but furious. 'We're not girls, and you have no idea what it was like. Get out. Go and pack up the car. We're leaving.'

She's never spoken to him like this before. He opens his mouth to respond but can't find the words. 'I'm sorry,' he says, and leaves.

Ruth's eyes turn to Jayne.

'The gun,' Jayne says. 'Please don't tell anyone I brought it with me. I'm so sorry. I feel so stupid.'

'I won't,' Ruth says. She means it. 'If you don't mention that I got so drunk and so lost and pointed it at you. Quid pro quo.'

'Of course. But we need to talk about it. The drinking, I mean. Not now, but soon.'

'I want to tell you something now.' Ruth knows that if she leaves here, she'll fall back into her old ways of keeping everything hidden. And after confessing to Jayne how Toby feels about Alfie last night, she's ready to share more. This, right here, is a moment she can't let slip away.

She's been thinking about Jayne's confession on the hillside, about the gun and Jayne's plans for it, about Jayne and Mark's struggles. It's emboldened Ruth.

And seeing Toby, who up here in this place suddenly strikes her as so ineffectual, so disconnected from the raw business of life, so furtive behind that bookish facade, so genteelly horrible to Ruth and therefore so possibly the sort of man to be living a darker existence away from their home, only encourages her.

If I don't say it here and now, she thinks, I'll never have the courage again.

She looks at the doorway, the space where Toby just stood and the hallway beyond. It's empty. From a few doors down, they can hear William Elliott's voice on the phone.

Ruth beckons to Jayne. 'I want to tell you something in return for what you told me,' she says. 'I can't keep it to myself any longer.' Jayne sits next to her and leans in. In a low, urgent voice, Ruth explains her fears about Toby. Her suspicions, his altered behaviour since she fell pregnant, the other small proofs she's accumulated, including the biggest of those: Lexi MacKay's Degas letter.

Jayne listens. When Ruth has finished, the silence in the room feels to Ruth as if it's pulsating in her ears.

'Toby was supposed to be staying with his sister last night, right?' Jayne says.

Ruth nods.

'Where does she live?'

'In Honeystreet, in Wiltshire.'

'What's the street name?'

'There isn't one. It's a houseboat. You park at the pub nearby.'

Jayne lowers her voice further.

'When I was with Emily and the driver outside earlier,' Jayne says, 'the driver said that Toby messaged this morning asking to be picked up from an address that wasn't your home, and it didn't sound like a Honeystreet address either.'

Ruth feels ice cold. 'Do you remember what he said?' she asks.

'Addison Court.'

'Did you look it up?'

Jayne nods.

Ruth blinks back tears. 'What's there?' But she thinks she already knows. It's a well-known address in the centre of the city because the development was controversial. It's near the University of Wessex, where Toby works. It's only a block long, and that block is occupied by one building, which the street is named after.

Jayne shows her phone to Ruth.

'Addison Court Student Accommodation' is the first result in her search. It is described as 'Bristol's best new student accommodation for undergraduates'.

Ruth stares at the page on Jayne's phone. She feels vindicated and horrified.

And Jayne feels as if her world is being turned upside down. If they're wondering if this is who Toby is, then should they believe that Edie can be a murderer?

Is Mark in danger?

She gets up and goes to stare out of the window, wanting a moment to breathe. To think. She cannot lose Mark. Her life will fall apart.

Where is he? What the hell has Edie done?

She sees another set of headlamps crawl through the fog into the farmyard, and her heart leaps, because it might be Mark, but a moment later it's obvious that it's a police car and she thinks, They must be here to tell me that Mark is dead.

In the car, outside Edie's house, I take a moment. I need to collect my feelings. If I'm honest, I'm exhausted.

Being in Edie's house wasn't easy. She was and always will be the love of my life.

My most precious memory of her is a night, long ago, which we spent by the beach.

Eighteen years ago, the gang stayed in a cottage near the coast in Wales owned by a friend of Toby's family. It was our first weekend away together. We were lent the cottage because we couldn't afford to rent anywhere. Nobody had any money back then.

Rob and Edie had only recently got together. I don't think I was the only one to be surprised. All of us men had been vying for her, in our way, and she'd flirted back with each of us. If you were feeling uncharitable, you could say she'd strung us along. And then, one day, out of the blue, she announced that Rob was the one for her. It was a shock, to say the least.

Their relationship changed us all. We all had to work hard to get used to it, which was more difficult for some of us than others. By the time we went to the cottage for the weekend, Edie and Rob had been a couple for a little over a year.

I say cottage, but actually it was a very basic place, practically a hovel, but it was magical because it was only a stone's throw from the sea.

It was our final evening. We'd spent three blissful days and two nights there, Edie was asleep on a daybed, partly covered by a gauzy scarf she'd worn across her shoulders earlier. Beneath it I could see her silky dress, and the way it draped over her body drove me crazy. I stood close and my parched eyes drank in the sight of her.

I'd been in love with her since the first day we met in school.

The others were on the beach. I'd watched them step down from the rickety terrace together and make their way towards the ocean. Moonlight silvered the fine sand and whitened the surf. They settled beside the rocks, huddled lazy and relaxed around a fire.

On the coffee table in front of Edie, a green marble ashtray containing three discarded cigarette butts, each pink with her lipstick. I picked one up and pocketed it.

I loved to see Edie smoke. It intoxicated me. I thought of her as a diva – not a modern diva but an old-fashioned Hollywood type. She would look fantastic in a black-and-white movie.

I feasted my eyes on her as she lay there. I stood so long in the half-dark that, eventually, touching her didn't seem wrong at all, but natural.

The back of her knee was pale, almost glowing. I ran my fingertips down her thigh towards that soft hollow of skin. She was a work of art, every bit of her.

She stirred, her thighs moved, one over the other, and I sank my hand between them. She didn't repel me when she opened her eyes and saw me, there was no shock in her expression, and, encouraged, I knelt beside her, and my heart skipped a beat as I felt her thighs tighten. She held my face, and I did the same to her. It was beautiful.

She told me she'd been fitted with a coil, and we made love, and the whole time our bodies moved together I could hear our friends on the beach, distant and so other. I laughed out loud as I came. I felt ecstatic. Her fingers pushed hard against my bitten lips. She shook her head and whispered, 'Shh. This has to stay our secret.'

My greedy eyes watched as she walked towards the bathroom. I thought of her cleaning herself up in there, wiping me from her. The intimacy was almost overwhelming. Years of wanting something and here it was, and it didn't disappoint.

When she re-emerged I opened my arms to her; just a few moments more was all I wanted but she walked past me, not even breaking her stride as she grabbed her scarf from the floor and draped it around her shoulders.

I hastily did up my shorts and followed her as far as the deck. She broke my heart as she strode down the beach towards the others and didn't look back and I felt cold all over in spite of the warm evening. She settled down beside Rob. I knew it was him. I recognised his silhouette. He put his arm around her, and she leaned into him.

I was hurting as I stood on the deck watching. I had just felt as if I had been brought alive, had just had one of the most incredible experiences of my life, but to her it was nothing. When that sank in, an involuntary shudder shook me from top to bottom and my thoughts became dark, slithering like hagfish. It was the first time I wished that Rob was dead.

I quelled the thought immediately, of course. It shocked and appalled me and I recognised that it was heinous. I resolved to put it away for good and to live my own life. I would stay close to Edie and that would be enough.

And for a long time I was successful. I got on with living. When Edie's pregnancy began to show, I didn't connect it to me. I was young, busy and, in retrospect, stupid. The timings were suggestive but nothing in Edie's behaviour led me to suspect that I might be the father. And when Imogen was first born everybody said how much she looked like Rob. I agreed. It wasn't until she grew bigger, and her baby features receded, that her resemblance to Edie took over and any sign of Rob was obliterated as she bloomed into a clone of her mother.

It was only this year, back in spring, when I learned that Rob was infertile that I began to join up the dots. Edie used me, I thought, to make a child. She hadn't been fitted with a coil. That was a lie because her husband was infertile, and they didn't want to admit it.

What was crystal clear to me was that she chose me to father her child. It was remarkable. Thrilling. I examined the idea from every angle to see if I could be wrong, but it made sense.

Rob probably was a better partner for her, perhaps a little easier, funnier, but it was me who she chose for the most important job of all. It was the ultimate compliment.

Why didn't she tell me? I don't know. In the moment after I choked the life from her body, I thought that I should have asked her. But it was too late.

Never mind. My life is about focusing on the positives now. About self-care and care for my daughter. I reflect on how perfect it seems now, that in the moments after Edie and I conceived Imogen, I first thought of killing Rob.

I believe my murderous impulse was a premonition of sorts. A hint as to what was to come in my life. It took me over seventeen years to interpret it. But better late than never.

I take a deep breath and feel strength return to my body and, with it, resolve that I'm on the right path. Imogen will be happy to join me on it, when I prove my paternity to her.

I feel very calm. The breathing is hypnotic. In. Out. I look at Edie's house and it looks back at me, squat and tidy, and reassures me. My little darling is safe in there and doubtless sleepy by now, possibly already in the Land of Nod. That's good.

I won't be too long.

I just have to deal with my wife. I've heard from her. She's on her way back.

Emily clutches the driver's phone. They're sitting in A & E just outside Newcastle. The pain in her ankle was so bad by the time they reached the city that she begged him to stop and wait while she got it seen to and got some painkillers.

The driver has Paul's number and he's kindly lent her his phone so she can keep trying to reach him. Every so often, the driver receives a text message from his wife, and the phone pings which shoots a lightning bolt of hope through Emily. Until she reads it.

Emily has been assessed by a nurse and had an X-ray of her ankle. Now she's waiting for them to fit a surgical boot. Then they can go.

She's jealous of the driver's messages from his wife. They're asking what he wants for dinner. Emily longs for the domestic mundanity, the normality.

When they're done at A & E, they pull into traffic. The satnav estimates four hours and six minutes to get home. If Paul doesn't call, she doesn't know how she's going to survive it.

'I need you to put your foot down, mate,' she tells the driver. He nods. She tries not to weep.

She considers whether she should phone the police and report Paul missing. Is it too soon? Will they take her seriously?

Minutes later, she feels the effect of the painkillers and her eyelids droop.

As the driver accelerates on to the M1, heading south, she can't stop herself falling asleep.

Jayne exhales. Of course the police aren't here to tell her Mark is dead. They're here for William Elliott. She finds him in a small office at the back of the farmhouse.

He's holding a photograph of his parents, on their wedding day. They look splendid in sixties fashion.

'They never fell out of love,' he says. 'If I can have a marriage like theirs, I'll be a lucky man.'

She feels a lump in her throat.

'I'm so sorry.'

'He shot himself,' William says. 'It wasn't an accident.'

'I'm sorry,' she repeats.

Times like this she feels as if she's back in the military, the mistress of sparse phrases, well used precisely because they contain the minimum of emotion. She wants to collapse on his shoulder, to draw him in tight, to say, 'I know how much pain you're feeling.' But she can't. She's not built that way. He probably would not want her to fuss over him like that.

'Your colleagues are here,' she says.

He follows her outside. Toby is loading their bags into the rental car. Ruth is already sitting in the back.

'We might have further questions for you,' William says. 'I don't know.'

'Your mum has my details.'

He nods and leaves her.

She is desperate to get away for herself, to find Mark, but also to give Maggie and William the space they'll need once John's body has been brought down from the peak where the burial chamber is situated.

When she heard John died at that location, she couldn't help feeling more personally involved. Her plans for burying the gun, for her and Mark to experience a sort of catharsis in that precise spot, seem like an intrusion on this family now, and so very wrong.

What was she thinking, wanting to dump her trauma on land that meant so much to someone else? How could she have thought it was OK to appropriate something so sacred to another?

She feels guilt. For being here with a bundle of selfish motives. For the trouble Emily caused the family last night and Ruth this morning.

Would John Elliott have killed himself if this chain of events hadn't led him up to the burial chamber at that moment?

Possibly. Probably. He had brought a gun with him. Maybe.

Jayne watches from the doorway as William crosses the yard and shakes the hand of an older officer. The man claps his hand on William's shoulder.

'We're ready,' Toby says. Jayne sighs. It's going to be a long drive and she doesn't feel up to it. She asks Toby to take the wheel and she slips into the passenger seat. Ruth takes the back seat and lies down across it.

Toby isn't a confident driver. He brakes too hard and too late, panics when he has to change lanes. He starts talking about the letter a couple of times. One minute saying it's obviously a hoax, the next mulling over the language in it as if he's taking it more seriously. Once, he asks her to phone Paul, and he looks worried when Jayne can't get hold of him.

She feels as if she's in shock. It's all she can do to listen to him, let alone respond. There is so much to process. Last night. What Ruth has just told her.

She tries to call Edie, because Jayne wants to give her a piece of her mind. But Edie's phone rings to voicemail too.

She thinks of Emily, riding home alone in Paul's car, and doesn't know what to think about that.

Her eyes fix dully on the motorway – the glare, the spatter, the speed – and the sound of the solitary bullet fired by John Elliott repeats in her head.

She tries to rest. What little sleep she got last night was terrible quality. But she can't relax.

Out of the corner of her eye, she's also aware of Toby continually checking the rear-view mirror which he's angled to get a glimpse of Ruth in the back.

He seems worried. About her?

Jayne's not sure.

But she does wonder, Who is he really?

The town car pulls into Emily and Paul's driveway.

Her home looks as beautiful as ever. It was Paul's originally, but she's never wanted to move. She loves it. It's newly constructed on the site of an old bungalow that Paul demolished and rebuilt as a two-storey home. He kept the original gardens, which had been beautifully landscaped. It's in a quiet, leafy suburb. Emily loved that he's never lived there with anyone else apart from her. She also loves the home itself. There's a lot of glass at the back, and it's full of light.

Paul's car isn't in its usual spot on the driveway. Emily swallows. The driver carries her bag to the door and waits while she unlocks it.

'Just put it in the hall,' she says. 'Thanks.'

The door dislodges a pile of mail as it opens. Paul would have picked it up if he'd been here this morning. Emily feels her fear like a cold trickle down her spine.

'Hope the ankle recovers soon. Do you need me any more?' The driver wants to go.

'No. I'm fine. Thank you for everything,' she says. 'My husband will be in touch to make sure you're paid for the extra time in the hospital, and for driving me home.'

He nods and walks away with a spring in his step. The end of a job. Time to go home to his life.

Emily wants to grab his sleeve and hold him tightly, keep him here. She's afraid. But he's done enough. She waves goodbye and turns and calls for Paul.

The house breathes silently around her in response. It's empty, she can sense it, a skill learned in childhood. Opening her front door as a kid had a measure of risk in it and she feels the same creep of trepidation now.

The sound of the car leaving makes her feel vulnerable. She regrets not begging the driver to come inside with her, just to check everything's OK.

'Paul!' she calls, again.

She clumps through the downstairs rooms in the surgical boot they gave her at A & E. Late-afternoon sun spills through the windows at the back of the house. The kitchen is clean and tidy, just how she left it, but that doesn't tell her much. Paul's a neat freak. He could have cooked a roast in here since she left, and it would look like this.

It's a slow ascent upstairs. He's not there either. She gets sick of calling his name. Every time he doesn't reply her anxiety levels hike up.

She has to pee.

As her bladder empties, she thinks, something's different in here.

She touches a towel on the heated rail. It's not the one she put out last week. That was one of the new, fluffy blue towels that match the bathmat. This towel is green. And the bathmat is draped over the side of the bath, not on the rail, where she left it.

Somebody has used this room. Paul hates taking baths, though, so who?

Edie? But why?

She stands and flushes. She'll call the police right away and report Paul missing. Enough is enough. She can't handle this on her own any longer. It's doing her head in.

A noise catches her attention. It sounds like the front door opening.

Hope and relief swell in her, messy, uncontrolled feelings. 'Paul?' Her voice shakes.

She hobbles on to the landing.

The front door slams shut.

'Paul?' she repeats, but all she can hear is silence.

*

They arrive at Ruth and Toby's house first. A Victorian semi in the middle of the city. Jayne gets out of the car so she can move into the driver's seat to take herself home.

The goodbyes are perfunctory and tense. 'Let me know as soon as you've heard from Mark,' Ruth says.

Jayne wonders if she should feel guilty about leaving Ruth, but if Toby has done something terrible it cannot be unpicked immediately. And Ruth looks ill. She needs to be home, in bed, to recover and Jayne is desperate to get to her own home to see if Mark is there, if he's left her a note, if there's any sign of him at all.

As Jayne puts on her seat belt, she watches Toby hold their front door open for Ruth. Ruth doesn't make eye contact as she brushes past him.

In the moment before she turns on the ignition, Jayne hesitates, considering knocking on their door and asking Ruth if she wants to come with Jayne to her house.

Something has rattled her about seeing them disappear into their home with such grim faces, seeing the door slam behind them. It's not a premonition of violence, exactly; more the thought of what can go on behind closed doors, when nobody else is watching. But she tells herself off. This is her own mind jittering because Edie has infected them all with the idea of violence and John Elliott's suicide has compounded it.

She needs to find Mark. That is her priority.

She heads home, hands tight on the wheel.

Their house is on a quiet, tree-lined street. Jayne wanted to live somewhere away from the sirens and noise of the city centre, to avoid PTSD triggers. It's an unremarkable sixties house, but relatively spacious inside, with large windows letting in a lot of natural light and a generous garden. Nothing fancy, but a place where she feels safe.

The drive is empty but that means nothing because their car might be in the garage. She unlocks the front door. There's mail in the cage mounted on the back of it, but that means nothing either. The job of collecting and opening it always falls to Jayne.

She pushes the door shut behind her and, as it closes with a soft click, the hair on the back of her neck stands up. Someone is here. She can sense it.

She glances left and right, down the hallway and up the stairs, and sees nothing out of the ordinary, no movement in the corner of her eye – hears nothing either. Her mouth feels sticky as her lips part. She intends to call out to Mark. It must be him. But before she can make a sound, she becomes aware of the scent, a perfume of some sort, an unmistakably bright, feminine, fragrance. It prickles her nostrils.

Edie?

Who else could it be?

Ruth slept most of the way home in the car and, as the front door of their home closes behind her and Toby, she's overwhelmed by a feeling of disorientation and claustrophobia.

In spite of the tragedy of what happened to the Elliott family, she knows she should feel as if she won the lottery this morning. Toby was the husband who arrived, after all. Mark and Paul are uncontactable. If the letter is to be believed, then Ruth is one of the lucky wives. If the letter is a hoax this is true too, because she's the first wife to be put out of the misery of wondering, What if?

But she feels no relief at all, except on Alfie's behalf.

Clutter and mess seem to close in on her as she walks through their house. In the kitchen she fills a tumbler of water and drinks greedily. It spills down her chin. Laundry has dried crisp and crumpled over a clothes rack in the corner, shoes are piled in a messy heap in the hallway. Washing-up lies waiting for attention. The highchair needs a wipe and traces of Alfie's last meal here before Ruth's mum picked him up are all over the kitchen floor.

When did I start letting everything go? Ruth wonders. When did the chaos of early motherhood segue into neglect? Neglect by her standards, anyhow. She would never have left the house in this state earlier in her marriage.

Where has Toby gone? When they came in, he slipped upstairs quietly. After everything she thought about him while she was away, it feels horrible to be alone with him now.

It's as if the air in the house has thinned, as if this place no longer harbours them but has conspired to ruin them, turned them into people she hardly recognises compared to the couple they were when they met.

She guzzles another glass of water.

A creak from above tells her that Toby is in the upstairs bathroom.

She thinks about going up there and confronting him with everything she suspects about him. She has to, now that she's told Jayne. She can't bury it any longer.

She remembers the shock on Jayne's face and wonders if she can trust Jayne not to tell anyone else. Jayne will tell Mark, for sure. Unless Mark's dead.

But Ruth finds it hard to connect to her earlier fear about the letter, since she has Toby with her and after what happened to the Elliott family.

So much has happened in such a short time. She feels as if her whole life has been turned upside down.

And she realises her fear only felt real when she thought that Toby was likely to be Edie's victim. She never considered whether the other two husbands might be in danger.

It seems impossible now. The letter is definitely a hoax.

What an unbelievably reckless thing for Edie to have done. A dangerous thing. A catalyst for a chain of events that has ended in a real tragedy. Her head is so muddled that she struggles to work out whether John Elliott's suicide would have happened anyway. Shamefully, there is so much that she doesn't remember about last night. She wonders if Emily will ever talk to her or Jayne again, after this.

And as for her own behaviour. The guilt and embarrassment are overwhelming. Did she really point a loaded gun at her friend this morning?

I need help, Ruth thinks, and admitting this to herself gives rise to more feelings of panic and claustrophobia. She is afraid of what needs to be done next, to put everything right. She's afraid of the confessions and confrontations that must happen and is unsure if she has the courage to face up to any of it.

She wants her domestic dream to be intact. She'd give anything to make it so.

She wants Alfie home, desperately wants him. She'll call her mum and tell her they're back early but not go into the detail of why. She'll just say she felt unwell, but she's better now and can cope with the baby.

But shouldn't she confront Toby first? She should. She will. They'll have a talk. Now. It'll be calm. They're in a difficult situation but perhaps he can explain everything, and it will all be innocent, and life can go on and Ruth can get help and this will eventually be a blip in their relationship that they can forget, or look back on as a challenge they overcame. Together.

I'll go upstairs now, she thinks. And say something.

She looks at the wine rack on top of the fridge. It's empty. Which is a shame because a drink would help her get through this conversation. Never mind.

I'll talk to Toby gently, she thinks, so he doesn't feel as if I'm flinging terrible accusations at him, so he knows I love him and doesn't suspect that I've been so horrified by what he might have done before talking to him about it.

She opens a pantry cupboard. On the top shelf, amongst old bottles of soy sauce and cider vinegar, she sees some cooking brandy.

Toby and I are rational people, professionals, we love each other, we're parents. We can have a calm dialogue about this. He'll explain to me why I'm wrong but understand why I'm asking.

She reaches for the bottle. It'll take the edge off her nerves, calm the trembling that seems to have taken hold of her whole body.

As she reaches, she catches a whiff of body odour. Gross, she thinks. I need a shower. Perhaps I'll take one first and then talk to him. It can't be a civilised conversation if I'm unkempt and smelly. If I disgust myself I'll surely disgust him too.

Her firm belief that there are limits to other people's tolerance of her, that she will offend or upset them if her behaviour is just a little off-kilter, means that the idea of presenting like this, of having been like this for most of today, even though she could hardly bathe at either of the Elliotts' properties while they were going through such horror of their own, repulses her. And she expects it to repulse Toby too. To reinforce his physical and emotional rejection of her.

She unscrews the lid of the brandy and puts it to her lips. Drinks. The liquid burns its way down her throat. She coughs.

'Ruth,' Toby says. 'What are you doing?'

She turns. He's behind her, his back to the light and his face in shadow. He's angry. Disappointed in her. Disbelieving that he's caught her like this. This, she knows, even before he speaks.

'You said you wouldn't do this any more,' he says. 'You said . . .' He raises his hand in a gesture of frustration before letting it fall, giving up on her. 'You stank of booze when I arrived this morning, and you still do.'

She looks at the bottle in her hand. 'I was just . . .' she starts to say but she has no lie ready, no explanation. 'I repulse you,' she says.

'What?'

She changes tack. 'It was the letter, Edie's letter. It started everything.' This isn't how it's supposed to be. She's supposed to be confronting him, not defending herself. And yet she feels she has to. 'You don't know what it was like,' she adds. Even to her ears, she sounds pathetic.

He tries to take the bottle from her. They tussle briefly over it, but her heart isn't in the fight and she lets go. She knows where another bottle is hidden.

'I think I know you better than you know yourself.' His sad expression enrages her. What does he know about her at all? Has he ever recognised her as a mother?

She watches him empty the bottle down the sink, and the way he does it, with his jaw set firm as if he's so superior to her, and the way he gives the bottle a final shake to get rid of every last drop, feels so purposeful and cruel, as if he wants to twist some final, desperate, craving feelings out of her and thwart them. The punishment aspect of it is unbearable and she says, 'I know you've been grooming younger women.'

He turns. The expression on his face is incredulous.

'Not this again,' he says.

'Where were you this morning?' she asks. 'I know you didn't get picked up from home, or from your sister's house.'

'Fuck you, Ruth. After everything.'

'Tell me!' she screams, and it feels as if all the frustrations and fears she's ever felt meet in that moment, as if in those two words she's letting the world know that she can't bear anything any longer.

He stares at her as if she's lost her mind. Her chest is heaving. The sense that this is the moment when everything comes out, when nothing is repressed any longer and she is as raw as she can be, is terrifying and also electrifying and she takes pleasure when she sees that she's got to him, that there is something as crazy and hurt in the backs of his eyes as there is in hers.

He throws the brandy bottle across the room and it smashes in the corner, into brutal shards of thick glass that please Ruth. We're finally our true selves, she thinks. She's forgotten she's even a mother. She's just a woman, facing a man and wondering why she ever let it come to this.

'I cannot deal with this,' he says.

When he walks out of the room, towards the front door, she feels as if he's robbing her of something, as if he's snatching a moment of catharsis from her and leaving her surrounded, as ever, by the casual, relentless rebuke of domestic debris that is hers to clear up, in the cage of their home.

The door slams behind him and she screams as long and as loudly as if she is no stronger than the shaking feral version of herself that Jayne discovered this morning, alone in the fog on the moor.

And in the heavy silence that falls over the house afterwards, she thinks, I'm not fit to be a mother, and if she's sure of one thing, it's that her failure is Toby's fault because he will not hear her or see her or touch her, and she's suffocating in the void that leaves her in.

Jayne inhales again, deeply. The scent is strong. It's not going away. There's no mistaking that it's lingering in the house.

It has, surely, to do with Edie.

For the first time since she read the letter at Dark Fell Barn, every last scrap of Jayne's rationality deserts her and she feels truly, viscerally afraid that Edie might have harmed Mark.

And she's not sure if she's alone in this house.

Her gun is right at the bottom of her bag. The bag is at her feet. But Jayne can't risk the time and noise it'll cost her to extract it, let alone to load it, and she reaches, instead, for a brass doorstop on the floor beside her.

It's a beloved object, in the shape of a shire horse, and now a weapon. Moving almost silently, it doesn't take her long to reassure herself that the downstairs rooms are empty, and the back door is locked securely. All the while, the sense that someone else is in the building grows.

Back in the hall, she looks up the stairs. Holding the brass horse by the neck, she climbs, taking care not to step on the tread that creaks, all her senses straining to protect her. At the top, she pauses.

Silence. No movement. The smell lingers up here though. It might even be a little stronger than it was downstairs.

Her bedroom door is nearest to her, almost closed, and she pushes it gently. It swings open far enough that she can see the room is unoccupied, and she steps in to where she has a view of the en suite, which is empty too. She backs out on to the landing and checks the spare room.

The bed is unmade. Her first, unwelcome, shocking thought is that this is an affair, that Mark's boyhood crush has survived into adulthood and he's fallen back in love with Edie, or never fallen out of love with her, and they've made love here. She imagines their bodies together. His hands on Edie. The pain of this possible betrayal feels like a punch in the abdomen.

The scent is stronger here and she has an impulse to sniff the bedlinen that's simultaneously irresistible yet repulsive. She doesn't do it but backs out of the room, turning suddenly when she reaches the doorway, realising with an extra jolt of fear that she'd dropped her guard for a moment. Adrenalin courses through her but also betrayal and anger and worry for Mark.

Where is he? The brass horse feels heavy in her hand. There's one more room to check. She enters the spare bathroom with breath held, but it, too, is empty.

A sense of desolation hits her. She perches on the side of the bath and puts the horse down. All her life, Jayne has pushed forward, determined to fix things, confident that she can, that she knows her strengths. Her whole purpose since she met Mark – since he surprised her by asking her, the plainest girl in the room, on a date – has been this marriage, and the mending of this man.

He made a statement, she felt, when he picked her. He chose a woman who could help him, who could be his equal.

So, now what? If he is having an affair, then, to Jayne, a future in which he has been unfaithful is no better than one in which he is dead. Her sense of morality is powerful. Compromise is not an option.

But it's only a suspicion, a fantasy. Based on an unmade bed. And a scent. She reminds herself that she is not her most rational self. That the events of the past twenty-four hours have driven her to this.

Edie has driven all of them to the limits of their rationality and beyond.

Her fingers start to jitter, bouncing up and down on her thigh. What to do next? Visit Mark's office, maybe? Call other people? But who? His friends are the gang. She doesn't have numbers for his colleagues.

She becomes aware of damp seeping into the seat of her trousers. It's the bathmat, a thick, useless thing that never dries out properly in the in-between seasons.

Mark never takes a bath. He hates them. Jayne thinks for a moment and puts two and two together. She reaches for a bottle of bath oil that she was given last Christmas and has never been used. The top unscrews easily, and its scent is identical to the one she's detected in the house.

She knows who loves a bath: Edie. Doyenne of bathtime, she is, ready to tell you how many candles she lights around the tub, which novel she just couldn't stop reading until the water went cold, how it's the only way to warm her bones in winter, a home spa, just a *gorgeous* way to spend an hour because self-care is so important, don't you think? Jayne?

Jayne doesn't. Lying in a bath feels, to her, like wallowing in dirty water.

Her hands clench around the mat. The extent of the dampness suggests that the bath wasn't taken very recently. It's only a guess, but she reckons it was yesterday. And it stinks. It's the source of the smell, for sure. Edie must have spilled bath oil on it.

She drops the mat and kicks it into the corner, feeling a sudden surge of anger and an urge to trash the room. She wants cracked tiles, smashed fixtures, a broken mirror, every bottle and tube emptied or squeezed out on to the floor; she wants noise and mess and destruction to blot out reality. Sometimes she dissociates, and sometimes she loses control. And when she loses control, it's spectacular.

The sound of the front door interrupts her rising anger.

She hears a sharp intake of breath, her own. 'Mark?' she says, a whisper.

The door slams. The noise seems to reverberate through her.

She stands up.

'Mark?' she calls.

When she's sure he's left the house, Imogen tips the hot chocolate down the sink and swills her mouth out over and over. She only pretended to take a sip of the drink in front of him and he fell for it.

She's been thinking about it. He must have slipped her a roofie. It's the only explanation Imogen can come up with for what happened to her last night.

It's terrifying, but nothing else makes sense. She's never going to eat or drink anything he makes her again.

But if he drugged her before, why did he do it? She knows why women get roofied. But she woke up fully dressed, tucked up in bed. There was no soreness or pain, no suspicion that he'd touched her inappropriately. She's sure she wasn't violated.

But he drugged her for a reason. She just doesn't know what it is.

If she had her phone, she would call the police. What about her laptop? She remembers it suddenly, gratefully, and searches all over but can't find it. Edie must have taken it with her, she thinks, even though she's not strictly allowed tech at her retreat. But Edie's never been afraid to bend the rules when she wants to and she has a habit of borrowing the laptop when she gets frustrated with her iPad, which Imogen can't find either.

Everything feels wrong and Imogen's very unsure whether to stay in the house or not.

If she lived on a street like Jemma's, with rows of semis, she'd feel safer. She thinks about running to a neighbour's house but they're a way away and Edie and Rob never cultivated relationships with them. If she leaves via the front what's to say he won't be waiting outside on the lane, watching to see if she tries to run away again? She doesn't feel it's safe to go back to the railway line behind the house either, because he'll find her there just like he did before. And what will he do then? She's afraid to think of it. He's a psycho.

Where will she be safest? She doesn't know the answer, but she realises she's more afraid of leaving the house than of staying.

She checks the time. It's after six o'clock and her mum was due home any time from five thirty so she could be back any minute and all of this will go away. But what if he comes back before Edie does?

Her chest feels tight, her heart rate so fast she's afraid she'll faint, but she paces the house and double-checks that she put the chain on the door properly. Even with a key, he can't push past that. She'll watch the front of the house, and if he gets back before Edie, she'll hide.

She wishes they had a landline. Edie got rid of it. Too expensive, she said, and pointless because they got such good phone reception here.

Imogen looks at her arm. He held her so hard earlier that it still aches. She can see a constellation of small bruises, like shadows on her skin. She feels as if he's marked her. It's a violation.

The memory of his grip on her arm won't leave her. He could have killed me. It would have been easy for him.

Her dad was enjoying himself on holiday and he died. She thinks of his drowning sometimes. Did he have his eyes open, underwater? Did his hair waft gently around his head belying the violence of what was happening to him? Did he forget which way was up as the water tossed him around or was he dragged silently and relentlessly beneath the surface by the efficient, unforgiving current?

Her fingers go to her mum's ring, on her necklace. Why was it on the floor? Imogen is sure Edie would have said something if the ring had become loose.

Surely it's only a few minutes before Edie gets here and Imogen can ask her. She goes upstairs and pulls a chair up to the window in her mum's room. She'll watch the driveway. If he comes back before her mum does, she'll flee again. Or she'll hide.

It's the best she can think of.

She feels as if she's in a horror film. She's seen enough of them. The solitary young girl alone in a house. The ultimate vulnerable victim. Is this her? Now? Her sense of unreality is crazy. But she's never felt so afraid, or so alert.

The driveway out front is stubbornly empty.

She feels faint when she wants to feel brave and certain.

She runs through her options again. Go, or stay?

She can't get the idea out of her head that he's waiting for her, just out of sight, waiting to pounce, like he did before. She thinks he's gone mad.

For now, this feels like the safest place. The chain is on the door.

Perhaps he won't come back at all.

And Mum will be here soon, she will, any minute now.

*

'It's me,' he says. 'Sorry. Did I give you a fright?'

'Toby?' Emily says.

He's standing in her entrance way, passing a set of chinking keys from one hand to the other. He's let himself in. It shocks her. Paul and his friends all have copies of each other's house keys but that's in case of emergency. They don't do this. They don't just let themselves in.

'Is Paul here?' he asks.

'No.'

'Have you heard from him?'

There's something heightened about Toby that makes her deeply uneasy. He looks more dishevelled than usual. Red blotches have crept unevenly across his cheeks.

'No. Why did you let yourself in? Did you think I wasn't here?'

'I'm sorry. I should have called before I came.'

No, she wants to say. You should have rung the doorbell before you let yourself into my house. But she's slightly mollified by his apology.

'How's Ruth?' she asks.

'Oh, she's sleeping it off. She'll be OK.' He clears his throat, a sharp, awkward sound, glances upwards and blinks rapidly as if he's beating back tears. It's disturbing.

'What's wrong?' she asks.

He collects himself. 'I really need to speak to Paul.'

'He's not here. I was about to call the police to report him missing and tell them about the letter. Did you see the letter?'

'I did. Can we sit down?'

'I need to make the call.'

'I'd like to talk to you first. Please.'

'It'll have to wait.'

'No!' he says. 'We need to speak before you make the call.'

Her heart's thumping but she leads him into the sitting room where she perches on the edge of a chair in a way that signals that she is not getting comfortable and he sits on the sofa opposite her. He looks even more agitated, and she feels intensely claustrophobic, as if someone has turned the heat up in the room.

'Why are you here?' she asks.

'I was meant to meet Paul yesterday,' he says, 'but he didn't turn up.'

'Paul was working. That's why he didn't come up north yesterday.'

'He wasn't.'

She won't have this, not another person claiming that Paul's lied to her. 'No,' she says.

'Paul and I had made a different arrangement,' Toby says.

She stares at him. 'What arrangement?'

Toby looks past her, into the garden, avoiding her gaze. She notes how pale he is, how much he seems to be struggling to put what he wants to say into words. It scares the hell out of her. 'Well, this is embarrassing, and it's going to sound very odd, but I'm not at liberty to say. I've been asked to keep it a secret and I don't know how much Paul told you but that's something we take very seriously as a group of friends. We don't betray each other.'

She couldn't hate him more in that moment. Everything enrages her, his faux-conversational tone, the embarrassment he's affecting right now, as if they're discussing some minor mishap. This fucking so-called loyalty. Her voice feels as if it rises up out of her from somewhere animal.

'Tell me right now what's going on.'

'I can't.'

'What does Ruth say about this?'

'I couldn't tell her. Not in the state she's in today. She needs rest. Frankly, she's not been herself for a while now.'

'She's a drunk.'

He doesn't flinch. He knows. She wonders if he cares, then decides she's not interested in the state of their marriage. Paul is all she cares about.

'Toby,' she says. 'You're delusional about your friends. You only need to look at Edie's horrible letter to know that. Tell me right now what's going on because I'm telling you that Paul's in danger.' Her voice rises until she's shouting.

He puts up a hand, as if to instruct her to calm down. It enrages her more. She realises she's shaking – not obviously, not so he would notice, but beneath her skin, an unravelling is happening, as if she's physically reached the limits of her patience.

'No,' he says. 'You see, I don't think he truly is. The letter's a fraud. Edie would never do something like that. But I'm worried about him. Not that he's dead, that would be ridiculous.' She notices that he's begun to wring his hands, fingers, knuckles and palms all in constant, nervous motion. 'But I'm concerned because I thought I'd have heard from him by now, to say why he didn't turn up to meet me yesterday.'

She stands. Her balance is precarious. She needs more painkillers. 'I'm calling the police.'

'No. No, don't. Please, don't.'

She has to pass him to get out of the room, to reach the landline, which is in the hallway. His lips look bloodless. She limps a few steps. He stands. He's very close to her. Within easy striking distance. The mood in the room has changed. She feels a rush of fear.

'Don't be hasty,' he says.

'Get out of my way.'

She's never felt as vulnerable as she does now. I don't even know this man, she thinks. I don't know who he is, really, or what he might do. In the world she grew up in, any man has the potential for violence.

She tries to straighten up, to present herself as strong, as not cowed by him. Pain shoots up her leg.

He doesn't move.

'Toby,' she says. 'You're scaring me.'

Something passes across his expression. A calculation. It terrifies her even more. If she can't get to the phone, she's helpless. Nobody would hear her scream here. The house is large, the plot it's in is generous. The windows are closed.

'That is the last thing I want to do,' he says. 'I'm sorry, but something has happened, and I've been asked to keep it a secret and so I must.'

She makes another attempt to walk past him, to the phone.

He steps in even closer. He is standing way, way too close. 'Emily,' he says. She can feel his breath on her face. 'I said no to calling the police.'

She pushes him, lightly, out of her way and keeps going but he grabs her by the upper arm, and she braces herself. Here it comes, she thinks.

'I can show you something,' he says. 'Proof. Please, look.'

He lets go of her and fumbles in his pockets looking for something. She doesn't want to know. Toby has lied to her about Paul lying. They all want her to believe that Paul isn't the man she thinks he is and she only wants to make sure that Paul is OK. She hobbles towards the door as fast as she can, half-running, the pain so bad it makes her cry out.

She can see the landline on the console table in the hall. She is almost close enough to reach it when he grabs her again, harder this time, and he swings her around to face him. She shuts her eyes, waiting for the blow.

They're inches from each other. She's aware of him breathing as heavily as she is. She opens her eyes.

'Look,' he says. He holds his phone up close to her face.

'Read it!' he demands.

She tries, but everything on the screen swims in front of her eyes.

'Please,' she says.

He shakes her, just a little.

It begins, she thinks.

'I'm begging you,' he says. 'Read it.'

He pulls it back a little and she makes another effort to focus and sees a text from Paul to Toby, sent on Thursday.

Meet me tomorrow night at 8 on the waterfront outside the restaurant. It's important. Don't mention this to anyone else and don't let me down.

'But he didn't turn up last night,' Toby says. 'I lied to Ruth about this. I've broken her trust. I told her I had to help my sister last night because Paul told me to keep this a secret, but when I went to meet him, he wasn't there, and I haven't been able to get hold of him since. I'm worried about him. But, do you see? Paul wants this, whatever it is, to be kept a secret. So, please, don't call the police.'

His hand is digging into her shoulder and his face is so close to hers that it's lost its definition. Its component parts look horrifying. Big pores, nostril hair, shot veins in his cheek, the fat muscle of his tongue, eyes bloodshot and with pink, fleshy edges. He seems to Emily to be nothing more than an animal – a needy, dangerous animal.

She doesn't know what to do.

How do you trust a man who lies and who is hurting you?

Ruth pulls a bottle of vodka from the back of the airing cupboard. Toby hasn't found all her hiding places.

He won't answer his phone.

She stands at the threshold to his office. She's never searched in here before. She's been tempted, but the thought of doing it always felt too close to an admission that things are wrong in their marriage. It made her feel dirty and furtive. And what if she actually found something? She was always too afraid of what that might mean.

But not now.

She opens the door. The room is narrow and snug, a desk beneath the window and bookshelves lining one wall: floor to ceiling, big monographs of Impressionist artists and other academic volumes. She runs her fingers along their spines as she approaches his desk.

It has a set of three drawers beneath it.

She sits in his chair, and it's strange, as if she's feeling what it's like to be him. The view from the window is pleasant. She sees rooftops and chimneys, wires and a docile pigeon. Her mouth is very dry. She takes another swig of vodka.

The two top drawers open easily. They're stuffed with stationery, a support for Toby's wrist, some household paperwork and a few personal bits and pieces he inherited from his father.

The bottom drawer is locked. Ruth rattles it but it won't open. It makes her feel angry. Who is he locking it against? The baby's too little, they can't afford a cleaning lady, so it can only be her. She fetches a screwdriver and wedges it into the gap between the top of the drawer and the desktop. She doesn't know what she's doing and feels a sense of triumph when she's able to prise the lock open without much effort.

There's a single piece of paper inside. She pulls it out and studies it. It's an obituary.

Her heart skips a beat when she reads the name: Alexandra MacKay, known as Lexi. The young woman who wrote to Toby and made accusations against him.

Born in 1997 and died just over a month ago. The text is brief, a short description of Lexi's life, mentioning her loving family, parents, siblings, friends, her hopes, dreams and short time at university. The cause of death is not specific, but the wording suggests suicide.

She feels shocked. What does this mean? Why has Toby kept it?

Perhaps Google can tell her more. She finds Lexi's Facebook page, which still exists. It's full of lovely tributes that bring tears to her eyes. And amongst them is a line from Toby:

I'm so sorry. Lexi was a talented student and a pleasure to teach.

Ruth feels as if the contents of her stomach have curdled. She makes more general searches for 'Alexandra MacKay' and 'Lexi MacKay'. Some of what she reads she's seen before, when she first looked up Lexi, after intercepting her note to Toby. But there's new material: testimonials from Lexi's friends. Ruth finds them profoundly sad. She learns what Lexi's interests were, what kind of a little girl she was.

Lexi's parents have been especially vocal. 'Our daughter was not a suicide risk,' her mother writes. 'She was a happy, sunny person who knew how to share problems and had a strong support network. Her death is inexplicable to us. We demand further investigation.'

Ruth feels a jolt when she reads that. Lexi's brother, Jake, has also given an interview in which he castigated the university for their lack of oversight of his sister's mental health. 'We did not see this coming,' he tells the interviewer. 'There were no red flags. To her family, Lexi appeared as she always had done until she began to withdraw from us during her last months. We strongly suspect that, during this time, Lexi may have got involved with parties who glorified mental health issues and persuasively contributed to her decision to take her own life.'

Ruth checks the date on which Lexi died: 9 August 2019. This summer. Just months after she wrote to Toby.

And how much of a support network did she have if she was writing to Toby the way she did? Making accusations? What was it Toby said about Lexi when Ruth confronted him with the letter? That she was 'troubled'?

She drinks again. Her stomach heaves but she keeps the vodka down. It feels as if a fog has spread through her brain.

Was Toby's pursuit of this young woman what drove her to her death? Did he tell her she was troubled to her face? Did he gaslight her, and twist her young mind from functional to paranoid to protect himself? He's smart enough and powerful enough to do it.

And it ended in her death?

It feels extreme but on the other hand anything seems possible right now.

Ruth drinks again.

And not just possible, she thinks. Probable.

She looks at an image of Lexi's face onscreen. It's easy to imagine her dead. Ruth thinks of John Elliott. What did he look like, up on the peak near the barn? She thinks of the cadavers she saw in medical school. Horrible.

But Lexi was probably beautiful, even in death.

Ruth looks at the pictures on the wall opposite Toby's bookshelves. There are many of them, pinned closely together. Mostly works by the Impressionists, and no shortage of images of Degas's work. She stands to look at them better. There they are, the nubile young women, the ballerinas, the women bathing. Degas was a voyeur, she thinks, just like Lexi said in her note to Toby.

There are also works by Manet and others. Nudes, everywhere. And in the middle of them, a colour print of the famous Pre-Raphaelite image of Ophelia by John Everett Millais. Ophelia, dead in the water, flowers in her hair. Death glorified, beautified, romanticised.

Does Toby love this image as much as the others?

And she can't help thinking, was Lexi's suicide something that he encouraged?

But that's crazy. She feels as if she's losing her mind.

She drinks again.

If she said this to Toby, he would say what he always does: 'Ruth, this is all in your head.'

And he might be right.

But is it in her head? Or not?

If he could pursue a younger, vulnerable woman with the intensity she accused him of, could he drive her to suicide too?

Imogen sits and stares out of the window of her parents' bedroom.

So far, there hasn't been anything to see, but everything out there spooks her. A squall of wind ruffling the leaves of the beech tree opposite. A movement across the corner of the garden. The dark shadow cast by the roof of her dad's workshop.

Neither she nor Edie have been in there since they lost him. Imogen can picture his woodworking tools as he probably left them. The shavings and dust on the floor. Components of some work in progress on the bench. He was making a chair for her when he died.

The weather has hardly changed in the time since she's been sitting there. The sky is a clear blue. Perhaps it has whitened a little, she thinks, but perhaps not. It will soon. It's as if time has stopped. And she wishes it had. Because the clock on Edie's bedside table tells Imogen that it's almost seven and Edie should have been home at least an hour ago.

She's late. Dusk isn't too far off and Edie hates to drive in the dark. She says the oncoming headlamps dazzle her.

Imogen wishes she'd paid more attention to her mum's plans. Edie is usually punctual. I'm sure she said she'd be back at five or five thirty, Imogen thinks, but she's not a hundred per cent sure.

Has something happened?

The fear she experienced earlier has settled into a low thrum while she's been waiting but her anxiety escalates now, so much so that she knows she can't possibly just sit here any longer and feel it because it will make her crazy. She needs distraction.

The drawer of the old chest in her parents' room is hard to pull out. There's a knack to it that her dad showed her. Imogen lifts it a little as she pulls. She takes out their family photo albums and kneels on the floor to look through them.

This is her favourite thing to do when she's on her own but instead of her usual comfortable, indulgent perusal of the photos, the gentle easing apart of the album pages that are stuck together, Imogen starts to flick through them with a more desperate, demanding energy that feels as if it's edging towards destruction. Her breathing is laboured.

She wants to see her parents' faces, wants to feel reassured by them, for them to make the fear she's feeling go away, but instead all she feels is certainty that both her mum and her dad are stuck in the photographs and that she will never see either of them again in real life and it's the most painful and frightening thing she's ever felt. She slams the album shut, gasping.

Her skin feels hypersensitive, as if it might peel away. It hurts, all of her does, inside and out. She wraps her arms around herself, unsure whether she wants to hug or hurt herself, and watches without acting as her tears fall on to the photo album cover and spatter there. Her weeping is silent. She didn't even realise she was crying.

She looks up when she hears the car. It's travelling up the lane. She hears it turn into the driveway. She casts the album aside and her knees ache as she gets up and she stumbles as she runs to the window and is too late to see whose car it is. She has a view of the entrance to the driveway, but not the parking area.

Mum?

She stands there, feeling the breath leave and enter her body as a solid thing that she might choke on.

She hears the front door open and catch on the chain.

The doorbell rings, a short, perky few blasts, the sort to tell you that you know who's here, the exact kind of ring that Edie makes when she gets home. Not something he would ever do. Imogen runs downstairs and sweeps the chain off the door and flings it open, ready to embrace her mum so hard she won't know what's hit her.

But when Imogen sees who's there her face falls and her gut twists hard because it's not Edie.

Toby is smiling.

And he has two deep scratches down one cheek.

Emily's been alone since Toby left. She's in shock. Her ankle is a blaze of pain. She feels unable to move.

'Paul,' she whimpers.

She's lying on the floor, her arms wrapped around her knees. Beneath the fingernails on her right hand are traces of skin and traces of blood, of Toby.

All she can think about is the letter. How it started this. How it's malevolent.

She knew it, when she first held it, and she was right.

But she doesn't know how this is going to end.

She lifts her head. There isn't too much distance between her and the landline handset, not really, not if she tries. A tear slips down her cheek. The handset lies on the floor in the hallway, where it spun in circles after Toby knocked it from her grasp before she could call the police.

She should be able to reach it. So long as he doesn't come back.

'Do you want to come in?' Imogen asks.

She's upset that it's not her mum at the door, but she likes Toby. Of all her mum and dad's friends, he makes her feel most comfortable. He has an easy way about him that she likes. It's compelling. And he's a good tutor. Fun.

But Toby looks uncertain, not his usual cheerful self; he glances over his shoulder. She pulls the door open wider.

'What happened to you?' she asks.

'I was gardening, and I lost a battle with a particularly ferocious rambling rose.'

He makes a face, and she giggles. That's more like him. He's silly. And it feels good to laugh, as if she's expelling some of the fear and tension from her body.

310

'I'm worried about Mum,' she says. 'I thought she would be home by now.'

'Oh,' he says. 'I'm hoping to have a word with her. Everything's gone a bit pear-shaped this weekend, to put it mildly, and I'm wondering if she can shed any light on it. I tried to phone her, but I remembered that she's gone to that hippy place where they make you give your phone up, so I thought I'd drop by.'

He sounds awkward, as if there's something he's not saying, or doesn't want Imogen to know. She can't decide if he's confused or distressed or neither, but he's being a bit weird.

'She was supposed to be home at five,' she says.

'Have you heard from her?'

She shakes her head. 'No, but I lost my phone. Can I borrow yours? To call her?'

'Oh, sure,' he says. 'Though, like I said, I haven't been able to get hold of her.' He hands it over. 'The code is 123456.' She smiles. 'I know, it's ridiculous, but I'll forget it otherwise,' he says.

She looks at the screen. 'You've got loads of texts and missed calls.' She hands it back. She doesn't say, 'From Ruth,' because that would embarrass them both.

He waves his hand, dismissive. 'Go ahead, call your mum and if you get hold of her, I'll have a word too.'

She phones Edie but it goes straight to voicemail. Imogen turns away from Toby and leaves a message asking when Edie will be back and begging her to call.

He takes the phone from her and puts it back in his pocket without looking at it. There's something wrong between him and Ruth, she thinks. It explains why he looks preoccupied and jumpy, like there's something weighing on him.

'Mum should be on the road by now,' she says. Her worries from earlier resurge. His arrival was only a temporary respite.

'Maybe her phone ran out of charge.'

'I don't know,' she says.

He checks his watch. Its gold face looks old-fashioned. The strap is worn brown leather. 'She hates driving in the dark,' he says.

'I know. But it's not dark yet.' This comes out as more hopeful than she feels. She has the feeling that she's not going to be able to act normal in front of him for very much longer, that she's going to have a meltdown and have to share everything that's happened. But she's afraid to. The men are all such good friends. What if Toby doesn't believe her?

'Do you want to come and wait for her?' Imogen adds. It would make her feel safer if he was here.

They sit. Toby's knee bounces up and down.

He looks around the room like he's a stranger there but doesn't seem to focus on anything. He doesn't talk for the longest time and Imogen doesn't know what to say. After a while, she feels like crying. He was supposed to make her feel safe and he's not. He's too agitated.

She wants him to talk about normal stuff, to make things feel OK. She tries to do it herself.

'How's Alfie?' she asks. She's babysat for Toby's son now and then. Alfie is a really nice baby. Funny and sweet.

'He's fine.'

'Does he still have that dimply smile?'

He looks confused.

'You know,' she says, putting a fingertip in each of her cheeks.

312

'Oh, right, yes, he does. He absolutely does.'

It's as if he's never noticed the cuteness of his own son.

'Do you think we should call the place where Mum's staying?' Imogen says. 'To see what time she left? Maybe it was running late.'

'That's a good idea.' He gets his phone out again. 'What's the name of the place?'

Imogen hesitates. 'I don't remember. Maybe wellness something. Valley Wellness?'

He looks online. 'Nope. Nothing coming up for that. Any other ideas?'

She tries to think but it's useless. She didn't pay enough attention. She knows Edie left the number at the music camp, but Imogen doesn't have it, and if she calls to ask for it, no one will pick up the phone at camp now. It's their final performance this evening. She shakes her head.

'Never mind,' Toby says, though he looks disappointed.

'Why aren't you on the holiday with the others?' Imogen asks. It occurs to her that he should be.

The weekend away has been the source of a lot of stress in her home. Edie was very upset when it was suggested, and even more upset when they went ahead and planned it. She felt it was an insult. 'They could have skipped a year,' she said. 'Out of respect for Rob and for me. It's like they're moving on without me.' Imogen agreed.

'Something came up,' Toby says. 'It's a bit complicated. It's partly why I'm keen to talk to your mum.'

He looks at her sharply, suddenly, and frowns, as if trying to understand something.

'Why are you home? I thought you were at music camp while Mum was away. Have I remembered that right?'

'I was always coming home tonight,' she says. 'But actually, I left yesterday.'

'Why?'

'It wasn't going so well.' She won't share more than that with him. It doesn't feel right.

'Are you OK?' He doesn't ask as nicely as he would usually. It's like he's distracted. Like Edie has been. What's up with him? Why is everyone distracted these days? It's like everything has suddenly got so fucked up and nobody is behaving how Imogen expects them to.

'Yeah,' she says.

'Do you want to talk about it?'

'Not really.' She wishes she hadn't mentioned anything now. Usually, the thing she likes most about him is how well he listens and sympathises, but her gut's telling her this isn't the moment to confide.

He narrows his eyes. 'So, who collected you if Mum's away?'

She exhales and looks down, afraid to meet his gaze. It's going to be hard to get the name out without starting to cry.

'Imogen?' he says.

'It was Mark.'

'Hey,' Mark says. 'Long time no see.'

Jayne didn't expect to feel this relieved at the sight of him, but there it is, a rush of emotion so intense it's almost overpowering.

It never ceases to amaze her that she feels so strongly about him, that she adores him so much, even after all these years of marriage. Jayne didn't expect to fall deeply in love. She thought she was the kind of person who wouldn't get that chance in life. Nothing in her cold upbringing prepared her for it and she didn't believe she was attractive enough. She'd made her peace with that. Until Mark began to show an interest in her romantically.

She didn't know what to do with herself at first; when he spoke to her, she felt like looking over her shoulder to see if his real love interest was behind her. And when he persisted, doggedly, and she finally accepted the situation, she gave into it wholly and found herself infatuated by him.

Jayne would never admit that, of course, to anyone apart from him, and their years together have tempered the strength of her infatuation, garnished it with reality, but it's still there, at the core of her, like an extra heartbeat.

She runs downstairs and throws herself into his arms. It feels like a release from the grip of all the fear and anxiety that's possessed her for the last twenty-four hours. Her eyes brim with relieved tears, but something doesn't feel right. There's a tension about him, beneath the surface, as if he's holding himself extra still.

Jayne pulls away carefully. 'What's wrong?' she asks. And then, 'Why didn't you come up to the barn this morning? Where were you?'

'I had an absolute nightmare,' he says. 'I'm so sorry. I'll tell you all about it, but more importantly, I just saw your messages so first you have to tell me what the hell happened up there. Are you OK?' He cups her cheek with his hand, and she leans into it and tells him everything.

She will deal with her suspicions about him and Edie later; she won't forget them, she can still smell the bath oil on her fingers. But for now, tough as she is, Jayne needs him to help her put herself back together.

Mark is appalled by the letter and by the suicide. 'How did the farmer seem to you? Was there any sign that he was about to blow his brains out?'

'He drove us up to the barn when we arrived, and I had a nice chat with him in the car, but that was all we saw of him. He had a love of the place, for sure. A deep love. And he answered my questions about the history up there very patiently. I liked him.'

'And the policeman? That was his son? He saw the letter?' he asks.

'He did. I think Toby took the letter but I have a photograph of it. Here.'

Mark studies it. She finds it hard to read what he thinks. He hands the phone back.

'What a truly horrible thing for Edie to do. Did you think I was in danger? From her?' he asks.

'No,' she says, leaning on the early confidence she felt, deciding not to share the fear that built. 'I thought it was a hoax.'

He gives her a look that she interprets as approval. 'But the others freaked out?' he asks.

'They really did.'

'Ruth should have known better. She knows Edie.'

'She was really drunk. You have no idea. She has a problem. I think things have been much tougher for her lately than any of us realised. Maybe you should talk to Toby.'

'She's always drunk.'

'I don't just mean tipsy. I mean proper blackout drunk. It was bad.'

He ignores this. 'That letter is a piece of work.'

'I know.' But she doesn't like the way he sounded almost admiring. Her adrenalin is crashing and so much that she wants to say is on the tip of her lips, ready to spill out. Years of resentment of Edie, the hatred of her that grew while they were at the barn, Jayne's biting suspicion about Mark and Edie. But she holds back, nervous of where it might lead. She sniffs her fingers again, discreetly. The scent of the bath oil is cloyingly feminine. But she mustn't jump to conclusions. This is a conversation best had when the dust has settled.

'Has anyone heard from Paul?' he asks.

'I'm not sure.'

'I wonder if he's home.'

She frowns. 'Are you worried?'

'Paul hasn't replied to any texts I've sent him since yesterday.'

Jayne knows how unusual this is. They stare at each other for a moment, and she realises that he actually looks worried. It sends a chill up her spine.

'What about Edie?' she asks. 'Have you heard from her? I tried to call her from the car, but she didn't pick up.'

He shakes his head. 'She's away on her retreat until later today. You know that.'

'Tell me what happened to you,' she says. 'I was worried when you didn't turn up. And why didn't you respond to my calls and messages?'

'I'm so sorry about that,' he says. 'Things have been a bit chaotic at this end and my phone ran out of charge this morning when I was at Edie's house. I couldn't get it charged until I was in the car on my way home just now.'

'Why on earth were you at Edie's house?' In her current state of mind, suffused with suspicion, it staggers her that he would say this so nonchalantly, but he explains about Imogen, and the crisis that led him to pick her up early.

'I hadn't realised how unstable Imogen is,' he says, and Jayne loves that he's such a Good Samaritan. 'Did you know she's been lying about self-harming? She's going to need a lot of support in the future. Edie really needs to step up.'

Jayne feels for Imogen, but the selfish part of her relaxes. It's a huge relief to know that it was Imogen who had a bath and slept here.

He barely draws breath as he describes how Imogen stayed the night here before he took her home and how she tried to sneak out for the evening with a friend, in spite of losing her mobile.

'I put paid to that,' he says.

'You know,' she says, 'you deserve a medal. Edie should be there for her own daughter. But she needs to do a lot more than step up. She's out of control. You saw the letter. Someone's got to talk to her. She's single-handedly wreaked havoc for all of us this weekend. It was carnage at the barn after we read the letter.'

Jayne wants Mark to understand quite how destructive Edie's words were. How quickly they drove wedges between the wives that could have repercussions for all of them.

'Emily was making accusations,' she says. 'About Dovecote. She implied that the money they lost might be a reason for Edie to want to harm you.'

'What?' His face reddens and his expression hardens in a way that unsettles her. She wishes she could take her words back. He's never been able to handle criticism and especially not about this. She should have known better. 'What a bitch,' he spits.

'She shouldn't have said it. It was nonsense and I would never have mentioned it, but I want you to understand how crazy the letter made us. You don't know what it was like, being stuck up there.'

He can't let go of it. 'Emily's got no right.'

'Emily spoke out of turn, but there's a reason for that.'

He looks angry and upset but also tired, she thinks. This was the wrong tactic. She was hoping that he might direct some anger towards Edie, who caused all of this, and who deserves to be knocked off the pedestal the gang keep her on, but he doesn't.

She takes his hand and holds it until he calms down.

'Bloody hell,' Jayne says. 'I missed you.' It's an understatement. She feels incredibly grateful to be back here, with him, in their home. She leans in to kiss him, but he doesn't reciprocate, which is disappointing, nor does he tell her he missed her too.

He looks preoccupied.

'What's wrong?' she asks.

'I think we should call Emily to see if Paul's home or if she's heard from him.'

'You *are* worried about the letter,' she says, and the realisation revives her own alarm in an instant.

'I am a little, if I'm honest,' he says. 'It's a bit strange. I'm going to call Emily, just for peace of mind.'

'She lost her mobile too. Last night.'

'I'll call their landline.'

Mark dials, puts his phone on speaker. Emily and Paul's landline rings and rings and no one answers.

I think about Jayne as she and I drive to Paul's house.

For a woman with so many talents, such an outstanding career, she is as blind as a bat when it comes to me. And so predictable.

She's sitting beside me now, biting her nails. She's swallowed up my narrative.

I'll miss her, in a way, when I start my new life with Imogen. There's no way Jayne is part of my long-term plan. But she's been fun to have along for some of the ride. She's played her part beautifully.

Her trauma helps, obviously, when it comes to manipulating her. She thinks I suffer from it too, and maybe I do, a little, but I'm not ruined like her.

I picked my wife because she was unlike any other woman I'd met.

She did not seek attention but nor was she shy. She never dressed to show off her body even though it was better than most. At work, she kept her cool more effectively than some of the most hardened and experienced men, even under circumstances that leave everyone scarred. It piqued my attention. I thought she was a rare thing.

I watched her closely for a long time before I made my move, and she was never aware of it because, in spite of her vigilance and intelligence, she wasn't a woman who expected to be watched in that way. That was her Achilles' heel, I suppose.

The first time I asked her out, I almost laughed. She looked like a deer in headlamps.

A woman usually concise, precise and thoughtful with her language stumbled over her response. My proposal that we go for a simple pub meal together was the first thing I ever saw fluster her.

Dating was a blast. I'd heard charity could be rewarding but had never given it a try, until then. How entertained I was as I watched the psychological contortions she went through to shatter long-held assumptions about herself. Her tight little forehead would scrunch right up. Not lovable! Not attractive! Prepared to settle! Well, with me, she started to believe that she could be more than that. She began to prise off all the dirty old badges she'd applied to herself and create new ones.

'Why me?' she asked once, after we'd been intimate. 'You could have had anyone.' She often likes to talk after sex, as if it's unlocked something in her. I like how much she needs me in those moments, but the talk can be tiresome, and we're intimate often because I take some pleasure in the tight, needy forms of her body, in my ability to make her relax beneath me, to render her vulnerable, to control her.

I thought before I answered. I wasn't going to tell her that I couldn't have the one person I wanted. Eventually, I said, 'Because I love you,' and felt a tremendous energy gather itself within her, a raw hopefulness. And afterwards, looking at my reflection in the bathroom mirror and remembering the moment, I chuckled.

Don't judge me. Jayne's an adult, and a highly skilled one at that, and adults should be responsible for themselves. I might have married her for show, so people couldn't suspect me of loving and wanting Edie, but at least I didn't stoop as low as Paul and pick up a girl young enough to be my daughter or settle for a woman as tiresome as Ruth. Wow! Toby bit off more than he could chew there. Ruth always was an emotional accident waiting to happen. A perfectionist to the point of self-destruction.

I look at Jayne. She's been silent for much of this drive. I told her she didn't need to come with me, that she'd been through enough, but she insisted. Of course she did. My apparent concern for Paul has got under her skin, made her doubt her own assessment of the situation. She's in the game with me now. Later, if necessary, she will be able to vouch for me, to relate my concern.

'Did you know that Edie suffered a psychotic episode when she was younger?' I ask.

Untrue, but I need to lay the ground for the scenario I've set up and that I'm hoping everyone will buy into. It's plausible, but only if I can get people to believe that Edie would leave her daughter to start a new life with Paul.

I mean, honestly, that part is correct in a way. Her body is on top of his in the freezer.

Everyone knows it's not the hardest thing in the world to paint a woman as unstable. There are road maps. Centuries of examples of best practice by gentlemen such as myself who are willing to indulge their heinous tendencies.

I'm watching the road, but I can feel Jayne's eyes drilling into the side of my head.

'I didn't know,' she says, as the car turns on to Paul and Emily's road. 'Is that why you all rally around her?'

'She's more vulnerable than people think.'

'Why didn't you tell me?'

I pretend I didn't hear that question and I hit the brakes to make the turn between the gates into Paul and Emily's driveway.

We get out. The sound of our car doors slamming shatters the peace in this suburban idyll.

I have a key to Paul's house. I put it in the lock.

'Shouldn't you ring the bell?' Jayne asks. So proper. Fancy maintaining your manners even on a day like this! She's a blast.

'It's fine,' I say and turn the key.

Darrell locks up his unit at the industrial yard. He's got twenty-three lawnmowers inside. Eighteen needing attention and five waiting for collection.

There's been something on his mind all day. The man who rented the unit down the end. The one who backed his car so far in that he looked trapped. It was the second trip he'd made there this morning, and something wasn't right about him.

He was very flustered, and it looked like he had nothing in the unit except for a massive chest freezer.

Darrell's husband Pete arrives to pick him up as he's pondering this, and Darrell shares his thoughts.

'A big chest freezer? Did you see what he was putting in it?'

'No, but he was sweating like a pig. Whatever it was, it must have been heavy.'

Pete stares at him. 'What? No! Don't be silly. You've been watching too many crime programmes. Come on, let's go. Shall we get takeaway tonight?'

'Listen, I'm not saying he's got a body in there but what if he's doing something illegal? That's the last thing we need.'

'Let's have a look, then.'

'What?'

'If you're so worried, we'll have a look. Then we can go home.'

'He's got a massive padlock on it.'

Pete smiles. They both know it'll only take him a couple of minutes to get past any lock. 'We'll be in and out in a jiffy. If everything's above board, and he's just got a few frozen lamb joints in there, we'll lock it up again and he'll be none the wiser.'

Darrell feels a sense of trepidation as they open the unit doors.

Right at the back, the chest freezer hums. It's very big and dented. A pool of liquid is gently spreading across the concrete floor beneath it.

'You open it,' Darrell says.

'Stand guard.'

Darrell positions himself by the doors and watches the entrance to the yard. There's no one else here. A warm breeze bends the nettles that have breached the crumbling tarmac. He yawns. From somewhere, he can smell a barbecue.

He watches as Pete tries to lift the freezer lid. It's a bit of an effort, and when Pete succeeds, the seal breaks audibly.

'Fuck,' Pete says. 'Oh, fuck.'

Darrell starts towards him.

'Stay there! Don't look,' Pete says but it's too late.

Darrell sees the body of the woman, a beautiful woman, lying face up. She's lifeless and, thankfully, her eyes are shut but beneath her, horrifyingly, is a man.

His eyes are open, and staring up at them, completely void of life.

And there's another detail, just as horrifying because it's so ordinary.

Tucked by their feet are two bags: an expensive man's messenger bag and a pretty woman's handbag, in canary-yellow leather, with a thick woven strap.

Pete reaches for them.

'Don't touch anything!' Darrell says and Pete snatches his hand back.

Darrell shuts the lid, stumbles out of the unit and calls 999.

The landline has been ringing and ringing, but Emily can't move. Through fear. And pain.

Every time she tries to pull herself up, she thinks she might black out. She has to rest, her head between her knees, and wait until the stars she's seeing recede.

She needs to call the police.

Her ankle has swollen up bigger than it was before. The pain is atrocious.

She tries crawling and it works but she has to stop every few yards.

She's made it almost to the handset when she hears the key turning in the front door.

'Paul,' she says again.

She thinks her heart might explode with relief at the thought that it could be him.

I push Paul's front door open. Jayne follows me in.

His house is beautiful, and I feel a little twist of envy every time we come here. The scale of it, the decor, the tech. Hard for him to leave it, the police will doubtless think, this home and his delicious young wife, but they'll only think that until they find the evidence I've hidden fairly well, but not so well it'll remain undetected by a reasonably competent professional hungry to make a name for himself.

'Oh my God,' Jayne says. She rushes past me. I tear my eyes from the chandelier that I've always envied and see what my wife has seen: Emily, lying on the floor at the other end of the hallway.

Jayne runs to Emily and holds her, helps her to sit up, starts to ask questions. I crouch beside them, concern plastered all over my face even though I can't help feeling excited to witness first-hand some of the fallout from my letter – for that, surely, is what this is.

Near to Emily, a phone handset. She is, apparently, trying to reach it. 'I couldn't move,' she says. 'It hurts too much.' Without embarrassment she cries plump, attention-seeking tears as the words tumble from her enhanced lips. She doesn't know where Paul is, she blubs. She hasn't had any contact with him since she was in the car on the way up to Northumbria. Her phone is lost, dropped in a puddle on a lane up there!

We look at her ankle. Bulbous! Wow. She has done a number on it. Though surely it wouldn't have stopped her getting to the phone if she really loved her husband. I suspect she just gave up and let hysteria overwhelm her. My steely Jayne would never have done that.

Jayne and I help Emily up, and we move her into the cavernous kitchen, where she sits pale and beautiful on a designer couch beneath a vast abstract painting. When the sobbing escalates and becomes uncontrollable, I step back and let Jayne deal with it.

I observe their interaction closely, though, because I will need some of these sympathetic skills, even ones modelled by a rank amateur like Jayne, with which to comfort Imogen. I note how Jayne sits, that she leans in and holds Emily's hand tightly.

Imogen is going to be very upset when her mother doesn't come home today. I plan to be there for her until it's clear that Edie is not coming back, and I'll remain by her side through the next difficult days and weeks – depending on how professional the investigation is – until it's clear that Edie has most probably disappeared with Paul. Because if I've done everything right, that's how it's going to look.

It feels fitting, to have set this up to seem as if those two have gone off into the sunset together. They'll be branded disgraceful, betrayers. It's what they deserve.

I had no choice, really, but to make it this way.

I don't know how, but Paul suspected that I helped Rob to his death and shared his suspicions with Edie. And his suspicions grew over the past few weeks until, ten days ago, I learned, because I cloned their phones, that they were considering telling the police.

All of this was particularly upsetting since I only killed Rob because I wanted Edie, Imogen and I to be a family together.

That was Plan A, but Paul ruined it for us.

It was heartbreaking when I realised that both he and Edie had to die as a result. I was not going to go to jail.

I started cloning phones when I was at a low point, after Dovecote. It's not difficult, if you know how. In retrospect, I was suffering a little paranoia because I felt like a failure when Dovecote imploded. I wanted to know what they were all saying about me.

But I learned so much more.

If I hadn't cloned Rob and Edie's phones, I'd never have seen the message where Rob mentioned his vasectomy, or his lack of a need for one. And I was also reassured that Paul hadn't told Emily what he suspected because Edie begged him not to.

Let's keep it to ourselves, she wrote. Until we're sure. Of course Paul obliged. I won't breathe a word, he replied. I wasn't surprised. None of us would think twice about lying to our wives for Edie.

It saved Emily's life.

So, this, here, now, live in action, is Plan B. Me and Imogen.

But I'm happy with that.

Imogen will be devastated when she discovers that her mother has abandoned her, and that's a regret, but I will comfort and support her through her pain while she processes her loss.

During that time, she and I will build our relationship as father and daughter. That's the plan.

Jayne's not part of the picture. But watching her now is helpful.

As Jayne and Emily talk, heads together, I zone out until they ask me to call the police. Paul should be reported missing, they insist. I don't disagree, but I need to give a moment's thought to how the optics work if it's me who reports him missing and I decide that it's fine but not before Jayne has snapped at me to hurry up in a way that I find unnecessary and unpleasant. Never mind. She'll get her comeuppance soon enough.

I make the call. They want to talk to Emily, so I hand her the phone. She chokes out the story semi-coherently. Jayne and I sit and watch her, which gives us front-row seats when she says, 'And also, I need to report an assault.'

Wow. It's so unexpected that I wonder if I've misheard her at first.

Jayne and I exchange a glance. She's as surprised as me to hear this, it seems.

'It happened at my home,' Emily says. 'No, not a sexual assault. He attacked me physically.'

She nods as she listens.

'Yes,' she says. 'It happened just now, about half an hour ago. He was out of control. Yes. It was a friend of my husband. His name is Toby Land.'

Ruth has finished the vodka. The empty bottle is on Toby's desk, like a reproach.

329

She tries to breathe slowly. In through the nose, out through the mouth. She has a terrible idea in her head, and she can't unthink it, even though it's dizzying her, horrifying her.

As a doctor, it's her job to pick up clues, big and small, from what a patient tells her and piece them together to reach a diagnosis. Sometimes it feels like detective work.

Which is what she must do now. She looks online, typing fast, locating the link she wants after a bit of creative searching.

Toby wrote the article when he had just completed his Masters. It was based in part on his thesis. She hasn't thought about it for years, but in the context of Lexi's suicide she's just remembered it.

She skims through the text, her heart in her mouth, and one sentence stands out to her in particular: a description of Vincent van Gogh's suicide. She feels the way she did when she first read it, years ago. She was shocked by Toby's language then, and she feels the same now.

His language glorifies the artist's death by suicide. It is sumptuous, almost poetic – Toby can write in a way that she's long admired – but so very wrong. It's as if he sees suicide as romantic, even seductive.

It's a horrific thought. She feels disgusted. Wounded. Repulsed. Never more aware of the difference between them as she's spent her career trying to save lives.

She wants more vodka and tries to drink the last dregs from the bottle.

Could Toby's interest in younger women be not sexual, or not just sexual? Is it worse?

Does he prey on vulnerable young women with mental health issues and encourage them to take their own lives?

What was he doing at a student accommodation building early this morning? Who was he visiting?

She needs to vomit. On her knees in the bathroom, she empties her stomach of its liquid contents. When she's stopped heaving, she wipes her mouth and sees that the bile in the toilet bowl has streaks of blood in it. Not good.

She staggers as she stands up and returns to Toby's office.

Everything about it enrages her. He has hidden in here, from her, for months. It has tormented her. And now she's possessed by the idea that he might be a monster.

She wrenches opens his study window and begins to throw his books out. She hurls them one at a time at first, but it isn't satisfying, so she gathers an armful and feels a flush of triumph when they hit the ground.

She keeps going until the shelves are empty and the books are scattered across their tiny front garden and the pavement. She stares at them for a while, her chest heaving long after she's recovered from the physical exertion, but her sense of satisfaction doesn't linger and, if anything, she feels hollower than she did before.

But not too hollow to text Toby. He needs to know what she knows.

She sends him one message, then another, and more, until her texts are a non-stop stream of consciousness that convey everything she thinks of him and everything she suspects about him and all the ways in which she wants him to be punished for it.

*

When Emily tells the police that Toby assaulted her, Jayne and I can't disguise our shock. Jayne pulls me aside, out of Emily's hearing.

'What the hell is happening?' Jayne asks, and I'm stumped. This I didn't see coming.

'She must be lying,' I say. 'I don't believe it.'

'But you know,' Jayne says, 'Ruth told me something very disturbing about Toby too.'

She repeats what she heard, about the student who Ruth suspects Toby of grooming, and I'm stunned. Genuinely. It's despicable behaviour. How could he? What kind of man is he? I mean, I lost respect for him long ago because he never seemed to grow up, but this is on another level.

'Did you know that Toby was tutoring Imogen?' she asks.

'No.' I feel immediately jealous.

'Well, I think Ruth was worried that he might have been inappropriate with her.'

I feel sick to my stomach. It's a struggle to remain calm. I can feel myself breaking out in a sweat. My heart begins to pound.

'Imogen?' I ask. 'Ruth thinks Toby might have made a move on Imogen?'

'She's not sure. She didn't say she had proof of anything untoward, it was more a suspicion, and I can't believe it's true. I mean, Toby's like an uncle to Imogen – you all are. I think Ruth was scared, and she only thought of this because she was looking for any motive that Edie might have had to hurt Toby. Because of the letter. She said she didn't believe it, but I think she did. And, of course, she was drunk. I felt really sorry for her.'

I've heard enough. I don't care about Ruth's problems. I feel a rage building.

The thought that Toby has sullied Imogen, or even considered it; the thought that he might have caused her pain, or fear, or be intending to prey on her is overwhelming.

What have I missed? Was I too obsessed with making my own plans to see what was happening right in front of me? Stupid, stupid, stupid. I can feel explosive anger brewing, deep beneath my sternum. It feels like a living thing. I hold it back as best I can.

'Do you know what, my love?' I ask.

'What?' Jayne's eyes are so round. She hangs on my every word.

'Can you cope here on your own? Can you support Emily?'

She nods.

'I'd like to go to Edie's house and check on Imogen. I want to see if Edie's back. If she is, I'm going to talk to her about the letter and also about Toby. She needs to know about this.'

'You could just call her. And don't forget this is Ruth talking about a suspicion. She might be wrong.'

'This is delicate. It's a conversation that needs to happen in person. And it does need to happen.' Of course Edie won't be there, but I'm not going to leave Imogen's side while there's a possibility that Toby might be predatory.

'Imogen is vulnerable,' I say and my voice cracks. Jayne lays a hand on my arm.

'Go,' she says. 'I'll look after Emily and I'll text you if we hear from Paul.'

'And if Toby comes back here,' I say.

'I won't let him in. Don't worry. And I'll call you.'

'Attagirl.'

I'm just leaving when she says, 'But what if Edie's there and she's dangerous?' I see real fear in her eyes. You can't believe how gullible people are, even those who think they aren't. Edie would never hurt anyone physically. 'We should let the police handle this.'

'I need to check on Imogen,' I repeat. 'That's non-negotiable. Whatever else happens, I'll deal with it.'

I give her a look which I know she'll interpret to mean that she and I are in this together, a team, more capable than other people because of what we've been through in the military. And she's so into the idea that she offers me a small salute in return.

'Go,' she says, again, and this time she packs the word with intensity. 'But be safe.'

'Mark picked you up from music camp?' Toby wants to confirm. He looks confused.

'Yes.' Imogen wonders whether to tell him about Mark's behaviour. She still feels nervous to and decides not to say anything for now. It's enough just to feel safer with Toby here.

'It would have been nice to hear from him,' Toby mutters. 'He didn't tell anyone else where he was.'

He seems upset but Imogen doesn't pry. She doesn't really care. Perhaps the long weekend away fell apart for all of them and nobody went on it. Her mum will be happy to hear that.

It's starting to get dark. She switches on a light, Edie's favourite, a standard lamp with a tasselled flamingo-pink shade.

Toby gets up. 'Do you mind if I use the bathroom?'

'It's upstairs,' she says automatically; then, 'but you know that.'

His phone has slipped out of his pocket and lodged between the cushion and the sofa arm. She reaches for it. He won't mind if she uses it to try to call her mum again. She's getting worried.

There are a ton of texts from Ruth on the phone, like, more notifications than Imogen has ever seen on one screen. She taps in '123456' anyway, makes a point not to read Ruth's messages, and tries to call her mum, but gets no answer.

Her fear feels like a restless weight in her chest. Something she wants to rip out. She longs to see the sweep of headlamps into the drive before it's black out there. Her mum will be freaking out behind the wheel by now, if she's not close to home. What if she's had an accident already?

She turns on the television to distract herself but can't find anything she can bear to watch. Toby is still upstairs. Out of the corner of her eye she sees his phone keeps lighting up.

She can't resist picking it up and peeking at one of the texts. She can say she opened it by mistake. It's long. And nuts. Wow. Ruth is kicking off. It seems like she *hates* Toby.

Imogen glances over her shoulder and turns off the TV. In the quiet, she'll hear the bathroom door when he comes out. The loo hasn't even flushed yet. Her and her mum's home isn't very big so you can hear everything.

She reads more. It's a very long text and it gets much worse. When she's finished that message she reads the next one. She can't look away. Ruth is accusing Toby of horrible things, of chasing girls not much older than Imogen. Of wanting to do things to Imogen herself. Of encouraging young women to kill themselves.

Are you planning to do this to Imogen too? Ruth asks. To take advantage of her grief? Then, You disgust me. You're a danger to young women and girls.

The loo upstairs flushes. Imogen's head snaps up. She has a few seconds before he'll be down and she can hardly process what she's reading. Should she be afraid of Toby, too? What should she do? She swallows. Her throat feels dry as paper. Her hands are clammy. She looks at the phone.

Where are you? Ruth has messaged to Toby, over and over again, between accusations. A new text arrives asking the same question as Imogen holds the phone.

She types a reply: At Edie's house with Imogen. Come quick.

She presses Send. Her heart is pounding so hard she feels as if her chest will explode. She can hardly get a breath in or out. The bathroom door squeals as it opens. She lurches across the sofa to replace the phone where she found it, tucked into the cushions. The screen glows, advertising the fact that she's used it.

Toby's calves are visible as he walks downstairs, then all of his legs, and his smile could be warm, but she reads it as sinister. He runs his hand through his hair. She swallows.

His phone screen is still glowing. She smiles back at him, but it feels robotic to her and she's worried he's going to pick up on her panic.

He sits heavily back down on the sofa. Only a few feet separate them. She avoids looking at his phone in case he follows her gaze. It's beside his thigh. The screen goes blank.

She tries not to let her relief show. She stands up. 'Actually, I might wait for Mum on my own, if you don't mind. I don't feel too good.'

'I'm here now,' he says. 'I might as well wait with you. If you want to go ahead and have a lie-down, go for it. I'll hold the fort. To be honest, I don't really feel like going home right now.'

She sees his coat on the chair at the bottom of the stairs. 'I need the loo,' she says.

He turns the TV back on. She walks behind the sofa, stepping quietly, and stops beside his coat. She glances back at him. He's glued to the screen. She feels the outside of his coat pocket. His car keys are inside it.

She wants to flee again, but she's not going to risk heading out on foot like before. Taking Toby's car would be better. She's had a few lessons and, though she doesn't have her licence yet, her mum says her driving is coming along well.

'What are you doing?' he asks.

She jumps. 'What?' she says.

'I can see your reflection in the TV.'

'I was just itching my leg.' It's a lame excuse. It's obvious she wasn't. He stares at her. She stares back.

'Do you need money?'

'No.'

'You were looking in my coat pockets.'

'I don't need money.'

He switches off the TV and swivels his body so he's facing her properly. Her skin feels as if it's humming.

'Listen, Imogen. If you have a problem, I'm here for you. I'm a great listener. I work very closely with a lot of young people. It's what I do. You've had a really rough time lately, so if you're experiencing some difficult emotions, that's perfectly understandable. You don't need to lie to me. You can trust me.'

She shifts from one foot to the other.

'All of us miss your dad horribly and grief can make us do some strange things, so if you want money, you only have to ask. Honestly. I'm on your side.'

Imogen is running calculations in her mind. She could drive to Jemma's house. And call her mum from there.

Because this is too much. First Mark, now Toby.

She plunges her hand into Toby's coat pocket and grabs his keys, turns on her heel and flees the house. Right before the door slams behind her she hears Toby's shout, hears his surprise and outrage, and they propel her on.

The gravel on the drive is sharp and her socks are thin. It slows her down. She presses all the buttons on his key fob until the car unlocks and she climbs in. Her hands shake as she hits the central locking and tries to get the key into the ignition.

He walks relatively calmly across the drive towards her. He looks confused. It's almost more frightening than if he ran. He puts his hand on top of the car and leans down, his face only inches from hers. She can't hear what he says. Her feet are pumping pedals, trying to find the one she needs to press to get the key to turn. His knuckles rat-tat on the glass and she screams, a noise so loud that it fills the car and hurts her own ears.

'Imogen!' His voice is muffled by the glass.

She lets go of the keys, covers her face with her hands and tries to cover her ears too. She doesn't want to see him or hear him, but she does hear the gravel crunch as another car pulls on to the driveway behind her.

'Mum,' she says and feels as if her heart might burst with relief.

When I arrive at Edie's house, I see Toby's beaten-up old Honda parked in front, and I feel as if I might explode with anger.

I'd intended to track him down and deal with him later, yet here he is, on Edie's driveway, waving at me and walking towards my car. No sign of Imogen. She should be drugged, safely inside. Hopefully she hasn't opened the door. Thank goodness I protected her from him.

I park halfway across the entrance to the driveway. There's no room for my car to fit on it completely.

It's very dusky now. Everything bathed in a strange grey pinky light that holds just enough brightness for me to make out Toby's asinine smile as he approaches me. His monstrous smile.

It was fun when we were younger, to have a friend so staggeringly unjudgemental, so prepared to disguise his intellect and play the clown – he ached to be liked – but it's worn on me as we've aged. And now I wonder, did I miss something? Was he hiding a more sinister version of himself?

I know he loved Edie as hard as the rest of us did. He wasn't as guarded about his feelings as Paul and me. He wept when Rob won her.

No wonder he chose the line of work he did, drawn into a painted world where he found meaning everywhere, but none of it was real. It electrified him, though. His concerns were minute (brushstrokes, pentimenti, the price of a particular shade of blue in sixteenth-century Florence) and also vast (love, death, history, mythology, religion, philosophy). He approached each one of them passionately and along the way he must have lost touch with reality completely.

He will never go near my daughter again.

'How's it going?' he asks.

'What are you doing here?'

'Mate,' he says, 'you sound like my wife.' He loves to say that sort of thing. He thinks talking in a faux-cockney accent makes him witty. I note that his laugh sounds forced.

I know who you are, I want to say. I have heard Ruth's concerns and I listened closely to what Emily told the police about how he turned on her inexplicably when she wanted to call them, how she fought like the alley cat we all know she is.

She did a good job. Now that he's beside me, I see scratches on his cheek that you might describe as gouges. They look angry.

But I say nothing because I want the advantage of surprise.

'Imogen's in my car,' he says, strangely, as if this is something that has happened by unfortunate accident.

My heart almost stops. I look. He's right and, inexplicably, she's in the driver's seat. Why isn't she sleeping like a baby after I dosed her? She must have been in there for a while because the interior light has gone off. Her back is to us, but I bet she's watching in the rear-view mirror. I make the effort to hold back any signs of my mounting anger.

'Why? What's going on?'

He throws up his hands. 'I have no idea. She took my keys and got in. I think she was embarrassed because I caught her stealing money from my coat pocket.' His mouth makes exaggerated, foolish shapes. He wants me to laugh at Imogen or raise an eyebrow at her 'antics'. His incompetence as an adult astounds me.

But this makes no sense. Why would she get in his car? Unless she's trying to escape him. What has really happened? What has he done to her?

I try to open the car door. She flinches when I rattle the handle. She's locked herself in. I rap on the window. 'Sweetie,' I say. 'Imogen. It's me. Can you unlock and hand me the car keys? I don't think you're experienced enough to be driving. Especially not in the dark. What will Mum think if she finds out?'

She tries to start the car. I hammer on the window. 'Stop!' I shout. She's only a learner driver. This isn't safe.

She gives up. Tries again. I bang on the window some more. I'm afraid she's going to do something reckless.

'You're parked in anyway,' I call through the window. It's not strictly true. You could get around my car if you had a bit of experience, but she doesn't, and she probably can't even see that there's a safe angle from where she's sitting.

I rap on the window hard. Behind me, Toby has realised this looks bad for him. He's blathering excuses as to why she's locked herself away from him that I don't even bother to listen to. My anger is burning hot now.

She gives up on trying to start the car. But she won't look at me.

'I'm not moving until you give me the keys,' I tell her.

Eventually, reluctantly, she unlocks the car, and as soon as she does, I open the door swiftly, reach in and snatch the keys from the ignition.

'Come on,' I say. 'Let's get you inside.'

She climbs out, refusing to look at either me or Toby. I whisper to her, 'Has he hurt you?'

She looks at her upper arm. I'm gripping it. I let go.

'Has he touched you?' I ask.

She shakes her head.

'Are you sure?' I try to keep my tone calm but there's menace in my voice, I can hear it. My anger is spilling out. She nods, recoiling from me, and I think, What am I doing? This is only going to traumatise her. I'll deal with it myself. I slip Toby's keys into my pocket.

He's standing a little apart from us, keeping his distance, scuffing the gravel with his feet, a hangdog, guilty look about him. When did he age so much?

'OK, listen,' I say to her. 'Don't worry about a thing. Go indoors and I'll have a chat with Toby. Do you want him to leave?'

She nods, then shakes her head. Nods again. Why is she so mute? 'I just want Mum,' she says.

Of course she does. It's natural. I try to relax a little and pretend to check the time on my phone. 'Oh my, she is a bit late.' I frown in a way I know to appear sympathetic. 'Look. Why don't you go inside? I'll ask Toby to clear off and maybe we can order a pizza or something for supper while we wait for Mum. That sound good?'

It clearly doesn't, but she's smart enough to know it's the best offer she's got.

'Toby wants to talk to Mum.'

'Don't worry about that. I'll talk to him. You go inside before you get cold.'

Imogen does what she's told. I watch her go back into the house and, as soon as the door shuts behind her, I turn to Toby. He's standing a few feet away, in the middle of the driveway, and he's about to say something when I reach him and grab him by the throat and push him into the lane, out of sight of the house.

His mouth gapes. The back of his head connects with a stone wall. His eyes are stretched wide, full of fear. He gasps for breath, his hands flailing like a girl's.

'I know what you did to Emily,' I say, 'and if you ever come near Imogen again, I'll kill you.'

I squeeze on his windpipe. Hold it. For longer. Release. He crumples to the ground, sucking in air. I breathe deeply, cool, calm breaths, invigorated by the sight of him struggling, by the justice I'm administering. Recrimination and fright spill from his bloodshot gaze.

He tries to move away from me, and scuttles, half-crawling, half-walking.

'You hurt Emily,' I say. 'If I hadn't done this, Paul would have.'

'Fuck, Mark, fucking hell. I didn't hurt Emily.'

'Don't lie to me,' I say.

He walks backward, hands up in a posture of surrender.

'And what did you do to those girls you teach? What is it you want to do to Imogen?'

My anger is taking over, disturbing my vision. I can't see Toby clearly. It's like watching someone move behind a gauze curtain.

'Nothing!' he shouts. 'Look, Ruth's got the wrong idea. Honestly, she's got it all wrong. You mustn't believe her. She's disturbed. She's become an alcoholic. It's escalated. She hasn't

343

been coping since the baby was born. She's got this idea and she's obsessed with it and it's all wrong.'

He's practically begging. It didn't take much.

Sometimes, weakness in others pleases me. If you understand what someone wants, you have identified their weak spot. It's easy, then, to manipulate them. At other times, weakness in others simply stirs the heinous part of me and the resulting urge to hurt them is very powerful.

Toby is breathing heavily, glancing over his shoulder into the gloaming as if there's a place of refuge for him there. He has a high opinion of his abilities and a high opinion of his intelligence. People can have this tendency, in my experience. Toby believes he can dredge something up out of his big brain to ameliorate this situation, to cajole me into believing him, into forgiving him. It's part of the fantasy world he exists in.

He doesn't believe I'll kill him.

He's jabbering. More excuses and attempts to justify himself. I tune him out. What's the point in listening? He's a threat to my daughter. That's all I need to know.

I am who I am and, unlike my wife, I've accepted that. I know that I'm capable of taking a human life, of murder, because I've done it and that is my story.

It is me.

It is I.

I have no shame.

My Jayney believes the experiences we've had in our past are so terrible that they bind us, and she entertains the delusion that we can heal one another, that we can remake ourselves and move on from this, but it's laughable. We're not soulmates, no matter what she believes.

And while I have to accept a lot of imperfection in my life, I can no longer accept this. I'm looking for the sort of love that doesn't ask questions, that doesn't require change. I want to be who I am and be loved anyhow.

It's the pure kind of love a daughter can bring you, because you share blood. And blood ties cannot be broken.

It's a forever bond.

Toby glances towards his Honda. I know what he's going to do before he does it. In fact, I step aside, out of the way, as he dashes past me.

He wrenches open the car door and gets in. He thinks the keys are still in the ignition and I smile as he reaches for them.

He didn't see that I took them from Imogen; he doesn't know that they're in my pocket.

The police arrived at Emily's house within half an hour of her calling them. She's talking to two officers in the kitchen. A man and a woman. Jayne sits in the room next door. She can hear everything.

Emily tells the officers how nobody has heard from Paul since he texted his driver yesterday. She's beside herself.

Jayne has been working her phone as they talk, trying to call Edie, and Paul. With no success.

'Did they have any kind of relationship with one another, Paul and Edie?' Jayne hears the policewoman say.

345

'No,' Emily replies.

'I'm sorry. I have to ask.'

Jayne wants to leave; she's got no desire to babysit Emily, even though Emily's distraught, even though she's going through something terrible. Jayne feels guilt about that, and a nagging sense that there's something wrong with her own self, that she's not maternal and should be. The only person she's interested in supporting is Mark. She hasn't heard from him and she's worried. What if he's encountered Edie? What if she's dangerous?

When Emily's finished giving her statement Jayne will ask whether she has any family members who might be able to come and sit with her, although there are no photographs of anyone Jayne can identify as such in the house, and she remembers that Emily's wedding was very sparsely attended on her side. But still, there must be someone.

Jayne was shocked by Emily's description of how Toby lunged for her and how he'd become violent when she fought him off. He'd wanted to stop her calling the police, Emily said. No, she didn't know why.

Jayne didn't tell Emily she thinks she knows why Toby didn't want police involvement. If what Ruth suspects about him is true, he will not want that kind of attention on their group. But she doesn't want to share this yet. She wants to talk to Ruth about it when Ruth is sober.

The voices from the kitchen sound more fraught. Emily is getting upset. 'You have to find him,' she says. There's hysteria in her voice.

Before John Elliott's death, Jayne had hoped that whatever happened at the barn might fade from memory once they were all home, but it will be hard to recover from feeling involved, however tangentially, in the suicide. And very hard to recover from this. Because it doesn't feel as if it's ended yet. The aftershocks are still happening.

And things may have gone too far, now, for Ruth and Toby. Only she and Mark, she thinks, have a chance. Paul and Emily, perhaps, depending on where he's been.

Otherwise, the repercussions are going to play out for a while.

'We'll call you with any information,' the policewoman tells Emily. 'And please call us immediately if you hear from your husband.'

They're getting up, putting on coats. Jayne stands and intercepts them in the hallway.

'Will you be interviewing Edie Porter?' she asks. She feels vehement, suddenly, about Edie taking responsibility for what she's done, for triggering this chain of events.

'We'll be talking to any persons we think are of interest,' the policewoman says. Her tone is calm and even, professional. Jayne bristles at being handled.

She shuts the door behind them and rejoins Emily who is in the kitchen, still hardly able to move without feeling sick and dizzy. Her leg is extended, resting on another chair, and it looks grotesque in silhouette in contrast to her slim form.

'Can I get you a tea? Or some food or anything?' Jayne says. Her tone sounds hard, cruel almost, under the circumstances, she knows, but she's exhausted and stressed and considers it a fault she can't fix just now.

'You can go if you like,' Emily says.

'Is there someone I can call, to come and be with you?'

'No.'

'Nobody?'

Emily shakes her head. 'I keep thinking he's dead and imagining his face with blue lips and cold skin.'

'Don't,' Jayne says. It's a horrible image and she's afraid it might trigger her. She tries to summon up some rationality. 'Even if you think Edie's capable of harming someone, why would she do it and admit to it in a letter? She has a daughter to think about.'

'I don't know,' Emily says.

'Unless she didn't write it,' Jayne says. The idea has just occurred to her. Why didn't she question this earlier?

'She wrote it,' Emily says. 'And I'm not going to stop believing that unless Paul walks through the door.'

The glass table between them reflects the window and the window reflects the room, where Jayne has put on the side lamps. It's as if there are alternate realities. Jayne wishes she could dive into one where none of this has happened.

'Are you sure I can't get you anything or call anyone?' Jayne says. 'Talk to me.'

Jayne feels wrung out, her limbs heavy. 'I'm sure they'll find Paul,' is all she can come out with.

Emily makes an exasperated sound. 'Jesus, Jayne, can't you ever stop trying to manage other people? Who are you, really?'

Jayne's not answering that. 'I guess it's time for me to go.' She stands. It occurs to her that whenever she's here, she feels diminished somehow by the money that's gone into this place, by its showiness. It's not her. She just wants a quiet life with her man.

But it is a very big house for a very young woman to be all alone in. She feels a twinge of guilt. 'You're not afraid that Toby will come back?'

'I'm not afraid of him. He won't come near me again.'

'What do you mean?'

'Nothing. You wouldn't understand.'

'Do you want to try me?'

'Get out.'

Something snaps in Jayne. She shuts her eyes. Sees things that she doesn't want to see. Pixelated death. A buzzing starts up in her ears, low-grade but persistent. She blinks. Emily looks hostile to her. Like an impostor. Perhaps none of this would have happened if she hadn't joined their gang. The buzzing increases in volume.

'You want to know who I am, but who are you, really?' she asks Emily.

'Who would you like me to be, Jayne? In fact, who do you think I am? A gold-digger? The girl who takes your husband's best friend away. The common little slut you don't want at your nice middle-class party?' Emily's expression is snarled with sarcasm, but Jayne also recognises self-hatred when she sees it, especially the brand that women love to direct against themselves, and she feels a little bit of sympathy for Emily.

She tries to hold on to reality, to ask herself whether she believes something might have happened to Paul and she should remain here, to support Emily. Is it the right thing to do?

The answer is yes. Mark has gone to support Imogen. He asked Jayne to do her bit here. And she should.

Emily's beauty is startling, even now. Strange that I should notice that in this moment, Jayne thinks. And, then, I envy her. Beauty is power.

But there is something else in Emily's face. Jayne's seen it before.

It's the look of a liar.

I walk towards the car. Toby is sitting inside it and he's realised that I have the keys. He's very still. There's a slackness to his skin that looks like cowardice. Out of the corner of his eye, I believe he can see me approaching.

I take my time. The lights are on in the front room of Edie's house but upstairs the windows are dark. Edie's bedroom faces the front. I lay in her bed, once, just for a few moments.

Rob had asked me round to help him build a playhouse for Imogen. I went upstairs to use the bathroom and couldn't resist sneaking into their room.

I burrowed my head into her pillow, felt the indent she'd left in the mattress and inhaled deeply, trying to rediscover the smell of that night we spent together beside the beach in Wales all those years ago.

Imogen is in the house but, as far as I can tell, she's not looking out of any windows, which is good. I'd hate for her to witness violence.

I don't intend to kill Toby. It would be very hard to explain away the loss of all three of my remaining close friends and exhausting to feign the appropriate level of grief for the appropriate length of time. But he deserves to suffer for what he did to Emily.

And for being here, close to my daughter.

He deserves to suffer mightily.

Ruth wakes up in her own bed. She feels hardly better than she did earlier, but she doesn't know if she's been out for a few seconds, or longer. She thinks it isn't long.

She has the sense that something woke her but she's not sure what. There's often noise on her street, so maybe it was something happening out there.

Her phone isn't on the bedside table. She doesn't know where she's left it.

She thinks about Toby. Maybe, if he agrees to move out and leave her and Alfie alone, if he leaves nicely, she won't report him to the police. It would be a dark deal, she knows that, but a mother must do what she can to protect her child. It would be a terrible burden for Alfie to bear if Toby has done those things.

She hears a noise from downstairs. A door slamming. She tenses up.

'Hello? Ruth?' It's her mother, Flora.

Ruth gets out of bed and looks down the stairs.

Her mother is in the hallway, coat on, Alfie in her arms. He's snuggled against Flora but when he sees Ruth it's as if he comes alive. He stretches out his arms and his whole body strains to reach her. She runs down the stairs and grabs him, showers him with kisses which he reciprocates by nuzzling her. She's never been so pleased to see him. She's not sure she can ever leave him again while he's so little.

'What are you doing home?' Flora asks.

'I wasn't well, so I came back early. I was going to call you, but I fell asleep. What are you doing here?'

Her mother studies her. Her nose twitches and Ruth keeps her mouth closed. Flora has accused her of drinking too much before. Ruth won't be able to stand it if she starts now.

'You don't look well, darling. I'm here to collect Alfie's hat. You forgot to pack it.'

Alfie is looking shyly at Ruth. His eyes are wide and bright. There is so much love in them. All the love in the world. Her heart melts. She squeezes him and feels her heart grow.

'There are books all over the pavement outside,' her mother says. 'They look like Toby's.'

Ruth shakes her head and blinks back tears. From Flora's tone of voice, she knows her mother is remembering when Ruth did the same to Flora's books, the psychiatry texts she'd spent a lifetime acquiring, causing both heartache and hundreds of pounds' worth of damage.

'Is Toby here?' Flora asks.

Ruth doesn't know how to reply. Her mother has caught her at rock bottom. Again.

'Do you want a cup of tea?' is all she can think to say, hating herself.

'I think we should pick up the books first, don't you?'

Ruth shakes her head.

'Darling,' Flora says, 'you don't need to have them back in the house. I'll put them in my car if you like. But they're too precious to leave outside. They'll be stolen or destroyed.'

Ruth feels judged, and it's horrible, but she understands that, in this moment, she deserves it. She is suddenly aware of her own appearance, again: her dishevelment, her unbrushed hair, her foul breath.

She holds Alfie as if he were a lifebuoy and watches from the window as Flora rescues the books. Alfie plays with her hair, and she thinks, How bad a person must I be if I can drink and get into this kind of state when I have this child? It's a question she's asked herself repeatedly over the past six months, and sometimes the only answer to it is to drink more. Drinking is the only thing that makes her feel in control, even though she knows how irrational that is.

And she knows that she doesn't have the strength to keep going the way she has been any longer. She's fallen too far to get back on her own. She's too alone. She has to finish what she started with Jayne and tell everything to someone she can trust.

She watches her mother lock her car, with Toby's books piled on the back seat, and walk up the path to the house. Flora's face is blotted with worry. She looks softer than usual.

Alfie touches Ruth's cheek, and examines his fingertip. It's wet. She's crying.

Flora will judge Ruth, and chalk up more failures for her daughter, and it will be painful but at least Flora will help. That's what she does. She might not hug, but she's effortlessly capable.

Flora pushes open the front door and pauses in the hallway, gathering strength for what she knows she must say. Her arms feel empty and strangely light after twenty-four hours of lugging the baby around. He's such a sweet soul; she's quite fallen for him. It's the first chance she's had to bond with him without her daughter hovering between them. 'Helicopter parenting' – isn't that what they call it nowadays? It's an apt description for her daughter, she believes.

But Ruth's problems are far more entrenched. Her daughter is drunk. Again. She looks unwell, mentally as well as physically. There's a grey tinge to her skin that speaks of alcohol abuse and deep unhappiness. And there's clearly been a terrible row between her and Toby.

Ruth sits down with Alfie on her lap. Flora settles beside her and watches as Ruth struggles to divert her attention from the baby and say what she means to say. Her daughter has always been like this: unable or unwilling to open up.

Ruth's childhood face, as Flora remembers it, was a portrait of tension. Ruth was her father's daughter, unable to relax, wanting to be the best at everything, piling pressure on herself relentlessly, a perfectionist in every area of life. She's Flora's greatest professional and personal failure.

Flora was delighted when Ruth met Toby, hopeful that his somewhat charming laissez-faire approach to life and his good humour would temper her daughter's terrible seriousness.

Has their relationship failed?

'Where's Toby?' she asks.

'He's gone.'

'Has he left you?'

'Why would you make that assumption? No, he hasn't left me. I kicked him out.'

Ruth's right to pick her up on this. Flora had always imagined it would be the other way around. 'I'm sorry,' she says. 'What happened?'

Tears spill from Ruth's eyes. The baby picks up on her distress, but she can't contain it.

'What is it?' Flora says. Ruth's silent crying has always bothered her. It's so unnatural. She puts her arm around Ruth's shoulders. Her daughter's body is humming with tension.

Alfie touches Ruth's face, her tears. He's getting upset. 'It's OK, sweetie,' Ruth says and summons a smile for him. Flora finds it moving.

'Ruth,' she says. 'Please talk to me.'

She is, she realises, afraid for her daughter's mental health. Very afraid. Again.

Ruth talks. She spills the whole story. About the letter, the night at the barn, John Elliott's suicide, her drinking until she blacked out, her suspicions about Toby and his students.

Flora doesn't interrupt. She notes that Ruth won't make eye contact. It's painful to witness her daughter's shame when Flora believes that Ruth has nothing to be ashamed of because we're all weak in some way, often in many ways.

But she is also relieved. She's been waiting for so many years for Ruth to open up to her. All of Ruth's life.

But what she's hearing is profoundly worrying.

This is my fault, she thinks. Mine and Toby's. They've hidden something from Ruth that they shouldn't have, and Ruth has become untethered. She's picking up clues to Toby's behaviour which are innocent and twisting them to fit a paranoid narrative she's fabricating. Flora and Toby should have been truthful with

Ruth and insisted she got help earlier. Flora needs to talk to Toby urgently.

'Ruthie,' she says. She hasn't used the diminutive for years but resorts to it now without thinking. Ruth has to be reeled in from the dark place she's descended into.

'Listen to me. What happened at the barn is awful, truly, but the rest of it, it isn't what you think. Toby hasn't done anything wrong. I can explain it all.'

Imogen leaves her home by the back door, just as she did earlier, but she's afraid to return to the railway track. Mark found her there too easily before. And now he has Toby to help him.

She doesn't know what's going on in her driveway and doesn't want to. She just wants to get away from them both.

Her dad's workshop is located to the side of the house, tucked into a sheltered spot in the garden. It has a lock on it. She needs a key to get in but it's in the house.

She creeps back inside. The workshop key isn't hanging in its normal place. Her breathing sounds horribly loud. She sneaks into the kitchen and rifles through the dresser drawers. There are bunches of spare keys – keys for the electricity meter, window locks – and she thinks she'll never find what she needs but she does. A single silver key on a leather fob.

She slips out into the garden again but stops right outside the back door. She can hear footsteps. They stop. A few terrifying moments pass before she takes her chances and bolts across the short patch of lawn and unlocks the workshop, eases the door open and slips inside. She locks the door behind her with shaking hands and feels a little bit of relief, but not much.

It's not a strong door.

She crouches down amongst the wood shavings and looks around the workshop. It's dark but she won't turn the light on. Mark and Toby would see it. She's not sure which of them frightens her the most.

There's only one thing visible that might be of use to her. She stands up and takes a small axe from its hook on the wall.

The wooden handle is worn and smooth from its years of use by her dad, and holding it feels as close as she's going to get to safety until someone comes to help her. She crouches down again and tucks herself underneath the workbench, out of sight of the window that faces the drive.

And tries to remember to breathe.

Alfie starts to grizzle and it's only moments before the grizzle turns into a full-fledged cry.

'He's hungry,' Ruth says. 'I'll get him a bottle.'

'I want to talk to you, Ruthie.'

'Yes, but I have to feed him!'

'I'll help.'

Ruth sees her phone on the kitchen table. She picks it up, wanting to know if Toby's replied, bracing herself to see his response to her accusations.

He has replied. But it's not what she's expecting. At Edie's house with Imogen. Come quick.

There's something about the text – its wording, the brevity, the mention of Imogen and Edie – that scares her.

'I have to go,' she says.

'Where?'

'Edie's house. Something's wrong. Toby texted me.'

'No, Ruth. You can't. You're drunk.'

'I'm going.'

'How about if I drive you?'

Ruth shakes her head and passes the baby to her mother who takes him because she's afraid, if she doesn't, Ruth will take him with her.

Flora watches, impotent, as Ruth grabs her car keys from the hooks on the wall and heads for the door.

I shouldn't drive, Ruth thinks, Flora's right, but this feels like the culmination of the horror of this weekend.

She has to go.

'Ruth!' her mother calls. Frantic.

Ruth ignores her. She slams the front door behind her and runs for her car.

Flora holds the baby close to her. What have we done? she asks herself. She tries to phone Toby, but he doesn't answer. She would try to follow Ruth, but she's got no idea where she's gone.

Alfie is crying hard now. Watching his mother leave has upset him.

Flora was surprised to get Toby on the phone last night. She'd called him to give him an update on the situation on a distressed student who lived at Addison Court, expecting to leave a voicemail because she knew that where Ruth and Toby were staying was off-grid, but to her surprise, Toby answered his phone.

What culminated last night had begun months ago when one of Toby's students, a young woman called Lexi MacKay, suffered a swift and serious decline in her mental health.

Lexi had tried to access the university's mental health services, but they'd been unhelpful and couldn't offer her an appointment for weeks, when she needed one urgently. The duty doctor could only offer her twenty minutes and she finished that appointment with a prescription for antidepressants that she didn't want to take.

She was desperate, her behaviour was deteriorating, and after she began to write accusatory letters to lecturers, including Toby, he'd asked Flora for help. Lexi, he said, was likely to be expelled from the university if she continued to behave like this without intervention. But she was very talented.

And there was another complication. Toby didn't want Ruth to know. It was news to Flora, but apparently Ruth's tendency to be possessive of Toby had escalated since she'd become pregnant. She was liable to be touchy about his female students, anyhow, but after intercepting a letter from Lexi she'd had a fit. Toby didn't think Ruth would be understanding, now, if she learned that he wanted to help this young woman. And Lexi badly needed help.

We should never have hidden this from my daughter, Flora thinks. The time to tell her would have been after Lexi's death, when she and Toby, reeling from their failure to help Lexi, had taken further action.

But Ruth had started drinking by then and was refusing to listen to either of them.

Flora and Toby carried on working together and kept it a secret. They were very concerned that there might be copycat deaths after Lexi's suicide. It was a known phenomenon at other institutions and could affect other students, just like Lexi, whose rapid decline had come out of a clear blue sky.

While Toby and Flora worked hard to shift the gears at the university to put some official support measures in place, it was obvious that any response was going to be woefully slow and likely to be underfunded and inadequate. In desperation, they'd organised an unofficial group of volunteers who would aim to respond to students in poor mental health immediately.

Last night, a call came in from Lexi's best friend, a young woman called Laura, also one of Toby's students. Flora took it. Stuck at home with Alfie, she organised another volunteer to visit Laura. When she rang Toby to let him know what was going on, intending to leave a voicemail, she was surprised to catch him in person.

'Boring story but I had to stay in Bristol tonight,' he said. 'A last-minute thing. I'm travelling up to the barn at the crack of dawn tomorrow.'

He listened as Flora told him about Laura, a shy but sweet student, who had rung feeling desperate, with suicidal thoughts.

'Who's on the rota for a visit?' he said.

'Becky.'

'She's pretty inexperienced. I might go with her.'

Flora wasn't sure. She thought he needed a break. 'Go to bed, Toby. And go away on your weekend. Becky and I have it in hand.'

But he insisted, spending most of the night at the Addison Court building with Becky, both of them talking to Laura. It was, apparently, a necessary and successful intervention. They would ensure follow-up.

And now, yet again, Ruth has twisted it into something ugly.

It's imperative that they're honest with her from this point onwards, Flora thinks and regrets bitterly that they haven't been from the start. But now's the moment to intervene with some muscle. We cannot handle this as a family any longer. We've helped our students but failed Ruth. We didn't recognise the seriousness of what was going on right under our noses and that's unforgivable.

She tries to soothe the baby, but he's red-faced and screaming by the time she gets her phone out of her bag.

She dials 999 and over the baby's cries she lets the police know that her daughter's out on the roads, driving drunk from her home address to the house of a woman called Edie Porter, and that Flora's very afraid that Ruth or someone else will come to harm.

I take Toby's car keys from my pocket and hold them up beside the driver's side window. He turns towards me slowly. It looks like it's dawning on him how much trouble he's in.

I jingle the keys and smile, but he doesn't reciprocate. I guess he's finally lost his sense of humour.

He reaches for the door handle.

The moment he steps out, we're going to take a little walk together, out of sight of Imogen.

But before I understand what's happened, I'm staggering backwards, bent over. I fall on to my backside and then the pain kicks in across my thighs and my abdomen, my groin. He slammed the car door into me.

I try to stand up, but the pain is white-hot. I'm so stupid. He approaches me and I'm afraid because he could kick the life out of me, but he stoops and picks up his car keys from where they fell from my hand. I lunge towards him and clasp his leg right behind the knee and he goes down fast, sprawling, and crawls out of my reach.

He staggers up before I can. As he gets into his car, I'm on my feet, fighting the pain, tears streaming from my eyes. But I'm too slow. He backs down the driveway towards my car, and swerves wildly as he reaches it, clipping the front bumper and Edie's gatepost. He's stuck momentarily but accelerates, and after moments of wheel spinning his car gets traction and explodes out on to the lane.

The sound of the impact is shattering.

In the aftermath all I can hear is my own ragged breathing.

I look at the house. No sign of Imogen. I look down the drive. Toby's car has been hit side-on by another vehicle. I see crumpled metal. Steam rising.

I stand up. The pain is nothing.

I hope Toby's dead.

The driveway's short, but it seems to take me forever to walk up it.

Imogen hears the collision, too, and gets to her feet.

She looks out of the window. Unlocks the door. Drops the axe. Runs.

'Mum,' she shouts. 'Mummy?'

*

'No!' I yell. I try to stop my daughter running past me. She needs to be protected from seeing this.

She dodges me, and runs towards the scene, screaming for her mother.

I work hard to catch up with her. At the mouth of the driveway, she stops. I reach her side.

The destruction is beautiful and terrible. The smell is intoxicating and unnatural. Toby's car is crushed on the driver's side where the other vehicle has slammed into it. I put my arm around Imogen and pull her towards me.

'It's not your mother's car,' I say. 'It's not Mum.'

She pulls away and runs towards the vehicles. I follow. I can see through the shattered windscreen of Toby's car that he's unconscious. His head is tilted back, his neck looks stretched, there's blood on his face and his eyes are beads of white.

It's hard to look at. Everything feels exquisitely painful, as if all my plans are falling apart right in front of me.

I look at the other car. Its bonnet is crumpled where it impacted Toby's Honda, its windscreen has partially shattered and the light inside the car has come on. I can see that the driver's a woman. She's hunched over the wheel and unmoving.

'Phone an ambulance!' Imogen screams at me. 'What are you doing? Phone for help! Give me your phone!'

She's tugging at my arm. I look at her. Of course. That's what I should be doing.

I take my phone out but find myself staring at it. She grabs it from me and dials 999.

I listen to her talking to the operator and I stare at the accident.

It's so potent. I feel almost bewitched by the sight, as if I've been the cause of all this and I don't know if that makes me a god or a monster.

When Imogen has finished making the call, she shouts at me, 'Why aren't you helping them? I thought you knew first aid,' and I realise I do, of course I do, and I should be helping and that perhaps I should be supporting her and not her supporting me. And I get the sudden conviction that she might never be able to love me after this if I can't pull myself together and prove myself to her.

Imogen runs to Toby's car and tries to open the doors, but they're stuck. She crawls on to the bonnet, trying to reach him via the shattered windscreen.

I approach the other car. Steam hisses from the bonnet. Imogen is calling Toby. Apart from that, the silence is other-worldly. I can't see the face of the driver in the car that crashed into Toby's, but it doesn't look good for her. Her door is jammed but I get the passenger door open and crawl across the seat and feel for a pulse in her neck.

It's there but weak. Her breathing is shallow. I daren't move her.

She moans. It's a shocking, inhuman sound. Through the front window I can see Imogen trying to reach Toby. She's lying on the bonnet, her hands through the gap in the windscreen, but it's not big enough for her to get to him. She's so unbelievably brave.

Imogen glances at me, desperation on her face, and immediately I lean forward, and talk to the woman the way Imogen has been talking to Toby.

'You'll be OK,' I tell her. My words sound stilted. 'If you can hear me, help is on the way.'

I don't care if this woman lives or dies but I want Imogen to see me doing the right thing, so I lean in even closer to pull the woman's bloody hair aside so that I can see her face, and I realise with a shock that it's Ruth.

An animal noise escapes from her mouth and her head moves a fraction. Her blood is all over the steering wheel. I can't get away from her fast enough. I scramble backwards out of the car and when I stand up I feel as if everything around me is moving and I am still, in its centre, in the eye of the storm, and I am finished.

Ruth is here, dying, in front of me. And so is Toby. She has driven into his car as he backed out. They might have killed one another.

Imogen is screaming for me to help her. She's given up trying to reach Toby through the windscreen and she's tugging again on his car door, the one that didn't receive the impact, but it won't budge. She keeps calling his name, but he doesn't move.

'He's dying,' she yells. 'Give me your phone again.'

Imogen calls 999 once more and puts them on speaker, her voice desperate, pleading with them to get here as quickly as they can.

'I'm afraid they're dying,' she says.

'Help is on the way,' the operator replies. 'They're very close. Are the victims breathing?'

'I don't know. I couldn't reach him to feel for a pulse. Mark, is the woman breathing?'

'It's Ruth,' I say. 'She had a faint pulse.'

'Ruth?' she says. She looks up from the phone and at me. 'Toby's Ruth?' she asks. I think she's cracking. This is too much for her. I need to take control of the situation. A young girl shouldn't have to deal with this, not when she has so much more trauma to come and has suffered so much already. I don't want my daughter to be broken beyond repair. But she doesn't move.

The operator is still talking to us via the speakerphone, the voice disembodied and strange. 'We'll check if the male is breathing,' I say. 'We know you're coming.' I hang up.

'Sweetheart,' I say to Imogen, and I force myself to sound gentle though I want to scream at her to get away from this mess. The sounds Ruth is making are bothering me. 'You need to go in.'

She ignores me and climbs into Ruth's car.

'Imogen!' I shout.

She starts talking to Ruth, her head right alongside Ruth's, telling her to hang in there, that it's going to be OK.

I lean into the car. I'm going to drag Imogen out of there and make her go back to the house. This is all wrong. Catastrophically wrong.

I try to grab Imogen but she lashes out at me, hard and unexpectedly. It's the shock more than the force of her reaction that causes me to fall on to my knees beside the car. I feel disorientated. Why won't Imogen obey me? She's supposed to do what I tell her.

I haul myself up and reach for her again and this time she reacts more savagely than before.

'Get off,' she screams.

'Imogen,' I say. 'I'm your father.' She's breaking my heart. She doesn't respect me.

I get hold of her, finally, and grip her so tightly she'll never be able to get away from me. I drag her out of the car and she fights it, twisting, raining blows on me however she can, but I succeed and pull her close enough to wrap my arms around her and envelop her. For a moment her body slackens and she feels as vulnerable as a young doe or a colt that has just taken its first few steps. But when I try to hug her tighter she goes crazy again, hitting me, shouting at me.

'Mark!' Her voice sounds strange, and I release my grip. It was too tight. I see that now. A mistake. 'I'm sorry,' I say to her. 'I was just trying to protect you.'

She coughs, her hand on her chest, and the look she directs at me makes me feel inhuman. I don't know if I'll ever be able to forget it.

'Please, Imogen, call me Daddy. I did a DNA test. I'm your daddy. I'll have the results soon, it should be any minute now, sweetie, and then you'll see that it's true.'

She backs away from me. There's blood on her face and on her hands.

And there's nothing loving in her expression at all.

'What is it?' Jayne asks.

She's exhausted by Emily's flip-flopping from friendly to hostile, exhausted by the fact that Emily might be lying now. She nearly left after Emily screamed at her, but she promised Mark that she would support Emily, and she will.

'I'm scared.'

'I know you are. I am too.'

'You are?'

Jayne nods.

'Were you scared when we were at the barn? Or were you really that cool about the letter?'

Jayne weighs up what to say and opts for the truth. 'I was calm because I believed it was a hoax, but now I think I was wrong. I'm scared now.'

'If we'd gone down to the farmhouse when I wanted to, this might not have happened.'

Jayne isn't sure about that, but she won't argue with Emily at this point.

'I think Paul's dead,' Emily says. 'I can feel it.'

Jayne goes to her and puts her arms around her. She half-expects Emily to flinch, but she doesn't.

'Let's wait and see what happens,' she says.

They sit for a while. It's dark around them, but neither of them moves to put on a light.

Emily cries hard and Jayne lets her.

Eventually, when Jayne's arms feel numb and neither of their phones has buzzed for far too long and the feeling of waiting for news is almost unbearable, Emily speaks again.

'I lied about Toby attacking me,' she says. 'And I feel terrible about it. I don't want Paul to know. He thinks I'm better than that. I am, usually.'

If Paul's alive to hear about it, Jayne thinks. If he is.

'You lied that Toby attacked you?'

'Yes.'

'Why would you do that?'

'I'm sorry. He was being weird about me calling the police and I got scared and I scratched him when he came near me. And then I didn't want to get in trouble for it. I didn't want to be accused of assault. But he never hurt me.'

'Oh, dear God,' Jayne says. 'Haven't we done enough to each other this weekend?'

Blue lights. So many of them. They're blinding.

Two ambulances. Four paramedics. Two fire crew. Four police officers. Shouts of authority.

I'm sitting on the side of the road. Dizzy. Drowning in my failure, in the awful pain of it. What's the bravest thing to do now? What will prove to Imogen that I truly love her?

A woman crouches down beside me. Green uniform. 'Are you hurt, sir?'

'He's not.' Imogen's voice. She sounds cold and hard. It's painful to hear.

I wipe away tears, ashamed for these people to see me weeping. They leave me on the verge.

A saw screams and sparks fly from Toby's car. They're cutting through the roof to get him out.

I stagger to my feet and sway as I watch. It's a lot to take in. The scene is overwhelming. The stink, the noise, the lights, the music coming from one of the car radios as if this was a gentle evening, not a scene of carnage.

A police officer approaches and offers me assistance, but I shake my head. I don't want Imogen to see me as weak. I am not weak. But my legs wobble, betraying me. It feels impossible to see anything clearly. I sit down again, heavily.

'I'm fine,' I assure her and meanwhile the metal saw stops, and I hear a roaring in my ears that's coming from inside my own head.

They have Toby on a stretcher, and they carry him past me to the ambulance. He's unconscious. I reach for him. I think I want him to be dead.

I get up again and stumble and fall against Ruth's car. I notice the baby seat in the back. I point at it, wanting to show it to Imogen and to say, 'You used to be in one of these.'

A policeman tells me I can't touch anything, that I must step away. 'I think we need someone to look at you properly, sir,' he says. Where have all these people come from?

'No, no,' I say. 'I'm fine.'

Except that everything seems to be collapsing around and within me. Apart from what I feel for Imogen, which is growing. It's colossal and beautiful.

Where is she?

I see her talking to a policewoman who leans in towards my daughter, intent on her every word. I'm so proud of Imogen. She gesticulates as she speaks and, at one point, they turn to look at me. I don't know what she's saying but the expression on their faces indicates grave concern. Is she worried for me?

I must go over there and introduce myself as her father, let them know that they don't have to look after her because I'm here.

I make my way towards them, strobed and disorientated by the blue lights.

*

Police Constable Rosie Jones puts her arm around Imogen. The girl is distraught, she thinks. She's been telling quite a story about the gentleman who we found with her at the scene. He looks as if he's coming over here now.

'Billy,' she calls. Her colleague's talking on the radio. He's sitting in their patrol car, which is parked behind the vehicle that's blocking the driveway of the house where the girl lives. The scene is chaos, but the paramedics and fire crew have just extracted the female driver from her car and are loading her into the second ambulance. She looks unconscious.

'Billy!' Rosie wants him to take Imogen into her house and look after her. The girl's in shock. They need to get her out of here to a place of safety.

Billy jogs towards them.

'Listen to this,' he says. 'The number plate of the car blocking the driveway has a marker on it. It's just pinged on the ANPR in our car.'

'What kind of marker?'

He pulls her aside and talks to her urgently, out of Imogen's earshot.

They've left Imogen on her own, standing amidst the carnage, and in the middle of all this terrible ugliness she's a beacon, a beautiful, angelic girl.

'Sweetheart,' I say, as I approach. 'I love you so much.' I smile. She doesn't hear me. She's staring at the cars. She looks distraught.

My legs feel like jelly, but I pick up my pace.

Imogen notices me and turns her back, edging closer to the two officers who are huddled by their car.

But I'm nearly beside her now, and I extend my arms because I need to hug her again, so she knows that she's safe, so that I know I am.

And I'm going to take her away from here and it'll be OK because she and I don't need Ruth or Toby or anyone else to be happy. We're going to start out all on our own, and in a way this makes it a bit easier. It helps me erase my past.

I'm almost with her, and although she's backing away faster now, I find a surge of strength as I cover the last few yards between us and I'm so close that I can almost smell her when a young policeman cuts in.

'Mark Pavey?' he asks. He has a brightness in his eyes, like a magpie eyeing a jewel.

'Yes?' I try not to snap because I have respect for authority, generally, but he's being quite rude.

'You're Mark Pavey?'

'I just said so, didn't I?' I try to see past him, to where Imogen is.

'Mark Pavey, I'm arresting you on suspicion of murder of Edie Porter and Paul Ramsay.'

Before I have a chance to respond, he seizes my arm and pulls it right up my back and his body pushes against mine as he tries to cuff me, but he fumbles, and fails to get the cuffs on, and I try to get out of his grip, but he yanks my arm harder and I cry out because I feel like it's going to break and I know from my training that, if I move, it will.

'Edie's my mum!' Imogen screams. 'That's my mum! What did you do?'

She flies at me like a banshee, and it takes one of the policewomen all her strength to hold Imogen back and I'm incapacitated and speechless and I never wanted this to happen, it's breaking my heart. I struggle to free myself again and Imogen almost breaks out of the grip that the policewoman has her in.

'Get him in the car!' she shouts at her colleague.

'He's not cuffed.'

'I don't care.'

With the help of another officer, he forces me into the vehicle, and I collapse on to the seat, out of breath from the struggle. The pain when he releases my arm is terrible and I nurse it and I also feel as if something frozen is melting down my spine because things weren't supposed to go this way. My plan was better than this.

They haven't slammed the door on me when my phone buzzes.

The DNA results. Must be.

I get my phone out of my pocket and unlock it, greedy to know, desperate to be able to show the result to Imogen before they drive me away so that, when I've explained why they're wrong about me and that Edie and Paul have absconded and I'm just a guy trying to do the right thing for a girl who's actually my daughter and they let me go, Imogen will be waiting for me and she and I can start all over again.

There's an email from the company who runs the tests. My hand shakes as I open it and I click on the link to the PDF that contains proof of everything I've ever wanted and it starts to download.

The police officer takes the phone out of my hand.

'Thank you, sir,' he says. 'I'll have that.'

He slams the car door and all the sound from the outside world becomes a little bit muted and I can see through the window that he's looking at my phone, reading the email, and I can't believe this is happening.

I bang on the window, but he ignores me, and I stop when I see the policewoman approach because I want to hear what they're saying.

'Is the phone unlocked?' Rosie asks Billy.

'Yes.'

'Brilliant. Don't let it lock itself again. Keep swiping. It'll save us a nightmare trying to get it unlocked.'

'I won't. Don't worry.'

'Jo's taken the girl inside, poor thing. I've called social services and requested a family liaison officer, and we need to make sure someone stays with her until they arrive, but drinks later, yeah? Just goes to show, you don't know what the day's going to bring when you get up in the morning. What an absolute result.'

Billy looks at the phone as the PDF finishes downloading.

'What was our friend so keen to look at do we think?' he says. 'Oh! Paternity test results.'

He scans down.

'Blah, blah,' he says. 'Technical stuff . . . OK, here we are: "The probability of paternity is 0%."'

He turns to the car and holds the phone up against the window so the perp can read the screen.

'Don't worry!' he shouts. 'The kid's not yours.'

SUNDAY – ONE YEAR LATER

Jayne hesitates before opening the email. It's from William Elliott. She hasn't thought of that name for so long that she feels as if the message has dropped into her inbox from another world.

She checks her emails as infrequently as possible. She's withdrawn from friends and they've stopped contacting her regularly. Journalists find her address periodically and hound her with earnest requests for interviews. They want her to tell her story and Mark's and sometimes they shamelessly offer bribes, the generosity of which often surprises but never tempts her.

Mark has been called a 'serial killer' by the press and this has created a market. People are slavering for details, for 'personal' stories about him. And who better to provide one than his wife?

The subject line on William Elliott's email is 'Hello' which encourages her. It makes a nice change.

As well as contact from journalists, Jayne also gets emails and messages from people who want to tell her what a disgusting person she is and how she must be partly responsible for what Mark did.

It makes her think of how much vitriol must have fuelled their presumably extensive efforts to find her and she wonders if they have a bottomless reserve of it, to be tapped into indiscriminately whenever they feel disgust or outrage, or if their vitriol is directed specifically at her, and at Mark because of what he did.

She wonders if they write to him at his institution or if they just target her, the wife, who should have known what he was capable of.

Some of them imply that she could have stopped him. Others accuse her of failing to do so.

She agrees with them. It's something she'll feel guilty about for the rest of her life.

Jayne believes she is responsible for the deaths of Rob, Paul and Edie because she was blind to who Mark is and the reason that she was blind is because she was selfish: she was on a mission of her own, to help him and, by helping him, to help herself.

She mistook his psychopathy – her shorthand for the multitude of personality disorders he's been diagnosed with – for PTSD, because she was in love with the idea of them both healing together. It was her own self-absorption and egoism that caused this.

Their friends died because she believed that she was guiding herself and Mark on a journey towards a perfect, happy ending.

Once, she told her therapist this, but her therapist countered by saying she thought Jayne should focus on defining her identity as a victim before exploring guilt, and Jayne was confused and felt another part of her mind break away to float in a soup of inert emotions.

But William's email has woken her up a little, and it's a nice feeling. She barely remembers how it feels to have her interest piqued.

She holds her breath as she opens it.

Dear Jayne

I got your email address from my mother. I hope you don't mind me making contact like this. Please ignore if it's an intrusion. We will understand.

Neither Mum nor I have been able to forget you and your friends and we're so very sorry about what happened to you.

I know we're strangers but the coincidence of our family tragedy and the horrific events you went through at Dark Fell Barn have made me follow your husband's case closely. I suspect it's fanciful to say that what happened that weekend links us in any meaningful way, but it has made me think of you and your friends often. I've kept in touch from afar and followed the progress of the case through my colleagues in Bristol. Your husband's confession must have been both shocking and devastating but I'm glad you were spared a trial.

We are fine, under the circumstances. My mother has borne a lot of guilt for what happened at the barn. We would both like to apologise for my dad's actions that night. As I believe you've been made aware by my colleagues, my father was not in his right mind and, while it was his intention to frighten you with the scarecrow, the man who did this was not the man we knew. An autopsy after his death revealed that he had advanced dementia with Lewy bodies. This means, to cut a long diagnosis short, that he was not only suffering the symptoms of advanced regular dementia but was also likely to have been experiencing hallucinations and delusions. My mother and I believe this to be the case and that it's what made him act the way he did. And we are so very sorry if it contributed in any way to worsening the horrific experiences that you went through.

We both send you our warmest wishes and hope that, now that a year has passed since then, you're able to find some kind of peace and a way forward.

William and Maggie

His mobile number's at the bottom of the email. Jayne looks at it, wondering if the fact that he included it is an invitation to call him, or if it's one of those automated signatures.

For the first time in a year, she feels a strong urge to reach out to someone. To him. It's as if he's been able to crack open the wall that she's built up around herself.

Before she can change her mind, she picks up her phone and dials his number. She holds her breath while it rings. He'll be busy, she thinks, with family, or friends; he won't pick up because hers is an unknown number and then she won't be brave enough to leave a message and she'll hang up and never dare to call him again.

'Hello,' he says.

'Hello. It's Jayne. Jayne Pavey. I got your email.'

'Oh, Jayne.' His voice is just as she remembers. Sing-song, measured.

It sounds as if he's settling down on to a seat of some kind. She imagines him staring out of a window as he does – at the moorland, perhaps. But perhaps not. Maybe he has the football on TV and he muted it.

Her mouth is dry. 'Thank you for what you wrote,' she says. 'Please, tell your mother there are no hard feelings, no blame. It's tragic what happened to your father. I'm so sorry.'

'That's very generous of you.'

She doesn't know what to do with compliments. 'Is your mother all right?' she asks.

'She is. She's done well, considering. We had to let the farm go but we managed to lease it to a family member, so she spends time up there. She lives in a cottage that's close. And the farm is being looked after well, the land and the flock, which is what my father would have wanted.'

'That's good,' she says. She doesn't ask about the barn because she's looked it up online and knows it's still being rented out for holidays. Its website has been beefed up and it's marketed as one of the few places in Britain you can experience the dark sky. It has wifi, a telescope, a driveable track to reach it and a boast about zero light pollution.

A holiday is not something Jayne can imagine any more. Her life now consists of work, of meals for one and of visits to a man who will spend the rest of his days incarcerated in a secure psychiatric institution. She's in a cycle of self-punishment that feels never-ending.

'How are you?' he asks.

She inhales and worries he hears it, that it's a sharp sound. 'I'm managing.'

'Well done,' he says. 'It's not easy, I'm sure.' She's grateful to him for not sugar-coating it.

'No.'

'My mum was asking after your friend, the lady who was lost on the moor that morning.'

'Ruth is fine.' Jayne weighs up how much to tell him and decides that for once she'll just be honest. That feels OK because he was a part of it. She's starting to understand the connection he says he feels. She feels as if something in her brain is warming up.

'It wasn't your dad's fault that Ruth was out there,' she tells him. 'She went out because she was drunk, and the letter spooked her terribly. She's an alcoholic. And she had some personal problems at the time that exacerbated things. But she recovered well from the accident, and she's been sober for a while now.'

A familiar stab of jealousy needles at her. How is it that Ruth, who was delusional about Toby, who fantasised that he was a paedophile, that he was encouraging young women to commit suicide, who pushed her husband about as far away from her as possible, got him back when Emily lost Paul, and Jayne can only wish that she was a widow?

She remembers a night when Toby came round, shortly after he left hospital. He explained it all. How he'd been working with Ruth's mum and they were wracked with guilt that they'd let Ruth's drinking get so out of control before intervening.

'I thought the weekend at the barn might help her,' he said. 'That getting away from home and from the demands of the baby might ease her paranoia. It was supposed to be a new start, until it all went wrong.'

He didn't mention Mark's name, or the letter, or the messages Mark had sent on other people's behalf, the ones which persuaded the men to stay behind that Friday night. Toby had got one from 'Paul'. Paul had got one from 'Edie'. But, of course, Mark had sent them all. Like a puppeteer.

And it was hard for Jayne to witness Toby's upset. Her situation was so much worse, Toby knew. He's tried to reach out to her repeatedly over the past year, but she doesn't want to see them.

'Ruth has a little boy, a toddler,' Jayne tells William Elliott. 'So, it's a relief to all of us that she's doing so well now.'

'Fantastic,' William says. 'I'll pass that on to my mum.'

She has a sudden urge to inform him more about her own situation, about how Mark isn't getting better. Whenever Jayne visits him, he harangues her, asking when Imogen is coming to see him, requesting that Jayne arrange a visit from her. He refers to Imogen as 'his daughter'. He lectures Jayne, in a tone so teachery and with such hollow authority that she wants to throttle him, that DNA tests aren't always reliable and sometimes he asks her to collect a sample from Imogen, so he can arrange another test.

He talks about the plan he had, how clever it was, how he'd set things up so that it looked as if Edie had run off with Paul by killing them both but leaving a trail of text messages from their cloned phones.

He repeats himself, his outrage that he was caught and his toxic self-congratulation on a loop.

And she wants to scream at him, every single time, that his plan was terrible. It was preposterous, utterly deluded, the fantasy of someone who had lost his mind so completely that he had become almost inhuman, and he will never, thank God, ever, bring a child into this world, or look after one.

Jayne wonders, sometimes, who Imogen's real father is. She believes Mark's claim that he saw proof that Rob was sterile, and she sometimes speculates that Edie may have slept with Toby and Paul, too, if she slept with Mark, with the intention of getting pregnant.

But Jayne won't mention her suspicions about this to Imogen. What good would it do?

If Paul is Imogen's real father, it'll be another bereavement for her to cope with. And if it's Toby? He hasn't bonded with his own son, and he has his hands full with Ruth. It's kinder, Jayne believes, to leave Imogen in peace, to try to rebuild her life, so she will not be the one to raise this, ever, because it would rob Imogen of her identity and change her perception of her mother. Imogen doesn't need to know any of it.

The only intervention Jayne has made is to reassure Imogen that Mark is mad and that any claims he made to be her father were grounded in insanity. Imogen had wonderful parents and she should cherish their memory and the years she had with them.

'And what about the other friend?' William asks. 'The one who hurt her ankle?'

Suddenly, she's finding his questions intrusive, and it occurs to her that this could be a set-up, that he could in fact have been persuaded by a journalist to call her and try to wheedle information from her.

'I don't know,' Jayne says. This is true because Emily sold her house and moved on, though Jayne's unsure where she went. Emily hasn't kept in touch with Ruth or Jayne and Jayne can't blame her for it.

William catches her tone and senses that she wants the conversation to end. 'Thanks for calling,' he says. 'I'll pass on what you said to Mum.'

And now she doesn't want him to go because she's changed her mind and she thinks he sounds entirely sincere, and she regrets her suspicion of his motives, but she doesn't know what to say to keep the conversation going. She's so out of practice. She's so lonely.

'OK,' she says.

'Well,' he says, 'keep in touch.'

'I'll do that,' she says but she's not sure she will.

She hangs up.

He didn't ask about Imogen. He'll have learned that she exists, no doubt, from the papers, but otherwise she won't be real to him. Jayne thinks about her all the time.

She knows that Imogen went to live with her friend Jemma and her family, and Jayne thought she saw them both in the city centre once, and she wanted to apologise to Imogen, but knew it was best to duck out of the way and let them walk on by. Mark has done enough damage to that girl.

When the doctors call a meeting, she asks them about Mark, about whether he's ever going to accept that Imogen isn't his. She's not sure she can stand to visit him while he still believes that she is. It's unbearable.

For a long time after the phone call with William Elliott, Jayne sits and runs over what they said to one another.

It was a good conversation, she thinks. For the first time in a long time she felt a connection with someone, felt that they didn't just pity her or see her through the filter of what Mark has done.

Not a widow. Not a serial killer's wife.

And on the back of that thought, she has another.

I might never visit Mark again.

I don't have to.

Imogen's phone pings with a notification. Lunch!

She pulls off her headphones, lays them on the bed beside her laptop and makes her way downstairs.

All the family are there. Jemma's getting something out of the oven and Imogen notices that she's wearing Imogen's new dress. Cheeky, she thinks, but she doesn't say anything. She's going to be out of here soon.

Andrea, Jemma's mum, hands Imogen a glass of prosecco. 'Here's our girl,' she says and envelops Imogen in a fragrant hug. 'You look lovely, darling.'

Imogen knows she doesn't. Unlike the rest of the family, who are dressed up, she's wearing jeans and a T-shirt. But she appreciates the compliment.

Andrea offered to take Imogen in just days after Edie's body was discovered, and she's been Imogen's champion ever since, lavishing her with support and attention.

It was a lifesaver at first, but Imogen feels as if she's suffocating a little now.

'A toast!' Jemma's dad says. David is brash and loud and doesn't enjoy being around people when they express their emotions, so he spends a lot of time at the golf course avoiding his wife and three daughters, and, Imogen supposes, herself as well.

But he helped her sell her mum and dad's house and put the money in trust for her along with their life-insurance payouts. He's ensured that she'll be financially comfortable for life and she's appreciated the quiet hours they've spent together, where he's helped her make decisions, and explained everything to her patiently, without being patronising.

Imogen has blanked out a lot of what happened a year ago. It's been the only way to make room for the future she wants to build for herself, to avoid being paralysed by grief. Her parents wouldn't want that, and she's determined to live up to their memories.

She has no contact with any of her parents' old friends – the ones who are left, that is.

Apart from Paul's wife, Emily. Out of the blue, Imogen received a parcel from her a month ago. It was a pretty necklace, with a sweet note accompanying it saying that Emily was thinking of her. The note was written on a postcard and sent from a small village in the South of France. Emily included a phone number and told Imogen to get in touch if she ever wanted to visit. 'I live here now,' she wrote. 'It's beautiful. I'd love to show it to you.'

Andrea insisted that Imogen get professional help in the aftermath of her mother's murder, and her therapist is patient and kind, but the sessions can be stultifying, and Imogen thinks she might make a change when she gets to London.

Andrea pours a glass of prosecco for herself, the twins fetch their drinks, and the family gathers around Imogen and Jemma.

'Here's to our big girls,' David says.

Imogen sees Jemma flinch a little. Jemma's been brilliant since Imogen moved in. But it hasn't been easy for her suddenly to acquire a new, and broken, sister, even if Imogen is one of her best friends.

Soon, Jemma can have her family back.

'Jemma, darling, congratulations on winning your place at Exeter to read psychology! Bloody amazing. We couldn't be more proud of you.'

Andrea wolf-whistles; they all cheer and drink and congratulate Jemma, who glows.

David turns to Imogen and raises his glass again.

'And Imogen, congratulations to you on winning your place at the Royal College of Music.'

They whoop and drink again and Imogen thanks them all.

Andrea is close to tears. She hugs them both tightly. 'You will come back and visit at the weekends, won't you? I'm going to miss you so much. It's going to be so quiet around here, isn't it, David?'

'Especially without that cello!' he says, and guffaws, and Imogen thinks, I knew he didn't like the cello. Though he never said so, and he cleared a room out for her to practise in and she'd never have won her place at the conservatoire without it. Andrea and David have been so kind to her. Rob and Edie would be so grateful.

Andrea serves lunch, piling plates high with the feast she's cooked this morning. On the side there's a sumptuous celebration cake for dessert.

Imogen eats quietly as the family hubbub rises in volume around her.

She feels happy and wanted, but content to let them chat about Jemma's plans for Exeter without her. She knows what she's going to do.

She'll live in student accommodation for her first year in London, to make friends. But she's going to hunt for a flat to buy, somewhere she can move into in her second year. She's got the money. She might ask David to help her in the search.

She wants somewhere she can play her cello, and she'll rent the second bedroom out to another student. She's kept the best bits of furniture from her parents' house, the photographs and artworks, and it's bittersweet to imagine moving them into her new place.

Her flat will be an investment, but also her home. She needs one.

ACKNOWLEDGEMENTS

I'm always grateful to everyone who supports my novels, both professionally and personally, but since Covid upended the world, I've never been more so.

Heartfelt thanks as ever to my brilliant agent, Helen Heller, for your unstinting support and brilliant creative input, neither of which faltered in the face of a global pandemic. Hours of intense Zoom chats at the start of the first lockdown generated the idea for this book.

To my editors, Emily Krump in New York, and Emily Griffin in London, warmest thanks for your patience, enthusiasm and vital input. It's been a pleasure to edit this book with your notes in hand and the finished product is so much better for it. Very grateful thanks to Sania Riaz and Julia Elliott, too.

For fantastic publicity and marketing campaigns, thank you to Kaitlin Harri, D.J. DeSmyter, and Camille Collins in New York and to Sarah Ridley, Isabelle Ralphs and Lydia Weigel in the UK.

The support of Liate Stehlik and Jennifer Hart at William Morrow and Selina Walker at Century means a great deal. Thank you.

I'm extremely grateful for the exceptional sales and production teams who get my books on to shelves. Warmest thanks to Linda Hodgson and Mathew Watterson in the UK and to the lovely Carla Parker and everyone else in the sales departments in the US.

Thank you to Elsie Lyons in New York and Ceara Elliott in the UK, for two incredible cover designs. I may be a little biased, but I think you both created something exceptional.

To all at HarperCollins Canada, what an incredible team you are! Thanks so much to Leo MacDonald, Sandra Leef, Mike Millar, Cory Beatty, Brenann Francis, Kaiti Vincent and everyone else who works on my books. I appreciate each and every one of you and the brilliant work you do.

Camille Ferrier, Jemma McDonagh and everyone at the Marsh Agency never fail to be a pleasure to work with. Thanks for everything, and thanks also to the editors and publishers of my books in translation. I'm very grateful to you for bringing my books to wider audiences.

Readers, booksellers, bloggers and reviewers create such a generous and supportive community for writers. Even though our interactions were necessarily online this year, they remained as creative, fun, warm and sustaining as ever. Thank you all.

My fellow authors are the best. I admire each and every one of you and am incredibly grateful for your support. To Claire Douglas, Shari Lapeña and Tim Weaver, especially, huge thanks for the chat, encouragement and support.

Heartfelt thanks to Jayne Pavey, winner of the CLIC Sargent Get in Character auction to have a character named in this novel. CLIC Sargent provide support to families caring for a child or young adult with a cancer diagnosis and are important to Jayne's family and to mine.

I'm thankful as ever for the two retired detectives who have so generously advised me on police procedure since I wrote my debut. I hope we can have lunch in person again soon. Mistakes regarding police procedure are mine.

Very special thanks to Craig Leathard and colleagues at Wansbeck General Hospital, to John Hepworth and Clare McCall, the paramedics who transferred me into the care of Northumbria Emergency Specialist Hospital, and the wonderful NHS staff there on Ward 3, who all treated me when a research trip for this book resulted in a medical emergency.

Rose Macmillan, thank you for your hawk-eyed checking of my copyedits.

To my family, thanks for putting up with me. Love you. To Jules, shame about the sourdough starter but thanks for the cookies. To Rose, Max and Louis, it's been crazy times, but I'm lucky to have had you alongside me and I'm in awe of your strength and resilience.